So Shall We Stand

ELYSE LARSON

So Shall We Stand

BETHANYHOUSE
MINNEAPOLIS, MINNESOTA

So Shall We Stand
Copyright © 2001
Elyse Larson

Cover design by Dan Thornberg

Published by Bethany House Publishers
A Ministry of Bethany Fellowship International
11400 Hampshire Avenue South
Bloomington, Minnesota 55438
www.bethanyhouse.com

Printed in the United States of America by
Bethany Press International, Bloomington, Minnesota 55438

Library of Congress Cataloging-in-Publication Data

Larson, Elyse.
    So shall we stand / by Elyse Larson.
    p.   cm. — (Women of valor ; 2)
    ISBN 0-7642-2375-5 (pbk.)
    1. World War, 1939–1945—England—Fiction. 2. World War, 1939–1945—Women—Fiction. 3. Americans—England—Fiction. 4. Women—England—Fiction. I. Title.
PS3562.A7522235 S6   2001
813′.6—dc21

2001001320

"WE SHALL NOT FLAG OR FAIL.
WE SHALL GO ON TO THE END, WE SHALL
FIGHT IN FRANCE, WE SHALL FIGHT ON THE
SEAS AND OCEANS, WE SHALL FIGHT WITH
GROWING CONFIDENCE AND GROWING
STRENGTH IN THE AIR, WE SHALL DEFEND OUR
ISLAND, WHATEVER THE COST MAY BE, WE
SHALL FIGHT ON THE BEACHES, WE SHALL
FIGHT ON THE LANDING GROUNDS, WE SHALL
FIGHT IN THE FIELDS AND IN THE STREETS, WE
SHALL FIGHT IN THE HILLS;
WE SHALL NEVER SURRENDER. . . ."
—WINSTON CHURCHILL, FROM HIS SPEECH ON
DUNKIRK AT THE HOUSE OF COMMONS, JUNE 4, 1940

DEDICATION

To our children,
each of whom is a hero to me:
sons,
Robin Richard Larson,
Paul Jonathan Larson,
and our daughter,
Diane Patricia Linden.

ELYSE LARSON is an author, photographer, and writing instructor. *So Shall We Stand* is her fifth published novel. Elyse and her husband live in Gresham, Oregon. They have three children and eleven grandchildren.

CHAPTER ONE

September 1944
Abergavenny, Wales

Nella Killian, desperate for a quiet moment to put an end to the headache that had plagued her all morning, quietly closed the front door of the Presbyterian manse and tiptoed to the kitchen. The silence in the gray stone manse indicated her baby, two-year-old Livie, was still napping.

When Nella entered the large old-fashioned kitchen, she found her mother, Elizabeth MacDougall, pegging Livie's freshly washed nappies to the clothesline.

Seeing Nella, she smiled, said, "Hello, love," and hoisted the line by its pulley up over the stove. With autumn bringing unpredictable rain showers, the washing would now hang above them in the kitchen. "Livie's still asleep. You look all done in. I rather hoped you wouldn't try to see Camilla so soon after she learned about the death of her husband." Camilla was the youngest daughter of one of the church families, the Flints, who had a farm just north of town. Camilla had been a widow for a day. Her husband of six months had been killed in action in northern Italy.

"I had to go." Nella went to the stove and tapped her finger against the black cast-iron teakettle. "Still hot enough for tea," she decided aloud and reached for a cup and the tea strainer. Scooping a measure of black tea into the strainer, she poured the steaming water over it into her cup. After she sat down at the table, she said, "I knew it would set me crying too, but I had to be there. I remember how I felt when Rob was shot down. To have someone come who has been through a similar tragedy is the only thing that brings any comfort at first. She needed me to cry with her. Mum, after sitting with her, I wanted to shoot some Nazis myself. To think what Hitler has done—the bloodshed and torture—and now all these weeks since the invasion our men are still dying while trying to stop him. Will it never end? I can't understand why God permits this horror to go on and on."

Nella thumped the table with her fist and burst out, "One and a half million people, Mum, died in that Polish concentration camp! For what reason? They were just people like us. It's so much worse than I realized back in 1940. And still the 'Fuehrer' goes on. Where in the name of God is God?" She knew she was close to using God's name in vain, but she didn't care.

Her mother moved quickly to her side and encircled her tight fist with her own hand, strong and warm. "It's not God's fault, Nella. We're none of us totally innocent. Nations as well as individuals suffer consequences from their sins. But I can't answer for the Lord when you beg to understand. For myself, I still believe there's a reason for everything . . . and many times the reasons are painful."

Nella drew a shaky breath, then took a sip of tea. She didn't want to go into the matter of faith with her mother. Ever since she'd been widowed while expecting Livie, her faith in God's care had wavered. After the first months of grief and following Livie's birth, she had not expected any supernatural help for the baby or herself. Her childhood notion that God took special notice of each person's needs had turned out to be just that—a childhood notion. God was too busy with the bigger things to bother with some individual's problems. Any other concept didn't make sense.

Not wanting to argue with her mother and her minister father, Nella kept this opinion to herself most of the time. Now she steered the conversation back to their grieving friends. "Mrs. Flint was glad I came. She said Camilla has always looked up to me. I don't know why. I never really spent time with her when working with the dogs out there. She usually stayed in the house with her mother. Well, at least Camilla can keep busy in the First Aid Nursing Yeomanry. She reports back for duty next week. In FANY she feels she's doing something important for the war effort, and it's something she can do in memory of her husband. If it weren't for Livie, I'd have joined the Women's Auxiliary Air Force again. I hate not doing more to help win the war."

"I know you do, but being with your baby is more important in the long scheme of things."

Mum's predictable answer irritated Nella more than usual. "You mean what little I could do for the war effort wouldn't make much difference."

Her mother stepped back from her side and glared down at her. With her hands on her hips, she said, "Nella Elizabeth! You know I don't mean that!"

Nella raised her chin, attempting an apologetic smile. "I do know, Mum. I'm just in a frump. I'd like to just sit here and sulk. My head aches as well as my heart."

"Why don't you go for a walk? Livie's still sleeping. The fresh air will do you good. And while you're out, you can pick up your father's cough medicine at the chemist's shop for him."

Nella would rather have gone straight to bed but couldn't refuse because of the prescription. "All right." She gulped the last of her tea, pulled on a raincoat, and quietly let herself out through the front door again.

The manse lay on the north edge of town, fifteen minutes by foot from the chemist's. The longer walk from the farm had not eased her headache, so it was unlikely that this shorter jaunt downtown would do much either. However, if she took a bit more time, she could keep walking through town and on to the river.

If the castle grounds above the river and meadow weren't filled with Nissen huts, military personnel, and vehicles, then she'd make that her destination. The huts, shaped like halves of steel drums lying on their sides, jarred her senses as much now as the first day she'd seen them. Nella and her best friend, Peggy Jones, used to play among the stone ruins and share their hopes and dreams with each other. All seemed possible back in those days.

Although it wasn't true, Nella called Peggy her adopted sister. The daughter of a coal miner, Peggy had come to live at the manse when she was eleven, to attend school in Abergavenny. Nella, who was nine at the time, had longed for a big sister. After a feisty adjustment to the life in the manse, Peggy had more than fulfilled Nella's wish.

As Nella strode down High Street, black clouds blew overhead yet dropped no rain. So she passed the chemist's shop and walked briskly on to Cross Street, thinking to head down to the river. With rising spirits, she stopped at Saddler & Son Tobacconist Shop to buy a newspaper for her father. The front-page headline declared the British 11th Armored Division had fought its way into Antwerp. Arrows on a map pointed out the current battle line in Belgium and also where the Americans were positioned in northern France.

Nella was counting out her coins on the counter when Mr.

Saddler said, "Did you read about the German spies that were arrested out by Crickhowell? Seems they were planning to sabotage the Brecon Canal. Had enough explosives to blow up half the town. Story's right there on the bottom of page one."

She hadn't noticed. "Nazi saboteurs here in the Usk River valley? Were they living in Crickhowell?"

"Nay, a couple of kilometers away, in the mountains. Our military happened to intercept their radio signals the other night and so traced them down. Bit of luck for us. Two women, they were. They'd been there since beginning of summer, working on the Miller farm. Good workers, old Mr. Miller said, so he asked no questions. Their hut didn't look like much on the outside, nothing to make a person suspicious, but inside was full of fancy radio equipment. Your father, the Reverend, will no doubt find it interesting reading."

"Yes, I'm sure he will," Nella replied. Her father carefully hoarded his petrol ration for his monthly drive to visit several elderly parishioners in Crickhowell. She wondered if he might have met the two women of the story. A poor quality photo of them appeared on page two. What was happening in Antwerp became secondary to the spies discovered so close to home. Nella lingered inside the tiny shop to finish reading the shocking report.

The news of the arrest would trouble her parents and would certainly frighten their upstairs guest, Giselle Munier. Giselle had fled from the Nazis in France the previous spring and had come to Abergavenny for safety's sake and to be close to her cousin Jean. A few weeks ago, Giselle's two children—eight-year-old Jacquie and six-year-old Angie—had been kidnapped and held hostage by a Nazi sympathizer named Andre who had followed Giselle from France. Apparently Giselle had been a person of importance in the Resistance. It had all ended with the children being rescued, but now Nella wondered if the two women had at one time collaborated with Andre. This probably would be Giselle's first thought too. Nella decided not to go to the river after all. She wanted to be with Giselle when she found out about the arrest—not that she could say or do anything to reassure her, but she'd at least be there.

Maybe Jean could stop by the manse for an hour or so. She had a gift for calming Giselle. Jean Thornton Kagawa was Giselle's American cousin and Nella's good friend. She worked in nearby Govilon at the military station hospital as a Red Cross recreational therapist. Govilon was less than four kilometers away. If Jean could get off duty, she could be at the manse soon. She'd been instrumental in rescuing Jacquie and Angie from their kidnapper. Getting her hands on a gun from somewhere, she had managed to shoot Andre. But if Andre hadn't been working alone, as the military authorities had said, then both Jean and Giselle needed to be on their guard now. The capture of two more Nazis could signal more danger.

Nella hurried up Cross Street, back over to High Street, and ducked into the chemist's shop just as rain began spattering the narrow sidewalk. At the counter she asked for Reverend MacDougall's prescription.

Mr. McPhee, who had known Nella her entire life, turned and raised his white eyebrows at her. "Nella. Good day to you. Yes, I've mixed my best cough prescription. I wish that man would take better care of himself. He's not much younger than yours truly."

"You'll have to tell him that, Mr. McPhee. I'm only his daughter who knows not a whit about how a man stays well by the very work he does."

"Aye. Well, when he comes in, I'll be telling him." He handed her a medicine bottle.

"How much will that be?"

The chemist smiled. "Six shillings, three."

Nella handed him a five-pound note, then scooped up the change he put on the counter. "Thanks, and I'll tell Father you want to talk to him," she said, only half in jest.

"You do that," he said with a wink. "I'll set him straight."

Nella laughed and then turning to leave, she crashed into the chest of a tall man standing behind her. "Oh, I beg your pardon! So careless of me!"

She looked up into a familiar-looking face, but belonging to a person she'd never spoken with before. Nella had seen Bryan Westmoreland from a distance when visiting Peggy in West-Holding, the village where she taught school. Peggy hadn't a good word to say about him. She had never looked kindly on the gentry, so Nella wasn't sure what was fact and what was Peggy's interpretation of fact. Not long after Bryan and Peggy met, Bryan had made the mistake of trying to kiss her without first asking permission. Peggy probably would have forgotten the kissing thing, but then Bryan nearly ran her over with his car while she was riding her bicycle. Then he lost his temper over the incident as if he owned the road. Peggy contended that his family acted as though they still owned the whole village and all the land surrounding it.

Now Bryan wore a friendly, unassuming smile. He caught her arm as if to steady her. "Apology accepted. I say, I'm afraid I was daydreaming, or I'd have moved out of your way."

But he didn't let go of her, and he kept staring into her eyes. Nella felt her face grow hot. She looked away and pulled her arm from his grasp. The man was downright offensive.

He stepped back as if she'd slapped him. "Excuse me. I was thinking—have we met before?"

Jean would call that "a line," words used by American soldiers to get better acquainted with girls. "No. We've never met." With a nod, Nella hurried out of the chemist's shop.

The accidental encounter left her agreeing with Peggy, who opined that he used his good looks for his own gain, that he was a spineless sort. Not caring enough for his country to join up with the other fighting men, she said. Instead, he'd waited to be called up and then got himself out again as soon as he could. Peggy figured Lord Westmoreland had taken advantage of some political debts so as to keep his only son home to help with the farming. And now that Nella had met Bryan up close, she suspected Peggy was more right than wrong.

On the way home, Nella's thoughts flipped back to the arrest of the spies less than an hour's drive from home. So much for walking off her headache. If anything, the distressing news made it worse. For even though the two spies had been captured, there could still be others.

It used to be that when she and Peggy were children, Peggy would often accuse her of possessing a "second sight." Still, neither of them was in any way superstitious. Then after Rob died, Nella decided her intuitiveness sprang from an instinctive fear of being hurt again and the desire to be prepared for anything. She'd had no sense of anything going wrong that day the officer came to tell her Rob's plane had gone down in the Channel. She felt betrayed by such a failure of her inner warning system. Now logical Peggy was the one who followed her hunches, while Nella had learned to wait before making decisions.

Nella stopped at the butcher shop and, using the family's accumulated ration coupons, purchased two beef kidneys that would do for the whole week the way Mum cooked.

Back at home, she carried the kidneys to the kitchen and placed them in the icebox. She then set the medicine bottle on the top shelf of the cupboard and stuck her mother's change in the empty sugar bowl. The newspaper she left on the table for her father.

Nella heard the steady whir of the treadle sewing machine coming from her parents' bedroom. Livie must still be asleep, or she'd be hearing her chattering away at her grandmother. Nella headed for Livie's room to check on her.

At that moment her father called from the front door, "Nella! Are you home?"

"Here, Daddy." She retraced her steps down the hall to the front door.

"This young man says you dropped some money in the chemist's shop, and James McPhee told him where to find you to return it."

A tall man stepped inside behind her father.

Startled, Nella moved forward to receive the money. Halfway there she recognized the visitor. She blinked and then forced herself to act casually, as if unsurprised to see this man twice the same morning.

"This is Bryan Westmoreland from West-Holding. He says he knows our Peggy."

"Mr. Westmoreland." Nella nodded formally. "Thank you for taking pains to find me and return my money."

"I was glad someone there knew you. It's a pleasure to see you again and learn your name, if I may say so."

She gave him a polite smile. "You may. It was good of you to look me up after I so clumsily bumped into you."

"A simple case of my being in the wrong place."

"Well, sir," her father said, "will you join us for *lunch*, now that you're here?"

Oh no! Please don't say yes, she willed Bryan Westmoreland.

Young Westmoreland smiled at her and graciously declined the invitation. After stepping outside, he turned and smiled down at Nella who was now standing by the open door. Lines crinkled the smooth skin at the corners of his warm brown eyes, suggesting he smiled a lot. This suited Peggy's description of him: not a care in the world while other young men, like Rob, were dying in battle. He appeared pampered, untouched by the war or any type of grief.

"Perhaps we'll meet again, Miss MacDougall."

"I doubt that," she answered firmly. "And my name is Mrs. Killian. Mrs. Rob Killian."

With a fleeting sober look, he replied, "Of course. I forgot that many young wives are living with their parents these days. Good day, Mrs. Killian."

As he marched down the sidewalk, Nella called belatedly, "Thank you again for bringing my money."

He smiled once more, casually saluted, and folded himself into his small car. Apparently the Westmoreland Estate could get adequate petrol for him to run his car as well as the tractors and lorries. It was all a bit disgusting, just as Peggy had said.

When Nella had closed the door, her father gestured toward the parlor. "Marge Emerson, Jean's nurse friend at Gilwern military station hospital, came by the church office and returned these books I'd loaned to some of the men. Would you mind putting them back on the shelf for me?"

"Not at all." Nella was relieved to think about something as mundane as replacing books alphabetically, as he required, on the parlor bookshelves. "I put your cough medicine in the kitchen cupboard on the top shelf, and the newspaper's on the table. Be sure to read the story at the bottom of page one. I want to talk to you about it later."

His blue eyes searched her face. "Aye. I'll have a look."

No sound came from the bedroom she and Livie shared, so she hurried back to peek in on her and found her still napping. She then made her way to the parlor and started shelving her father's books. There were a couple of theological tomes, some biographies, a book on Welsh history, another on Welsh farming methods. Then she came to *The Pilgrim's Progress*. She gazed fondly at the old volume. She'd had her own children's version of the classic yet always loved best her father's copy, because of its dramatic old engravings. Even the texture of the familiar worn cover soothed her.

Nella took the leather-bound book and sat down on the sofa for a quiet few minutes. This book had guided her first steps as a believer when seven years old. She sat there for a while without opening it, thinking about how simple and comforting her faith had been in those days. Until the war, she'd believed unwaveringly that God attended to her every prayer. She sighed, wishing she could return to those days of innocence. Life was much more complicated now. Being both Mum and Daddy to Livie had pulled her a dozen different directions. Nella longed to build a future for the two of them, but with the war still raging on, such a wish was a road to nowhere. So she focused her efforts toward her next wish: to do her part in the war effort now that Livie was old enough to stay with her grandmother and grandfather. With her mum's attitude, though, this seemed impossible too.

Beyond her unfulfilled longings, Nella simply wanted a life of her own. After becoming a war widow at age eighteen and returning to her parents' home in the Presbyterian manse, she wasn't quite sure what having her own life might mean. But while Livie had been growing more independent, Nella felt she'd been doing some growing up of her own. She'd always had a streak of independence. She needed nobody to tell her that. After all, she'd run away and lied about her age to get in the WAAF. However, when Rob's plane went down, Nella found she'd lost her will to strike out on her own.

Now life and desire had returned, though not the desire for a man. No one could take Rob's place in her heart. Tender and passionate, he'd been an ideal husband. He'd been her hero and had died a hero's death for his country. No, she wasn't eager to marry again. And despite what Peggy told her, she wasn't running from reality. She aimed to create for Livie the kind of life she and Rob had hoped for following the war. She knew she could do it, but not while living with her parents.

Nella leaned her elbow on the armrest of the aging sofa and, with her chin on her hand, stared out the parlor window as she thought about her dilemma. Since her brother Charles was killed in action last spring, her mother and father had shown that they needed her and Livie. She couldn't trample their feelings to go her own way. They'd have to agree with her wishes. Yet this didn't seem likely to happen.

Feeling a growing frustration, Nella straightened and turned her attention to *The Pilgrim's Progress*. The book fell open to where someone had stuck a thin envelope as a bookmark. Beside the envelope staring up at her was an engraving of Christian struggling in the slough of despair. The last time she'd looked at the book, she hadn't yet experienced despair. Now she didn't need a picture to remind her of its miry grip. Before turning to a different illustration, she picked up the envelope, for the words written on it caught her attention. An unfamiliar bold scrawl announced, *Open in case of my death*. She turned the envelope over. The seal on the flap was unbroken, and the envelope wasn't all that old. The paper was modern airmail stationery, so thin she could almost see through it to the writing inside.

A dozen unnerving scenarios flashed through Nella's mind. After a few seconds of hesitation, she pulled up the flap, removed the thin stationery, and smoothed it against her lap. The same awkward writing said, *For my mother*.

> *Dear Mom,*
> *If you are reading this you know I been killed. I know they'll try to make it look like suicide, but believe me I'd never kill myself. I want you to know I done my level best to come home and take care of you. I always wanted to protect you from the old man when he was drunk. But I never did know what to do. I thought I found a way to set us both up fine after the war. Now I see I didn't choose smart, so I'm trying to get out of it. It's best you don't know how I*

went wrong. I don't want these guys to go after you. If somehow they get hold of this letter, MY MOM DON'T KNOW NOTHING.

Mom, I have a buddy who knows where I put the money I got so far. He has your address. I trust him like a brother. If he hears about me being killed, he will bring it to you. If he don't make it either, well, I guess it just wasn't meant to be. I love you, Mom, and I will do my very best to stay alive for you.

Your boy,
Rufus

At the bottom of the paper was written a name and address: *Please deliver to Mrs. Arvid Johnson, 134 SE Market St., Coreyton, Illinois, USA.*

Nella stared at the letter in a state of shock. She knew Mrs. Johnson and felt as if she knew Rufe. He had drowned in the Usk River three months ago, shortly after D day. Nella was on a walk with Jean, when they discovered his body downstream from the military station hospital in Gilwern where Rufe had been a patient. The authorities had determined his death to be a suicide.

She had gotten to know Rufe's mother from writing to her. Nella had been sickened at seeing Rufe's drowned, bloated body. She kept thinking that was how Rob would have looked, crashing into the water as he did.

Finally, because of her own pain, she had sent Rufe's mother a note of sympathy. So through the mail Nella and Mrs. Johnson developed a surprising friendship. The brokenhearted woman said she was so relieved to tell a sympathetic person about her only son. For many of Mrs. Johnson's friends had indicated they thought less of a young man who would take his own life. Nella's heart ached for her. It was hard enough to lose a loved one to a hero's death. She couldn't imagine the unique pain her new friend was suffering.

But would the information in this letter make Mrs. Johnson feel better or worse? Nella looked again at the writing, wondering if she should destroy what she'd just found and let the matter die with Rufe.

CHAPTER TWO

Nella had planned to call Jean right away in case she hadn't heard the news about the spies out at Crickhowell. Now, having read Rufe's letter, she decided to call Marge Emerson first. Marge, an Army nurse who had known Rufe better than anyone, could turn the letter over to the authorities at the hospital.

Nella hoped Marge would be able to identify Rufe's writing. She rang up the Gilwern military hospital and left a message for Marge to call her. Then she called the station hospital at Govilon and requested the same for Jean.

Jean had visited Rufe more than once in the mental ward at Gilwern. Both Jean and Marge were shocked when the authorities had ruled out accidental death, holding that Rufe must have killed himself. Marge said he would've had to wade out into the middle of the river to reach enough depth to drown himself, an image that tormented her again and again. Neither she nor Jean could imagine Rufe wanting to do such a thing. Marge felt sure he was faking his mental illness by refusing to talk with the hospital's doctors.

With Marge certain Rufe hadn't committed suicide, Nella, too, began wondering about foul play. Peggy, who wasn't one to speculate, accused Nella of over-dramatizing the situation. Yet Jean agreed with Nella, and so did Marge. Still, nothing ever came of Marge's efforts to convince her supervisors, for trainloads of wounded men began arriving, and the subject of Private Johnson's mysterious death was soon dropped in the rush to tend to the living.

Nella pressed her hand against her chest as if her touch could calm her distress. She read the short letter again. It must be authentic.

If Rufe had not written it, then who did? Someone playing a joke on her father? That seemed unimaginable. Daddy had a friendly way with the soldiers. He always listened more than he talked. She remembered his grief over Rufe. He felt he had failed the eighteen-year-old boy.

Would this letter ease some of his pain regarding Rufe? She sat frozen in place. One thing for sure, the letter was bound to stir up a new investigation. On impulse Nella decided against telling her father and mother until they needed to know. After losing Charles, they'd been through enough. The letter would worry them. They'd wonder if the murderer was still around posing danger to those who might know about this new evidence. Yes, it was best not to tell Mum and Daddy just yet. She'd better remove the letter from the manse quickly to eliminate any risk of their finding it.

Nella never thought she'd be this close to a murder. Such things happened somewhere else. But then she never thought she'd see a kidnapping either. Jacquie and Angie, Giselle's little girls had been abducted from the street right in front of the manse. Without question, the war had brought violence to her hometown.

Poor Rufe. Because he was only a private in the American army, if someone had murdered him, the circumstances tied to the heinous act were probably unrelated to the war. And if further investigation revealed that Rufe had gotten mixed up in some illegal activity, then his mother would be grieved in a new way. But since the possibility of suicide troubled her so, Mrs. Johnson deserved to know her son hadn't killed himself.

Nella folded and placed the stationery back in its envelope, then tucked it into her apron pocket. After returning *The Pilgrim's Progress* to its place on the bookshelf, she walked straight to her bedroom with the idea of hiding the letter till she could give it to Jean.

Livie was awake now. "Up, Mummy!" She reached her chubby arms over the crib rail and performed a bouncing jump. Nella laid the letter on her dresser and lifted the baby out for a hug. "Did you stay dry, love?"

"Want to go to loo," Livie announced with pride.

"That's wonderful," Nella commended as she carried her to the bathroom.

Nella's mother appeared in the doorway. "How's your headache? Shall I watch her so you can lie down?"

"My head feels better." After Nella said it, she realized it really did. "Thanks anyway, Mum."

"So you'll be off to the USO tonight, then?"

"Yes. I'll have a go at it. Do me good, I think."

Her mother nodded. "Aye. Then I'll be making muffins for you to take along."

To Nella's relief, her mother left without noticing the alien envelope in full sight on the dresser top. Holding Livie in one arm, she snatched up the letter and shoved it under her handkerchiefs in the top drawer. Then she hugged Livie and pressed her lips against the fat wrinkle in her neck and blew, making a silly blubbery noise.

Livie giggled uproariously. "More, Mum!"

Nella obliged while walking slowly toward the kitchen. Her mum stood at the stone sink, washing vegetables, and her father sat at the table with his tea, the newspaper spread out before him.

Nella put Livie in her chair and gave her a cup of milk and half a muffin. She then sat down across from her father. "So what did you think of the story about the spies?" she asked, keeping her voice casual sounding.

"What?" Mum asked.

"The paper says two women were arrested recently near Crickhowell, arrested for spying," Nella said. "They had explosives and were planning to destroy the Brecon Canal. They also had sophisticated shortwave radios."

"My word!" Mum exclaimed. "Ian, what else does the paper say?"

Her father read the report aloud.

"Well, thank the Lord they were caught before they blew up anything," Mum said.

Nella asked what had plagued her mind from the beginning. "Daddy, do you think these women could've been connected to Andre in any way? Sounds as if they appeared at Crickhowell about the same time Andre came to Abergavenny. Giselle said he used the pretense of working on the canal locks for coming here from London."

Nella hoped her father would soothe her fears with a good dose of his solid common sense. Instead, he frowned and said, "I hadn't thought of that. This may be bad news for Giselle. If she hasn't already seen the paper, we'd better tell her. Nella, would you see if she's in and ask her to come down?"

"Now, Daddy? I was wondering if Jean shouldn't be here for this."

"Giselle will be all right. She's much stronger now than she was four months ago."

Nella nodded. "I'll go fetch her."

Giselle was home and had not yet read the paper. "What is it?" she asked, her face going pale.

Nella could see she had better tell Giselle right away. "It's not concerning Claude. It seems they caught some spies up at Crickhowell."

Giselle hadn't known for most of the past year whether her husband, Claude, was alive or not. She'd worked at his side in the French Resistance before they were both arrested. Giselle and Claude were later rescued from the Gestapo, yet had been separated from each other during their escape. She hadn't heard from Claude until just a week ago. Now he was fighting under General De Gaulle, after having served in a French guerilla army known as the Maquis.

"Spies at Crickhowell?" Giselle repeated. "German spies?"

Nella took her hand. "I guess they seemed to be English. Come downstairs and read it for yourself."

Down in the manse kitchen, Ian said, "Giselle, I thought for the sake of the girls you'd want to know about this in case it turns out to be a worry."

Nella handed her the newspaper, pointing out where she should begin reading.

Giselle sat down at the table and read the report. Then, looking up with an anxious expression, she said, "Spies in the Brecon Beacon mountains. You'd think there's little here to make it worth their time."

"Well, the canal's important," Ian said. "Destroying it would cut off a huge portion of our coal supply and cripple some key industries. But there may be more to it than that. We don't know what could be hidden up in the mountains. Remember how surprised we were to learn about the hundreds of tanks the military concealed in those hills as they waited for D day? To ease your mind, Giselle, I'll try to find out more about the two women arrested. I just thought you might want to talk to the girls. Or maybe you want to keep it from them. . . ."

"They may hear the news from other children. I'll tell them first and assure them there's nothing to worry about." With a grieved look, Giselle shook her head. "I've never believed a lie would protect my children as well as the truth, but I find myself lying a lot. Who knows, maybe these spies *were* with Andre. Maybe there are more still out there. . . ."

Hearing Giselle put her worries into words chilled Nella. She waited for her father to reassure everyone there was nothing to be concerned about.

Instead, he said, "I was hoping you'd see it that way. One can't be too careful these days. We need to be watching out for each other, especially for the children. It's not likely any more spies are lurking about, but we still shouldn't take any chances."

As Nella listened to her father's cautioning, Rufe's letter—hidden in her dresser drawer upstairs—suddenly became more ominous. She knew she must get the letter out of the house and into the hands of the authorities immediately.

Her father left for the church office while Giselle returned to the apartment upstairs, looking as calm as one could be after receiving such unsettling news. This was a relief.

Nella took down the dry laundry hanging in the kitchen and folded everything that didn't require ironing. As she was separating the clothes, the phone jangled out in the hall. "I'll get it, Mum," she called but heard no response. *She must be outside again,* Nella thought to herself.

"Hello, Nella," Marge said. "They said you called. What's up?"

Nella cupped her hand around the mouthpiece and spoke in a low tone. Quickly she described Rufe's note and related the contents as much as she could remember.

"Good grief!" Marge exclaimed. "He personally handed me that book and made a big point about returning it directly to your father. I brought the book to my quarters, and then we got so busy, I completely forgot it. Em found it yesterday under a pile of magazines while looking for a place to put her typewriter. Did Jean tell you Em is here?"

"No. I hope she'll come see us." Em was Marge's sister and a war correspondent for a magazine in America. "Do you think Rufe wanted my father to read that note? Or did he think you would discover it?"

"I only remember how he wanted to make sure I'd hand-deliver it." Marge went silent for a moment, then said slowly, "He made a point of it, all right. I thought . . . oh, I don't know what I thought. Then when you found him drowned, I forgot all about the book."

"Well, did he say anything to you about being afraid of someone?"

"Sure he did, when he first began talking to me. His remarks seemed so farfetched. Like everyone here, I thought maybe he was mentally ill. First, delusions of grandeur, then paranoia. But maybe he was telling the truth the whole time."

"What did he say?"

Marge emitted a loud sigh. "He said he was in on a big operation that could end the war. Then later he kept raving about how 'they'—he wouldn't say who—were after him. Once he said something like, 'Tell my mother, I'd never betray my country. I'm going to throw a monkey wrench in the works.' During the two weeks before he died, he seemed so rational that I figured he'd said all those things to convince me he was crazy."

"Did he tell anyone else?" Nella asked.

"Not that I know of. He didn't respond to anyone when he first came here. Then, for some reason, one day I got through to him. After that, they called me in several times to deal with him. Little by little he cooperated with me. I sort of got attached to him . . . he was so young and reminded me of my kid brother. I visited him as often as I could."

"Did you tell anyone about the things he said to you?"

"Sure, at first. The doctors said my reports confirmed he was mentally ill."

"What about later when you thought he was faking it?"

"I didn't have the heart to report him. I should have, but he wasn't as tough as he tried to sound. I guess I decided on my own that he needed to go home. And I didn't have to lie. The doctors already agreed he was unfit for duty."

"What made you think Rufe wasn't as tough as he sounded?"

"The way he looked when he talked about his mother. That's what made me write to her."

"Did you tell her about his wild claims?"

"Of course not. After they decided he'd killed himself, I kicked myself for weeks for not realizing he really had been sick. I felt I should've been able to help him more. No, I didn't tell her about the things he told me."

Nella glanced down the hall to be sure her mother was still busy elsewhere. Not seeing her nearby, Nella continued, "Can you remember anything more that Rufe said?"

"I can't remember his exact words," Marge replied, "but I remember thinking what he said sounded crazy all right, like a spy movie with him cast as the hero saving the world."

Nella swallowed hard at the word *spy*. "Spy movie? What made you think of that?"

"He mentioned more than once something about a big secret hidden in the green hills of Wales. Crazy stuff. Especially when he said he had outwitted the enemy. That fit a man driven to insanity from the fighting. If he wasn't mad, you have to admit what he said made no sense."

"War doesn't make sense," Nella said slowly. "What if he did know about some military secret? What if he was killed because of what he knew?"

"Good grief, Nella, if there was a secret mission going on in Wales, your government wouldn't murder anyone for discovering it—"

"Not us. The Germans. The secret service just arrested two German spies out near Crickhowell. Have you read about it?"

"No!"

Nella told her the story and said, "I have to get Rufe's letter to you right away. What he wrote may be important. If you can identify his writing, the authorities will need to be contacted as soon as possible."

"This is all moving too fast for me. I can't imagine the boy I knew being tied to spying! But I'm game for turning in the letter."

"Can you come to church tomorrow?"

"I'm not sure. If Jean can, you could give it to her."

"That would be fine. If my worst fear comes true, I don't want to be connected with this letter."

"I can't blame you for feeling that way. I just don't know what to think," Marge said.

"I'd better go, but I'll make sure you get the letter tomorrow after church, one way or another."

"Sounds good."

Nella rang off and went back to folding the laundry.

When her mother came in, they prepared supper together. With onions, cabbage, carrots, and potatoes from their garden and part of the kidneys she'd bought from the butcher, they made pasties and set them in the oven to bake.

The phone rang again. This time Jean's voice greeted Nella. "What's going on?" she asked.

"Can you make it to church in the morning?" Nella added more quietly, "There's something I want to talk to you about."

"Of course," Jean replied. "I wanted to see Giselle, so I planned to get the time off. How's she taking the news about the spies?"

"Pretty well, but you'll be able to judge that better than I can. I'm so glad you're coming."

"I thought I'd better. By the way, did you know Em is back and staying with Marge? She said to send you her love and that she'll try to see you before she goes back to London."

"I talked to Marge this afternoon, so I knew, but thanks for remembering. Look, do your best to come tomorrow."

"Well, sure, Nella. Are you okay?"

"Yes. We just need to talk. I'll explain when I see you."

After Jean rang off, Nella sighed and rubbed the back of her neck as she entered the oven-warmed kitchen. "Mum, Em Emerson is back at Gilwern and working on another story for her magazine."

Her mother brightened. "Is she, now? Well, did you invite her to stay with us again?"

Nella smiled. "No, but I will. Jean's coming to church tomorrow, so I'll send word back with her. Knowing how Em works, I expect she'll want to stay with Marge till she finishes her interviews. Then she could come here to write."

"I do like that young woman. We must be sure to tell her she's always welcome."

"I'm sure she already knows that."

Em worked for *USA Living & Review*, a thinking man's magazine, Em called it. She'd told Nella once that "Those who run the magazine admit some women read it too, but still refuse to change the original name. I'm their one concession to the 'weaker-sex' readers. I was hired to give a woman's perspective on issues." Her feature story, which covered the problems of battle fatigue, was reprinted in several other magazines, including a military periodical and a medical review. One of the people Em had written about was Private Rufus Johnson.

What would Em think if she found out that Rufe may have been murdered for knowing too much about a military secret? Trying to imagine this brought Nella up short against the incredibility of her speculations. Em would probably blame the theory on Nella's flare for drama. It would be just as well if she did. Nella didn't want to believe the possibility herself.

CHAPTER THREE

Saturday evening Nella tried to put aside all thoughts of spying and murder. Watching after Livie and working with her mother on the routine surrounding suppertime had helped to distract her. Later on, she tucked Livie in, focusing all her attention on the cozy bedtime ritual they had established.

The baby's crib stood against the wall near her own bed. Nella laid her down and pulled a light blanket over her. Livie loved bedtime, a real blessing, her grandmum said. Nella sang, "Lullaby and good night, with roses bedight. With lilies o'er spread is baby's wee bed. . . ."

Livie smiled. Another blessing, that beautiful smile so like her father's. If only Rob could see her now. He would have been so happy.

She finished the song and then helped Livie say a short prayer that Nella herself made up because she hated "Now I lay me down to sleep," which went on to say, "if I should die before I wake . . ." The possibility that Livie could die terrified her. Babies can die, just as young husbands can die. She had to work hard not to show her dread around Livie.

"Say it with me, love, 'Thank you, God . . . for this good day . . . tomorrow bless me . . . as I play.'" Then she named people for God to bless. As she did so, she wished she could believe wholeheartedly that God would protect them all. Still, it was important that Livie believe. A child needed that.

By the time Livie repeated each of the names, she was nearly asleep. Nella kissed her and adjusted the window drapes to shade the room, for it was still daylight outside. The clouds had blown away now, and the September sun would soon be setting.

She removed her apron and laid it over the antique bedroom chair. Before supper she had changed to her second-best dress, a blue rayon with fitted bodice and lightly gathered skirt. The women from church served one evening a week at the USO canteen. Nella enjoyed this opportunity to offer hospitality to the soldiers. Most of them came from the two sprawling station hospitals located upriver from Abergavenny. Jean said that once their wounds had mended enough for recreation in town, they'd soon be off to the war again. This made serving them a special privilege. With the servicemen sacrificing so much, Nella felt she couldn't do enough toward the war effort.

She turned to face the crib and made her voice a caress. "Nightie night, Livie."

"Night night," came the tiny, lilting voice.

Nella closed the door softly and paused to lean against it. Inside the small bedroom lay her reason for living. Returning home as a widow to face childbirth without Rob had been so painful, but her first glimpse at that little face became her salvation. Whenever she felt blue, Livie perked her up.

Tonight, however, the shock of finding Rufe's letter had cast a shadow over everything. Peggy said she was always borrowing trouble. But Rufe's words, the news about spies, and then Marge's remarks all combined to stir up an unreasoning fear that something dreadful could happen to her family because of her accidental discovery of this new evidence.

Nevertheless, when Nella stepped to the kitchen to say good-bye to her mum, she put on a cheerful smile.

Her mother's face brightened. "You look fetching tonight. That blue brings out the gold highlights in your hair."

Again Nella made herself smile in a carefree manner. "Thanks, Mum. I never thought of my hair having any gold in it. I'm sure not a blonde anymore."

"Well, you're not a redhead either. Livie looks so much like you did at her age."

"Really? I thought she looked more like Rob."

"Rob too, but it's easier for me to see the image of my little girl. Nella, do the soldiers at the USO ever ask you out?"

"Sure, but I always tell them about Rob, and then they leave me alone. Why do you ask?"

"It's no business of mine.... I just want you to enjoy yourself. Some of the women tell me you want for fun. They say a girl your age needs more. I want you to know we'll care for Livie should you ever want to go to a movie or have dinner with one of the soldiers."

Nella sighed. "I wish the ladies would say as much around me, and I'd tell them a thing or three. Don't you worry about me, Mum. They're wrong. I have a good time in my own way." She hugged her mother, hating that she could feel her bones where she used to feel a comfortable padding of flesh. "Thanks for watching Livie. Because it's Saturday night, I'll be staying late to help clean up, so don't wait up. Good night." They kissed and Nella left.

The USO was downtown, a distance in the old market town that couldn't be counted in blocks. Nella counted her walks about town in terms of minutes, the USO being roughly twenty minutes away. She had plenty of time to get there and help make sandwiches before the evening crowd arrived.

After an hour of serving hungry soldiers, Nella almost forgot about the letter signed "Your boy, Rufus." Records played continuously on the jukebox while local girls and the Land Army girls who worked on nearby farms danced with the boys. Often a soldier would linger at the sandwich counter where Nella worked and chat with her after she'd said she didn't care to dance. The men had come from all over the United States, and they all loved to talk about home.

Tonight several of them were talking about the recent battle in Belgium. "Did you hear we've crossed the Albert Canal? My buddies are there. I wonder how far they'll be by the time I get back in the action."

Listening to them, Nella thought how schoolchildren nowadays knew more about the towns and villages of France and Belgium than she'd ever learned. They also followed the news on the wireless and studied the maps printed in the newspaper, which showed the whereabouts of the Allied forces fighting their way toward Germany.

While the Americans wagered about how long it would take for the Allies to get to Berlin, Nella took orders and handed out sandwiches. Finally most everyone had eaten their fill, and orders now dwindled to requests for coffee, tea, or fizzy drinks.

When she had finished serving, a man approached her, not to ask that she dance with him but to talk. He looked very young. Nella smiled a warm greeting. "Hello, Corporal. Have you been in Abergavenny long?"

"Just got in today, on leave."

"Oh, then you're not from one of the military hospitals. What made you choose to come to Abergavenny?"

"A buddy of mine was here, and he liked it."

"Well, that's good to hear. Will you be staying long?" Nella paused to open two bottles for a couple of men.

When she turned back, the corporal said, "My buddy died, and I came here to kind of . . . remember him, you know."

"Oh, I'm so sorry."

"Thanks. His death hit me pretty hard. I didn't think he'd do a thing like they said, but I made him a promise so came as soon as I got leave."

"That's very nice," Nella said softly. "I'm sure your buddy would be glad to know you're remembering him like this."

Then came several requests for coffee. When they had all left, the young blond man was still close by. He caught her eye, came forward, and leaned on the counter. "You ever visit the military hospital at Gilwern?" he asked.

"Yes, I've been there. Many of these men are patients there."

"That right? I wonder if I could hitch a ride out there with some-one."

"Well, I don't know all the rules, but you could sure ask."

Suddenly he leaned in closer. "Were you here in town when that soldier drowned in the river a couple of months ago?"

The question so startled Nella that she took the simple route and answered with the truth. "Aye, yes. Actually my friend and I . . . we found his body."

The man's eyes widened. "You did! Then you saw him up close."

"Not very well. I was the one who ran for help."

"Must have been an ugly situation."

"Heartbreaking. . . ." Recalling the gruesome scene, Nella sup-pressed a shiver, then set to wiping the counter where someone had dripped some cola.

As if to himself, the corporal muttered, "I could hardly believe he'd take that way out. It just wasn't like him."

"Rufe Johnson was your buddy?" she gasped.

"You sound like you knew him."

"No, but my friend did. I'd never met him. Did he . . ." She strug-gled to phrase her question carefully. "Did Rufe ever tell you about . . . anything he wanted sent to his mother back home?"

His young face suddenly grew hard as he studied her. "You said you didn't know him."

"But I didn't."

Now the man turned red with anger. "Lady, if you managed to weasel him out of all he saved—"

"I told you, I didn't know him or ever speak to him!"

"Then how'd you know about his wanting to send something to his ma?"

Should she tell this man about the letter she'd found? Surely he had confirmed the authenticity of it. What would be gained or lost by letting him know?

"Hey," called a soldier, "can I have a ginger ale, please?"

"Sure thing, Sergeant." Nella pried off the cap and handed him the bottle. Hoping Rufe's irate friend would leave, she made conversation with the newcomer for a few minutes.

Her ploy didn't work. When she turned back, Rufe's friend stood leaning on the counter and staring at her. "You better tell me how you know about Rufe's business."

"I came upon a letter I think he wrote, addressed to his mother. I've written to Mrs. Johnson myself, so through her I've come to feel I almost know Rufe. Well, in the letter I found, Rufe mentioned a trustworthy friend who would send his savings home if anything happened to him."

"Did he say anything that made you think he might kill himself?"

"No. Actually he said he was afraid he'd be murdered—" The instant the words were out, Nella wanted to snatch them back.

Behind her a disgruntled voice said, "Lady, if you can tear yourself away, I'd sure like a cup of coffee."

She jumped and hurried over to pour the man his coffee. "Sorry, soldier. I . . ."

But he quickly turned his back and stomped away. She felt her face go red and wished she would get over this childhood tendency.

"Pay him no mind," the corporal said. "You didn't make him wait long."

Nella shrugged. "Well, I should have been watching. That's why I'm here."

"Look, forget him. I'll help keep an eye out next time. Now go on. You said Rufe thought someone was out to kill him, right?"

She nodded. "But I don't know for sure yet if the letter was really written by Rufe. I found it in a book my father had loaned him. My father is a minister."

"So he knew Rufe?"

"Yes, he visited him in the hospital."

The man leaned closer again. "Hey, I'm sorry I blew up at you. Like I said, it hit me hard losing Rufe. I think I know where his savings are. As soon as I pick up his cache, I've got to hotfoot it back to London. If he *was* murdered . . . I'd hate to think of the killer or killers getting off scot-free! Only I can't stay to do anything about it."

"Did he ever hint to you that he was afraid, maybe into something dangerous?" Nella asked.

"Not Rufe. He wasn't afraid of anything. You should've seen him on D day. Nothing slowed him down. He saved my life more than once, which is why I owe him. You think you could find out the truth of what really happened?"

"Not me personally, but I'm going to give his letter to someone who can."

"Good. There ain't nothing I wouldn't do for Rufe, but I got to report back tomorrow, or I'll be AWOL. You said your father's a minister. Maybe he can help."

The last thing Nella wanted was for her father or any of her family to get involved, but she said, "I'll do what I can."

"That makes me feel better."

"I'm glad to help. Would you like me to write and let you know how things go?" she offered, wishing he could stay a few days. His word would give credence to the letter.

"I sure would, thanks." On a napkin he scribbled *Corporal James Peterson* along with his military address.

"Thank you," Nella said as she tucked the napkin into her purse. She then opened a soft drink for a soldier who stood waiting. Turning back, she saw that Corporal Peterson had vanished without saying good-bye. She glanced uneasily around the room. The crowd was thinning now, as it was nearing curfew time. So Nella closed down the sandwich counter and walked toward the kitchen to help wash the dishes.

About a half hour later when Nella was preparing to go home, she learned no one else was heading her direction. She didn't worry about going alone, though. Having walked it many times in the blackout without the benefit of an electric torch, she knew every curb and stone. And tonight she'd remembered her torch. With the glass shielded for the blackout, she set out. The dim light illuminated the sidewalk a few steps ahead. All of Abergavenny had settled down for the night except for the army personnel carriers, which could be heard rumbling out of town to take the men back to their wards.

A vehicle entered the street from behind her. Nella turned and saw that the blacked-out lights resembled those of a jeep. She then resumed her walking. Sounding closer now, the vehicle slowed down. *Probably wants to offer me a ride,* Nella thought. She turned again. Still behind her, the jeep was barely moving now. She prepared to greet the driver and refuse a ride, for she'd rather walk.

Suddenly the engine roared, and the vehicle lunged forward. It then swerved, jumped the curb onto the sidewalk, and came straight at her. She threw herself into the recessed doorway of a shop to avoid being hit. The jeep raced past and screeched back into the street.

The crazy driver had nearly killed her! Was he drunk? Shaking, Nella peeked out of the doorway. The jeep had stopped and was turning around now in the middle of the street. Maybe it wasn't an accident. Maybe someone did mean to kill her!

Terrified, she darted across Monk Street and into the garden of St. Mary's Church. She'd dropped her torch when she dived into the store doorway. So without a light she stumbled and fell flat. Scrambling to her feet, she ran to the shrubbery behind the church and hid. She strained to see her pursuers in the darkness. The jeep's engine shut off. Then she heard voices and footsteps approaching. They were searching for her!

She wormed her way through the bushes and then dashed for the closest street toward the hill. At the end of an alley, she spied a vehicle driving slowly up Lion Street. She froze and listened again. The sound of the motor faded, so she started running again, feeling as if in a nightmare. At last she made it to the back gate of the manse garden. Breathless, she sprinted to the house and let herself into the kitchen, locking the door behind her.

On wobbly legs Nella staggered across the dark room and slumped down onto a kitchen chair, her heart racing. Someone had tried to kill her and had nearly succeeded. But why?

Then she heard herself telling Corporal Peterson that Rufe's letter said someone was trying to kill him. In her mind's eye Nella saw the group of soldiers who had been standing close enough to hear. Someone who knew the truth about Rufe could've overheard her. And if they felt threatened, there was no telling what they might try next.

Nella sat in the dark kitchen for several minutes as she tried to collect her thoughts. She hesitated to awaken her parents, and it was too late for the constable to do anything that night. They'd be long gone. Anyway, she couldn't identify either the vehicle or the driver. She hated to think how upset her mum and dad would be over what had just happened. Although it wasn't her way to keep quiet about such things, this time silence seemed the kindly course to take. She'd decide in the morning whether to tell them. Right now she was too confused about everything.

She went straight to Livie's crib and gently tucked her blanket around her small body. The old manse remained cool in the daytime but was downright chilly at night. She listened to her baby's even breathing and couldn't pull her hand away from the curve of her shoulder under the covers. *If that jeep had hit me, she'd be an orphan,* Nella thought, with a shiver.

Livie stirred and mumbled softly. Nella gently rubbed her back. After the baby's breathing took on a sleeping rhythm again, she finally pulled herself away and changed into her nightclothes. She knelt beside her bed for the first time in what seemed ages. Praying had become difficult after Rob died. Even though it still wasn't easy, tonight she had nowhere else to turn. She'd never doubted God's existence. "Heavenly Father," she whispered, "you know how I feel . . . not filled with trust like I used to be. But I don't know what else to do except ask you. Please keep Livie safe and keep me safe for her. Please . . ." She couldn't go on. Her doubts loomed up and held her tongue captive.

So Nella slipped into bed and closed her eyes, trying not to think of all the frightening possibilities. After a while, feeling frustrated over not being able to fall asleep, she got up and pulled on her robe. She slipped into sheepskin slippers and, grabbing her electric torch, tiptoed to the desk and opened her journal.

She'd kept a diary since childhood, except for those months of grieving following Rob's death. Then, for Livie's sake, she began to record memories of her brief marriage. She also wrote about Livie's baby months, her weight and length as she grew, and all her baby firsts.

In the dim glow of the light, she wrote, *Tonight I faced what my death would mean to Livie. . . .* She hesitated. She mustn't write anything that would reveal this night's danger in case Mum, or anyone for that matter, should ever see her journal. Nella had never made a big to-do about her writing being private.

With this in mind, she continued more carefully now, focusing on her feelings and not actual events. *I looked at Livie sleeping so calmly, safe in her crib, and thought about how she'd be an orphan without me. I'm thank-*

ful for Mum and Daddy being around, yet I believe Livie really needs me as she grows up. And I want to be with her when she has children of her own. Tonight I realized I could die young just like Rob did. I looked death in the face, but I lived. I must remember this. I lived, and I will live. Her pen left a wet droplet on the period at the end of the last sentence. She took a blotter and soaked up the excess before it could spread.

The poor lighting made writing all but impossible, making her want to lie down again and close her tired eyes.

Strangely her mind became clearer. She was sure now she'd done the right thing in not rousing her parents so late at night. If they must be told about the incident with the jeep, tomorrow would be soon enough. Either way, Nella would be careful not to go walking alone at night again.

As she was putting her journal back in the drawer, she noticed the last letter she'd received from Rufe's mother and so picked it up. The envelope contained a snapshot of a grinning boy, his arm wrapped around a large dog's neck. On the back was written, *Rufus loved this dog. He only got to keep it awhile, as his father never liked dogs. I was planning to get him a fine dog when he returned home.*

Nella shook her head sadly, then unfolded the letter to read again.

Dear Nella,

I can't tell you how much it means to me to be able to write to you about my son. He was such a good boy. Nobody here knew his goodness. His teachers were always scolding him for not getting his lessons done on time, but he was working to take care of me. I couldn't get him to do anything different, so I finally gave in and let him be the man he wanted to be.

I wish you could have known him, always smiling, always saying he loved me. I still find myself sometimes expecting him home for supper, a habit that's hard to break.

I have a job in the shipyard now and get good pay. If Rufus were here, he could go to school and not worry about me. The biggest mistake I ever made was to marry his father, but if I hadn't, I wouldn't have had Rufus, then, would I? I did my best to protect him. Looking back, I should've left his father long before I did. It was Rufus who gave me the courage and hope. Maybe if I'd left his father sooner, Rufus wouldn't have killed himself.

I'm sorry for going on about this. It's just that you're the only one I can tell how I feel, you losing your husband and all. It's such a comfort to write to you about my boy. Nella, girl, do you believe in God? Rufus always did. He used to sneak off to Sunday school, and I know he said his prayers. Some say you can't go to heaven if you

*kill yourself. Since you're a minister's daughter, can you tell me if
this is true?*

*Thank you for writing. I look forward to each letter. I love to
hear about Wales, such a peaceful place that my son got to see with
his own eyes.*

Your friend,
Mrs. Arvid Johnson

Her own faith being what it was, Nella had done her best to comfort Mrs. Johnson and also asked her father to enclose a note. Ian had spoken with Rufe in person about his spiritual readiness, so he had assured her that Rufus was indeed at home in heaven.

Nella hadn't yet received an answer to their two letters. She smoothed the photo of Rufe and studied his narrow face. He had one front tooth missing and a new tooth that appeared too big for his face. He looked so content with his arm around his dog. Tears came to her eyes. Such a short life he'd had and such a hard time of it.

Nella placed the photo and letter back in its envelope and laid it in her drawer on top of the recent addition, the envelope inscribed *Open in case of my death.*

She returned to her bed, and surprisingly, this time sleep beckoned.

CHAPTER FOUR

In the sunlight of Sunday morning, the terror generated by the jeep chase had diminished in Nella's mind to a state of uncertainty. Maybe the driver thought she was someone else. Maybe he was crazy drunk. Or maybe it was just mindless rage. If none of these more acceptable reasons, then she shuddered to think of the other possibility: The attempt on her life was carried out by someone who had overheard her remarks about Rufe's letter. Not having a solid answer yet, Nella decided against telling her parents about what happened the night before.

Once she was at church and surrounded by friends, Saturday night slipped into the background, where, like a bad dream, it infected the day with anxiety. She couldn't wait to talk to Jean and Peggy; they'd help her to make sense of the whole thing.

Peggy had bicycled in from West-Holding, and Jean had ridden to town with several other Red Cross women. Nella thought how fortunate she was to have two good friends so close to home, for the war had separated so many people from their friends and families.

It ended up that Jean and Peggy were invited to Sunday dinner at the manse. During dinner Jean brought up the subject of the spies at Crickhowell, her main concern being how Giselle felt about the news. Nella said that, despite outward appearances, Giselle seemed deeply troubled.

"I don't believe for a minute that those spies had any connection with Andre," Jean said. "Andre had his own agenda, thinking only to save himself by turning in Giselle. And the best efforts of the British secret service have disclosed no plot that involves Giselle." She turned to Nella. "I hope you'll help me convince her there's nothing to worry about."

"I'll try," Nella said, taking care not to let slip some of her own worry.

While they ate and later when cleaning up, Jean glanced at Nella from time to time, looking curious yet apparently understanding that Nella preferred not to discuss further the matter with the spies and whether or not there was any present danger.

As was her custom, Nella's mother offered to keep watch over Livie during her nap time while Nella, Jean, and Peggy went for a walk. When Nella changed out of her dress into slacks, she slipped Rufe's letter into her front pocket.

Out in the warm September sunshine, the three walked along the street that led north toward Flints' farm. Before Nella could bring up what she wanted to talk about, Peggy spoke.

"Jean, have you heard from Tom?"

"Oh yes. He's written almost every day."

"Too bad he had to go back into action after his arm was twice wounded," Peggy said. "It doesn't seem fair."

Jean smiled. "Uh-huh, but he wouldn't have been happy if he couldn't. He was bent on rejoining his buddies in the Nisei Combat Team."

"I can understand that," Nella said. "If I were a man, I'd want to be in the action and get this war won. Do you have any idea where Tom is?"

"No, but it hasn't been two weeks yet since he left. He may still be in England, waiting to be shipped out."

Nella saw the flash of loneliness and longing on Jean's face. "Surely the war will be over soon, and he'll be coming back. I hope he comes to Wales, and you could both stay for a while at the manse."

Jean brightened. "They'll probably send him directly to the States. But no matter what, we'll make our way back here. Wales has become a second home to me. Giselle feels the same way." They had reached the edge of town, and from the first hedgerow lining the country road, Jean picked up a walking stick. Swinging it along in a rhythmic tap, she added, "I love this town and the people in it." Then she gave Nella a serious, searching look. "Nella, is everything okay? You sounded worried on the phone."

"I wanted to show you this." Nella pulled the letter from her pocket and handed it to Jean.

"What's wrong?" Peggy asked.

While Jean read, Nella explained the letter and the way she'd come upon it in her father's book.

Jean walked slowly while reading the letter. Then she stopped, read it quickly through a second time, and gave it to Peggy.

When Peggy finished, she let out a big sigh. "You think this is true?"

Nella nodded. "I do. I hope Marge Emerson can confirm it's Rufe's writing. I told her about it, Jean. She's waiting for you to bring the letter to her."

"You say the letter was stuck in your father's book?" Jean asked. "So did you show it to him?"

"Not yet. I thought I should find out first if it's really Rufe's handwriting. Can you tell?"

"No," Jean answered, "but Marge ought to know. She visited him often and helped the nurses on his ward gather up his personal things to mail home to his mother. She must've seen his writing somewhere. But if Marge can't tell, maybe you could get a sample of his handwriting from Mrs. Johnson."

"I never thought of that," Nella said, "although I'd hate to have her know why I needed it. I think neither she nor my parents should be told anything until we're positive the letter's authentic."

"Good idea," Jean agreed. She took the letter back from Peggy and read it yet again. "This will interest Em too. It changes one of the case histories in her article about battle fatigue."

"I suppose so," Nella replied, "that is, if Rufe wrote the letter. I'm almost certain he did, but no one would believe me at the moment, not until I've verified the handwriting."

"Then how can you be so sure?" Peggy asked.

"Because of what happened last night at the USO. I met Rufe's buddy, the one he mentions in the letter. He came to get Rufe's money to send home to his mother."

"You what?" Jean exclaimed. "Why didn't you tell us?"

Nella shrugged. "Well, first you needed to read the letter."

"Nella!" Peggy scolded. "We're not in a three-act play here, where such revelations must be saved till the proper dramatic moment!"

"That's not why I waited," said Nella. True, she enjoyed telling a good story, especially one with a surprise ending. And she had performed in every play during her school days. But this was no time for Peggy to get sidetracked. "I just thought it would make better sense if you read the letter first, that's all."

"Okay, you two," Jean interjected. "Now go ahead, Nella. What about this friend of Rufe's?"

She told them all she could remember, then added, "I promised him I'd do what I could to get someone to look into the cause of Rufe's death."

"Did Corporal Peterson see the letter?" Jean asked.

"I didn't have it with me."

"Well, as far as I'm concerned, Corporal Peterson's existence proves the letter is real," Peggy said.

"Still, shouldn't someone like Marge identify the writing?" Nella asked.

Their walk had led them to the road to Crickhowell, as the afternoon sun warmed their backs. They stopped for a moment at the junction of the two roads, and Peggy pursued her line of reasoning. "You have Corporal Peterson's mailing address, right? Well, all the authorities have to do is call him back for questioning. How can they not look into it?"

"I think you're both right," Jean put in. "I'll give the letter to Marge this afternoon. She can take it from there."

"Good," Nella said. Then she added cautiously, "If she does recognize his writing, we could be getting into something very dangerous."

Jean halted. "Better explain yourself, Nella."

"Marge says Rufe had raved about his being a part of something important, something that could put an end to the war. He talked about some military secret hidden here in the hills. At the time, Marge thought he was acting irrational. Then Rufe suddenly became frightened, thinking someone was out to kill him. That seemed to fit a pattern of mental illness. Jean, you should talk with her yourself about this. Anyway, after listening to her, I think Rufe might've been mixed up in some kind of espionage. And I think the two spies arrested at Crickhowell could be linked to Rufe's being drowned. If that's true, then there may be more of them."

As if drawn by a magnet, Jean and Peggy turned and gazed up the road leading to Crickhowell.

Peggy's eyebrows climbed halfway to her hairline. "Are you out of your mind?" she exclaimed. "How can you imagine such a wild scenario? In the name of good sense, Nella, please stop this wild speculating—"

"Wait a minute, Peggy," Jean interrupted. "If Rufe *did* write this letter"—she did an about-face and headed back toward town—"then come on, we've got to find out right away. I'll hitch a ride back to Govilon from the Red Cross canteen."

They set out at a fast pace.

"I was hoping you'd both tell me I was making too much of all this," Nella said.

Peggy looked to be too flummoxed to talk anymore.

As they approached the manse, Nella said, "Remember not to let Mum and Daddy know about this yet."

"You're right," Jean agreed. "It's best not to tell anyone right now. When Marge turns the letter over to the authorities, they may want to keep it hushed up while they gather information."

"I can't believe this," Peggy muttered. "Spies and military secrets... here?" She shook her head and glanced at Nella from the corner of her eye, as if wondering about her sanity.

"Are you talking to yourself or to me?" Nella asked. "If it's me, I have to say I agree. Yet there's the possibility that someone's already after me because of Rufe's letter."

"What makes you think so?" Jean asked.

Nella explained how she'd said out loud information concerning Rufe at the USO where others could have overheard. She also told them about the jeep that had nearly run her over.

Peggy grew so pale the freckles on her nose stood out like cinnamon sprinkles.

Then Jean said firmly, "It's too pat that someone involved with Rufe's death should just happen to be at the USO when you said more than you should have. I'd guess that the chase was coincidental. Does the constable have any leads?"

"I didn't call the constable—"

They exploded at her, both talking at the same time and leaving no doubt as to what they thought of her judgment.

When they paused to take a breath, Nella said, "Listen. Mum and Daddy are missing Charles so much, I didn't want them worrying about me. By the time I ran home, the vehicle I never got a good look at was gone. So what could the constable do?"

"Nella," Peggy sputtered, "I can't believe you didn't report what happened!"

Jean looked as upset as Peggy, yet she spoke more calmly. "Well, it's not for you to decide what the constable can or cannot do."

"I suppose you're right," Nella said. "This morning I thought all my speculations were just that—speculations. So I kept quiet. I was hoping you two would help me think straight."

Jean gave her words silent consideration, then replied slowly, "Okay. Now that you've come this far, I think it's smart to keep on acting as if you've never seen the letter."

On hearing Jean agree to secrecy, Nella's thoughts shot ahead to her worst fear. "Livie and Mum and Daddy could be in danger, as well as me. Isn't that right?"

"I wish I could say you're wrong," Jean said. "If they are in danger, the hardest part will be walking the line between keeping them ignorant while doing all you can to assure their safety."

Peggy gripped Nella's arm. "But, Nella, whoever it was, they didn't see where you live, or they would've followed you there."

"Peggy's right," Jean said matter-of-factly. Jean glanced all around as if she felt someone watching them right then. "Look, let's assume, for safety's sake, that Rufe was murdered and that his killer is still around. As soon as we get back to the manse, I'll go to the canteen and find a ride. Nella, I think you should stay home tomorrow. Don't even go to the market for anything. Keeping this to ourselves may buy the necessary time for the authorities to look into it without the suspects finding out."

"You're really making me nervous, Jean." Peggy's sharp words shattered the country quiet.

Jean sighed and shook her head. "Sorry, but for one day it can't hurt to keep this a secret. Don't you agree?"

"Of course," Nella said.

Peggy nodded, but Nella could read reluctance on her face.

They hurried home, each lost in her own thoughts and the implications of what they'd decided.

After Peggy and Jean left, Nella spent the rest of the early evening in the back garden watching Livie play with Jacquie and Angie. Giselle remained upstairs, busy with sewing school dresses for the girls.

When bedtime for Livie arrived, Nella sent the older girls inside to their mother, hoping her precautions didn't appear unusual. They cheerfully obeyed, so she must have succeeded.

Not wanting to upset Livie with her nervousness, she took special pains to speak calmly as she took her in for her bath. After going through their nightly ritual, tucking Livie into her crib, she sat beside her for a long time and hummed lullabies, waiting for her to drift off to sleep.

Once Livie fell soundly asleep, Nella stood up and stretched. Her neck felt tense, and her head began to throb again. She wished she could believe the case of Private Rufus Johnson would be resolved simply and without stress to her family, but then more frightening scenarios played themselves out in her mind.

CHAPTER FIVE

At West-Holding Elementary School where Peggy taught a class of twelve-year-olds, she had a hard time Monday keeping her mind off Nella and her close call with the jeep. The thought that spies might be after Nella utterly terrified Peggy. Surely this would be proven wrong and soon.

She wished Nella had told Mother and Father Mac and the constable about it. Yet, like Nella, Peggy didn't want to see her beloved "adopted" parents become needlessly upset when they were still struggling with losing Charles. She stared out the window, her thoughts jumbled.

"Miss Jones!"

She jumped, so far was her mind from her business. Peter Hilliard had his hand up. "Yes, Peter."

"I think Annie wants something."

"Thank you, Peter." Turning her eyes to Annie Nelson sitting across the aisle from Peter, she met the blond girl's intense gaze. Annie was deaf and could only mouth a few words, which were difficult to understand.

Peter was the only pupil of gentry in the class. In hopes of keeping him safe from the bombing, his grandmother had enrolled him in the village school. At first Peggy struggled with being fair to Peter. She kept reverting to her childhood resentment of the wealthy, finding herself being especially hard on Peter whenever he got the slightest bit out of line. Of course, after Peggy snapped at him, she would then feel guilty and ashamed. But Annie had helped to change all this. Actually Annie had changed Peter. To Peggy's surprise, the boasting and demanding boy had made himself Annie's protector. Since then, he had become more considerate toward the rest of his classmates.

Now Annie caught Peggy's eye and signed, *"I've finished my work."*

Peggy awkwardly signed back, *"Good job, Annie."*

"Come see." Annie held up her painting.

Peggy smiled. The class had been drawing and painting pictures for their geography folders. Annie was a gifted artist. Although she'd been at the West-Holding School since the first evacuation of children from London, her extraordinary talent hadn't been encouraged by her other teachers.

However, it was understandable how the special needs of one quiet little girl could get overlooked. For with the great influx of children—distressed over being snatched from their homes—had come the reality of overburdened teachers, and the whole village, for that matter. Some teachers came from London along with the children and stayed on to teach, but it had still been chaos. When many decided to return and risk the danger of being bombed, the pressure on the village eased somewhat. Peggy hadn't been here then. She was attending school herself during the time of the blitz. Yet the newspaper photos depicting the frightened eyes of the children and the ragged grief of their mothers had haunted her ever since.

As soon as Peggy was qualified to teach, in the spring of 1942, she applied for a position in a village where displaced children were still being harbored—in nearby West-Holding. She'd been glad to find the work.

Knowing that Annie would be in her class this year, Peggy had gone to visit the girl's home during the summer to learn sign language from Annie and her mother. She had possessed a smattering of skills in signing, as did many of the children, because Annie's mother always gave lessons to Annie's class each year.

During the visits to Annie's home, Peggy had seen beautiful watercolor paintings decorating the walls of the rooms they leased from Miss Blackwell. At first Peggy couldn't believe a child had painted them. Then she saw Annie work.

Peggy was enough of an artist to win a scholarship to the Art Institute in London, but with the war and the blitz, she'd put this aside temporarily to teach the evacuated children.

When many of the evacuees had returned to London, Annie stayed on in West-Holding. Her mother had explained to Peggy that she couldn't bear the thought of Annie not being able to hear the air raid warning to take cover. The fact that Mrs. Nelson never left her deaf daughter alone didn't remove her maternal horror. She'd done well for Annie, perfecting her own signing skill and then working tirelessly to teach Annie to lip-read too. The latter effort was still in process, she explained, as she taught Peggy the signing.

Annie had two sisters, younger by only one and two years, who watched out for her like little mother hens.

Miss Blackwell, mistress of Brookside, an old manor house at the edge of the village, had been happy to let some of her many rooms to Mrs. Nelson. To everyone's surprise, the stern spinster had taken to the three Nelson girls, especially to Annie. Annie was small for her age, but possessed bright blue eyes that never missed anything. Her elfin face wore a chronically serious expression, which, Peggy learned, came from the child's constant effort not to miss anything. Despite her oddly adult soberness, Annie was quite lovely to behold and not nearly as fragile as she appeared. She often ran footraces with the boys and won, and she climbed trees fearlessly.

Now near the end of the day, Peggy stood beside Annie's desk and took delight in looking at Annie's rendition of a handsome tiger for her folder on India. Peggy smiled and signed, she hoped, *"Excellent! Good job. This is lovely."*

Annie grinned and nodded, her cheeks flushed with pleasure. *"Thank you."*

"She made a splendid tiger, didn't she?" Peter whispered.

"Yes, she has a talent," said Peggy.

Peter wasn't eager to let Peggy see his drawing, but he'd done a credible sketch of a mahout directing an elephant that was lifting a huge log.

"Very good, Peter." She straightened up and announced, "Class, it's time to put your work away. Those of you who have finished your drawings, please tack them up on the bulletin board. Be sure to write your name on them."

After the hubbub of hanging their drawings, the children lined up at the door. Once they were quiet and in order again, Peggy opened the door and dismissed them. And as they'd been taught, each one politely said "Good day, Miss Jones" as they passed her. Annie signed her farewell, then dashed out of the school building to meet her sisters on the sidewalk.

Peggy considered her teaching the children in West-Holding to be her wartime service, a detour in her life much like the army was for most of the soldiers. She wasn't sacrificing anything compared to them, but she did have her own battle of sorts: a continuous friction with her supervisor, Lady Clementina Pryor Westmoreland. Lady Westmoreland had been appointed originally to oversee the evacuees from London. Now, five years later, she served as an overseer of the basic education of all the village children. She took this responsibility very seriously—too seriously, Peggy thought. Lady W., as Peggy referred to her privately, didn't approve of creative projects in the classroom, whereas Peggy saw them as essential.

Peggy had found unexpected enjoyment in teaching. She thrived on the opportunity to help the children think new thoughts, enjoy the process of creating something beautiful as well as useful. Her pupils seemed to enjoy activities such as today's assignment, though the boys were usually more enthusiastic when Peggy came up with a leatherwork project or something using wood, such as constructing models.

This new class was no different from her previous ones, except for Annie. The girl displayed such artistic talent that Peggy had spent her off-hours thinking of ways to develop her gift. So far this meant plenty of art lessons in class.

This year she had a group of children who seemed to be thriving in the area of art. She hadn't yet turned to the traditional woodworking for the boys and sewing for the girls, the course other teachers took. She felt that when she offered such crafts, *all* of her pupils should have a hand in whichever project she assigned. Also, Peggy found that they were more inclined to learn when she prepared art projects to go with their other lessons.

Through her classroom window she watched the children disperse toward their individual homes. She waited until she saw Annie's sisters meet her and the three of them set off together toward Brookside. Then Peggy returned to her desk to correct arithmetic exams. If she hurried, she'd be done in a half hour and be free to bicycle into Abergavenny, in case Nella called and needed her.

A few minutes later when a quick rap on the door interrupted her, she wasn't surprised to see Lady W. march into her classroom.

Peggy stood and said, "Good afternoon, Lady Westmoreland. If you please, come and be seated."

"Good afternoon, Miss Jones," Lady W. responded crisply. "I trust you've had a good day." Without waiting for Peggy to answer, she said, "It has come to my attention that you have used an inordinate amount of watercolor paint in the short time since school began. I fear you are emphasizing the frivolous. What exactly have you been doing?"

They'd gone over this subject many times, so Peggy didn't give an extensive explanation. She kept herself composed, while inwardly she seethed. "We were doing a geography project today."

"I see." Lady W. went over to the bulletin board and scanned the children's colorful papers. Peggy hadn't yet straightened them, so the arrangement looked a bit helter-skelter.

Lady W. then spun around and walked back to stand in front of Peggy's desk. "Sit down, Miss Jones. I need to talk to you."

Peggy obeyed, and her supervisor did the same, sitting with perfect posture in the wooden chair beside the desk. "Some of the teachers have complained to me that we do not have enough jars of paste or boxes of chalk or colored pencils. It struck me that you, because of your personal interest in drawing and painting, may be using more than what is reasonable or your fair share. I'm sure you will agree that we must all adjust to help one another during these wartime short-ages."

"Of course, Lady Westmoreland."

"Then I will count on you to keep your art projects at a bare minimum as the others do."

Peggy wanted to tell her that the "bare minimum" would stifle her pupils, but she kept her mouth firmly closed. For if she let the woman talk, perhaps she'd get up and leave sooner. She wished to hurry home to her room at Gatekeep. What if Nella had called while she sat trapped with the Dragon Lady?

Poor Nella. What was behind that horrifying experience the night before? Peggy had her doubts about the plan to keep quiet. *I hope Jean and Marge can clear up the business with Rufe quickly so we can call in the constable*, Peggy thought. *Nella must be terribly worried.*

She kept her eyes fastened on Lady W., nodding from time to time to reassure her that she was listening.

Once begun, Lady Westmoreland could talk forever. Peggy silently sat at her desk and wished God would put a stopper in the woman's mouth. The thought of how she'd look made Peggy want to laugh.

As the woman droned on, Peggy's mind wandered again, this time to Annie and the handsome tiger she'd just drawn. Her art could open a door to many wonderful possibilities for Annie. Somehow the child's work should be evaluated by someone qualified to judge the full extent of her talent. Maybe Nella would have some ideas about this. Even Lady W. would take notice if little Annie attracted the favor of someone notable.

Surrounded by the smell of chalk dust, the cloying scent of paste, and the cheap water-based paint the children had used on their drawings, Peggy struggled to maintain her respectful mask. The sound of the older woman's voice suddenly ceased.

Peggy snapped to attention.

Lady W., with emphatic correctness, said, "Miss Jones, I have the distinct impression you've not heard a word I've said. One would suppose a teacher would have learned to be attentive to her superiors."

Peggy, who hadn't once taken her eyes off her supervisor, blinked, hoping she appeared innocent and surprised. "Oh yes. One would. Please continue, Lady Westmoreland."

The woman had the power to make her feel like Cinderella, the unwanted stepchild, if Peggy chose to dwell on it. So as soon as Lady W. resumed her lecture, Peggy let her mind roam free again while feigning attention. She thought about how she'd come to West-Holding. She'd made the mistake of picking up the *Daily Telegraph* and looking at the bewildered faces of children boarding trains to escape London. Patriotism and her heart got in the way of her ambition to go to art school, war or no. Later she discovered she couldn't have finished art school anyway, even if she had gone to London. Most of the teaching staff were called up for service, and the bombing of London made Peggy glad she'd stayed in Wales.

With the war going on over five years now, a lot of the children she'd come here to help had returned to London. But some fifty children, like Annie Nelson and her younger sisters, had remained in the village to wait out the war.

Lady Westmoreland's voice broke through her thoughts.

"... study the details of my outline for providing practical training for your pupils. You must stop projecting your own interests onto them. Many will go from West-Holding School straight into service in the great houses. The girls need to be prepared for maid service and homemaking. The boys will need the practical skills that men use in farming. This"—she flipped one hand toward the freshly painted pictures on the bulletin board in a manner that conveyed contempt—"so-called art instruction only wastes their time. I must insist that you stay within our established curriculum."

Peggy cleared her throat. "The children are learning their practical skills. They also read, write, and calculate quite proficiently. They've learned geography by following the war news around the world. I believe many of them understand more about the British Empire than do some of their parents. Lady Westmoreland, you should know that I only offer art projects when their assignments for the required subjects have been completed and are satisfactory. Surely a short art class at the end of the week will not hamper their future work skills."

"Young woman, you obviously need to learn your place. I am responsible for the children in this village." She stood up. "Their parents want them to learn in the same manner they did. They want no frivolous, impractical ideas put into their children's minds. If you cannot follow proper guidelines, I can certainly acquire a new teacher who will."

Peggy clenched her teeth to hold back words that would most likely result in losing her job. Her greatest disagreement had to do with the remark about practicality. If children had a talent for something different, Peggy was sure their parents would agree with her. Some had already told her so. Peggy's passion was to help them realize their potential, to be whatever God had endowed them to be. Unfortunately, in the past, the village children ended up following their father's trade, which kept them at their *proper* social level. Although she was boiling inside, Peggy managed to say calmly, "I shall do my very best, Lady Westmoreland."

"Well, see that you do, Miss Jones!" With that, Lady Westmoreland marched out the door like the queen herself.

Peggy sighed in relief when the door closed behind her. She wasn't sure how much longer she could keep her lips sealed over her anger. She'd come to love the children, especially the evacuees, and had made it her mission to show them some of the beauty in the world, beyond their disadvantaged lives. Lord knows they'd had little enough of loveliness due to the privations of war. *Well, Lady W., you're going to be surprised come war's end. A lot of us won't fit your mold anymore. And some who you think belong downstairs in the kitchen will no longer stay there. Me included.*

She thought of the young soldiers who had never hoped for a higher education yet had now become leaders of men. They weren't thinking to come home from the war and stay in the mines or on the docks. They wanted and deserved more. And the children would have a brighter future after the war. She thought of Annie, a sensitive and competent painter already, and twelve-year-old Betsy Harding, who wrote profound and moving poetry. Or Tim Sievers, who was so gifted in mathematics that she'd have to send away for more advanced texts for him. *No,* Peggy thought, *I can't let my pupils down by not showing them the possibilities out there. I won't be a part of holding them back.*

But if I push too hard for what I believe, I could lose my position. And if I do, who else will care enough to risk breaking the traditional rules of Lady

W.? The other teachers kept their place and kowtowed to Lady W. They probably agreed with her.

Peggy swept up the remaining arithmetic papers, placed them in her briefcase, and headed for home. She strode down Great House Road, hoping not to have to talk to anyone. She was upset and anxious to get home to see if Nella had called. Eyes straight ahead, she walked quickly past the chemist's shop, the post office, The White Horse Pub, Drury's Bake Shop, and Miller's Co-op. By the time she reached Gatekeep, where she lived with Mrs. Lewis, her anger had been reduced to a simmer.

Then a lorry came roaring down the road from behind and braked noisily alongside her. Bryan Westmoreland grinned down at her. "Miss Jones."

"Mr. Westmoreland," she responded politely, while groaning inwardly at how fast her wish to be alone had been violated. "You were driving too fast again. You seem to forget that classes have been dismissed and children are out and about playing."

"And you seem to forget that you're in charge only in your own classroom," he replied sharply. Then, as he often did, he switched character and gave a friendly smile. "I'm sorry, Miss Jones. I do watch, you know. And this old relic makes a lot of noise, which sounds like speed but isn't." He waited for her response, but getting none, added, "That day I nearly ran you down scared me as much as you."

"I doubt that," Peggy countered. She still felt sick at the thought that if she'd been a child, unable to get out of the way . . .

"I assure you, I have reformed my driving habits."

To be fair, she hadn't seen him speed on the narrow hedge-lined roads around the village since the day she crashed her bicycle into the hedge to avoid being smacked by his Bentley. In fact, she hadn't seen him in the Bentley since then. She looked up, hoping he'd go on his way. "Is there something I can do for you?"

"As a matter of fact, there is. I understand you grew up in the Presbyterian manse in Abergavenny."

"Yes," she said cautiously.

"I wonder if I might impose upon you to deliver this book to Reverend MacDougall. He said he'd like to read it." He held out the old leather-bound book, which looked like a legal tome. "It's the history of the Westmoreland family here in Wales."

She received it and turned it carefully in her hands. "This must be pretty old."

"It was published in 1892. The history in it goes back to A.D. 1200."

"Is this your only copy?"

He shrugged. "There are copies in a few university libraries. Will you deliver it the next time you go into town?"

"Yes, but may I read it too? I'd like to use this book to prepare a few lessons for my class."

"Certainly. Keep it as long as you deem necessary." He reached for the key in the ignition, then paused. "Tell me, how is Mrs. Killian?"

"Nella? She's fine."

"Having a husband in the service while she has a baby to care for must be difficult."

"She's a war widow. That's even more difficult."

"Oh. I'm sorry to hear that. Please give her my regards, won't you?"

"You know her?"

"Not exactly, but we've met. Good day, then." He raised a hand in a half salute and drove away.

As Peggy watched and listened, she had to admit that he was right—the very noise of the lorry made it seem that it was moving faster than it actually was. Nevertheless, she neither liked nor trusted Bryan Westmoreland.

She had disliked him even before that day he'd kissed her, presuming she would welcome his bold move. The kiss in itself wasn't worth her staying angry. Besides, he had apologized and then never bothered her again. And Bryan had been consistently polite except for the few times she'd challenged him. Today, for instance. She sighed. Nella would say she was behaving unfairly because he was gentry.

She tried to teach her pupils not to treat others this way, yet in spite of her best efforts, every time she had to deal with Bryan Westmoreland, her feelings tended to overrule her good intentions. She despised her own resentment and lack of control. It contradicted her deepest Christian beliefs. Furthermore, if she couldn't change herself, how could she then expect better of others?

Frustrated, she stepped inside Gatekeep. "I'm home, Mrs. Lewis," she called to her landlady, who was making supper by the sound of the pans clattering in the kitchen. "Did I get any phone calls?"

Mrs. Lewis popped her head around the corner in the hall, looking like a pink-cheeked jack-in-the-box, and waved a floury hand. "Not a one, love. Funny, someone usually calls."

"Well, no news is good, they say. Do you need any help with supper?"

"Not a whit, thank you. If you didn't bring home any schoolwork, you'll just hafta sit on your hands." She chuckled at her own cleverness, then disappeared into the kitchen again.

Peggy headed gratefully to the privacy of her room. If Nella didn't call, she could only assume everything was okay. It was a bit awkward for her to phone Nella, as it meant going through the switchboard. Then she had to be sure she squared the charge with Mrs. Lewis when the bill came. And Mrs. Lewis was inclined to argue against her paying.

She sat down and looked out the window, past the main road that wound through the village and up the hill toward Whitestone Manor, the Westmoreland family mansion. She wasn't sure whether Lady W. could actually remove her from her teaching position, but she knew the war had changed many of the old ways. Lady W. was domineering, but she'd never given Peggy a reason to think she would lie. So she probably did have the power to dismiss her.

Now that Peggy's anger had cooled, the idea of getting dismissed frightened her. Such a thing would be a blot on her employment record, something that would follow her for a long time. She might not be allowed to teach again in the public schools. Or worse, her dismissal could cost her the scholarship to the Art Institute. She remembered from her interview what a persnickety bunch they were. Already having delayed in her acceptance of the scholarship because of the war, she might be in a precarious position. She mustn't take any chances. Without the scholarship, the Institute was simply beyond her reach.

Just looking at Whitestone Manor gave her a sense of oppression. She could almost feel the presence of generations of powerful Westmorelands staring back at her. No wonder the villagers told ghost stories about the ruling family.

She bit her lip, turned away from the window, and pulled out the student work she'd brought home to correct. She couldn't sit idle while waiting for Nella to call.

CHAPTER SIX

Nella had remained indoors at the manse all day Monday, wondering if she'd run out of good excuses for not going out. Later in the evening, while anxiously waiting for some word from Jean, Marge's sister Em called from Gilwern.

"Nella, hello. I'm wondering if I might stay at the manse until I can board a train to London. I'd love to see you and your family before I leave Abergavenny. You did say to come again when I got the chance."

"Oh yes! Mum will be delighted. We were afraid we might miss you this time."

Em laughed. "I'd never leave without at least stopping to say hello. But I wasn't sure I should invite myself to stay."

"For you, our door is always open."

"Thanks so much, but don't you need to clear it with your mother first?"

"No. She'll be so glad. Only today she asked about you, and I told her you were in Gilwern."

"Then is it all right if I come right away, even though it's near bedtime?"

"Absolutely. I'll get the bed turned out for you."

"Thanks. I'll be there within the hour." She suddenly lowered her voice so Nella had to ask her to repeat herself. "Have you stayed out of sight as Jean suggested?"

So Em knew too. "Aye. All day."

"Good." Em's voice rose to its normal level again. "See you soon."

"Righto," Nella said lightly. She hung up the receiver and went to put fresh sheets on the bed in the room that had belonged to Charles. After he'd been killed in action the spring before, her mother hadn't wanted to remove even his clothing from the wardrobe, not until Em needed a room and came to the manse. Her folks loved Em. Em's visit had turned out to be a good thing for Nella's parents, to have someone use Charles's room again. Even so, the furniture and the pictures on the walls remained untouched.

Now as Nella tucked in the clean sheets, turned down the comforter, and plumped up the pillow, she remembered the last time her brother had come home.

She'd brought him tea in bed the final day of his leave. He patted the edge of the bed and said, "Stay and talk, Sis."

Nella smiled and sat down, glad he'd asked.

"I remember how determined you were to go do your part by joining the WAAF, and how you finally won over Dad when he was dead set to get you out after you lied about your age to get in. You've become a strong woman, Nell, and I'm proud to be your brother."

"Well, Charles . . ." she had stammered, embarrassed and yet pleased over his wanting to say this. "You're the hero of this family. I'm so proud of you."

"Oh, it's not the same for a man. A boy thinks it's a noble and great adventure to go off to war. But girls, they're different. You always liked things peaceful-like and to your own ordering. It isn't just that you went and took your chances, but then coming back home like you did after Rob was killed and starting over . . . well, you're a dab-hand at so many things. I just wanted to say, in case you ever wonder, you're a woman who can do anything she sets her mind to. You're a winner, Nell." Now he looked a bit embarrassed, not being one to put his feelings into words like that.

To help him out, she said simply, "Thank you, Charles. It comforts me to no end to hear this from you."

He had looked pleased and also relieved, as if it was important for her to take his words seriously.

Nella had been surprised over what Charles had said, a little puzzled too. More than once since then, however, she'd taken courage from recalling his last words to her. In spite of his teasing ways, he'd been a good big brother, always helping her when she needed him. She was grateful that she'd leaned over and kissed him that day before returning to the kitchen.

Now in his empty room Nella sat on the edge of his bed and let the tears come till they washed away some of the pain from missing him. Wiping her eyes, she slowly stood and went to tell Mum that Em was coming.

When Em arrived, Nella invited Giselle down for tea. Giselle brought scones she had just baked. "The girls are already in bed asleep. So tired they are, now that they're in school."

"How are they liking school in English?" Em asked.

"They've had a few months to adjust to the Welsh way of speaking, and you know how children are. They pick up language quicker while playing than we can teach. I think it's being in the classroom that tires them so. In Lyon Jacquie went only one year to school, and then I taught her at home. Angie I taught from the beginning. Their teachers say they are far ahead in reading and even in English spelling, but both need help in arithmetic."

"Poor tykes," Em said. "Will your husband get leave to come see you after being out of touch for so long?"

Giselle shook her head. "We must be patient. He is needed in France."

Nella's father came in from his den. "Em! How good that you've come. We didn't hope to see you again so soon."

"Hello, Reverend MacDougall! Thank you. I never know from one week to the next where they'll send me, but I jumped for joy to be coming back here."

"Do join us for tea, Ian," Nella's mother said. He sat down at the kitchen table, and she poured tea and milk into his favorite big cup.

Then Em pulled out a box of real chocolates she'd acquired from her travels. "Be sure to take some to Jacquie and Angie," she urged Giselle.

"Oh, thank you. I will." Giselle chose two pieces, taking the paper cups with them.

After they had caught up on personal news and finished their tea, Em stretched and said, "Excuse me, but I'm very tired. Do you mind if I go to my room now? A good night's sleep will be pure heaven after camping with Marge in that Nissen hut with six nurses coming and going."

"You go right along, dear," Nella's mother said. "You know where everything is. Don't hesitate to tell me if you need anything."

Nella stood up. "I'll go with her, Mum, to help get her settled. Excuse me, please, Giselle."

"But of course. I should be getting back upstairs now."

Once Nella and Em reached the bedroom, Nella closed the door behind them. This was their first private moment to talk freely about Rufe's letter.

Em got right to the point. "Marge said the writing looks like Private Johnson's all right. Jean seemed to feel I should leave Abergavenny without attracting notice so as not to become involved. For my safety, she said. I'm sorry you're in such a fix, Nella. I hope there's no danger, but you're smart to be cautious. How did it go today, staying indoors and all?"

"I managed all right, but I can't keep on like this. I'll just have to take my chances and be extra careful."

"I know how you feel about being shut in. Wish I could help."

"I guess this is something I have to do by myself. Jean's right. It's better for you to leave. And who knows, maybe you'll see a way to expedite an investigation. You know some important people."

"I don't know about that, but I'm willing to try. I think the one who can help you most is right here in your house—Giselle. That woman, with her experience, is wiser than all of us put together. You should tell her everything and then trust her judgment."

"But Jean says wait—"

"Still, I really think you should talk to Giselle and also to your parents. If there *is* danger, having everyone informed may protect them as well as you."

Nella hated the feeling of deception that had dogged her all day. "Maybe you're right. I'll talk to Giselle, but I won't tell my parents just yet. I'll wait till I hear more from Marge."

"Nella, this is no time to hide things from your parents," Em said.

"I won't for long. I just want more information before telling them."

Later on, long after going to bed, Nella couldn't sleep. The fact that she'd had to keep her worries to herself all day had worked to magnify them. Now tired and sleepless, she went over and over in her mind all that had happened and what it might mean. If a killer wanted to silence her, would he try to get at her through her loved ones? With sick dread she remembered how Jacquie and Angie had been kidnapped to get at Giselle. The thought that something could happen to Livie utterly terrified her. Finally she decided she might as well get up. Maybe sit in the chair by the window.

She retrieved an old comforter from the closet shelf to use for a wrap. At Livie's crib she pulled the coverlet up again and lightly smoothed the baby's curls. The sight of her, so serene and angelic, made Nella want to scoop her up, carry her to her own bed, and hold her in her empty arms. The feel of her small, warm body snuggled up close might ease the fear that threatened to overwhelm her. How could she, by herself, know what to do to keep Livie safe? She thought of the terror Giselle had endured when her girls were kidnapped, and shuddered.

Sinking to her knees beside the crib, Nella remembered how Charles had told her she could do anything she set her mind to. She had a feeling his words would be tested in the days ahead. She rose, took the comforter to her favorite chair, and wrapped up in it. Then she tried to pray.

But her stumbling pleas to God brought her no peace. Instead, Em's advice to go to Giselle echoed in her ears.

The next morning, while Em went to purchase her ticket at the train station, Nella knocked at Giselle's door at the side of the manse. With Jacquie and Angie at school and Nella's mother and Livie at the church, now was a good time to talk to Giselle.

Giselle opened the door and smiled in surprise. "Good morning, Nella. Would you like to come up and have some tea?"

"Thank you. I surely would." Nella said as she followed her up the steep stairs.

Giselle poured them each a cup and then sat down, giving Nella her full attention.

Nella got right to the point. "I have a problem, and I need your advice."

Giselle sobered. "What is it?"

"Well, I guess I should start with what happened Saturday afternoon." Then Nella told Giselle about the letter, about meeting Corporal Peterson, and about later being chased.

As she poured out her story, Giselle grew quieter and quieter, never taking her eyes from Nella's. At last when Nella had stopped talking, Giselle said, "I wish you had called the constable right away."

"But as I said, it was too late! Then in the morning, I thought it would be better not to worry anyone. Don't you see?"

Giselle shook her head. "No. But it's done now. So you gave Marge the letter, and you still haven't told your parents."

"Right."

Giselle sighed and took a sip of her tea. A slight frown creased her brow. She seemed far away in her thoughts. Finally she said, "I was hoping the fear and danger would be over now, but from what you've just told me, that doesn't seem to be the case. We may still be in danger."

"Are you thinking about Andre? Surely that's over for you."

Giselle gave her an agonized look. "I can't be sure. Not until the war is over. I'm glad Marge is turning in that letter, but you still must talk to the constable. Let him report to the military if he thinks there's a connection between the assault on you and Private Johnson's death. You must tell him immediately," she repeated.

"But then I'd have to tell Mum and Daddy too. I didn't want them to know unless there was a clear danger."

"Nella, you don't know what you're dealing with here. The law must take over now and decide things. Has your father left for his office yet?"

"I think so."

"Let's go down and see. If he's still home, I want you to tell him what you've just told me. Everything."

"But shouldn't I wait till I hear from Marge?"

Giselle sighed. She pressed a hand to her forehead, then rubbed her temples. When she looked up, her former, haunted expression had returned. She'd looked this way last spring when first coming to the manse to be near Jean.

The force of Giselle's fear made Nella catch her breath and instantly offer, "Look, I'll go myself to the military police. And if Marge and I go together, they're sure to take this seriously."

Giselle nodded. "That's a good idea. Go see Captain Andrew Evers at the Gilwern military station hospital. He's the one who interrogated me and directed a search here for Andre's accomplices." She stood up. "I think I still have Captain Evers' phone number." She hurried away, and Nella heard her opening a drawer in her bedroom.

In a moment she was back. "Here. I hope he's still there. If he isn't, you can ask for whoever replaced him."

With trembling fingers, Nella took the piece of paper. "Try not to worry, Giselle, and please don't tell Mum and Daddy. In the meantime will you help me watch out for them?"

"Yes," Giselle said firmly. "I can do that."

When Nella went downstairs she found the privacy she needed for the telephone call. Em had returned but was busy typing furiously in her room, and her mother and Livie were still away at the church. She rang the three-digit number and made her request.

In a moment a businesslike masculine voice came on. "Captain Evers here. What may I do for you?"

Nella introduced herself and mentioned Giselle, whom he remembered. "Mrs. Munier felt I should talk to you. I have new information concerning the death of Private Rufus Johnson. Do you remember him, the soldier who drowned?"

"Yes, indeed I do," he replied brusquely.

"May I meet with you about this?" She lowered her voice. "I think someone tried to kill me. Mrs. Munier suggested I talk to you before going to the constable."

His answer was slow in coming. "I don't know about that, but can you come this afternoon? Say at fourteen hundred. That's two P.M. I'll send a driver for you at one-thirty."

"Please, for the time being... I'd like to keep this from my parents, until they need to know."

"Not a bad idea. How about meeting my driver down at the castle grounds? Tell the MP who you are. Does that suit you?"

"Yes. And thank you."

As she rang off, she heard the front door open and Livie calling for her. "Mummy! I home!"

"Coming, Livie," Nella called back, quickly devising a plausible reason for her need to be gone for the afternoon.

At the castle she found Captain Evers' driver waiting for her in his jeep. Riding to Gilwern, she tried to organize her thoughts. She must impress the captain with solid evidence, so he would see that what had happened to her was somehow linked to Rufe's death and determine whether Giselle's worry—about there being more Nazi sympathizers in the area—was in fact justified.

A sergeant escorted Nella into Captain Evers' office, and with one look, she found herself wishing the man in whom she was about to confide inspired more trust. He had the blond good looks of an English gentleman, yet even with his military correctness, he appeared too casual. Nevertheless, she filled him in on what had transpired from the time she discovered Rufe's letter to her narrow escape Saturday night. The captain made quick notes, as did a man who seemed to be his assistant.

Then he commenced asking her questions. Had she ever seen Corporal Peterson before? Why did she believe his story? Was there anything Peterson said that might suggest he would try to run her over later with his jeep?

Nella was shocked at such a suggestion. She had no doubt that Corporal Peterson was Rufe's "buddy" from the letter. She gave her reasons and handed Corporal Peterson's address to the captain. "You can question him yourself."

He took it and said, "I'll follow up on this. Who else came to the sandwich counter while Peterson was there?"

"I'm sorry. I'm afraid I wouldn't know any of them again if I saw them," she said, discouraged over her lack of specific details.

"I expected that. Just checking." He made a few more notes and then dismissed his secretary. Standing up, he led her over to the door. "Thank you for coming. Your driver's waiting where he let you off. I'll do what I can to get to the bottom of this. For the time being, please trust it to me. At the right time I'll call in the constable. It is wise, as you say, not to worry your parents about it for now. Go about your daily business as usual, but don't go out alone at night. Not a good idea, even in peacetime, for an attractive young woman like yourself. But I think you've learned your lesson there." He smiled and opened the door for her. "I'll call you if I find out anything."

"Thank you, Captain Evers. I hope that will be soon."

"So do I. Good-bye."

"Good-bye." Nella walked down the narrow hall and outside to the waiting transport, wishing she felt more comfortable about the outcome of the meeting. Had he taken her seriously or not?

CHAPTER SEVEN

Upon reaching home, Nella decided that as soon as she could she'd tell Giselle about the secret meeting with Captain Evers. However, until then, she must act as if she had nothing on her mind more unsettling than the usual household chores.

Except for Em's typewriter clicking steadily in Charles's room, silence greeted her. She found Livie's crib empty. Assuming her mother and the baby were in the garden, Nella stepped out the kitchen door.

Sure enough, Livie was picking up new potatoes as Elizabeth unearthed them.

"I'm back, Mum," Nella said, love for them welling up in her throat.

Her mother smiled. "Did you have a busy afternoon at the USO?"

This had been Nella's pretense: the need to fill in for someone at the canteen. "It was pretty slow," she lied again. "I don't think they really needed me."

Livie was so busy filling her little pail with potatoes, she didn't even look up.

"I imagine they were glad to have you," her mum said. "Did anyone tell you that twelve thousand German soldiers surrendered yesterday, when the British First and the Americans took Le Havre?"

"No. What a struggle that's been and not far from where they landed on D day."

"Giselle says Le Havre gives the Allies a deep-water port instead of the beachhead docks for unloading troops and supplies. Which is why the Germans have hung on so desperately. Now the advance across France will proceed faster. Giselle's so eager to return to Lyon. I'll greatly miss her when she leaves."

"Me too. She and the girls are like family now. Livie will feel lost without Angie and Jacquie around." Nella moved to her mother's side and knelt to help her. Tossing the potatoes into the basket reminded her of her school days before the war. Even though the work could be backbreaking, she had loved getting excused from school to help with the local potato harvest. On impulse she asked, "Would you mind if I helped with the harvest this year?"

Her mother glanced at her with a pleased smile. "I think working out of doors would do you a world of good, and you know Livie and I will get along just fine."

"Yes, she dearly loves her *mamgu* and *dad-cu*." In place of her previous baby talk, Livie had recently adopted the Welsh for grandmother and grandfather. She spoke the words with a mischievous smile, delighted with the new sounds. Nella threw another handful of potatoes into the basket. "I wonder what it would be like to serve in the Land Army."

When war was declared, the women of Britain had turned out en masse to work the land and keep the farms producing food while the able-bodied men left to fight. The Land Army wasn't new. Nella had heard how in World War I, the Land Army had kept the farms operating at top production. Now in this war, even though other branches of service had opened to welcome women, a surprising number chose to work on farms. Many city girls had put on the brown and green uniforms and milked, plowed, planted, harvested, ditched fields for drainage, laid hedges, and did all the work the men had been doing. Nella had met some of the girls who had been assigned to farms near Abergavenny.

"Being a Land Girl is heavy, hard work," her mother said. "I hear tell the girls even fell trees for lumber."

"Yes. I sometimes wish I'd volunteered for the Land Army, seeing as how I love farming and have always wanted a small landholding of my own. But then if I'd become a Land Girl, I'd never have met Rob, now, would I?"

"That's a fact."

They both turned at the same instant to gaze at Livie, who had begun digging in the dark soil at the edge of the victory garden.

When the war was declared, all those who owned a bit of earth had turned it to producing vegetables. The task of raising one's own food was a patriotic duty, and everyone called the private plots victory gardens. So in a way, all the women who had access to a few feet of soil could be called Land Girls.

Like other gardens once given over to flowers, the manse garden had been transformed, enlarged to produce vegetables by the peck. They often shared the excess with parishioners. And Nella helped her mother bottle the remainder, the only way to ensure them having something other than potatoes and cabbage to eat during the long winter.

As Nella watched Livie dig enthusiastically, her mother said, "I gave her some late peas to plant. A few might actually grow for her."

"You're so good with her, Mum. I'm so grateful we could come home, so she could be near you and Daddy."

"We're grateful too, love. It helps . . . after losing Charles and all."

"Mum, when I was preparing Charles's room for Em, I got to thinking . . . I want you to know if anything ever happened to me, I'd be at peace knowing Livie has you and Daddy."

"Nella! Why ever are you talking like that? Don't even think of such a thing!"

"I'm sorry. It's just something I want you to know. I don't expect to leave Livie, but who's to know what the Lord has in store for any of us?"

"Don't bring the Lord's good name into this, and I don't want to hear any more of this talk. You're sounding like you did when you first came home after losing Rob. You've got nothing to fear. Oh, honey,"—she reached out and took Nella's dirt-stained hand—"I know you've had a heavy burden for one so young. But you must realize that most of the time life is filled with good things. This war will be over soon, and then you'll see more beautiful, ordinary days."

"I understand, Mum." She squeezed her mother's hand. "I'm fine. Really. I know what you say is true." All the while Nella was thinking how wise she'd been not to awaken her parents the night she'd almost gotten run over. As much as the deception distressed her, she was also glad she had successfully concealed her visit to the military police.

That evening when Em was getting ready to leave and board her train, Nella's father insisted on walking her to the station. Nella was relieved at this, for it meant she could go along and see Em off. Otherwise she wouldn't have dared, but she didn't want Em out walking alone either.

She and her father stood with Em on the station's platform, filling the waiting with talk about the weather and cautions to take care and to write and to be sure to come back, as people do when they are about to say good-bye and the important things have already been said. At last Em boarded her train.

Nella and her father strode home through the blacked-out town. They chatted about church activities, Livie, and the potato harvest. When they came to the doorway that had protected her from being hit by the jeep, Nella found herself listening for approaching vehicles. She wished they were on the other side of the street where no one could trap them against the solid stone wall ahead. Unable to quell her fear, she asked her father to cross the street with her. He didn't question her reason, for it was normal to walk that side sooner or later as they made their way back to the manse.

Wednesday morning Livie woke up at her usual early hour. Nella just groaned, lingering in her bed for a moment. The next thing she knew, sunlight was pouring into her bedroom and Livie was gone. Surprised that she'd fallen back to sleep, she shot out of bed, slipped on her robe, and hurried to the kitchen. There sat Livie in her high chair, eating her porridge. Her mother was having her tea and toast at the table.

"Sorry, Mum. I didn't mean to oversleep."

"We just got up ourselves a little while ago. I put Livie in bed with us, and we all fell asleep again," she said, reaching for the teapot. "Your father went to the church already. Said something about needing to go to Brynmaur to see old Henry Clyde. He's failing fast."

"Oh, that's too bad," said Nella. "Until the war took the petrol, he was always at church. I've missed him."

"I have too. Remember how he used to stop by to make sure we weren't in need of anything? Such a sweet man."

"Aye. I wonder if I could ride with Daddy as far as Govilon. I could deliver those table games that folks have left at the church for the wounded soldiers."

"I don't know why not. Run over to the church office and ask him. He won't be there long."

Nella gulped her milk-cooled tea and hurried to catch him.

At the Govilon military station hospital, Jean scolded Nella. "You shouldn't have come here! You should've waited for Marge to call you."

"But I often come to see you, so it won't look out of the ordinary." With Jean so edgy, Nella avoided saying anything about her having been to Gilwern to meet with Captain Evers.

Yet, as was her way, Jean calmed down quickly and then rang up

Marge to see if she could get out for lunch. It turned out that Marge could; she suggested they all meet at The Blue Bell. Only a ten-minute walk from where Marge was, the cramped pub was frequented mainly by older farmers.

Nella and Jean set off right away. They avoided the main road and instead walked the path beside the canal. Along the way, some women at the helms of the long narrow coal barges waved jauntily as they chugged by.

"They look to be having a good time," Nella remarked.

"I wonder if the women will be able to keep on after the men come home."

"I suppose not. They'll be needing their jobs back. Besides, most of the girls will probably be glad to go home and have babies. Although Peggy thinks a good many may want to keep working for the freedom of it."

"It's hard to guess what everything will be like after the war." Jean glanced at her wristwatch. "We'd better hurry. Marge must be at The Bluebell by now."

When they got there, Marge was waiting in front of the small stone building. They walked in, ordered sandwiches and tea, then sat down at a table in the back where it was private.

Marge sipped her tea and frowned down into her cup.

Unable to wait as patiently as Jean, Nella said, "What's wrong, Marge? Did you get into some kind of trouble because of the letter?"

Marge shook her head. "No. I just hate to have to tell you. . . . I gave the letter to my supervisor Monday morning. Then before coming here, I asked her what the doctors thought about it." She held up both hands in a gesture of helplessness. "I'm so angry. She said they all think it's a cruel hoax. They insist that Rufe was paranoid as well as depressed. And, of course, I'm the only one who feels certain he wrote the message."

"But can't they compare the letter to something else he wrote?" Nella asked, feeling herself get upset.

"All of his personal things were sent home right after his death. We have nothing in the hospital records containing his handwriting."

"You must have his signature somewhere," Jean protested.

"No, I looked through his files, and there's nothing. Absolutely nothing."

"Well, did you tell them someone tried to run over Nella the night she talked with Rufe's friend?" Jean pursued.

"And what about Corporal Peterson?" Nella put in. "He exists, just as the letter said."

"I mentioned all these things," Marge said, "but they think it's just coincidence. Nella ... they think the corporal could've been feeding you a line. And when some drunk soldier almost ran you over with a jeep and chased after you, you then imagined a plot, a connection with Rufe. They've seen how attractive you are and even mentioned that your red-gold hair and fair skin has been a turn-on for their patients. They know you've led a sheltered life, growing up in the manse as you have, and so figure you aren't an objective judge of what happened."

Nella groaned. "I can't believe this. All they have to do is contact Corporal Peterson. He'll tell them he was Rufe's buddy and that he'd promised to mail Rufe's money to Mrs. Johnson."

"I told them all that. They said finding the corporal will take some time. So far they've received no response from their inquiries about him."

"Surely they'll keep trying," Jean said fiercely. "He may be on his way to the Front."

Marge tapped her fingers nervously on the tabletop. "I'll do what I can to push them, but I have to say that's not much. I just don't understand my supervisor. Monday she was as concerned as I, but now she comes back to me with all this disbelief."

Nella decided it was time to reveal her own efforts. She shoved her plate aside and straightened herself on her chair. "I spoke with the military police yesterday, a Captain Evers. Maybe he'll be able to do something."

"You what!" Jean exclaimed. "You went to the MPs...? I thought we agreed to wait for Marge to give them the letter."

"Well, now I'm glad I didn't wait," Nella flashed back. "Maybe the doctors and nursing staff will pay more attention when Captain Evers questions them."

"But you promised to let Marge handle this," Jean exclaimed. "Nella, you don't realize what might be at stake."

"I didn't exactly promise. I agreed and then later changed my mind. I did it because of Giselle—"

"You mean you told Giselle?" Jean exploded.

"Yes, I did. I decided I needed her advice more than she needed to be protected from everything connected with Rufe's letter."

Jean slumped back on her chair, shaking her head. "I can't believe this."

"Come on, Jean," Marge said. "Now that it's done, it might be better to have Giselle know what's happened."

Jean sighed. "Well, how is she? How did she take it?"

"It scared Giselle that I was chased and almost lost my life Saturday night. Which is why I took her advice and went to the military police, to ease her mind. She gave me the name and phone number to call."

Again Marge intervened. "If we want an investigation, then Nella did the right thing. The MPs won't let the matter drop now. The doctors and nurses are probably too busy taking care of the wounded, so they don't have time for thinking about a patient they lost. Nella, are you still writing to Rufe's mother?"

"Yes. I've grown very fond of her. She's really broken up at the thought of her only son taking his own life. She's part of the reason I want to pursue this." She turned to Jean. "I'm sorry I betrayed your wishes, but I just had to talk to Giselle. I needed her advice."

Jean straightened. "It's okay. Let's just go on from here. Have you told your parents too?"

"Not yet. Captain Evers agreed that they don't need to know until something definite turns up."

Marge took a sip of tea. "You know, despite your talking with the captain, this may go nowhere. We only have my opinion on the handwriting. I hate to say this, Nella, but I'll play devil's advocate. How do you know it wasn't a drunk who chased you? Some men go crazy when they're drunk. A criminal mind would be capable of everything you've described without being drunk. What if the guy chased you simply because he didn't want you to report him?"

"You could be right," Nella replied, "but—"

Jean broke in. "Marge does make sense. I may have become too jumpy after what happened to Giselle. I can understand how Rufe's death might appear to the hospital staff. After all, they diagnosed him as mentally ill."

Nella looked from one to the other. They waited for her response. "The theory that the chase was happenstance does sound more reasonable than the idea of a plot. Actually that was my first reaction." She sucked in a breath and let it out slowly as she sorted her thoughts. "So if the chase isn't an issue, then what's left is that Rufe's killer should be brought to justice, for his mother's sake if nothing else. I hope that, with the help of Corporal Peterson, the military police can find out who was behind his being murdered."

"Maybe you should reassure Giselle by telling her what we think,"

Marge said. "That it boils down to just the letter and a possible murder investigation."

"I can do that," Nella agreed. "I'd better be getting back to Govilon. I have less than an hour before Daddy comes to get me." The truth was she needed time to think. Nella didn't feel settled about anything they'd discussed.

CHAPTER EIGHT

In her schoolroom Wednesday afternoon, Peggy walked from desk to desk, viewing her pupils' efforts to draw and color their renditions of the large basket of vegetables they had put together with produce taken from their own victory gardens.

She'd tied the art lesson to a study of farming methods for the boys and, for the girls, of how to raise victory gardens. She felt such a plan would stand up before the rest of the school committee in the event that Lady W. decided to continue to make an issue of Peggy's overemphasizing art in her classroom.

She paused for a moment in front of the window. The soft September rays had set a green glow over the fields and pastures surrounding the village, reminding her of springtime rather than the approaching autumn. It looked peaceful to her, as if there could never be war here, as if an evil such as murder could never occur in this gentle valley of the Usk River.

Then she thought of Nella and hoped no news from her meant everything was all right. If she didn't hear tonight, she'd for sure call her. Even if Nella couldn't speak freely, Peggy figured she could tell from her voice how things were going.

"Miss Jones?"

She turned. "Yes?"

Allison Barr, the postmaster's daughter, waved her hand frantically as though having been at it for an hour.

"May I be excused to go to the loo?"

It seemed Allison had to use the loo every five minutes. At first Peggy had thought this to be her way of putting off her schoolwork.

But she soon changed her mind. Allison had proved to work hard on her assignments, yet was one of those high-strung children who over-reacted to nearly everything, so her frequent need to run to the loo turned out to be an honest need.

Peggy nodded to the thin, dark-haired girl. "Do come back quickly. I have something to show the class when you return."

Ducking her head, Allison hurried out. Allison acted more nervous than usual today. This morning she'd been upset and had gotten several other girls all worked up about the Whitestone ghost, of all things. She insisted that her big sister, one of the Land Army workers out on the Westmoreland Estate, had seen the ghost. By the time Peggy came upon the huddling group of girls, the boys were bragging about how they were planning to go up to Whitestone that night to see for themselves. The girls shrieked at this, but Allison turned pale. She said her sister had run home, refusing to ever go back. She immediately requested service somewhere else.

Peggy had thought the so-called ghost sighting was nothing more than a lot of nonsense. Apparently, however, it was all very real to the superstitious girl. So for Allison's sake, she began the day by talking about how ghost stories get started, then grow as people add more to the stories with each telling. After the children talked about this, she had them form a circle to play a whispering game. First she whispered a message to one child, and that child whispered what she heard to the next. On and on from one child to another the message went until everyone except Annie had heard it. To Annie, Peggy signed the original message. And when the last child in the circle announced what she'd heard, Peggy turned to Annie again and signed what was said so she could understand how much the message had been changed. Then the entire class laughed uproariously, including Annie.

"Boys and girls, this is how ghost stories come about. Something happened that started the story. Then over the years as different people told the story over and over, the story changed and became more and more fantastic."

After their game, the children worked on their regular assignments and stopped their whispering about ghosts. But then at lunch Peggy heard Allison again telling some of the girls about the "Whitestone ghost" and what her sister had seen.

Seeing their teacher approach, they all fell quiet—all except Allison. She looked up from under her long bangs and said, "Ruthie really did see a ghost, Miss Jones. She would never ask to work somewhere else if she hadn't."

"All right, Allison," Peggy said. "I understand that she really saw something. But please don't worry about ghosts. Maybe she thought she saw a ghost because she'd heard the story before. Probably she saw an animal or even a person who looked strange for a moment."

Nevertheless, the rest of the day Allison behaved like a mouse in the presence of a cat. Peggy wished she could do something to counteract the influence of superstition on the child's wild imagination, yet she couldn't think what.

She walked up to the blackboard to demonstrate with chalk as she taught, signing to Annie at intervals. "Students, we'll begin a new picture now. When we draw with colors, there are many ways to begin. I noticed that some of you start by drawing lines to create the shape of an object, then you color it in later. That's fine, but I want you to try something new. Take a crayon, lay it sideways on your paper, and color a shape like this . . . then draw the lines around it, or don't draw any lines at all. Just make a colorful shape or design. And it doesn't have to look like the squash or beets or cabbage or potatoes. For example, think about using vegetable shapes for making a design of colors."

Because Peggy had white chalk only, all she could do was block in different shapes as she talked. "For the next fifteen minutes I want you to think about different shades of color and different shapes to create your own new designs. Have fun with it. See how one color looks next to another color or over another color."

Some of the boys sighed but then bent their heads to the task. The girls, as usual, delighted in the assignment, although they'd groan next week when it came time for woodcrafts. Peggy felt there was no reason why the girls shouldn't learn how to use a hammer and saw.

Peggy signed to Annie, "Do you understand?"

Annie nodded, smiled, and signed, "Yes."

Then Peggy began correcting their spelling assignments while they worked. She was pleased to see Peter signing to Annie and offering his help. Annie signed back and then bent over her drawing.

When it was nearing time to quit, Peggy walked around the room again. Unsurprisingly Annie's work was outstanding. She smiled. "Very good!"

Peggy reached Peter next, who looked up and said, "This is fun, Miss Jones." His paper had become a pleasing abstraction of bright colors, a nicely balanced composition.

"This is very good. May I hold it up for the others to see?"

He blushed as he nodded.

"Class, here's a good example of what I described earlier. You're all making handsome designs. Do you see now how easy it is to create beauty without drawing a particular object?"

"Yes, Miss Jones."

Several waved their hands. "Look here at my paper, Miss Jones!"

"Look what I did."

She held up one colorful drawing after another for the whole class to see. "Let's turn that wall beside the blackboard into our art gallery. We'll display your designs there to brighten up our classroom."

After school that day, Annie stayed back and handed Peggy an envelope. She grinned as if knowing its contents, yet had kept it as a surprise for the end of the day. Peggy opened the envelope and read. When she finished, she signed, *"Tell your mother I would be happy to visit for tea this Friday after school."*

Annie's blue eyes widened with pleasure. *"Very good!"* Giggling, she sped out of the classroom to meet her sisters on the sidewalk.

Annie had barely closed the door when it swung open again.

In walked Bryan Westmoreland. "Good afternoon, Miss Jones."

His manner appeared so naturally arrogant that he immediately brought out the worst in her. "Your neighbor Peter left fifteen minutes ago," she said abruptly.

"Oh? Well, I didn't come for him. I came to see you." He sauntered over to her desk and, without invitation, sat in the chair she reserved for parents. "I'm hoping I may enlist your help."

Peggy remained standing, leaning against her desk. "Help? What kind of help?"

"My father wishes to sponsor a harvest party for all those connected with the potato harvest. He asked me to oversee the arrangements. But I'm not very good at planning such things or carrying them off for that matter."

"But your mother . . . Lady Westmoreland is the one to do this. Why ask me?"

"Because my mother will be away. She's to leave Saturday to stay a month with my aunt Helene, who will be recuperating from surgery. Actually, Mother suggested that I ask you to assist me in staging the festival."

"What?" Peggy gasped. Lady W. had treated her with such little respect. Why then would she suggest Peggy help organize this festival—something she was ill prepared to do? Did the woman just want to see her made a fool?

"I realize this is an imposition," Bryan continued, "but by myself the harvest festival will be a disaster. I thought . . . well, you and Nella MacDougall, I mean, Killian, are like sisters, so Reverend MacDougall said. Surely she would help you—us. Growing up in the manse together, you two must've learned a great deal about putting on celebrations and the like."

Bryan looked so sincerely worried and wistful that she began feeling guilty for her disagreeable attitude. It was true that if Nella helped, the task would be done well. Nella possessed a knack for unique ideas, and Peggy could handle keeping everything in order. Yet she didn't know how Nella would feel about the idea.

Peggy smiled as she shook her head doubtfully. "I don't know what your mother was thinking about to suggest me, but if I could get Nella's help, I might be willing to give it a try. I'll ask her and let you know."

"And if she can't . . . you wouldn't leave me to do this alone, would you?"

"Mr. Westmoreland!" she blurted, showing her exasperation.

Bryan's congenial smile and boyish look faded, suddenly replaced by the expression of a man accustomed to handing out commands and being obeyed. The abrupt change startled her.

He told her bluntly, "This festival is not for me. It's for the village, particularly the children. Although there's been little enough celebration for their parents, either, these past five years."

Peggy glared at him. He was betting on her love for the village children, and if she refused, she would appear selfish and spiteful. Suppressing her anger, she answered in a teacherly tone—calm and logical: "I know better than most how badly the children need a bit of fun, and their parents too. It's simply that I don't think I'm the one to plan the harvest festival. But again, if Nella should agree to help—"

"Thank you," he cut in. "I hope you won't change your mind and disappoint the children. You see, if the arrangements are done by me alone, it will surely turn out a disappointment." His words were followed by a grin, as if showing his helpless humility, then he stood up to leave.

An idea popped into Peggy's mind, and she figured this to be the perfect time to pursue the plan. "I wonder if you might do a favor for me in return."

Bryan's grin disappeared. "What can I do for you?"

She told him how upset some of the children had been over the so-called legend of the Whitestone ghost. "Your family has that history book I'm to take to Reverend MacDougall, but I didn't see anything in it that tells of the Welsh bride. Do you have any other resources that would give the true story for my pupils? I'd like to dispel this superstitious ghost nonsense in my classroom."

"As a matter of fact, we do have such a book," he said. "I'll need to ask my father, but we have an English translation of the Welsh bride's own diary. You would have to read it to your students, however. We wouldn't want the children to handle it."

"Of course. I could read it at home and then relate the information in class. I expect the truth will change their minds about ghosts."

"Well, good luck with that. Most believe what they want to believe."

"Then I'll have to find a way to make them want to, now, won't I?"

He smiled in his flippant way. "That's the spirit my mother must have counted on when she suggested you for arranging the festival. If Father says it's all right, I'll bring the diary the next time I come down to the village. Good day, Miss Jones, and thank you."

After he'd left, Peggy wondered if she had just allowed herself to be manipulated. Still, if she didn't have to work with "The Bryan," as she'd dubbed him when she first met him, she would've counted planning the festival as exciting and fun. More importantly, now she might find out the facts about the Welsh bride for her class.

Leaning against the window frame, she watched as Bryan drove away in one of his farm lorries. He was a strange one. All she'd ever heard about him suggested a soft, weak man. Yet he'd managed to get her to accept a job she didn't exactly want. She went about straightening up her classroom, her thoughts preoccupied now with what she and Nella could be getting into if they worked with him. In the brief moment he'd quit acting the empty-headed playboy, she saw his other side, commanding and tough. Well, he wasn't going to dictate to her. If she worked on the festival, she'd do it her way.

Later, at Gatekeep, while Peggy was getting ready for bed, the phone rang, and Mrs. Lewis called for her. "It's your friend, Nella," she said, holding out the receiver to her.

"Hello, how are you keeping?" Peggy said.

"I'm purely wanged out. I'd like to be in bed, but I had to wait till Livie was tucked in and Mum and Daddy had left before I could ring you. Peggy, I'm so upset. Marge just called and said someone has lost Rufe Johnson's letter."

"Lost the letter! Did—" Peggy glanced around to confirm that Mrs. Lewis had indeed gone to her bedroom and closed the door. She lowered her voice anyway. "Did the authorities get a chance to read it first?"

"I don't know who read it. Marge handed it to her supervisor. Those who read it thought it was a hoax and said I was a naïve, distressed witness. So they disregarded the whole thing. Then tonight, seeing as how nobody believed the letter, Marge asked to have it back. That was when they admitted someone had misplaced it."

"I can't believe this. What will you do now?" Peggy asked.

"I don't know, but deep down I know that Rufe was murdered."

"Did they also discount the fact that someone tried to kill you?"

"Marge made a pretty good case that it was probably a coincidence that the chase happened right after I talked to Corporal Peterson. And by all that's reasonable, she's right. It could've been someone who wasn't specifically after me. For Giselle's sake, I told the military police about it. Now without the letter, I suppose they won't do anything. But I'd still like to know the truth about Rufe. He was all his mother had. I can't stand the thought of her thinking he killed himself if it's not true."

"I understand, but don't you go taking things into your own hands. I hear that tone in your voice."

"Not to worry. You coming to town for church Sunday?"

"I'll be there."

"Good," said Nella. "We can talk more then."

"Sounds right." Peggy could tell tonight was hardly an auspicious time to ask Nella about helping with the harvest festival.

After Peggy hung up, she walked slowly to her room. She hadn't wanted to get Nella even more upset, but it sounded too convenient to say someone had misplaced Rufe's letter. Some fancy skulking was going on at the Gilwern military hospital, but why?

CHAPTER NINE

Nella awoke in the middle of the night from a dream so vivid that she'd been crying real tears in her sleep. She had dreamed she was in a small town in the United States with her brother, Charles, and Peggy at something like a family reunion.

The American town had looked exactly as she'd always imagined. In the center, where she was standing, lay a village green. Across a street on one side stood a white wooden church, and on the opposite side, a square brick building fronted with white Grecian columns. Carved words above the portico said *CITY HALL*. Tables laden with every kind of food imaginable were set up in the park, and a small band played in a nearby gazebo. Children chased one another in the bright sunshine, dodging between adults, and nobody worried about their safety.

The war was over. She could hardly believe Charles had come back. He looked so well, as if he'd never been hurt. A group of young men persuaded Charles to show them how to play rugby, so Nella and Peggy decided to watch. Then Nella changed her mind. She wanted to wait for Rob. She hadn't seen him yet, but he must be at the celebration.

Suddenly someone called, "Nella! Nella!"

She turned. Hurrying toward her was a woman and a tall blond youth. As the woman drew close, Nella realized this was Mrs. Johnson, Rufe's mother, looking exactly like the small photo from one of her letters. And the young man at her side was Rufe. No wonder Mrs. Johnson's face looked so radiant.

"Mrs. Johnson! I had no idea you'd be here," Nella exclaimed.

"I wouldn't miss it. I had to come and thank you for all you did for us. Rufus is home again! Isn't it wonderful?"

Rufe grinned, his eyes as blue as his mother had described.

"Oh, Rufe, I never thought I'd see you alive...."

At Nella's words he choked and grabbed at his throat. His face turned purplish, then he collapsed. Rufe was dying all over again! He ended up looking like he did that day Nella and Jean found him in the river.

Mrs. Johnson screamed and fell to her knees beside him.

"Help! Help! Is there a doctor?" Nella shouted.

But the people milling about went on talking and laughing as if deaf and unable to see Rufe lying on the ground. Charles had disappeared, and Peggy too. Nella ran to the nearest person, a man. "Please, sir, help us!"

He ignored her and continued his conversation with someone else.

Nella rushed back to Rufe. "Help me turn him over," she said to Mrs. Johnson. "We've got to get him breathing!"

But they couldn't move him. "Someone help us!" Nella screamed again.

No one paid them any attention. Mrs. Johnson was sobbing. So was she.

This was when Nella woke up, weeping, and with her stomach in knots. She drew in a big breath and wiped the tears from her cheeks. Had she cried aloud? She glanced over at Livie who was sleeping soundly in her crib.

Whatever had made her dream she was in the United States? Like most dreams, not much made sense except the feeling of despair over Rufe's death. *His poor mother,* she thought. *When the war is over, she'll still be grieving.*

Nella finally fell back to sleep until morning. The sadness of the dream remained with her, however, as she got up and went to start breakfast.

After eating, Livie played with her grandmother while Nella washed and hung the baby's nappies and playclothes on the line in the kitchen. As she finished pegging up the last tiny stocking and pulled the laundry up out of the way, an idea came to mind. If she could somehow locate Rufe's letter and then get a sample of his writing from Mrs. Johnson, the truth might come out. Maybe the letter had simply been filed away in the wrong place. If she could get into the medical records room where charts were stored, she might be able to find it. Nella knew they wouldn't allow her to volunteer for such a task, yet there might be a way. Marge would know.

So she rang up the hospital at Gilwern and asked for Lieutenant Marge Emerson, saying it was an emergency. Soon a woman answered who knew Marge. "I'll have her call you right back," she promised.

A few minutes later, Marge returned her call. She sounded as though she'd been running. "What's wrong?"

"I'm sorry, nothing's wrong. I just wanted to get you to the phone right away. Listen, would it be possible for me to visit and stay overnight in your quarters?"

"Yes, we can put up guests, but only for a good reason."

"You could say I'm there to observe the staff at work, because I'm thinking of becoming a nurse."

"What's on your mind besides nursing?" Marge asked with an edge to her voice.

"I was hoping we could get into the medical records room and search for Rufe's missing letter."

"Nella, they don't let outsiders just walk in here and sift through medical records."

"I know that, but I thought if I were with you, and if you could get both of us in the room using some kind of pretext—"

"I have to obey orders. What you're asking just isn't possible."

"May I come anyway in case we can think of a way?"

The line went silent. Then Marge said, "Your idea is impossible. Besides, I thought we agreed to let the military police take care of this."

"Have you told them the letter disappeared?" Nella asked.

"No, I haven't had time."

"Because I could call Captain Evers—"

"Look," Marge interrupted, "if you want to come, I'll try to get you clearance, but you must leave the search for the letter up to me—in my own way and on my own time. Do you understand?"

"All right," Nella agreed quickly. Once in the hospital she might learn something of value.

Arranging the visit went more smoothly than Nella had expected. Marge had told her supervisor that Nella wished to observe the nurses working their shifts and assist wherever a volunteer might be of use. Permission granted, Nella told her mother the same story.

At two P.M. Nella coasted her bicycle down the narrow road from Gilwern village to the sprawling military hospital situated along the bank of the Usk River. Acres and acres of brick barracks, functioning as wards for wounded and sick soldiers, had obliterated the once-green pastures.

She parked her bicycle at the gatehouse and then met Marge at the nurses' office. Nella was introduced to the nurses on duty, including the supervisor, Captain Gray. Several of the nurses offered to take Nella with them on their afternoon rounds to dispense medication.

"Sorry, but I'll be leading her on her first tour of the hospital," Marge said. "After all, she's my guest."

"Okay, Emerson. You always work things to your benefit," one girl said, laughing. "But before supper she can help me change bandages, get a picture of the real thing. My patients will love her."

"That may be," Marge replied, "but my boys enjoy a new face just as much as yours."

The other nurse laughed good-naturedly again and left.

Nella accompanied Marge as she read her patients' charts, checked temperatures, and administered their medications, taking time out to chat with the soldiers.

When Marge led her to the next barracks, she pointed out the mental ward. "That's where Private Johnson was before he took his walk. I can't take you in, but we can walk around the building so you can see the layout."

The ward was one of several brick buildings dedicated to mental patients. "Do the men go home from here?"

"Either that or to other hospitals for long-term care. The doctors here evaluate their condition. A few recuperate enough to return to active duty, mostly desk jobs or other such work."

"What about Rufe? Was he to be sent home or given a noncombatant job somewhere?" Nella asked.

"I'm not sure. That's why I kept quiet when I thought he was faking illness. He was so young, I hoped he could go back home. I figured the war would still be won without him." Marge shook her head sadly. "He was barely eighteen, you know. He had lied about his age, gotten into the army at sixteen. Before long, he'd seen hard fighting and so had good reason for battle fatigue."

They strolled between two mental-ward barracks, circling back to the road on the other side of the building.

While they walked, Nella studied the windows and the emergency exit at the back. "I should think anyone with determination could get into the ward at night from the back there, overcome Private Johnson, and carry him away. Is the nurses' station in the same area as the patients?"

"No, but there's a window and a nurse is on duty twenty-four hours a day."

"Still, she might miss a clever intruder if at night. And if the other patients were either sleeping or mentally incapable, nobody would see to report it."

"That's what I thought," Marge said abruptly, as if she'd long ago dismissed the idea.

"About the medical records room," Nella persisted, "can we simply ask to see Rufe's file again? Or maybe I could volunteer to help with some of the routine filing?"

"Not a chance, Nella. I told you, patient records are confidential."

"I wonder if a person might be able to sneak in there at night . . . after hours."

"Nella! Don't even think about it."

"Listen. You told me you kept information to yourself about how Rufe seemed to be faking his illness. Is it any worse to sneak in and look around for a lost letter?"

"This is a military hospital, and I'm in the army. You don't break rules here without serious consequences. I could never sneak in there—"

"Not you. Me. If there's some kind of emergency exit, I'll go in that way. If it's locked, there must be a key somewhere."

"So you want me to steal a key," Marge countered. But her voice was quieter as though calculating the idea. "Did I ever tell you, you remind me of my sister Em?"

"No, and I'll take that as a compliment."

"In this case, you shouldn't," Marge said. Her tone had definitely softened now.

Sensing her friend may be relenting, Nella pressed her point. "I could sneak out during the night after your roommates are asleep and be back before they wake up. No one would know, unless . . . Marge, do they guard the area where the records are kept?"

"No, but guards do keep watch at night, as on any military base." She stopped and studied Nella. "You really want to risk this for a boy you never even met?"

"I feel as if I knew him from his mother's letters," Nella responded passionately. "Mostly I want to do it for Mrs. Johnson's sake. She's blaming herself for not seeing how hurt he must've been, for not getting him away from his abusive father sooner. When I think how finding his letter could bring her comfort, I just have to give it a try."

Marge started walking on. "Nella, you're an incorrigible do-gooder.

You probably don't need as much of a logical reason as you already have. But I've never met a do-gooder I liked as well as you, so I guess I'd better help you. I have to get back to my rounds. I think I can get a key. Remember, if anyone catches you in the act, you'll have to think up a good story, because you can't involve me. That way I can protect the person who gives me the key. He owes me a big favor. So I'll do this for you . . . and for Rufe and his mother."

"That's wonderful! And my searching for the letter will be all my doing. You knew nothing about it when I asked to stay with you."

"You think you can carry off a story like that, you being a minister's daughter?"

"I've been told I'm a good actress. I'll worry later about whether it's right or wrong." Even as she said this she knew she was violating her own deeply held beliefs. However, if she found the letter, she felt this was one time when the end would justify the means. She told herself that she was fighting for the truth.

"Now I'm going to take you to the medical records building," said Marge. "You'll need to memorize the route. Luckily it isn't far from my quarters." Marge guided her from the records building to her Nissen hut and back again to give Nella a clear sense of direction. Nella prayed it would seem as easy after dark. The buildings would all look alike at night.

By the time Marge and Nella made their way back to the nurses' office for tea, Nella's back and legs ached. Marge informed her she still had bandages to change before sitting down to supper.

When mess call finally came, though Nella couldn't remember a moment when Marge had left her sight, Marge had already obtained the key. She slipped it into Nella's hand on their way to the chow line and whispered, "When you're finished with it, place it just under the soil at the left end of the steps by the exit door."

Nella tucked the key in her pocket. "I will. Thanks." She felt like shouting her excitement. Maybe the letter was there just waiting to be discovered. How she would later explain the manner in which she'd found it, she didn't yet know.

After helping Marge with her evening rounds, Nella gratefully lay down on her cot and snuggled under the covers.

The lights were switched off, and someone said, "So, Nella, are you going to become a nurse?"

"I don't think I can answer that tonight," she said, laughing. "I never make important decisions when I'm this tired."

This brought chuckles from all the women. One responded, "You might make it, then. No romantic ideas to blind you."

Nella waited for a long time in the dark, wondering when she should get up and tiptoe away. Some moments later Marge reached out from her bunk and touched her shoulder. Nella quietly dressed.

Marge opened the door and stepped out with her. "I'll be watching for you."

Nella squeezed Marge's arm and slipped into the dark night, wishing she could use the electric torch in her coat pocket. Fortunately she had worn dark clothing. As she walked, easing each foot silently ahead, the thought came to her that a murderer could creep through the hospital grounds without detection just as easily as she was doing now.

The thin moon low in the clear sky shed a little light. Once Nella's eyes became adjusted, she could make out the shapes of the many barracks. She decided to count the barracks as she walked. Before long, she stopped in front of the records building, then listened and strained to see in all directions. No one in sight. She then went around to the rear door, inserted the key, and stepped inside. Nella had taped her electric torch so it would let out only a tiny streak of light. Even so, when she switched it on, fear shot through her, for it gave off too much light. She kept it low, aiming at the floor. All around her stood shelves and file cabinets. Marge had said to look first in the shelves where records of past patients were stored.

She managed to find the archives area and the shelf containing records with patients' last names beginning with J. Then she came upon a large number of Johnsons. Many were privates, though none with the first name Rufus. Nothing. Suddenly she realized the charts all belonged to patients still living. Records for the deceased must be stored somewhere else.

Nella walked back and forth among the rows of shelves, studying their labels. At last she came to a separate section labeled "Deceased." Soon she found a folder marked "Johnson, Pvt. Rufus P." Quickly she pulled it from the shelf and then paused to listen. All was quiet, so she opened the file folder and read.

Much of it meant nothing to her, but early in the record a doctor had written, *No discernable psychosis. Return to duty.* This had been heavily crossed off. Further down the chart, close to the bottom, the diagnosis had been changed to *Manic-depressive, paranoid tendencies. Return to U.S.*

She noticed that after a number of medical entries, his death had been recorded. *Suicide.* The information confirmed what Marge already had said. There was nothing else on the chart she could understand. Disappointed, Nella shoved the file folder back in its place on the shelf and began to search the files of other Johnsons or any similar names where someone may have filed Rufe's letter by mistake.

None of the files she pulled contained any type of correspondence. After a while, she beamed the torch at her watch. She'd been in the building more than an hour now, which was pushing the laws of chance. Any minute someone might detect her small light glowing in an otherwise blacked-out camp. She returned the file she had in her hand and snapped off her torch.

It appeared she'd taken a great risk for naught. Now she must get back to the Nissen hut and into bed without anyone knowing. She quietly let herself out and hid the key in the damp earth beside the back step. Having done that, she breathed easier.

Heading up the walkway, Nella began counting the barracks again to find her way back. Suddenly a male voice shouted, "You there! Halt!"

She stopped, frozen in her tracks. Her heart about stopped too.

A soldier's boots crunched on the gravel path behind her. Had he seen her coming from the records building? Nella turned toward him.

He flashed an electric torch in her face. "Who are you? What are you doing here?" he demanded.

CHAPTER TEN

Nella squinted as she tried to see the face above the electric torch. "I'm Nella Killian from Abergavenny." She saw no way to avoid mentioning Marge. "I'm visiting my friend, Lieutenant Marge Emerson. She was given permission for me to stay overnight with her to learn about nursing."

He stepped closer, his light still pointed in her eyes. "Mind telling me what you're doing out here this time of night? It's highly irregular."

"I needed some air. I was about to suffocate being shut up in that small Nissen hut. I couldn't sleep." Nella then realized she couldn't be accused of anything beyond wandering out after curfew. Thankfully she'd hidden the key by the step and placed all the files back on the shelf. Slipping easily into the role of an innocent young girl, she added, "I'm terribly sorry, sir, if I've done anything against the rules. If you're concerned about who I am, you can call my father, Reverend MacDougall, in Abergavenny."

"The Reverend is your father? Well, I guess I don't need to call him. I can see you're telling the truth." He lowered his light. "But, miss, you can't just wander around the station hospital at night. Only the doctors and nurses are allowed to do that. Can you find your way back to your hut?"

Nella looked around. To her horror, she couldn't remember which direction to take. "I'm not sure. . . ."

"Well, I'll take you over to the women's quarters. When we get there, I'm sure you'll be able to recognize which hut is your friend's."

"Yes. Thank you."

"I'm Captain Blaine, by the way. In civilian life they called me Doctor."

"Are you on night duty?" Nella asked, then realized it was a stupid question.

He didn't seem to mind. "Yes, but just getting off." After a short distance, he paused. "On your right is the first of four Nissen huts, all female personnel. Over there, see?"

"Yes. I think it's the second one."

"Should I wait until you know?"

"No, I'm sure that's the one. I'll be all right. Thank you for escorting me, Captain."

"You're welcome. If you should visit overnight again, stay indoors after dark. The MPs might not be so easy on you. Good night now."

"Good night. And thank you again, sir."

The sound of his footsteps faded quickly down the walkway.

Nella tiptoed to the door of the hut she thought was Marge's. The door swung open before she could reach it. Marge stepped out, closed it, and whispered, "Nella, what on earth happened? I saw you talking to someone."

"Everything's all right. That was a doctor. He just warned me not to leave your hut at night."

"I was getting worried. You were gone a long time. Well, did you find anything?"

"I'm afraid not. We can talk about it in the morning. I put the key where you said."

"Good. Let's get some sleep."

In spite of all the excitement, fatigue overcame Nella soon after stretching out on her cot. When she opened her eyes again, everyone was up and getting dressed.

Nella reported the results of her search to Marge on their way to breakfast. "It was fruitless," she complained.

"We risked a lot for what you accomplished," Marge said, "but it wasn't a total waste. You ruled out a number of places where it might've been."

"I suppose you're right," said Nella. "Marge, maybe the letter wasn't lost by accident."

"I find that hard to believe."

"Well, we're out of options," she said, wondering how Giselle would see things now. Then Nella made a swift decision. "I think I'd better go home right after breakfast. No need to hang around here."

"Okay. I'll be in surgery all morning anyway."

When Nella went to fetch her bicycle, she passed the military police office. On impulse she retraced her steps, entered the building, and asked for Captain Evers.

The man at the front desk left and came back a short moment later. "He will see you now. Follow me, please." He led her down the narrow hall she'd walked once before.

"Mrs. Killian for you, sir."

Slouched behind his desk, Captain Evers quickly rose to his feet. "Please come in, Mrs. Killian. Won't you be seated?"

"Thank you." She settled into the hard chair facing his desk.

Evers sat down again and reached for a cigarette pack. "Smoke?" he offered.

"No, thank you," Nella replied.

He lit the cigarette and inhaled deeply. Through a cloud of smoke, he said, "Your visit today comes as a surprise. I was planning to call you."

"You have news then?"

"Not exactly. I wanted to tell you that we've gone through all our leads and have eliminated the possibilities for the time being. First, we can't find Corporal Peterson. That doesn't mean we won't find him. He's somewhere out of touch, probably near the battle line in northern France. That's where his division is fighting. Second, even when we find him, he can't help us unless the letter turns up. I presume you've heard that the letter you discovered has been lost?"

"Yes. One of the nurses told me."

"Without it, we have no evidence to suggest foul play," he said.

"Were you able to read the letter before it disappeared?" Nella asked.

"I'm sorry, but no."

"Well, Lieutenant Emerson, who knew Private Johnson quite well, did read it, and she says it looks to be Private Johnson's handwriting." She cleared her throat. "So if the letter was written in his own hand and both of us have read it and verified this, then can't we be witnesses?"

"Not without having the actual letter. Your testimony carries no weight by itself. Don't you see? I need the letter to open an official investigation. Even with that the case is weak. Maybe after the war the truth will come out, as they say."

Nella's anger warmed her to the roots of her hair. "I see. One young man and his mother are expendable when it comes to fighting a war."

Evers frowned. "Sadly, many young men *are* expendable. That's how wars are fought." He stood to his feet again. "I can only do my job. With no concrete evidence, I haven't a viable reason to investigate."

Nella stood up also. "Will you at least keep searching for the letter? Someone in the hospital may have an idea where to look."

"I can't promise anything. The doctors who treated Private Johnson all agreed that his illness drove him to suicide." While Evers talked, he walked her toward the door. "I'm sorry, Mrs. Killian. You've put up a valiant effort for your friend, but maybe it's time to let this go."

Then a young MP appeared and escorted her out of the building.

Back at home Livie greeted her with a hug and kiss, yet had not seemed to miss her.

"So are you thinking you'll go into hospital work now?" her mother asked a bit anxiously.

"No, Mum. I decided nursing isn't for me."

Her mother sighed in obvious relief. "I'm so glad. You belong at home with Livie. You can still help with volunteer work like rolling bandages at the church, as you've been doing."

"I know, but I keep wishing I could do more. I'm young and strong. Older people can do the things I've been doing."

"Still, I'm glad you won't be going away to do nursing." Her mother handed a small basket to Livie, and they went out together to the garden.

Nella closed her eyes as she pressed her fingers against her temples. She needed to talk to Giselle.

After Giselle let her in, she immediately asked, "Have you any news?"

"No. Listen, I didn't want to tell you ahead of time, but I spent last night at the Gilwern military hospital, and Marge helped me sneak into the medical records building so I could look for Rufe's missing letter."

Giselle's eyes widened. "You didn't!"

"Don't worry, nothing happened. Nor did I find the letter. I looked through a lot of files but finally had to give up."

"Nella, you could've been killed if the murderer is still about and saw you."

"By the time I left, I realized that."

"You know, with all that's happening, someone on the inside has to be involved," Giselle said.

"You mean someone on the hospital staff? Marge didn't want to believe such a thing," Nella said, thinking fast now. "Imagine if I'd been caught and my presence tied to Marge...."

"You would've put her in real danger," Giselle finished for her. "You've got to stop delving into this. Leave the matter to Captain Evers. You've done as much as you can, more than you should have."

"You're probably right."

"But back to last night. Did you notice *anything* out of the ordinary on Rufe's chart?"

Nella told her about the difference between the first and final diagnoses.

Giselle leaned back, a thoughtful expression on her face. "So at first a doctor thought Private Johnson was not mentally ill, and then they decided later that he actually was and planned to send him home?"

"It looked that way."

"I can see the possibility of suicide if he were depressed and scheduled to go back to the battlefront. However, if they were about to send him back home, why then would he kill himself? It doesn't make sense."

"Maybe he didn't know he was to go home," Nella offered.

"Did you see the date of the doctor's entry, whether it was a long time before his death?"

Nella thought a moment. "There were many entries written before the final one that said death by suicide. So quite a bit of time must have passed."

"I suppose we can't know for sure, but what you read on Private Johnson's chart harmonizes with the information in his letter—that he was frightened and not depressed. What you learned could be useful if more evidence turns up."

"Captain Evers didn't give me much hope of that. I talked with him before I left Gilwern. He said the case is closed and cannot be reopened without the letter. He won't be doing any investigation."

"Then we must be extra careful," Giselle said. "The officials, they have their rules, but we must look out for ourselves."

"It's so frustrating to sit helplessly waiting. Maybe I could tempt the killer to reveal himself—"

"No! Don't say that. To take such a risk, you've got to have someone like the constable or the military police, who can jump in at the right moment. But you have no help, no one you can trust."

"Giselle, tell me honestly, do you think it was just a couple of drunks who chased me?"

Giselle's mouth tightened. "After what I saw the Nazis do in France, I'll never again ignore a so-called coincidence. I already told you that I must live as if there are agents in Wales secretly working for Germany. All this week I've taken the same precautions I did in France. For Angie and Jacquie, I must."

Nella knew most people would think Giselle was overreacting because of her terrible experience in occupied France. But Nella, remembering her own terror while fleeing for her life, didn't feel her words were that extreme. "I'm sorry it's come to this, Giselle. I'll help you in every way I can. So will Jean, you know that."

"Only Jean knows what to do if Andre has friends here, and she thinks there's no more danger. Nella, if you really want to help me, then give up this crusade for Private Johnson. I don't know whether his death is related to the possibility of German spies here, but I can't take the chance. Please drop it."

As far as doing something for Rufe's mother, Nella could let go of that for the time being. Whether Giselle's fears about spies were justified or not, Nella wanted to ease her fears. "It was a childish idea to think I could help solve a crime," she said. She chose her words carefully, thinking to remain free to use her own judgment without having to break her word. "As far as I'm concerned, my crusade, as you call it, is over. I won't do anything foolish."

"Good," said Giselle, yet her wary expression showed that she guessed Nella's reservation about making a specific promise.

Sunday morning, while walking to church with Peggy and Giselle and the children, Nella didn't regret her promise to Giselle. She watched Livie toddle along between Jacquie and Angie, holding their hands. "I love the way your girls care for my Livie," Nella commented to Giselle. "We're so lucky to have you staying at the manse."

"It's been wonderful for them too. Even though I can't wait to return to France and to Claude, I shall miss all of you." When she said Claude's name, she looked happy again and ten years younger.

As soon as the service was over, Livie ran to stand by her grandfather while he greeted the parishioners. Nella followed, stationing herself close enough to keep an eye on Livie. Jean, Peggy, and Giselle soon joined her. Then someone called Giselle aside, and while they chatted, Nella asked Jean, "Have you talked with Marge? Did she tell you I visited her recently?"

Jean nodded. "She said to assure you she's not giving up."

"Good for her!" Peggy exclaimed. "Nella, what's this about staying overnight at the Gilwern military hospital? What have you been up to now?"

"I think I'd better tell you later," Nella said, looking around at the people nearby. "Can you both come for Sunday dinner?"

"I'd love to," Jean said, "but I'm scheduled to take a group of the men to White Castle today. So it's back to Govilon and mess-hall food for me. Thanks for asking."

"Sure," Nella answered. "Next time, I hope."

"I hope so too," Jean said.

Nella and Peggy walked with Jean to her waiting transport, an old ambulance, and then returned to the church steps to fetch Livie. Ian was holding her while he discussed farming with Mr. Flint. When they paused in their conversation, Nella said, "Excuse me, Daddy, but I can take Livie now. We're going on home to start dinner."

He gave Livie a squeeze. "She's doing fine. I'll watch her and bring her home with me."

Livie grinned and waved. "Bye, Mum."

"You rascal. You be good now." Nella caught her chubby hand and kissed it.

Livie giggled. "I good girl, Mummy."

Nella hurried back to Peggy, smiling and shaking her head. "That little girl! I've worked so hard to help her be independent that now I wonder if she even needs me."

The three blocks to the manse took but a moment to walk. When they reached home, they found the wrought-iron gate standing open.

Peggy hesitated. "Funny, I was the last one out when we left for church, and I know I latched the gate. I remember thinking we ought to take more precautions than we used to."

"Maybe Mum or Daddy had to come back for something," Nella said. "It wouldn't be the first time."

"Aye."

But as they opened the manse's front door, a feeling of strangeness came over Nella. She stepped inside and hadn't gone two steps before seeing the broken vase and water and flowers spilling from the parlor doorway. She rushed into the formal old room and cried,

"Peggy, someone's been into everything!" Books from the shelves and papers from the rolltop desk covered the floor.

Peggy rushed to her side. "I'm calling the constable."

Nella gasped, "Yes, right away!" Her heart pounded. Was the intruder still in the house? "You call. I'll look about." She raced from room to room, looking in each room and thinking she must be ready to flee if she confronted anyone. Once she made sure they were alone in the manse, she ran back to Peggy, who was hanging up the phone. "Look, no matter what, let's keep quiet about Rufe's letter," Nella cautioned. "I still don't want Mum and Daddy to know. The fewer who know, the less risk."

"Risk of what?"

"Giselle thinks Nazi agents may have killed Rufe. And if we get too curious, they'll be after us."

"But surely you don't believe that! I mean, he was in the U.S. Army and only a private. What use could he possibly be to German spies? It's natural for Giselle to react that way, but you know how things are here. There's not a chance—"

"Now wait," Nella cut in. "First, I don't mean to try to change your mind, so you needn't argue. Second, I as much as promised Giselle I'd drop the whole thing with Rufe. Still, the two spies arrested at Crickhowell prove that most anything is possible. And just look around you at what's happened today in the manse."

"But . . . it sounds so farfetched," Peggy said.

"So was Hitler's takeover of Europe. No one believed it at first."

"All right, I'll do what you ask. But you'll tell the constable now that someone tried to kill you."

"Not if I can help it. Captain Evers out at Gilwern may have already told him. If not, please don't bring it up. You know how it would worry Mum and Daddy. We'll let Constable Burns investigate this just for what it is—a break-in and robbery."

"Okay, I'll keep my mouth shut. I just hope it's the right thing to do."

Nella nodded. "Me too." Then she went back to look more closely at each room. Every bedroom had been ransacked. Contents from drawers and shelves were strewn on almost all the floors. In the kitchen every cupboard and drawer had been gone through and now stood open.

Standing in the main hallway, Peggy said, "I wish we could clean up this spilled water on the parlor rug, but I suppose we'd better leave everything till the constable arrives."

"I agree. Leave it as it is. But I think I'll run and tell Daddy. I don't want him or Mum to walk into this as unprepared as we did."

"Why don't you stay here to meet the constable and let me go tell them," Peggy offered.

"That's fine, but I can hardly think straight enough to talk to him. I feel muddleheaded, I'm so angry. How dare someone break into our home like this?" Nella pushed her hair back from her eyes. "I just can't believe it! Giselle is bound to think this is part of everything else that's happened. Is it, or is it just another *coincidence*?" She stopped as she grappled with the confusing possibilities. Then she said, "Sorry. I'm rambling, aren't I?"

"It's all a shock, Nella. I'll go prepare the folks. Maybe you should sit down."

"I'll be okay. You go ahead."

Peggy started for the door, then halted and returned. "After thinking about it, I should stay with you. What if someone wants to get at you while you're alone?"

"Peggy! There's no need for that." Nella glanced around. "I've looked everywhere. Besides, the person who did this wouldn't likely linger after making such a mess."

"I'm still staying. I'll watch for the folks and then run meet them at the gate."

"All right." Then Nella had a chilling thought. "Oh no! What about Giselle? You don't suppose they did this to her apartment too!"

"I'll go upstairs with her when she gets home."

Nella couldn't stifle a groan. "If they did, she'll be so frightened."

With that, they both sat down to wait. A few minutes later, the constable arrived.

CHAPTER ELEVEN

While Nella took the constable inside, Peggy went out to the gate and watched for the rest of the family.

Giselle and the girls arrived first, and before Peggy had finished explaining to them, Father and Mother Mac appeared. They hesitated only long enough to hear the news.

As Father Mac hurried up the front steps, he called back, "Peggy, go with Giselle and let us know immediately if her apartment was broken into also. Mother and I will speak with the constable and see what needs to be done."

Peggy nodded and turned to Giselle whose face had paled. Jacquie and Angie held their mother's hands, both girls looking too afraid to move. "How about me running up first to check?" Peggy said.

"No. We will all go. Jacquie, Angie, don't be scared. Whoever did this is gone now. If they went upstairs, it will only be a mess to clean up. Come, we'll have a look." Giselle marched to the side entrance of the manse, which led upstairs to her apartment. She tried the doorknob. "It's still locked."

"You locked it? Giselle, that may have saved you. The Mac-Dougalls have never locked the front door."

"I know. I couldn't get used to that when I first came here." She went inside with the girls close behind.

Peggy followed them upstairs, observed the normal orderliness, and breathed a sigh of relief. "I'm so glad you locked your door."

The girls let go of their mother's hands and walked cautiously to their room. After peeking in, they entered. "No one's been in here, *Maman*," Jacquie called.

"That's good, dear. Change into your playclothes while I go downstairs to help clean up. Jacquie, make lunch for yourself and Angie, please. And stay up here till I come for you."

Jacquie came to the door of her room. "We'll hurry. We want to help too."

Down on the first floor, the constable and two of his assistants made notes as they inspected the different rooms. Mother Mac and Nella had cleared the kitchen table and were busy setting out scones, blackberry preserves, wedges of cheese, and tea.

"We decided to eat," Mother Mac said to Giselle and Peggy. "Then we'll feel more up to the task." Her cheeks were flushed, her eyes a bit too bright.

"We'll all work on it together," Peggy assured her. "I can stay as long as need be, just so I get to school in the morning."

"The girls are coming down to help too, soon as they eat," Giselle said.

The constable came into the kitchen. "Well, ladies, the Reverend says he can't find anything missing. Maybe one of you has noticed something gone."

"I've a notion I'll not be able to spot anything until we get things back in order," Mother Mac said. "But so far, I've not noticed anything missing."

"Nor have I," Nella said.

The constable cleared his throat. "Let me know the minute you do. It gives me a turn to think anyone would do this to the manse. It looks to be plain mischief, and I've never seen the like of it here in Abergavenny."

Mother Mac nodded. "It's a torment for Ian. I fear he'll be wondering where he failed in his witness and his preaching."

"Don't you let him harbor such thoughts, Mrs. MacDougall. He's always been well thought of in Abergavenny. Not a single upstanding man here that wouldn't fight to defend the Reverend's honor. It's bound to be somethin' mean that never originated from the townsfolk."

"Constable Burns is right, Mum," Nella interjected. "We can't let Daddy think for a second he's failed someone. It's just that there are spiteful people in the world."

"I'm thinking you know that for certain," the constable said, "after those drunks chased you last Saturday night. The war has sure enough changed our way of life here."

So Nella's secret was out. Captain Evers must have informed the constable.

"Chased you?" Father Mac exclaimed. "Nella, what's he talking about?"

Peggy was relieved that Nella had to tell her parents. Both appeared shocked and shaken, as Nella had anticipated. They also were angry.

"Young lady," her father said, as if she were a schoolgirl again, "what were you thinking not to wake us up and call Constable Burns?"

"I . . . I didn't see how it would do any good. I wasn't able to identify the vehicle, so how could anyone trace it? No harm was done. I didn't want to worry you."

"Don't you ever do such a thing again. And don't you ever walk out alone at night again either," he ordered.

"I won't," Nella assured him.

Constable Burns cleared his throat. "Don't be thinking that you don't need to report anything. You can't know whether or not the culprits may be caught after all. I did lock up two drunks Saturday night for dangerous driving, but I let them go in the morning once they were sober. So don't behave this way again, lass. Mind what your father says."

"Yes, Constable. I will." She looked properly put in her place.

Then Father Mac asked, "Do you think, Constable, there's any connection between this break-in and Nella's getting chased?"

"Nay. Not a bit. Anyway, she says they never followed her all the way home. They wouldn't be knowing who she was or where she lived."

"I'm glad you pointed that out," said Mother Mac. "One never knows what to think when things like this happen."

"Aye, it's a shock," he said.

Peggy had to speak up. "Constable Burns, I hope you'll come up with some clues soon to lead you to whoever's responsible."

"My men are searching around the house right now. We'll do the best we can."

Father Mac turned to Giselle. "I understand your apartment wasn't touched. That at least is good news."

Giselle's face took on a distant expression, and Peggy couldn't help but wonder what she was thinking. Now she seemed to come to herself with a start. "Yes. I'm especially thankful for the girls' sake that I locked the door."

"Aye, a blessing amid the trouble," Father Mac said. "I hate to be locking the manse door, but it looks as though it's come to that. Well, Constable Burns, can we offer you tea before you leave?"

"I thank you, but no. We must get on with our business. I'll be in touch, sir. And mind what the young lady says about locking her door. You do likewise."

"I will. Thanks," he said while walking the constable to the front door.

Giselle called after them, "Constable Burns, will you be leaving some of your men to keep watch on the manse now?"

"Aye. I'll do that till we get this solved." He waved a salute and left.

Nella turned back to the tasks at hand. "I'll put Livie down for her nap. In another minute she'll be asleep in her food." As she went to pick up the baby, she made a small gesture to Peggy, an old childhood signal between them that meant "help me."

"I'll come along," Peggy said. "Be back in a minute, Mother Mac."

Elizabeth nodded. "No hurry. This isn't exactly a sit-down Sunday dinner."

In the bedroom, Livie's eyes closed almost as soon as Nella laid her in her crib. She spread Livie's favorite blanket over her and then walked over to the window seat and sat down.

Peggy sat beside her and asked in a low voice, "What's wrong, Nella? You look as if you're about to be ill."

Nella responded in a stage whisper. "While you were upstairs with Giselle, Jean rang. She said Marge was suddenly shipped out before daybreak. And without warning. She was transferred to the Front in France, the other nurses are saying."

"Well, even though we'll miss her, that's what nurses do."

"But this wasn't the usual way. No one else in her unit has been sent anywhere. Only Marge. Singled out and sent without anyone hearing about it till after the fact. Jean thinks it's an attempt to silence her questions about Rufe. When I told Jean about the manse being ransacked this morning, she said . . ." Then Nella's whisper broke off.

Peggy finished for her. "Someone may think you have the missing letter here. Right?"

Nella nodded. Keeping an eye on Livie, she said, "Aye, it's crazy. Maybe they know I stayed with Marge that night and so think I found the letter. And with Marge being shipped out . . . it could be she's been taken somewhere. Oh, Peggy, what if someone has . . . killed Marge?"

"Nella, calm down. Your imagination is running away with you. I know you've been frightened, but you're making too much of all this."

"But listen. Jean's friend Mary O'Leary said there was a big fuss Saturday morning at the Gilwern hospital. Someone pulled out a bunch of files in the medical records room and left them scattered about the room. The Red Cross workers were questioned by the MPs. Don't you see? Someone else must've been looking for the letter too. And now this break-in and Marge being sent away..." Nella's eyes filled with tears. "Peggy, I think Giselle is right. Something really dangerous is going on. I should leave the manse. Me and my supposed knowledge may be endangering everyone here."

"No!" Peggy said, struggling to keep her voice quiet. "You can't do that! You've got to tell all this to the constable and get his help."

"But it's all circumstantial. I have no convincing facts."

"You're not thinking clearly. Even if you left, how would anyone know you haven't already told Mother and Father Mac about the letter?"

"Because the constable doesn't know and so he won't be investigating anything."

Peggy leaned back against the cool window casing. This was all moving too fast for her. Too many complications. "Look," she said, "even if you're right about leaving the manse, where can you go? How can you go without explaining everything to the folks?"

"I don't know! I'll think of something," Nella said, her desperation coming across as anger.

Peggy reached out and gave her arm a squeeze. "Why don't you come stay with me?"

Nella sighed. "I can't just up and go for an extended visit with you. Anyhow, West-Holding is too close. I need to go farther away."

Peggy took her hand, which was cold. "Now they've had their look and found nothing, so maybe it'll be fine to stay here."

Nella's eyes met hers. "You really believe that?"

Peggy glanced down. Nella's imaginings had gotten to her. "I-I don't know. I just want you to calm down and not do anything rash."

Nella nodded and rose to her feet. "Let's finish cleaning up. Maybe by the end of the day, things will come clearer."

Peggy followed her back to the kitchen, deeply aware that Nella needed wiser advice than she could give.

By teatime many things had been placed back in drawers and

shelves, and when Constable Burns came in and said he'd found no obvious evidence, Nella's mind was made up. She'd tell him her worst fears.

After he drank a cup of tea and reassured her mother that one of his men would keep watch overnight, he made ready to leave.

Nella stepped forward. "I'll walk you out, Constable Burns. I'm wondering if your men took notice of the damage to my favorite roses. I've pampered them so much, I miss even a blossom or two. And I saw some broken stems."

Immediately Peggy said, "Father Mac, one of the kitchen drawers won't go back in place. Will you please help me slide it in right?" Ian didn't insist on going along to see the constable out.

Outside, Nella led the constable to her rosebushes, but then she spun around and said, "I wanted to talk to you privately, Constable Burns."

He smiled and nodded. "I figured you might. Captain Evers out at the Gilwern military hospital told me how worried you were, imagining all kinds of foul play from that letter you found in one of your father's books."

"Then you know all about it?"

"Aye, and I agree with Captain Evers. That the poor lad was sick in the head. You can't count on anything he may have written to be the truth."

"Captain Evers said that?" she gasped.

"Aye. As for the ones who almost run you over last week, I'm convinced those drunks were the culprits. If you had seen them, you would agree. A mean-looking pair, they were, but without your complaint"—he shook his head—"I had no reason to hold them the next morning. I'll be looking out for them, you can be sure about that."

"Good. And until you catch them, you'll keep someone on watch here at the manse, right?" Nella wanted his word.

"I'll do what I can. Now you let me do the worrying. You're too smart a lass to be turning a single unfortunate experience into a plot against your whole family."

"But . . ." She was so astounded that he wasn't taking her seriously that she groped for words. "Maybe you don't know this, but yesterday someone at the Gilwern hospital searched the medical records and left everything in a shambles just like at our home. Doesn't it follow that whoever did that might've come here, thinking I had the letter? Don't you think they would be dangerous if they're that desperate?"

"I think you're overwrought about all this, and that's all there is to it. You just need a good night's sleep. Everything will look better to you tomorrow."

Nella wanted to scream. She had to work hard to keep her voice down, but found she couldn't keep the tremble out of it. "Yes, I'm frightened, Constable Burns. Mrs. Munier is terrified. She also thinks there's a plot, and she's had a lot of experience with undercover operations. I think she makes sense. I'm afraid for my baby and for my parents. Why won't you even consider the possibilities here?" Despite her efforts, her voice had risen a key higher.

He stared at her a moment, then said firmly, "Miss Nella, I want you and your friend to calm down. She's been in a mental hospital too, the way I heard it. You mustn't let her fears upset you anymore than that letter by the poor, sick lad. Everything is going to be all right. It's your task to reassure Mrs. Munier. This here"—he waved his large hand toward the manse—"is just a case of vandalism, and you're reacting exactly the way a vandal would be wanting. Now, when you go back in the house, don't be repeating your fears to that dear mother of yours or to the Reverend. They've had enough to bear, what with losing your brother so recently. I'll take care of the criminals when I find them."

Nella nodded miserably and managed a polite good-bye.

So much for telling the constable. According to him, even Captain Evers had dismissed her as just too excitable. So she was on her own, just as she'd been before confiding in Constable Burns.

Later, when she and Peggy were alone, she told her how the constable had responded.

Peggy looked glum. "I hoped he would've at least taken you seriously."

"Well, he's known me since I first learned to walk. I suppose he still sees me as a scatterbrained, impulsive girl. After all, he led the search for me when I ran away to join the WAAF."

"Like a father, he is," Peggy said. "He can't recognize when the kids have grown up. The offer's still open for you to come out to West-Holding and stay with me, if it will help."

"Thanks, Peg," Nella said. "I'll think about it and let you know."

Once the house was straightened up, Nella's mother declared nothing had turned up missing. To Nella, this seemed proof that someone had been searching for the letter.

It was so late by this time that Ian insisted on driving Peggy, bicycle and all, back to West-Holding in his old auto. Then Nella went to her bedroom and literally fell into her bed. Unable to think any longer about her plight, she hoped she'd know what to do in the morning.

She awoke to the fragrance of toasting muffins and the sound of her mother's voice as she talked with Livie. While washing and getting dressed, she noticed that there were still some things scattered about on the floor from the break-in. She'd have to finish picking up before Livie carried away something she shouldn't have. Nella followed her nose to the kitchen and there sat Livie in her chair, eating bites of mixed fruit.

Her mother exclaimed, "We not only had nothing stolen, but I found money!"

Nella looked at the money her mother pointed to. "Oh, that's your change. I left it in the sugar bowl. I dropped it at the chemist's the other day, and Bryan Westmoreland picked it up and returned it."

"But this is near ten pounds. I didn't send that much with you."

Nella took the money in her hand and stared at it. "I didn't think about whether it was the right amount. Well, then, I'll have to give some of this back to him." She didn't look forward to facing Bryan again; something about the man hit her wrong. But maybe she was only reacting from Peggy's assessment of him.

She couldn't think on anything as trivial as money. The night's rest and new day hadn't diminished her fears. Now she had to decide what to do to keep her family safe. Maybe Giselle could help.

When Giselle came in after the girls had left for school, she talked about a battle in the Vosges mountains of France, what the land was like and what the soldiers faced. She said this was probably where Claude was located. Nella decided not to add her worries to Giselle's anxiety.

All morning long Nella felt jumpy. Over and over again she had to ask her parents to repeat themselves, for her mind kept wandering to her own problem. She caught them watching her with the same anxious expressions they'd worn back when she came home newly widowed.

She wished she could be honest, tell them the truth, and just move out. Although she wasn't certain moving away would remove the danger from her family, she thought about how some mother birds fled their nests, how animals sometimes ran away to protect their young. She prayed that fleeing might work in her case.

If only she could get her enemy to believe she indeed possessed the letter and had taken it with her—but how could she communicate this fact? She wrestled with the problem until her head ached.

By afternoon when her mother asked if she was feeling ill, she could honestly admit she was. "I just need to stretch a little. I'll go gather the vegetables for supper." She picked up a basket and took Livie with her out to the garden. Livie carefully placed little brussels sprouts in the basket, as Nella pushed her shovel under a potato plant and turned out the new potatoes.

Soon her mother came out with a pan and began to pick the last of the runner beans. Livie didn't even look up, she was so busy putting the smaller potatoes in her own pail. Her hands and chin were brown with dirt. Nella reached over with her apron hem and wiped the child's face.

Mum worked quietly for a few minutes, then said, "The break-in upset you badly, I expect."

"Aye, it has," Nella answered, hoping she could avoid having to lie to her mother.

"Me too. I never guessed how violated a body feels when her own home has been invaded."

Nella stopped and studied her. "You scared, Mum?"

"I am. I know it won't likely happen ever again, but the dreads won't go away."

"Yes. It won't happen again," Nella said, feeling protective. As she spoke, her fog of uncertainty began to lift. "You know how long we've lived here without anything like this happening. Besides, the constable said he'd be watching the manse, and the church too."

"I suppose we'll feel better as time goes on."

"Sure we will. It was a shock, is all. I'm just glad Livie doesn't even know what it all meant." Nella crouched beside Livie and tossed some larger potatoes into the pail. She loved the moldy smell of the rich, clean earth. "Potatoes are early this year, don't you think?"

"Aye. I couldn't believe it when the tops began to die back. I imagine the whole harvest will be early, and if the big fields are like ours, the farmers will need every hand they can get."

Nella pictured acres of dark soil turned up. Without giving it much thought, she said, "Mum, I'd like to be in the Land Army." After she said it, she realized this was the answer to getting away. That is, if Livie could remain at the manse.

"You don't really mean that," her mother said with a little laugh.

"But I do, Mum." She made her voice firm. "I've thought about it from time to time for ages. I want to do more for the war effort, and as you've said, the need out on the farms is great right now."

"But you're a mother. Whatever would Livie do without you?"

"If you're willing, she has you and Daddy. You know how she loves you. She'll do fine. And remember, the Land Army is the one service that takes mothers and allows for part-time schedules for the sake of the children."

"I never raised a daughter to go off and abandon her child. I can't imagine what you're thinking of," her mother said heatedly.

Her angry tone brought a knot to Nella's throat. She hadn't seen her mother this upset since the time she and Peggy had climbed out a window one night to watch a rugby game after they'd been told to stay home and finish their schoolwork.

But instead of backing down and pacifying her mother, Nella heard herself snap back, "You don't know everything!"

"God didn't give you this beautiful child to have you abandon her and go chasing off to war. You think that's what God wants of mothers?"

This was an old bone of contention between them. "I don't know what God wants! How can I understand a God that allows wars in the first place?"

"God doesn't make war. Men do."

"Yes, but God made the men. You taught me that God foreknows all that happens. Well, He began the whole thing knowing there would be murders and wars." When Nella saw the hurt on her mother's face, she tried to rein in her anger. "Oh, Mum, I can't pretend to have faith like yours, but I do hope someday I will. Right now, I'm doing the best I can. Enlisting in the Land Army would be an investment in our future—Livie's and mine." The more she talked, the more she saw this was a move in the right direction. "You know that I've always wanted to have my own farm someday. I could learn a good amount to help us later. Please say it's all right with you."

Tight-lipped, Elizabeth just looked at her. "I don't see how you can even think of leaving Livie. But I can see we both need to pray and think about this for a while."

Nella nodded, not trusting her voice. She noticed Livie frozen and staring at them with round eyes.

Her mother picked up her pan of beans and marched back to the kitchen. Things were getting out of control. Since neither Constable Burns nor Captain Evers believed her fears were justified, Nella felt she had to do something on her own. Leaving the manse without telling her parents the real reason might help. Why couldn't they just let her go?

CHAPTER TWELVE

Nella watched her mother who, with one hand on her stiff back, disappeared through the back door and slammed it shut. How had it come to this? The last thing she wanted was to upset her parents, yet she couldn't tell them the whole truth.

Without question, only Giselle would be able to understand Nella's thinking now. Maybe Giselle could talk with Mum and Daddy. Or would they, like Constable Burns, discount her opinion as the mere result of all she'd been through?

"Mummy?" Livie whimpered.

Nella jumped. "It's all right, Livie. Mummy and Mamgu just disagreed. We're not angry anymore. Come, love, take the basket of sprouts to Mamgu while I go pick flowers for the dinner table."

Livie sniffled, then lifted the basket and tottered toward the kitchen door with the load.

"Step careful," Nella cautioned and watched till she'd made it safely indoors. Then she hurried to the front dooryard and with her garden knife cut a bunch of yellow and russet chrysanthemums for the table—a peace offering to her mother. Turning around, she saw an envelope lying just inside the gate. She stooped and picked it up. When she turned the envelope over, her own name stared up at her, printed by hand with a student's blacklead. *NELLA KILLIAN, PERSONAL*, it said, without any address or postage stamps.

"What is this?" she muttered to herself. Her pulse began racing. She ripped open the envelope and pulled out a sheet of thin paper. Her eyes took in the words, and her mind went blank for a moment. She read it again. *YOU KNOW TOO MUCH, BUT IF YOU COOPERATE,*

YOU ARE WORTH MORE TO US ALIVE THAN DEAD. IF YOU WANT TO STAY ALIVE AND KEEP YOUR FAMILY ALIVE, THEN FORGET RUFUS JOHNSON AND LEAVE ABERGAVENNY. IF YOU DON'T, YOU WILL SEE YOUR FAMILY DIE. TELL ABSOLUTELY NO ONE ABOUT THIS NOTE AND BURN IT IMMEDIATELY.

Nella ran to the gate and looked up and down the street. Nobody was in sight, not even the neighbors. "Oh, dear God!" she whispered. "Now what do I do?"

She reread the threatening note and then crumpled it into a tight ball and put it in her apron pocket. Now for sure she couldn't tell Mum and Daddy the real reason she must leave the manse. She couldn't even tell Giselle.

Flowers in hand, she walked around to the back garden and paused at the kitchen door to try to slow her breathing and at least appear calm. She then stepped inside as if all were normal. Elizabeth was busy tending a steaming pot on the stove.

Nella struggled to recall what she'd planned to say to her mother. The shock of the note had jumbled her thoughts. "Mum, I'm sorry for talking to you the way I did. I don't know what came over me. Please forgive me."

Her mother laid down the stirring spoon and came with arms outstretched. "I'm sorry myself, dear. Please forgive me too. I know I sometimes treat you like a little girl instead of the grown-up woman you are."

Nella moved forward and hugged her tightly. The tremble in her knees crept over her entire body.

Her mother's familiar arms comforted her. "There now. We've all had a fright. We just need a bit of time to get over it."

Nella nodded and gave the best smile she could muster. She hated deception but knew it was necessary for her family's protection.

Supper that night was subdued and polite. Nella noticed that her father kept looking from her to her mother, but thankfully he asked no questions.

Later in bed Nella agonized alone. She couldn't bring herself to tell Giselle about the note. She couldn't trust anything to the constable. Captain Evers might take the note seriously, but she couldn't think of a way to reach him without the risk of being discovered. One thing was clear. She knew now she had to move from Abergavenny and right away.

Her worrying over Livie drove her to near hysteria. *Will she be safe if I leave her here? What if Mum and Daddy refuse to care for her in hopes of keeping me home? Then I'd just have to take her with me and disappear.*

The thought of placing her baby in the care of strangers was too much. No. If Mum and Daddy refused to keep Livie, she'd run away alone. Then they'd have to care for Livie. Somehow she would find a way to communicate with Captain Evers. But could she trust the captain? What if he were in on whatever happened to Rufe's letter? Her terror made everyone suspect.

On the edge of panic, she decided she must obey the note exactly. She must persuade her parents that her enlistment in the Land Army wouldn't hurt Livie, but would be an investment in their future. Then she remembered her intention to write to Corporal Peterson. A letter from him might convince the authorities of foul play, though she couldn't at the moment see how.

So Nella got up out of bed and, by the light of her electric torch, began a short letter to him. She was afraid to mention the attempt on her life or the threatening note. Someone besides the military censor might find out and report the information to the wrong persons.

Dear Corporal Peterson,
I hate to bother you with this, but I thought you would want to know. Without evidence from you, the authorities will not be investigating your friend's death. They told me they haven't been able to reach you. And the people at the military hospital said they would try to contact you, but they are busy tending the wounded and are convinced that your friend killed himself. So I hope you get this letter and soon. If you do, please write back immediately and include in your letter the same information you told me when we met in the USO. Thank you so much, and I promise I will try to write about more pleasant things in the future.
Yours truly,
Nella Killian

She sealed the letter in an envelope and addressed it.

A moment later she wanted to crumple it up and throw it in the dustbin. Why even bother? Surely it was hopeless. Marge, who had promised to keep looking for Rufe's letter, was gone now, and Captain Evers said the matter was closed.

No. I can't think that way, she chastised herself. *I've got to stand firm.* She snatched up the letter, tiptoed to the front door, and placed it on the hall table with her father's outgoing mail.

Crawling back into bed, she felt less trapped. The act of writing the letter had prevented her from sliding into despair. Maybe a letter from Corporal Peterson would help. In the meantime, she would leave the manse and quickly, with or without her parent's blessing.

The next morning Nella got up early, switched on the wireless, and started breakfast for the family. On BBC a man announced in a clipped voice, "In France yesterday, the Justice Commissioner, François de Menthon, ordered the arrest of Marshall Petain and all the members of the Vichy cabinet for their alleged collaboration with the Germans." A bit of good news for Giselle. Petain had been a puppet in Germans' hands. He'd created the Milice, a military police organization as cruel as the Gestapo. Nella added more flour to the muffin batter and worked it in.

Her mother, wrapped in her old chenille robe, came into the kitchen, blinking at the light.

Nella handed her a cup of hot tea. "Good news. They've arrested Petain and his men."

"Ah. That'll be a relief for Giselle. The stories she told me about the Milice about made me ill. Incredible that Petain, a World War I hero, could turn against his own people like that. But then he's very old by now."

"A poor excuse," Nella remarked. "His age should make him wiser."

Her mother sat down at the table and stirred tinned milk and a little sugar into her tea. "Would that age always brought wisdom. Nella, I confess my failure on that point."

"What do you mean?"

"I had no business lecturing you. I keep forgetting you have to live your life your own way—"

"Aw, Mum, forget it. I do understand how you felt."

"Well, if you're still set on joining the Land Army, I won't argue."

"Do you really think it would be all right?"

Her mother gave a tired smile. "I've been thinking that maybe I never gave you a proper chance to speak your mind when you were growing up. I didn't listen to you as well as I should have."

"You always listened to Charles and me and Peggy. It was me that didn't listen."

"That's good of you to say, but I want to do better now. There's one thing more I want to say, and then we'll forget about last night. Don't ever think that God is too small to handle some yelling at. He loves you no matter what. When you can't understand something, I believe He'd rather hear you yell at Him than ignore Him. Now that I've said that, what about the Land Army? Are you still for joining up?"

Nella poured tea for herself and sat across from her mother. "Aye, I am, Mum! If Livie can stay with you and Daddy."

"Your father and I have talked, and although we don't feel all that comfortable about your going, we do trust you. Knowing how much you love Livie, we expect you have a great need to do this. It looks like the war is far from being over, with those V–2 rockets falling on London and the battle going so slow in France and Belgium. So your country does need you. Of course we'll care for our Livie if you go."

Nella jumped up, went around the old oak table, and kissed her mother's cheek. "Thank you. I'm so glad you'll be watching over Livie. I know you won't let her out of your sight."

Elizabeth stood and hugged her. "Of course I won't," she said, sounding surprised that there should be any question. "I'll go get dressed now that we have that settled."

Nella sat back down with her tea, feeling as if her mother had lifted a great weight off her chest. Now she only had to enlist and hope that the person who wrote the note would see she was obeying the demands to tell no one and leave town. As for coming back home to visit, she'd work this out later.

Her hand brushed against a lump in her apron pocket. The note! She'd meant to burn it last night. She hurried to the kitchen stove, quietly cracked open the door, and tossed the paper ball onto the glowing coals.

Peggy hoped that, after the break-in at the manse, Nella would decide to come to West-Holding and stay with her for a while. Working on the harvest festival might help to get her mind off the frightening things happening.

When Nella phoned her after supper, she sounded tense yet enthused about something. Peggy promptly dropped her thoughts of the harvest festival. "Nella? What's happened?"

"Good news, I think," she said, her voice brittle bright. "I'm going to join the Land Army."

"The Land Army! Well..." Peggy gulped in surprise. "How soon will you leave then?"

"Daddy's taking me Friday to Newport to enlist."

"Friday! So he and Mother Mac think it's all right for you to go off and leave Livie?"

"Not really, but they're willing to help me do what I think is right."

"You expect this will accomplish . . . what you want?"

"I hope so. It's the best I can think of. I'll be able to apply for part-time service later. The Land Army allows that for mothers. Then when it seems a good idea, I can come home to visit."

"I hate to bring this up, but . . . what if someone were to take Livie to get at you, like they did to Giselle."

"Peggy! Please! I've thought this through, and I know what I'm doing. There is no good solution. You know I hate to leave her."

Peggy could tell Nella was less positive than she was putting on, but she also knew that arguing now wouldn't change her mind. "I know, but I had to bring it up. It scares me."

"I'm sure Livie will be safer with me gone."

"One of your hunches?" Nella had made some impulsive decisions in the past that she and everyone else had regretted later.

"Aye, if you want to call it that."

"You don't need more time to think about it?" They had an agreement that Peggy always should remind her to take three days to make an important decision.

"I know what you're saying, that there's time to change my mind between now and Friday. I promise, if I think of a better solution, I won't go."

"Good. If you do join the Land Army, I wonder how soon you'll be given your assignment. I was hoping you could help me with the harvest festival."

"Help you with what?"

"I'd planned to talk to you about it on Sunday, but with all that happened I forgot. Lady W. wants me, and you, to organize the harvest festival for all the workers here, especially for the schoolchildren."

"She doesn't even know me. What made her think of me?"

"Actually it was Bryan—you know, the son of the Westmore-lands—who asked about you helping out. He's her emissary. Lady W. and I, we don't speak to each other if we can avoid it. Seems Lady W. has to be away, so she up and dropped this project onto Bryan's lap and told him to get me to organize it. He said he knows nothing of such things. He then suggested that you assist me. I told him if you were willing, I'd take on the job."

"I'd be glad to help if I were staying home. But I'm guessing they'll put me to work as soon as possible, seeing as how the harvest is going at full tilt in many places."

Peggy sighed. She hated uncertainty. "So when will you know?"

"Soon, I hope. I'm sure you and Mr. Westmoreland will do fine without me."

"He and I wouldn't likely do fine even with you, but you'd be a good buffer and keep me sensible. I may just tell him to find someone else."

"Well, I'll let you know what I find out on Friday. By the way, when you see Mr. Westmoreland again, please tell him I'll be returning the money he left here. Turns out Mum isn't short in her change, so it must've been lost by someone else. I'll give it to you at church."

"I'll tell him. Any more news from Jean . . . about Marge, I mean?"

"Not a word. Maybe she'll know something by Sunday."

"I can't help but hope you'll be available to help with the festival."

"I'll let you know. And Peggy, I wrote to Corporal Peterson myself. If he gets my letter and writes back, his word might persuade Captain Evers to look into Rufe's death and also to assign someone to protect me and the family."

"Sounds like a wise move. Good for you."

When Nella rang off, Peggy replaced the receiver and strolled thoughtfully to the front window of her room in Gatekeep. Nella had sounded torn up about all that had happened, and why shouldn't she be? Peggy hated being stuck in West-Holding when the family needed her. Not that she could do anything. Nevertheless, after school on Friday, she would bicycle home for the weekend. The manse was still home, though she loved having her own quarters here in the small stone house. Gatekeep had been the old gatekeeper's cottage back when the entire village was part of the Westmoreland Estate.

She rested her eyes on the little dooryard garden that she loved. Someday, after she made a name for herself in the art world, she wanted to own a cottage like this one, somewhere in a quiet village where she could paint by the hour instead of squeezing in a few minutes after teaching all day.

Despite the deprivations of war, the village hadn't lost its ageless, pastoral appearance. From her window, Peggy could view a piece of the countryside. Pastures full of sheep lay just beyond the stone wall across the road, and then meadows and fields stretching eastward. In the middle of the nearest meadow stood the thicket of trees Annie Nelson had chosen for her private hideaway. Annie had shown her the lovely glen in the midst of the thick growth. It was one place Mrs. Nelson allowed her to go alone to draw and paint. To the west, quaint stone cottages lined the village street. The sight always roused a feeling of nostalgia in Peggy, probably because it reminded her of an illustration from her old nursery-rhyme book.

She knew that life in earlier times had been hard on the villagers. Still was. Even now the people depended too much on the residents at the manor house. The older folks still looked up to Lord Westmoreland, just as much as anyone had in the past. The servile attitude lingered, ingrained and perpetuated by traditions like the harvest festival.

Coming abruptly back to the present, Peggy thought, *What possessed me to say I'd do the festival if Nella could help? Good thing she won't be available. I should pick up that phone right now and tell Lady W. I won't be doing it.*

She didn't, however. She decided to wait and tell Bryan instead.

CHAPTER THIRTEEN

The following afternoon on the way home from school, Peggy saw Bryan Westmoreland standing with a tall stranger outside the post office. She stopped and said, "Mr. Westmoreland, I want to warn you, you may have to do the harvest festival by yourself. My friend Nella is going to Newport on Friday to sign up for the Land Army."

"Friday, you say. Well, thank you for telling me." He turned to the stranger and said, "Laurie, may I introduce Miss Peggy Jones, one of our schoolteachers. Miss Jones, this is Laurence Barringer, a longtime friend of mine. His cousin once removed is one of your students—Peter Hilliard."

"Oh," Peggy said, smiling. "How do you do, Mr. Barringer."

"Pleasure to meet you, Miss Jones," he responded.

He looked strangely familiar. He had a long narrow face to go with his long narrow frame, dark eyes, and sun-bleached brown hair. She focused again on Bryan. "You do understand that you're on your own with organizing the festival, don't you? Unless somehow Nella doesn't leave right away."

Bryan raised an eyebrow and grinned. "Then we'll wait until after Friday and see. Maybe the Land Army won't accept your friend. If she is still available, I'll hold you to your word. Also, I meant to tell you that Father is pleased you want to teach about our family history to your class. I'll bring you the Welsh bride's book as soon as I locate it."

"Thank you." Peggy then nodded to Bryan's friend. "Mr. Barringer, it was nice meeting you."

"Again, the pleasure is mine." His tone and warm manner gave the trite phrase sincerity.

She walked on, wondering why he reminded her of someone. Although he hadn't said much, he had smiled each time she'd glanced in his direction. The effect of his friendliness disarmed her normal caution toward men born to wealth, as he obviously had been. On the way to Gatekeep, she puzzled over her unexplainable reaction. One moment she lectured herself about the foolishness of taking a liking to someone so similar to Bryan, yet the next she felt drawn to him regardless.

When standing before Mr. Barringer, Peggy had caught herself checking her shoes to make sure they carried no streaks of coal-blackened mud. She hadn't done so in years. Seeing him had thrown her back to feeling like the little girl she'd been in a coal-mining town. How then could she be wishing to know him better? Confused, she retreated into the haven of Gatekeep.

After class the next day, Peggy decided to correct the last of the geography papers in the classroom rather than take them home. She'd just settled into the task when a knock on the door announced a guest. She called, "Come in, please."

Bryan stepped in, and behind him came his friend, Laurie Barringer. Taller than Bryan, he reminded Peggy of a figure in an El Greco painting.

Bryan marched in and declared, "Miss Jones, I found the Welsh bride's book!" He thumped it down on her desk and turned to the man beside him. "I guess Peter has gone home."

"Yes," Peggy volunteered. "About fifteen minutes ago."

"That's fine," Mr. Barringer said. "I just thought I'd give him a lift if he hadn't." He approached her desk, walking with a limp he appeared to be trying to hide. She saw that his eyes were not brown but a striking dark blue. Up close they seemed to have a light of their own when he smiled. He looked as unassuming as a friendly villager or perhaps one of the teachers. His eyes crinkled at the corners, which gave him a boyish appearance.

"I'm pleased to see you again, Miss Jones."

"Thank you, Mr. Barringer." His name seemed familiar to her. "Do you live around here?" she asked.

"No. My father held an interest in the mines near Blaenavon, but we've always lived in Cheltenham."

"Blaenavon!" She still visited her mother and sisters near there. For some unknown reason, connecting this stranger to her hometown had made her uncomfortable.

"You've been there?" He looked startled.

"Yes. Of course. It's not that far away." She turned to Bryan. "Did you want to talk to me, or were you just dropping off the book and looking for Peter?"

"Mostly the book and Peter. But I would like to discuss ideas for the festival. Since your friend in the manse hasn't yet been accepted and sent anywhere, maybe in the meantime she'll consider helping us with the planning stage."

"I don't know. I'll see her Sunday. If you want to plan on a meeting Monday without knowing for sure, that's fine with me."

"Did you say she was signing up for part-time service?"

"I don't know if I said, but I think she is. She has a little girl and so doesn't want to leave her for full-time work."

His eyes narrowed as if he were doing arithmetic in his head. "So she'll enlist part time. Maybe she can still help then. Come up to Whitestone Monday evening, and we can discuss the preliminary plans."

"Excuse me? Mr. Westmoreland, if I help you, I'll want any meetings necessary right here in my classroom!" He'd sounded so presumptuous that the words exploded from her. Now she wished she could take back the remark or at least modify its tone. What would Mr. Barringer think, for goodness' sake? Her cheeks began to burn. Still, she raised her chin and glared at Bryan to make it clear she wasn't about to comply with his thoughtless plan. It was enough that she had agreed to help him.

Bryan bobbed his head in subservience and said with exaggerated submissiveness, "Yes, Teacher Jones. We'll meet here in your classroom." Like a schoolboy, he was making fun. Well, she had treated him like one of her pupils. It should be no surprise he would then act the part.

But Peggy refused to smile. Instead, she nodded in a businesslike fashion, hoping he'd take the hint and leave.

Appearing unruffled, he strolled toward the door. "Until Monday then. Let's be on our way, Laurie."

"Good-bye, Miss Jones," Mr. Barringer said. "I hope we shall see each other again soon." For a moment she thought he was going to say "under happier conditions," but he didn't.

"Thank you." For him she smiled. "Oh, Mr. Westmoreland, I almost forgot. Nella asked me to tell you that someone else must've dropped the money you returned to her. She counted and found her change to be correct. She'll be giving me your money on Sunday."

He raised his eyebrows. "Is that right? Well, tell her to take it to the chemist's instead, and he'll see if anyone complains of missing it."

"All right, I'll tell her."

Bryan swung open the door and held it for Mr. Barringer, who cast one last look at her over his shoulder before limping out. The fleeting look on his face, like a small boy being herded somewhere against his will, suddenly pierced Peggy deep inside. Laurie. Laurence Barringer the Fourth. How could she not have remembered the name? But they'd met so long ago, and one tends to forget even the happiest experience when it ends in pain. She shuddered as she thought back.

Peggy composed herself. It was pointless to allow something so long ago to distress her all over again. She returned to checking geography papers, putting Laurence Barringer the Fourth out of her mind.

But then the image of his backward glance drew her into the past, to the memory of one morning in Blaenavon. She could almost taste the coal dust that blackened the mining town where she'd been born.

Suddenly Peggy couldn't sit still any longer. She snatched up the papers and stuffed them into her homemade briefcase, carefully placing the Westmoreland book in the middle for protection. Walking home in the September sun, she greeted villagers with a smile or a word or two, but in her thoughts she was five years old again, back home with her little sister Winnie.

It was when that immense car had driven up the muddy road between the houses of the miners and then stopped at the mining office across from their meager cottage. She and Winnie stood by the dooryard and watched. She could still see the scene clearly with the eyes of her memory: the black shiny car, Winnie beside her. A tall man got out. Behind him hopped out a boy, not much bigger than she. He was a tidy looking boy with short-cropped blond curls and wearing a sailor suit, much like the boy in a storybook she'd once seen.

"Don't you get muddy and upset your mother," the man ordered. He didn't bother to see if the boy obeyed, but marched into the mining office.

"Let's go play with him," Winnie had said.

Being a year older, Peggy knew better. But she had agreed anyway. "Okay. Maybe he'll come over here." Da had warned her and Winnie to stay on their side of the road, out of the way of the miners. But except for those in the office, everyone was underground at the time.

A voice pulled her out of her reverie. The postman, calling from the doorway of the post office, said, "Miss Jones! Hold up a minute. I've got ye a package."

She stepped over to the post office and waited, while he scooted behind the counter, bent out of sight, and then popped up again. "I was watching for you. Didn't want to be leaving this package on your doorstep."

"Thanks, Mr. Owen. I appreciate that."

He grinned, peering at her through his thick glasses. "I heard you'll be giving us all some real celebrating after the harvest. We're sure needing it. The children haven't had a party like this in ages."

It was for people like Mr. Owen, as well as for the children, that she had let herself be talked into doing the festival. "Aye. We all need a bit of fun now, don't we?" She thanked him again and went back out to the street. A glance at the return address on the package told her that her mother had sent something from the farm. It wasn't very heavy, so she tucked it under her arm.

While her feet continued to carry her toward home, her mind traveled back to Laurie Barringer. Who would have thought he'd grow up to be so tall? She had liked him the minute she saw him. She had taken Winnie's hand and had run across the street to him. Seeing him smile at them, she'd said hello.

He'd looked at Peggy with his large blue eyes and declared sassily, "I can jump higher than anybody."

"Then do it," she said back, not at all disturbed by his boasting.

The boy bunched himself up, crouched down, then leaped straight up in the air. When he came down, he splashed mud all over his shoes, and theirs too. But he truly had jumped higher than she expected.

"That was good," she said, giving him his due.

"Now you try," he said in a friendlier tone. "Let me show you how. You have to bend down like this." He lowered to a half squat and beckoned for Winnie to do the same. "Now jump!" He leaped in the air. Winnie followed and did pretty well. He turned to Peggy. "You try."

She jumped and felt as if she could fly, even though she knew she didn't do as well as he. She got an idea then. "Let's run and then jump. It'll be like flying." The boy was game, and so taking care to stay away from the middle of the road, they ran and leaped with their arms out like wings till they were panting. When they stopped, he asked, "What's your name?"

"I'm Peggy. She's my sister Winnie."

"I'm Laurie. That's short for Laurence. My father is Laurence Barringer the Third, and I'm Laurence Barringer the Fourth. I have a pony that I can ride. His name is Shadow. Father let me name him. Do you have a pony?"

She shook her head. She'd never seen a riding pony, only Welsh ponies that stayed down in the mines until they couldn't work anymore. "We have a cat. We found her when she was a kitten. Mum says she's a good mouser."

They had run some distance from the mining office, so Peggy led the way back. When they reached the big car, she suddenly realized they all were very dirty. "Oh, our Mum will let loose on us for getting so dirty and washday near a week away. Will your mum be mad?" She leaned over and tried to brush some of the dirt from his dark blue trouser leg. She was used to taking care of her little brothers.

Suddenly there was a beastly roar behind her. Even now, remembering made her heart lurch. She had turned, too scared to speak, and there was the tall man with his mouth twisted and his face mean. "Get your filthy hands off my son, you little urchin!" He had grabbed her by the back of her dress and shaken her. Fear had so clogged her throat that she couldn't cry out.

Winnie had screamed and run home.

"How dare you touch my son!" the man yelled. He gave her another shake, so much so that she stumbled and fell. Then she saw his big foot raised to give her a kick. Peggy became so terrified that she wet herself. "Filthy commoner," he spat. He turned away. "Get in the car, Laurence!"

Muddy and wet, she picked herself up off the ground. Laurie had turned and gazed back at her through the car's rear window. She thought he looked sorry and would've liked to stay and play.

This was the look that had triggered her memory today in the classroom. He'd given her the same glance back over his shoulder, as if he wished he could stay. How could a man be recognized by an expression seen only once on his childhood face? Peggy shook her head, confounded. *I thought I'd forgotten. I wanted to forget.* Well, that wasn't quite true. She'd made herself remember, so she'd never allow herself to get into such a horrible situation again. But it had been years since she'd thought of the boy and that day.

When the boy had looked at her from the car's window, she was suddenly thankful she was so dirty and in a dress, so he wouldn't see that she'd wet her pants. Just before his father pushed him into the car, Laurie, keeping his hand from his father's sight, had waggled his fingers in a secret good-bye.

Peggy reached Gatekeep and turned into the welcoming dooryard.

She set down her briefcase and package and fumbled in her purse for the old iron key. Mrs. Lewis, her landlady, had said she'd be gone to the church to help put together gift packages for the servicemen. Soon Peggy was in her own cozy room, yet she didn't feel comforted. Strange how remembering something even a long time ago can still bring back the bad feelings.

She laid the package on her desk to open after she'd heated water for tea on the hot plate. Then she cut the strings her mother had wound around the package. Inside she found two jars of fresh black-current jelly. *How did Mum save up enough sugar coupons to make jelly?* she wondered. *What a treat.* As much as she'd felt at odds visiting the farm after her mother had married Mr. Edwards, she always felt close to her mum.

That day Mr. Barringer had shaken and shamed her, her mum had come running to comfort her. "Oh, what has he done to ye?"

She gathered me up and carried me, dirty and big as I was, into the house. I couldn't stop crying. I felt so ashamed, not just of wetting my pants, but ashamed in a new way. I didn't know why, but I wasn't fit for being friends with tidy kids like Laurie, and he had been such fun.

She had asked her mum why the man wanted to hurt her, when she was only trying to clean up the boy.

Her mum had seemed ashamed herself. "There, there. Ye shouldn'a crossed the street, but ye didn'a do wrong to the boy. I did wrong not to warn ye about the gentry. I just didn'a think it need be so soon. Ye must never go near the gentry. It's safer that way. Stay away from the lords and ladies and their young masters and mistresses."

Then she ladled hot water from the stove to a pan to bathe her and repeated how she must learn to behave around the gentry. As her mum talked, she felt she'd never feel clean again.

The teakettle whistled. Peggy jumped up and poured the boiling water into the teapot, being careful not to wash the leaves over the edge of the strainer. While the tea steeped, she spread out students' papers to correct.

She began marking papers, pausing from time to time for a sip of tea. She couldn't help thinking again of the tall man she'd met as a child. Under that seemingly friendly surface he was probably just like his father. With luck, she'd never see him again. Working with Bryan Westmoreland on the harvest festival would be hard enough.

Friday dawned gray for Nella. When she went to kiss Livie good-bye, her heart constricted in her chest. Livie didn't know it, but this would turn out to be a long good-bye. Unless, of course, the Land Army wouldn't take her. Nella climbed into the old car beside her father, looked back, and waved one more time. On the front steps Livie waved cheerfully from her mamgu's arms.

After driving silently for a while, her father said, "So you're on your way back into service again. I hope you'll be assigned close enough to come home regularly. Part-time service, like you told your mother."

"Yes," she said but knew she wouldn't be coming home anytime soon. "Daddy, you know how I hate to leave Livie, even though I'm doing what I feel's right."

"Aye. Your Mum and I understand how you're pulled two ways at once. You mustn't worry about the babe, Nella. Now that you've set your mind to serve, trust her to God and to us. She'll miss you, but will do fine. And Lord willing, the war will soon be over."

"I truly hope so." As far as trusting her baby to God's care, she could trust her father more than she could trust a distant God. God and her prayers hadn't done a thing for Rob.

"Daddy, Giselle thinks there may be more German spies nearby that haven't yet been caught."

"Aye, and it's natural she would think that."

"She could be right, don't you think?"

He glanced at her. "I suppose. Lately I've come to believe anything is possible."

"That's what I think too. It makes it harder to go away and leave Livie. Will you try to persuade Mum to be extra careful? I mean, if it wouldn't worry her too much."

He nodded slowly. "I've been thinking that myself. Mind you, I don't think there's a danger to Livie, but I've taken to locking the doors and to watching out for strangers. The Lord did say to be wise as serpents." He reached over and squeezed her hand. "I'll talk to Mum, and we'll be watchful. But I worry more about you than Livie. It's hard to be a father of a grown daughter and not be able to protect her. It's especially hard when I can't hand you the trust in God that gives me peace of mind."

Nella bit her lip and fought back tears. His tenderness undid her. All she could do was nod. When she regained control of her emotions, she said, "I feel better, Daddy, just knowing you realize there could be danger. Thank you." She didn't want to hear about trust and faith.

And she certainly didn't want him to guess the reason for the panic driving her to have to leave home. So she changed the subject, discussing the fields they passed and the coming harvest. She diverted him easily, just as she'd wished.

All the way to Newport, rain showers misted over the green hills. Then as they approached the city, the sun burned away the clouds as if in celebration, and before them lay the port city, freshly washed and drying under a light breeze.

Her father parked against the curb near the enlistment center. "I don't suppose you'll be wanting me to come in with you?" he asked.

She laughed. "I'm old enough this time to sign up on my own."

"I'll do a bit of shopping for your mother then. She's hoping the stores here have some things she needs, things she can't get back in Abergavenny."

"If I finish first, I'll just wait in the car."

"Aye."

He walked off on his chore, as Nella entered the building. She felt as though she'd walked into a cave after being in the bright sunlight. The room looked like a warehouse full of desks and file cabinets, with signs everywhere about joining the military. She finally found the area for the Land Army. An older woman sitting behind a desk smiled up at her, friendly but businesslike.

Nella recalled when she joined the WAAF. They were so glad to get her, it hadn't been very difficult to lie about her age. Now she didn't need to lie.

"Twenty-one," she said. "I heard I could do part-time work in the Land Army, and that's what I'll want after a bit. I have a little girl who will be staying with my parents."

"We do allow part-time service for mothers. May I have your name, please, and your home address."

"Nella Killian. I live in Abergavenny. However, I'd like full-time service to start with and to be stationed some distance away from my home, please."

"Well," the woman said, "I'll see what I can do. You fill out these forms, and I'll work to find you a proper farm."

The induction process took the rest of the morning, but by lunchtime Nella was outfitted with the brown and green uniform of the Land Army and given leave to return home for the weekend.

A different woman, with a no-nonsense frown, explained her assignment. "We've just received an emergency request, and I think you will fit nicely there. The Land Girls we've already sent report excellent treatment. Monday morning you will report directly to Lord West-moreland at Whitestone Manor in West-Holding. Perhaps you know the place, it being close to Abergavenny and all."

"Yes . . ." Nella said faintly, "I know the place." All the while, she was thinking, *No! That's too close to home!* But what could she say? "Are you sure I'm not needed a bit . . . farther away?" Nella asked.

The woman glared at her. "Mrs. Killian, do you want to serve in the Land Army or not?"

"Of course I want to serve."

"The Westmoreland Estate needs a girl as soon as possible, and you are uniquely qualified. Your experience in the WAAF has prepared you for the discipline of service so you may go right to work. At the end of the harvest season, you will report to us here in Newport for more formal training. I'm sure you will do fine until then. Oh, and until the harvest is over, you will live at the farm full time. After that, Lord Westmoreland will adjust your hours according to the needs of your child. This arrangement sounds quite agreeable, does it not?"

"Yes, ma'am, it does." Even if Nella could get out of this, it would take time to find another means of escape, and then she'd have to explain to her parents. She couldn't do that. So she straightened, sa-luted, and said, "Thank you, ma'am." Marching out, she felt she'd just joined a boarding school rather than a wartime service. The woman must've run a school before the war. She had made it impossible to get placed on a farm farther from the manse. Nella hoped the killer would accept her assignment so close to home as a valid sign she was obeying the note's demands. For the note hadn't stated how far away she should go.

On the way to her father's car, she worked herself into acting a role and put on a happy face. After all, her parents would be overjoyed to have her at West-Holding, so she'd better pretend to be pleased too. Maybe after Lord Westmoreland's emergency was over, she could transfer somewhere else. Also, for all she knew, being close to Aber-gavenny might serve to draw the killer's attention away from the manse, as she'd once calculated. The horrible truth was she had no way of knowing what was best.

At the car her father looked up from the newspaper he was read-ing. "Well! I had no idea they'd put you in uniform already. They that eager for you to get to work?"

"It just happened that Lord Westmoreland out by West-Holding put in an emergency request for a Land Girl. Isn't that amazing?" she said, keeping her voice light.

"Ah, an answer to prayer, Nella. Your mum will be so pleased to have you nearby."

Nella wasn't so sure her placement had been handled by God. She'd feel a lot better if she could believe it was.

CHAPTER FOURTEEN

Peggy came home from school Friday with a sore throat and wanting nothing more than hot tea and her bed.

Mrs. Lewis insisted on covering her with her best down comforter and bringing her a cup of broth from the oxtail soup she'd made for supper. Next she produced her home remedies: an evil-smelling flannel wrap for Peggy's throat, a hot-water bottle for her feet, and a cool cloth for her forehead.

Finally she turned up the volume on the wireless, so Peggy could listen to music on the BBC. The news came on every so often and announced the latest on the fighting in Belgium and France. Peggy thought of Giselle when she heard that the Americans had taken Nancy and Epinal. So much destruction in her homeland must be difficult for her. And Claude remained in constant danger.

Like everyone else, Peggy had heard that pushing Hitler's armies back to Berlin wouldn't be easy, yet she'd hoped it would go much faster and easier than it was currently going.

As she struggled to swallow the soup, she got to thinking. What would it be like to come down sick on the battlefront, with no warm bed and no hot drink? War was rotten, no two ways about it. It must be the ultimate torture to be sick on top of being shot at.

After supper Mrs. Lewis brought a mug of hot water into which she'd added a spoonful of vinegar and two of honey. She refilled the hot-water bottle for her feet.

By bedtime Peggy began feeling a tiny bit better. She climbed out of bed, pulled on her robe, and went to ring up Nella. Her "Hello" gave away the effects of her sore throat. "I won't be going to church Sunday," she croaked.

"I'm sorry you don't feel well," Nella said. "What will you do Monday about teaching?"

"I should be well by then. Don't you know teachers never get sick?"

"Seriously, what happens if you can't teach?"

"Emma Wilson would take my class along with her own. It's hard to double up, but we've all done it before. The children are pretty good about cooperating in such a pinch."

"Then you'll stay home if you're still ill?"

"If I have to. I didn't call to talk so much about me. What happened in Newport? Did they take you in?"

"I'm a Land Girl now, and you'll never guess where they assigned me. I'm to be at the Westmoreland Estate. They made an emergency request for someone. I'm to report there Monday morning. I suppose the harvest is about to begin."

"Aye, but I happen to know they just recently lost two girls. The girls who swore they saw the Whitestone ghost and ran for their lives."

"Really? I didn't think anyone would fall for that ghost story nowadays."

"Well, they probably did see something. Add to that the fact that some here in the village swear the ghost *is* real. One of the Land Girls was the older sister of one of my pupils. The children were fairly upset over it. We had to talk in class about how such stories get started."

"That's too bad."

"Aye. You know, if it weren't for you wanting to be farther away, I'd say it's wonderful to have you come to Whitestone."

"I hope it will do. I can't say more than that," Nella remarked quietly.

Peggy guessed that Mother Mac must be within hearing. "I understand. Listen, just say yes or no. Do you still think Giselle's fears are justified?"

"I do keep that in mind."

"I'll take that as a yes."

"Peggy, how can I know for sure?"

"Uh-huh. Time to change the subject. I wonder if Bryan will assign the festival as part of your duties. That would be good luck for me." When she said the word *luck*, she could almost hear Father Mac saying *There's no such thing as luck, Peggy*. Because of his insistence, she'd often noticed in hindsight that God had indeed guided and protected her.

In this case, however, Peggy suspected a human element as part of the coincidence. "Nella, I'd wager that somehow The Bryan—that's short for Bryan-the-Great, which is what he thinks he is—well, that he's managed to influence your assignment."

"Oh, he couldn't. The Land Army isn't influenced by politics or personal requests. Anyway, he didn't know I was going to enlist."

"He knew all right. I told him you were heading to Newport today to sign up."

"Still, such maneuvering couldn't be done. And certainly not because he's wanting help with the harvest festival. They told me Lord Westmoreland himself put in the emergency request."

What Nella said made sense. A village festival held no importance for those outside the village. "You're probably right, but like father like son. Because the son of the lord is skilled at working the odds, I can't help but wonder about the father . . . or what the two of them together may finagle."

"Bryan does come off a bit presuming and overbearing. If I do get to help you, I hope we can work without having much to do with him."

"Me too. Between the two of us, I fancy we can manage that. Let's make it our personal project."

Nella laughed. "We do make a good team. Remember when you were trying to avoid Henry Harrison, and we set up Cynthia as a decoy to sidetrack him?"

Peggy started laughing but then went into a coughing spell. When it was over she choked out, "Good old Cynthia. Sidetracking boys was her specialty. I wonder where she is now?"

"Didn't I tell you? She was in the Auxiliary Territorial Service when I was in the WAAF. She was having the time of her life. I saw her right after Rob and I married. She couldn't believe I'd be settling on one man for the rest of my life, me being so young and all."

Peggy coughed and said, "I'm afraid we won't have another Cynthia to help us out. We may have to think harder this time."

"That's a fact." Nella rang off with the promising words, "One way or the other, I hope to see you next week."

By Sunday morning Peggy's sore throat was on the mend, so she dressed and attended services in the village. When she first had moved to West-Holding, she'd attended St. Mark Church regularly, hoping to get to know the parents of her students. Now she felt quite at home in the Anglican service. She liked the liturgy and colorful traditions, some that had begun with the villagers, like Thanks and Blessing Day. Each fall farmers brought one sheep to the churchyard to represent their flocks, and Father Thomas gave thanks and asked God's blessing on the crops and animals through the coming year.

The prewar harvest festivals had grown out of Thanks and Blessing Day. After the Sunday of blessing, every night the rest of the week the villagers would put on folk dances, concerts, and plays. Games, a puppet theater, and carnival rides entertained the children. Now the challenge would be to offer some of the same delight with using only local talents.

As Peggy entered the church and quietly chose her usual seat halfway toward the front, she noticed Lady W.'s absence from the family pew. Sitting in the Hilliard pew across the aisle were Laurie Barringer, Peter Hilliard, and Peter's grandmother, Eunice Hilliard. Beside Mr. Barringer sat a handsome dark-haired woman. Laurence Barringer certainly bore no resemblance to his aunt Eunice. Neither did the dark-haired woman. Her profile, however, matched Peter's. She must be his mother, home from India.

When the service ended, Father Thomas detained Peggy at the door. "Miss Jones, I hear you're to organize a harvest festival this year. A fine service for the village. Let me know if there's any way I can be of assistance."

"Thank you, Father. I may need to consult you."

"We'd have a hard time putting on a festival without Miss Jones, Father Thomas," came Bryan's voice from behind her. "Mother personally selected her for this project. And you know how Mother feels about reestablishing the festival."

"Yes. She's wanted to do this for the past two years. The festival will be a healing thing, especially in these hard times. At the risk of offending, I have to say that sometimes I think the Sabbath was meant for play as well as for rest."

"Miss Jones will be receiving the help of the Presbyterian minister's daughter, which should add another dimension to our celebration," Bryan added.

"I know Reverend MacDougall well. Maybe his parishioners will wish to participate in some way. Do you think so, Miss Jones?"

"I can certainly ask." She hadn't considered that the festival might also attract the townsfolk. "I'll let you know if that can be arranged. Thank you for the suggestion." With that she excused herself and stepped outside.

Before she reached the street, Bryan called from a few paces behind her. "I hear your friend Nella is coming to our farms. This must be good news for you."

She turned. "Yes. I trust you'll see that she has release time for working on the festival."

"I've already talked to Father about it."

"You don't seem surprised that Nella will be at Whitestone Manor."

He raised an eyebrow and grinned. "I consider it an act of God himself that we should be so blessed."

"How did you manage it?" Peggy asked.

"What?" he blurted. "My father did mention that he'd made an emergency request, scarcely hoping it would be honored in time to help with the harvest. But you understand, even if I wanted to, there would be no way I could influence a service appointment."

Behind his glib, innocent speech, she saw a flicker of wariness sharpen the lines around his eyes. This man was conniving. Why, she couldn't guess. Neither could she imagine how he'd managed to get his way, but she felt certain that somehow Bryan had used the family name to get Nella assigned to the Westmoreland Estate. And he definitely didn't want anyone to know.

She shrugged. "I understand."

He called after her, "Have you had time to look at the Welsh bride's book?"

"No, I haven't. I'm looking forward to it, though." Peggy hated being beholden to Bryan when all she wanted was for him to keep his distance. Nevertheless, she was grateful for the use of the heirloom book. She turned and said as politely as she could, "Thanks again for loaning the book."

Monday morning Nella pushed her bicycle up the hill the last kilometer to Whitestone Manor. She had cried all the way to West-Holding, grieving over having to leave Livie. Saturday morning she'd told Livie she had to go away for a while. Together they had turned Nella's bedroom into Livie's very own room with a small single bed instead of the crib.

Saturday night and Sunday Nella had slept in Charles's old room. Livie seemed proud to have her own room and calm about the idea of change. While Nella worked toward making things easy for Livie, Nella's heart felt to be cracking. She hated to miss any day of her baby's life, and yet she knew she must.

In a state of panic, Nella had made the decision to obey the threatening note. Now, with more time to think, she still felt Livie was safer with Mum and Daddy than if she'd taken Livie away with her. Anywhere they went, she'd have to work and leave the baby with someone, and no one would watch over her as carefully as her own grandparents. So leaving her at the manse was best.

Now trudging up the hill, she wiped away her tears and forced herself to concentrate on what lay ahead: fulfilling the demands of the note and becoming a competent Land Girl. Dressed in her brown and green uniform, she carried her work shirt, coveralls, and gum boots in a bag tied on the bicycle rack behind the seat. Later in the day her father would bring her large suitcase.

Nella finally reached the mansion's wrought-iron gates halfway up the hill and entered the estate proper, suddenly feeling as if she'd crossed into enemy territory. She stopped and drew in a quick breath. Why this feeling of danger? A case of nerves, for sure. Giving herself a mental shake, she straightened and pushed her bicycle on up the hill.

The great house with its towers and many chimneys dropped out of sight behind a rise on the hillside. As she continued walking, she reflected that she had good cause to be jumpy. Besides the terrible threat to her family, in the space of two days she'd left her baby and joined the Land Army. Such changes were enough to unnerve anybody.

By the time she approached the graveled turnaround in front of the manor, Nella was perspiring, and the sharp sorrow she felt over leaving Livie had eased some. Hopefully working on the farm would teach her useful skills for when she owned her own land someday. She must remember she was building a future for Livie. Leaning on her bicycle, she gazed out across the Usk Valley to the tree-thatched, rounded peak of Ysgyryd Fach.

Nella had visited the Westmoreland Estate a few times when she'd participated in sheep dog trials with the Flints, but she'd never been up here to the house. The view from Whitestone Manor contained all the beauty she loved about South Wales. The great house's manicured lawn and formal gardens stretched down the slope toward the fields and meadows that surrounded West-Holding. The village nestled on the valley floor looked like a child's play village with its tiny stone cottages and twisting streets laid out on both sides of Shearing Creek. All around the village, almost as far as she could see, the manor's farmland blended with that of the smaller farmers' holdings in a tidy checkerboard of fields. Many of them burgeoned with this fall's potato crop.

She walked past the front door of Whitestone and circled to the back of the mansion where she assumed the kitchen must be. A side door looked like the servants' entrance. She banged the old iron knocker and waited. Just the size of the mansion was intimidating. She comforted herself with the thought of Peggy being down in the village just a few minutes away. Of course, they'd both be busy, but there should be more opportunities to be together than they'd had since the war began.

It didn't seem likely she could help Peggy with the festival, not with the needs of the harvest coming first. But maybe she could offer a few ideas and be a moral support.

The door swung open, and a slim dark-haired girl who looked to be about fourteen said, "Oh, ye must be the new Land Girl. They'll be wanting you down at the stable, no doubt, but let me go ask." She closed the door, leaving Nella to stand and wait on the stone steps.

The girl's rudeness irritated Nella. Yet she had wanted to be taken on her own merit, not to be treated differently because she was a minister's daughter. *So, Nella Elizabeth, you certainly got what you wanted.* She inwardly laughed at herself.

In a short time, the door opened again. "You're to come with me," said the girl.

Nella grabbed her bag and started to bring it along.

With a toss of her head, the girl said, "Ye can leave that there inside the door. Old Thompkins will get it for ye later."

Nella set the bag against the wall and followed empty-handed. Their footsteps on the slate floor echoed around them as they proceeded down a narrow corridor. At the end the girl opened a heavy wooden door into a long, shadowed hallway. There the thick carpet allowed them to walk noiselessly. They passed several rooms where the massive furniture had been draped with white dust covers. Apparently, as in most great houses, the servants had gone to war, and the family lived in only a few rooms now. She supposed that as soon as the weather cooled, even more rooms would no longer be used.

Already the place may as well have been an abandoned castle, for all the silence. Or maybe a mausoleum, she reflected.

Her reaction probably grew out of local tales about the days when the Westmoreland family had wielded so much power over the Welsh people. And then there was the creepy ghost story Peggy had mentioned, a tale of a beautiful Welsh girl smitten with love for the young lord. Shortly after the birth of her baby, she had taken a fatal fall from one of the upstairs windows. Six months later the young lord had married an Englishwoman of nobility and had doubled the family's fortune.

Years had added spice and mystery and more evil to the tale. Some said her personal maid had seen the bruises and a wound on her throat that a rope would have left. Other servants claimed to have seen a weeping apparition of the beautiful girl in the garden at the back of the mansion.

Nella never took seriously any ghost story, but this lifeless old mansion oppressed her. She wanted to throw open the windows, let in some fresh air and warmth from the sun. Instead, she drew in a deep breath and followed the saucy servant who went to an open door near the bottom of the wide staircase, where she announced, "Here is the new Land Girl for you, sir."

A man's voice responded, "Bring her in, please."

The girl bobbed her head, stepped inside the doorway, and beckoned with her hand for Nella to enter.

The room turned out to be an enormous library filled with books from floor to ceiling on either side. Morning light spilled through tall windows that looked out onto the front drive. Across the room from the windows, a fireplace big enough to take man-sized logs dominated most of the wall. Old family portraits occupied the wall space around the fireplace. Bryan Westmoreland rose from a vast desk. "Thank you, Ruth. You may go now."

His eyes were on Nella. "So we meet again, Mrs. Killian." When the girl was gone, he said, "Sorry Ruth left you stranded on the back stoop. She's new here and didn't grow up in household service as maids of yore used to." He raised one eyebrow, and she couldn't tell if he was complaining about these present conditions or criticizing the old. He quickly clarified himself. "Mrs. Harrison, our cook, is from the old school and has tried to teach Ruth the old ways. The result is sometimes ridiculous. The poor girl should be educated for some other kind of work, but it seems all she wants is to be a servant in a large house. And Mrs. Harrison does need help. Our regular servants all left for military service or factory work. Thompkins, our butler, has become house and garden man."

He gestured toward a chair beside the desk. "Please be seated. We've a few things to talk about before Ruth shows you to your quarters."

Nella obeyed, eager to know her duties.

"First," he said, "you need to know I call the Land Girls by first name. And they address me simply as Bryan. One Lord Westmoreland is enough. Call my father and mother by their titles and use *sir* and *ma'am* when not using their titles."

She nodded, uncomfortable at the idea of calling this near stranger, and he being her employer, by his first name. However, she said, "I see."

He chuckled, yet didn't sound amused. He was *supercilious*. Yes, that was the word.

"I can tell you don't see, but in a short time you will. Farming is backbreaking, dirty, and sometimes dangerous work. I find it most inconvenient to use a formal address when I ask a Land Girl to muck out the stalls, yell at her to slow down a tractor, or to get out of the way of a falling tree. Extra words only get in the way." He paused and looked searchingly at her. "Does this meet your approval, Mrs. Killian?" His voice was soft, but somehow the words held a bite.

She wasn't sure whether he was being sarcastic or serious. She hated ambiguousness. She studied him for a moment and noticed that his eyes were exactly the same chestnut brown as his hair, an odd harmony of coloring that she'd only seen in certain sheep dogs, not in people. She wanted to laugh at this vagrant thought but kept her mouth straight and said respectfully, "Anything you say, Bryan."

For the briefest instant, honest human warmth flashed over his handsome features, but then it was gone so fast she decided it might have been a trick of the morning light spilling over him as he turned sideways toward the windows to sit at the desk.

When he spoke again he was all business, with no hint of sarcasm, no suggestion of double meaning. "I understand that Miss Jones discussed with you our proposed harvest festival. Your first assignment, beyond routine chores, will be to work on the harvest festival with her. So you are to stay here full time for at least the first month. I presume you were told about this full-time arrangement."

"Yes. They said they'd waive my usual training period because of my former service in the WAAF and because of your urgent need with the harvest coming so soon."

"You were in the WAAF?"

"For most of a year. When they discovered I had secretly married and was expecting our baby, they mustered me out. Soon after that I became a widow." She didn't know why she volunteered this bit of information except that she wanted Bryan to know she loved Rob and hadn't divorced him.

His expression softened. "I'm sorry. That must have been very hard for you. Your parents are caring for your baby now while you serve?"

In a more casual way than she felt, she said, "Yes, I felt I needed to do this for her future and mine. I intend to have my own farm someday." To prevent him from commenting on this, she said abruptly, "Livie's in good hands and will make do. The war's hard on everyone."

His sharp look made Nella uncomfortable. She wondered if her reason for leaving Livie sounded convincing. To her own ears it did not. She'd never leave her baby just for the purpose of learning more about farming. Peggy always said she was a poor liar. She must be careful to act her part consistently so there would be no reason for speculation on why she left home.

CHAPTER FIFTEEN

Nella throttled a sigh of relief when Bryan stopped staring at her and glanced down at the papers on his desk. Picking up his fountain pen, he said quietly, "You're right. The war is hard on everyone. I'm sure you have good reasons for deciding to serve in the Land Army. All right then, I've had them make room for you in Garden Cottage. We like to place new girls close to the house."

He glanced at his wristwatch. "When the rest of the Land Girls come to the kitchen for lunch, I'll introduce you. One of them will show you around the property. At three-thirty I'll take you down to West-Holding School to meet with Miss Jones, and the two of you can get the festival plans underway. Tomorrow morning you will start your farm work, up at four-thirty to feed and water the stock. At Garden Cottage you can make your own tea before early chores and then come to the kitchen at seven for breakfast.

"I hand out each day's work assignments at breakfast. You'll work on the estate during the day, and then after supper, you'll work on the festival. Miss Jones may have told you my mother is away right now, and you won't be seeing much of my father either. If you do, please remember that I'm the one who gives the work assignments."

This came as a surprise to Nella. Was there some kind of family feud? Well, she wasn't about to get into it. "What if he tells me to do something?"

"You will obey but tell me about it as soon as possible. I'll deal with my father."

She decided his attitude seemed protective rather than angry. "So when they said Lord Westmoreland urgently needed help, they actually meant you."

"My father rang them up, but he doesn't always know what is an emergency and what is not. He was upset to lose two Land Girls right before the harvest. Understand, Mrs.... Nella, I am in charge here. But my father must never realize it."

"I ... I'm sorry. I didn't mean to pry."

"No harm done. Just remember, you report to me and you will take orders from only me."

She nodded as if she understood, assuming that when she met Lord Westmoreland, the situation would become clear.

"Good." Bryan stood up and pulled an old-fashioned bell cord beside the window.

What an anachronism, Nella thought, glancing around the room. The whole house gave one a trip backward in time. She wondered if the Welsh bride had ever stood in this room and pulled that very same cord to summon a maid. Being in this room made the old legend come alive. How long ago would she have lived—and died—here?

Ever since childhood Nella had felt that old homes developed personalities according to the families who lived in them, and this great house felt unfriendly.

Defensively Nella sat up straighter on her chair. Miss Lucretia Agee, her favorite teacher at St. Catherine School, used to say excellent posture increases one's courage.

Her gaze fell on a painting hanging to the left of the fireplace of a strikingly beautiful girl. Formal as the portrait was, the artist had captured a sense of vitality unusual for the period in which it must've been painted.

As if reading her mind, Bryan said, "I suppose you've heard the tale of the murdered bride."

Nella caught herself just in time to conceal the nervous start that his perceptiveness gave her. She relaxed and nodded. "Yes."

"That's her portrait there, to the left of the fireplace."

She let out a slow, quiet breath. He wasn't a mind reader after all. He'd simply noticed her interest in the painting. Nella shrugged. "I've heard the tale, but I imagine it grew from much less dramatic facts."

"You're right about that. If you're interested, you might like to read her diary. I gave it to your friend Peggy. You're welcome to borrow it when she's finished."

At this revelation, Nella couldn't maintain her disinterested façade. "The bride kept a diary?"

"Indeed she did, and my family has treasured it. She wrote some poetry, which she called word songs. Some say her talent lingers in our genes, but I must confess it certainly missed me." With a wry shake of his head, he laughed.

Nella found herself smiling with him, though every fiber of her being warned against friendship with this man. She regretted that she'd have to deal with him instead of his father.

Then Ruth appeared in response to Bryan's pull on the bell cord. She gave an awkward bow and led Nella back to the carrier she left by the kitchen door. As Nella followed her, she decided on closer inspection that the girl wasn't as young as she'd first thought. Her eyes held a glint of canniness that befitted an older person. Her small stature misled one, this and a certain angular awkwardness like that of a colt not fully grown.

"Are you from around here, Ruth?"

"Nay. I'm from Swansea, but came up here to stay with my aunt in Llanfoist, and then I heard tell they needed help at Whitestone. I've always fancied being in service. Nice quarters, good food, and usually a bit of excitement between the lords and ladies." She grinned suggestively.

"You never wanted to go into the military?"

"I did think on it. Then I decided this is the life. Besides, I have me a boyfriend in the RAF. Mrs. Harrison, she's good 'bout letting me off anytime he gets leave. He flies them mosquito bombers, you know." Her smile turned her face ingenuous and pretty.

"My husband was in the Royal Air Force too," Nella remarked without forethought.

"That right? You say *was*?" Her smile faded.

"I'm sorry. With you having a boyfriend in the air force, I shouldn't have told you like that. The Germans shot down Rob's plane during the blitz. But surely the risk isn't so bad now. . . ."

Ruth still looked stricken. "Oh, it's me that's sorry. I hate to think what you been through."

Nella suddenly liked the girl very much. "Thank you," she said. "We have a little girl—Livie is two now. Rob never got to see her."

They had reached a small stone cottage located behind the mansion on the edge of what had once been an enormous kitchen garden. A wisteria vine climbed up one side of the cottage and onto the slate roof. On the other side, lush hydrangea bushes snuggled against the walls.

Ruth banged on the door. No one answered so she opened it and walked in. "Master Bryan, he had me set up a bed for you in this room over here. This chest will be for your clothes. Now I'll get me back to the kitchen 'fore Mrs. Harrison gets twitchy." She paused at the bedroom door. "It would cheer me if I could talk with ye now and again about how it was to be a flyer's wife."

"I'd be happy to, whenever we both have time. Thank you for showing me to my room."

The girl bobbed her head as if Nella were gentry now and left with a polite, "My pleasure, ma'am. You need anything, just let me know."

Nella smiled to herself. So much for first impressions. This girl was no child, neither was she totally lacking in manners.

Edith, the Land Girl assigned to show Nella around the estate, was a sturdy-looking city girl from Birmingham. Nella discovered they shared a deep love for country living, for animals, and for growing things. In a few minutes they were chatting like old friends. Hiking across the hillside over several acres, Nella learned where all the outbuildings were and what purposes they served. The horse stables had been built close to the house, and now that farming had turned to mostly using tractors, only two teams of working horses remained. Lord Westmoreland still kept half a dozen horses for hunting, but most of the large stable stood empty. The long loft upstairs had been converted into a dormitory. Twelve of the Land Girls lived there, while six, including Nella, stayed in Garden Cottage.

After seeing all the farm buildings, Nella noticed what looked like a church spire in the midst of oak trees up the hill from the house. "What's that?" she asked, pointing. "Is it part of the estate?"

"Oh yes. That's an old chapel left from the days when the family had their own worship services here instead of going down to the village. There's also a cemetery there, with family graves dating back to the first Lord Westmoreland and his wives."

"Wives?"

"He had nearly as many wives as King Henry the Eighth. He had five wives, to be exact, and they all died before he did. Nothing evil about it, though, like the stories about the Welsh bride. The gravestones say three died in childbirth, one of the plague, and the last poor woman was lost at sea on a journey to Cornwall.

"Some of the girls insist they've seen ghosts in the woods up there. I told them they'd be more likely to see downed Nazi flyers trying to hide. They didn't think that was very funny. They avoid the place. Just before you came, two of the girls swore they saw a ghost in the kitchen garden. They were so scared they left straightaway. Just packed and left at daybreak. I don't know what they saw, but I still don't believe in ghosts. If you'd like to go see the church, we can. There's time to climb the hill before supper."

"I'd like to, but I have to meet Bryan at the manor at three-thirty."

"Well, we'd better be moving that direction then. It's near time."

Nella found Bryan waiting in a farm lorry to take her down to the village.

"I could have bicycled," she said as she climbed in.

He nodded. "That'll be fine later, but I want to be present for this first meeting." He started the engine and headed down the hill. Over the chugging of the engine, he called, "Can you find your way around the estate now?"

"I think so. I saw the stable, the paddock, the animal barn, the shearing barn and pens for the sheep, the storage buildings for the potatoes, the building for the tractors and equipment, and—let me think—the kitchen garden and greenhouse, the old millpond and mill on Shearing Creek, the poultry building, and the roads to the upper and lower fields. I even saw where the old family chapel is."

He glanced at her sideways. "I suppose Edith told you about the ghosts the other girls claimed to have seen at the cemetery."

"Well, yes, but she's sensible and doesn't believe such things. She said she'd take me there sometime."

"It's really no place for you women. The woods are a vicious tangle. I got lost there once when I was a kid and never did figure out how I became confused. Besides, there's an old mine shaft and rock quarry that make wandering about downright hazardous."

"Really. That sounds pretty Gothic."

This time he gave Nella a straight-on look. "Stay out of the woods. If you really want to visit the old chapel and cemetery, wait until I can take you."

She wasn't eager to spend any more time than necessary with Bryan Westmoreland. She hated to promise. Nevertheless, since he was the boss, she felt compelled to say, "All right."

In her classroom Peggy heard Nella's voice before Bryan escorted her inside. As if he owned the school, he strode to her desk and gestured for Nella to take the chair while he stood. He glanced at Peggy's desk where she had laid the two family history books next to the Oxford dictionary.

Bryan touched the books. "Before I forget," he said, "I told Nella she could borrow the Welsh bride's book when you have finished with it. No hurry for either of you. It only stands on the shelf at Whitestone, collecting dust, waiting for the next generation to read it."

Peggy picked up the book with the faded blue cover and held it out to show Nella. The front had been embossed with flowers. And the title, set in white letters, read, *Gwenyth's Diary.*

Nella touched the decorative cover. "How beautiful! I can't wait to read it."

"I'll soon be done with it. I've been reading with the intention of telling the action portion of the story in my own words to the children. Some of what she writes is beyond them and some of it . . . well, I'm thinking some parts Gwenyth wouldn't have wanted children to hear."

Bryan rocked back on his heels and then to his toes. "Sounds like you've taken a liking to the lady."

"Indeed I have. You have an admirable ancestor."

He chuckled. "And you are surprised?"

"Not a whit," Peggy replied, allowing he could take it seriously or not. She didn't care. Clearing her throat, she said, "Well, let's get on with the festival business." She stepped over to the craft table, seated them on student chairs, then handed them her notes of ideas to look over.

Bryan was first to finish reading. "You've plenty of good ideas here. Are you sure you can implement them all?"

"You mean without spending money?"

"Partly. Mother wants the villagers to enjoy a fair of sorts. Games, booths for food, handcrafts for sale, bowling on the green, and the like. We'll provide all the food, but we're short of hands to do the work."

"Not to worry about that," Peggy instantly said. "The mothers and grandparents in the village are eager to help."

"Where are you thinking to set up for the stage show and dance?"

"In your shearing barn. It's large and presumably unused this time of year."

Both of Bryan's eyebrows shot up. "Not a bad idea. Work out the details and let me know what you'll need. While you make the list, I'll drive over to the Hilliard Estate and pick up Laurie. I'll be back in about an hour, Nella, to drive you up the hill."

"I can walk."

Bryan frowned. "I'm sure you can, but be here when I come back."

After he was gone, Peggy said, "So what do you think of The Bryan?"

Nella shrugged and said, "So far he only seems notional and demanding."

Peggy let out a laugh. "You're always determined to see good in people. Consider that you've seen him on his best behavior."

"Then I won't be in a hurry to see his true self."

An hour later they had a good outline of projects and list of possible volunteers and needed materials.

Bryan showed up on time with Laurie Barringer and introduced him to Nella. Then he said, "Laurie is your first volunteer for the festival. I told him you'd be glad for his help."

Well, jolly for you, Peggy thought, but she didn't say a word. Then Nella gave her a funny look. Was her reaction that obvious? But one look at Laurence Barringer the Fourth, and she knew it was. He, too, was studying her with a quizzical expression.

Peggy said carefully, "We have everything planned. We really don't need more help now."

"All the same, you will have to deal with the both of us from time to time," Bryan stated coolly. He started for the door. "Come along, Nella."

Nella's eyes narrowed. At the same time she clamped her lips tight and obeyed. Before leaving the classroom, she called back, "Tomorrow night then, Peggy."

As Peggy watched her leave, walking between the two men, she wanted to laugh. Little did Bryan know what he had ignited by barking a command to Nella as if she were his dog. Her own irritation with Bryan subsided as she thought about what Nella probably would like to tell him right now. She grinned to herself. At last Nella would see that her opinion about The Bryan hadn't been totally biased.

She cleaned off the craft table in preparation for class in the morning. As she did so, she thought again of Bryan's reaction when she'd accused him of arranging Nella's assignment to the Westmoreland Estate. In spite of his flippant denial, she'd wager that the odd expression he had so instantly veiled involved a deadly serious matter. His expression was out of character, which is why Peggy had been so startled. She shook her head.

Maybe she was just overreacting to The Bryan. The frightening incidents in Abergavenny had unnerved her. The crazy driver's attempt to run over Nella and then the break-in at the manse had left her feeling as if she were on quicksand. There was nothing outwardly threatening about Bryan—except that Nella might fall for him. For he was handsome and could be disarmingly charming when it suited his purpose.

Before Nella went to bed that night, she pulled out the small notebook that she'd been using for her diary. She had to jot down some of her impressions of this first day in the Land Army, or she might forget.

18 September 1944

Today I toured the estate. It's still a vast landholding. The other Land Girls have been very friendly. It seems that most of them come from cities. I think they never guessed how hard farm work is. But my, they do look fit! I shall have to work myself to a frazzle to keep up.

I haven't seen Lady or Lord Westmoreland yet. Don't like to be taking orders from Bryan or even calling him by his first name. I wanted to hit him with a chair tonight. He nearly snapped his fingers at me when he said "Come along"! I treat the sheep dogs with more respect. I can see he will test all my powers of acting.

He forbade me going to the woods. We'll see about that. The other women obviously went and so shall I. Little does he know, I'll be safer here in the forest than in my own home in Abergavenny.

CHAPTER SIXTEEN

Nella's first day's assignment, as Bryan had promised, began with feeding the horses and the small herd of dairy cattle, then cleaning out stalls. The mucking out and carrying hay for fodder and straw for clean bedding left her aching with fatigue. Later on she worked in a pasture laying a new hedgerow, cutting saplings, staking them into the ground, and weaving in smaller branches for the bushes to grow around. Muscles she hadn't used for ages quivered from exhaustion.

As she followed the other girls to the house for lunch, something cool and wet touched her hand. She jumped and turned. "Oh! And who are you?" she asked the handsome gray dog.

The dog barked in reply. Nella laughed and knelt to pet the friendly animal, obviously a herding dog but different in appearance than any she'd seen. The dog gazed at her from pale blue eyes. Its coat was the usual long fluffy hair but mottled gray with black and white streaks and foxy red markings on its ears and above its eyes. She ran her fingers through the silky hair. "Well, you are a fine one," she murmured affectionately.

The dog peered into her eyes and barked again. She was a talker. One of the dogs on the Flint farm had answered her every remark in the same way.

"That's Ember," Dora said, pausing beside her. "I think her name ought to be Ashes to match all the gray, or Cinderella!" She chuckled at her own cleverness.

Nella laughed with her and stood up. She automatically signaled the Stay command to the dog. "Good-bye, Ember." The dog stayed. Nella smiled. "I love dogs. I've worked with sheep dogs a lot in the past."

"Then what are you doing mucking out the barns?" Dora asked.

"Dora's right," Edith said. "Have you told Bryan about your experience with dogs? By the looks of the doddering old man who herds with the sheep, he could use some help."

Nella's heart quickened. It would be pure pleasure to work with the dogs and sheep. However, she felt compelled to say, "Actually, the older the shepherd, the better, but maybe I'll mention it to Bryan."

After supper when Nella retrieved her bicycle from the carriage house to ride down to Gatekeep for her meeting with Peggy, Ruth popped out the kitchen door and waved good-bye. "Ye'll be careful riding down, now, won't ye? It's steep on that sharp curve. I nearly went over myself the other day on 'count of the loose gravel."

"I'll go slow," Nella called back. "Thanks!"

Bryan rode up on a tall bay horse. "Be back before dark," he said.

"What?" He sounded like her father. Was this part of her duty, to be under orders every second, as she'd been in the WAAF?

Her irritation must've shown on her face, because he added a bit more explanation. "We don't have an official curfew here, but your safety is my responsibility, so please come back before dark."

His use of the word *please* didn't exactly soften the clipped demand. His attitude awakened her childhood resentment to rigid rules. *So much for my adult freedoms. Mum and Daddy never took on such a hard look as his. Peggy's nickname, The Bryan, fits him well.* She'd have to be careful not to use it within his hearing. She assumed a respectful air. "Yes, sir."

He nodded curtly, reined the horse away, and headed for the stable.

At Gatekeep, while Nella helped Peggy figure out the materials they'd need for the booths and stage for the festival, she dutifully kept an eye on the sun and on her wristwatch.

Finally Peggy said, "Do you have work to do when you get back to Whitestone?"

"No. But I'm supposed to return before dark."

Peggy laid down her pencil. "Is this another rule of The Bryan?"

"Aye. I didn't know about it until I started down here this evening."

"What's he worried about? I run around the village and countryside after dark. So does everyone else."

Nella put her note pad down, leaned against the prickly back of Peggy's mohair couch, and drew her feet up under her. "I can't stand his bossiness, although in a way I don't mind getting indoors before dark. I hope it's safe here, but I can't help thinking another jeep might come racing out of the dark again to hit me. When it's dark my fears tend to take over."

"I can imagine. Tell me, do you still think Rufe Johnson was mixed up in some kind of big plot like he told Marge?"

"The way I see it, I can't take the chance. Just in case he was."

Peggy studied her with a worried expression. "I've been thinking a lot since you decided you had to leave the manse. I was wrong to jump on you for blowing things out of proportion. I mean . . . what if there *is* a plot and your fears are justified? I wish you'd get help from the authorities. If you have no faith in the constable, then how about that military policeman at Gilwern? Won't he think twice now that both the manse and the medical records room have been ransacked?"

Nella tried to conceal the flash of fear that streaked through her. She couldn't let a hint of the threatening note slip out. She had no intention of speaking with Captain Evers until she received a letter from Corporal Peterson. The waiting would be easier if she could tell Peggy the whole truth, but then if Peggy ever let her knowledge slip out, all could be lost. After all, Nella herself had started the trouble by talking too much at the USO. "I will contact him. I just had to get away first in case he chose not to do anything."

Without a suggestion of suspicion, Peggy nodded. "In the meantime, I'm kind of glad The Bryan has his rules and takes them seriously. It just makes me angry that you can't feel as safe as all the rest of us now that you're out here."

"I suspect I won't feel safe till Rufe's killer is caught." Ever since losing Rob, death was no longer something that happened only to the elderly or to other people. The threatening note had fed her chronic fear of losing Livie or dying young so Livie would be orphaned.

Nella desperately wanted to tell Peggy about the note. She curbed the urge and instead gave her a different reason for her distress. "I don't suppose I'll ever be able to erase the image from my mind of how he looked down there in the water. For his sake I hate it that his killer may never be brought to justice." She picked up her pencil again. "We'd better make good use of our time or The Bryan and Mr. Barringer may insist on helping us. I don't think you'd like that."

Peggy grew still. "Nella, was I too adamant against working with Mr. Barringer?"

Nella chuckled. "You made yourself plain. If I hadn't known better, I'd have thought you had a quarrel going with him. Had you met him before?"

"Briefly."

Peggy looked more troubled than usual for committing a social blunder. Nella teased, "He's handsome. Are you attracted to him?"

Red spots blossomed on Peggy's cheeks. "He's the last person on earth that I would likely be attracted to!"

"Oh. Sorry. None of my business, I know."

"No, I'm the one who's sorry. I . . . I guess I should tell you who Laurie is. Do you remember my telling you about the man who humiliated me when I was five years old, the man who scared me so bad that I wet my pants?"

"Aye," Nella answered slowly. "I don't think I'll be forgetting that."

"Well, Laurie is that horrible man's son. He's the little boy who played with Winnie and me."

Nella's mouth fell open. "Are you sure? You recognized him after all this time?"

"I'm sure. I know it seems impossible, but I never forgot his name and the way he looked at me and waved good-bye after his father shoved him into the car. It all came back."

"Does he know you recognized him?"

"No, thank the Lord. When I realized who he was, I felt as if I were five all over again, back home playing with Winnie. It was a bit of a shock to remember. That's why I feel so uncomfortable when I'm around him. I keep hoping he'll go away and return to wherever he came from, but he seems to be settling in with the Hilliard family." Peggy leaned back on her chair. "So you see, I'm not attracted to him. I just feel extremely nervous in his presence."

"I always thought you liked him a lot when you were little. Maybe you still do. He seems nice."

"Hah! With the kind of man who sired him, how could he be? I get an ugly feeling just thinking about how he must've grown up."

"Even so, just working with him shouldn't be so bad."

"If I'm lucky, I won't have to find out. Putting up with The Bryan is about all I can take."

Nella sat very still, watching her with concern. "What did your mother say when she found out how Laurie's father treated you?"

"She hugged me and carried me into the house, then heated water for a bath in the washtub. She told me about how I must always stay away from the gentry."

"No wonder you have such a hard time dealing with Lady Westmoreland."

Peggy gave her a startled glance. "I hadn't thought about that . . .

but no, she is a dragon. Even if I'd never been abused by old Barringer, she'd still be a dragon."

Nella laughed and then shook her head. "I hope you won't set your mind to becoming a dragon slayer."

Peggy smiled. Nella sometimes seemed naïve, but she'd always had a way of gentling a person's anger. "A dragon slayer. I think I like that."

"Oops! Sorry I gave you the idea."

"Say, the sun is setting. Have you noticed?"

"No. I'll have to be going then. Should I take today's list of materials to The Bryan?" Nella asked.

"Sure. And tell him I'm getting more volunteers from the village."

On the way back to Whitestone Nella pedaled fast as far as she could up the hill and then dismounted to walk the rest of the way to the manor. The narrow drive led through a section of dense oak trees where the shadows stretched long. It had grown darker than she'd realized. The sound of the bicycle tires and her footsteps crunching on the gravel would carry deep into the woods if anyone were listening. She paused to do her own listening. Once she heard the snap of a twig and froze. Hearing nothing more, she walked on but watched now in all directions.

When she'd left the woods behind, the amber sky still brightened the grassy slopes on the hillside between her and Whitestone. The soft light comforted her. She didn't need Bryan's warning about being out after dark. She wasn't over the memory of that jeep nearly killing her. Common sense told her she couldn't count on surviving such a narrow escape twice. She'd likely have no warning if her enemy knew where she was and decided she was worth more dead than alive.

At Gatekeep Peggy spent the evening reading the Westmoreland family history and making notes about what she wanted to present to the children. Then she got ready for bed and picked up Gwenyth's diary.

Most of the pages had been typeset and printed in English, but in the back the girl's faded handwriting in Celtic had been preserved. Peggy wondered if anyone could still read the old language. She settled for struggling through seventeenth-century English, the time when the translation had been made.

The first section was written by Gwenyth while still in her father's house, before her marriage. Details of daily life filled the pages. But it was the short verses and the written prayers that caught Peggy's eye. She flipped through them, reading some critically. She thought they were quite good for one so young.

Curious, she turned back to the beginning.

25 May 1403

> *Yesterday Father took Mother and me to visit his good friend, Lord Westmoreland. It was a long drive so we stayed the night. I liked Young William. He was very kind. He was teaching some of the servants' children to read, so I listened. Father says William will be sorry one day for educating servants, but I think it is very good of him.*
>
> > *If I were blind,*
> > *I'd want someone to hold my hand.*
> > *If I were lame, I'd want a helping arm.*
> > *If I could not read,*
> > *Oh! I'd want someone to teach—*
> > *To teach me!*
>
> *That is my song for bonny Young Master William. Of course, I won't sing it to him. Gwenyth*

Peggy smiled. Gwenyth's word song reminded her of the pleasure she felt when teaching. That she truly enjoyed teaching had come as a surprise in the beginning. She'd thought she only wanted to be an artist.

As a teacher she wanted to help all the children. Was she giving too much attention to Annie at the expense of the others? No. Truly she wanted the same for each of them. It was just that Annie had higher barriers to surmount if she were to get the chance she deserved.

She opened the old diary to a later date.

> *Today my father was killed. Mother is terrified. Father's brother, Uncle Myrthyd, says I must marry Rowan now, that he will protect both of us during this rebellion against the English. I would rather die. Rowan makes me feel like I did when I came upon a nest of squirming snakes. There is something very evil about him. Oh, Father, Father, if only you did not die!*
>
> On the next page: *Mother says I must run away tonight if I want to be safe from Rowan. Mother will stay here with her brother, Uncle Ellwell. Dear God, please protect Mother and me. . . .*
>
> Further on: *I am safe! I am at Whitestone. Lord and Lady Westmoreland agree that I should never be given to Rowan. They will protect me as their own. Master William was glad to see me. . . .*

Peggy skimmed through the diary and added Gwenyth's information to the more general family history as she prepared the lesson for the next day. Hopefully Gwenyth's true story would wipe out the spooky tales the children half believed.

Dawn came quickly for Nella after her first full day of farm work. She stifled a groan when she sat up on the edge of her cot in Garden Cottage. Her muscles were so sore, she felt crippled. The other two girls in her room, the wiry farm girl Dora, and Edith, her guide on her first day, dressed hurriedly while she was still trying to wake up. She stumbled to the washbasin and poured fresh water, splashed it on her face, and toweled dry. A glance in the mirror told her that although her hair was hopeless, it would do for wearing under a bandanna.

A few moments later, wearing her farm shirt, coveralls, and work boots, she clumped into the cottage kitchen. Dora handed her a cup of creamed hot tea. Nella had been assigned to do the early chores with Dora.

"Thanks," Nella said, taking the cup.

"You're welcome."

"So what's on the news today?"

Dora raised her eyebrows. "Huge bombing raid on Germany and the Siegfried Line. Hitler's getting it back now."

Nella nodded. "Sounds like our troops may soon be in Germany."

"Aye, we'll show them then," Dora said. "I'm finished with my tea, so I'll go ahead and start with the cows."

"I'll be along in a minute," Nella replied.

Dora grinned and said, "You're not moving so swift this morning."

"How right you are. I hope the work limbers me up some."

"Don't count on it. It took me all of a week."

"Oh, don't tell me that!"

Dora laughed as she stepped outside.

What Dora said proved true. By the third day, Nella made a valiant effort to hide her stiffness, for she hated looking so tender. When Nella and Dora headed for the house for breakfast, the gray dog Ember appeared beside Nella. She petted the friendly dog's head and waved her back to the barn.

Nella had missed the dogs out at the Flint farm. After breakfast, she lingered in the kitchen to ask Bryan if she could help with the sheep. She thought he'd be glad to hear that this was one thing she could do without any training, but she was wrong.

"You're going to drive tractor," he said. "Your experience with lorries in the WAAF makes you more valuable with the machines. Even so, you'll need practice to be able to root up potatoes without destroying the lot."

She nodded, feeling disappointed. "Why is that gray dog always around the barns instead of out with the sheep? She looks like a herding dog to me."

"Ember? That poor beast is my father's fiasco. He got her from some man who imported dogs from Australia. He persuaded Father the dogs were superior to any seen around here. Father hoped to raise litters of champion herders. But the minute I saw that dog, I figured she was a loss. You can see she's got dingo in her blood. That's where the red markings come from. Dingoes are wild dogs. Everyone but my father knows dingoes are hunters, not herders."

"Did she fail then in her training?"

"Dismally. But Father's still fond of her. She follows him about whenever he's here."

She wanted to ask the whereabouts of Lord Westmoreland, but this being inappropriate, she said, "The dog seems lonely. Maybe that's why she obeys me so well."

He looked at her as if he wanted to laugh, a devil dancing in his eyes, as Peggy would say. "She's a notional beast. She knows how to get what she wants."

"So you think I'm a soft touch?"

"I wouldn't be surprised."

The offensive gleam was still in his eyes, suggesting he fully intended a double meaning. Nella's face grew hot. She hated how her fair complexion betrayed her at times like this. Hoping her face also expressed her disgust, she whirled around and left.

All the way to the stable, she fumed. The nerve of him, and she a married woman with a child. Then she heard herself. She still felt as though she were married, maybe because of Livie. Thinking about her baby after not seeing her or holding her all week filled her with anguish. Just as she couldn't turn off a blush earlier, she couldn't hold back the tears now, which welled up and streamed down her cheeks. But afraid someone might notice, she angrily brushed the tears away and marched toward the barn to muck out the stalls.

Driving tractor proved to be a pleasant surprise. After some practice in an open area near the barn, Bryan, who was on horseback, led Nella and tractor to a meadow.

He halted the horse beside the tractor. Waving a hand, he said, "The government has ordered us to till this hillside for crops next spring. Which is a pity. This lush meadow hasn't been touched for generations. Still, even if the war ends by summer, we'll have rationing and food shortages for a long while."

On the BBC that morning, Nella had heard a sobering report on the fighting in Belgium. "You think the war will be over by summer?" she asked, turning to face him.

He sat on his tall horse in a regal manner, unlike her childhood friend, Tommy Flint, a typical farmer's son who rode any old way. Tommy had a crush on her right up to the day she married Rob. She'd felt sad for him, but could never see him as anything but a brother.

Watching Bryan hold his spirited mount in check, she supposed his grace on horseback came from growing up in a lord's family. Maybe after a few generations it was in their blood.

He frowned. "Only God knows."

For a moment, she forgot her question. Then she put it together with when the war would be won.

He pointed with his riding crop. "Anyway, we till. Go down to where the swale becomes brushy and then back up here in line with that old tree."

She began the task of turning virgin sod to prepare it for spring planting. After two furrows, she had a feel for how to set the plows and for keeping to a straight line.

From the side of the field, Bryan waved her on and rode away. The gray dog Ember had followed them out and now decided to stay with Nella, trotting beside the tractor, then finally lying in the shade at one end of the field to supervise from a distance.

Midmorning, when Ruth brought Nella some hot tea, she parked the tractor and dismounted to sit beside Ember. "You really need a job to do," she said, scratching the dog's neck. "Watching me will make you lazy."

"Master Bryan says the dog's daft," said Ruth, "but I like her. 'Course I have no reason to make her mind me."

"You like dogs then?" Nella asked.

"Aye. Though I'd crave a tidy little corgi if I was to have a herding dog. Auntie has one. Old Baskerville, Bask for short. He's a sharp one. Even knows red from yellow, he does."

Nella chuckled and said, "I've only seen one corgi. But they're more for driving cattle, running behind as they do." She scratched Ember's ears. "How's it going for you in the house, Ruth? It makes for a long walk to be delivering tea a distance like this."

"Me, I like to walk. Old Thompkins takes tea to the closer Land Girls. I wonder if you'd mind... if I was to get permission, I could help you and Miss Jones on the festival fixings."

"We would both appreciate your help. Go ahead and ask."

Ruth gave a sigh of pleasure. "Thank'ee. I would enjoy the doing. I'll ask Master Bryan and Mrs. Harrison right away. Maybe I can go along with you tonight."

"That'll be fine. Let me know at supper."

Ruth nodded, rose to her feet, and nearly skipped away, again giving the impression of being younger than her years.

Before climbing back on the tractor, Nella decided for the fun of it to put Ember through some basic herding commands. Having no livestock present, she signaled for the dog to run around the tractor and come back. Ember was happy to circle the machine as if it were a cluster of sheep.

"You'll get my dog killed, teaching her to race around machines like that," a gruff voice called.

Ember yipped in excitement and dashed off toward the voice.

Nella turned around. A gray-haired replica of Bryan came striding toward her. It had to be Lord Westmoreland, and he didn't sound or look impaired in any way. "I beg your pardon, sir. I didn't think of that. Ember is intelligent.... I guess I assumed she'd only do it on command."

The dog danced around Lord Westmoreland. His frown smoothed, and his dark eyebrows eased upward. He knelt and petted the dog, then straightened. "So you find my girl intelligent. And what gives you the ability to decide against the opinion of professional trainers?"

"I've worked a lot with dogs, sir, and led many to first place in trials. I'm sure Ember has the qualities of a winner. She just needs a bit more personal attention than most dogs."

"You've trained dogs, eh? Then you were a farm girl before coming here."

"No, sir. I'm just a town girl who loves farming and dogs."

He nodded. "Well, I'll have no more of this training to herd tractors. Give her some practice with the geese, and if she stays steady on them, I'll have my man bring you a few sheep for her to work. Of course, this would be after you've finished your regular work. Come, Ember!" He strode away. Ember barked a farewell to Nella and trotted after him.

Nella started up the tractor and continued her plowing. When she turned at the end of the field and reset the plows, she spied Lord Westmoreland watching her from a side road. As far as she could tell, there was nothing wrong with this vigorous man's judgment. Maybe he and his son were at odds about something. She rather liked the lord of the manor. But then, Nella liked anyone who offered her the chance to work with a good dog. And The Bryan shouldn't mind as long as she finished the projects he assigned her. Surely she could take a few minutes a day to work with Ember.

CHAPTER SEVENTEEN

Peggy decided to condense and paraphrase the material for her class to make it more interesting, more memorable. She began with Lord Hugh de Bracie Westmoreland, who had been granted the estate known as West-Holding by King Henry IV. She went on to describe life in the fourteenth century and then gave her pupils thirty minutes to search their history books for more details of the period that they could later share with the class.

At the end of the afternoon, she told them about the Welsh bride, Gwenyth. "She was only fourteen when her father died at the hands of one of Owain Glyndwr's men. Owain had organized many Welsh chieftains to fight against the English. Gwenyth's father was killed because he favored English rule. Afterward, her uncle arranged for her to marry Rowan, a brutal man whom she feared. She escaped by night, and traveling alone for two days through the Brecon Beacon mountains, she finally reached Whitestone. Whitestone was the home of Lord William Hastings Westmoreland, her father's longtime friend."

The children listened, quite spellbound. Peggy tried to sign for Annie, but wasn't sure if she conveyed the story clearly.

"At Whitestone, Gwenyth felt safe again. Lord Westmoreland didn't like Owain or fear his power so was happy to take Gwenyth in. When young William Westmoreland the Third fell in love with Gwenyth, Lord Westmoreland arranged for them to marry secretly. It still wasn't safe to let anyone know she was staying at Whitestone.

"Gwenyth loved William, and they were very happy together. She was a Christian girl. In her diary she wrote poems to her unborn baby about God and about heaven, where she would see him if she were to die. You see, in those days many women died during childbirth.

"Then tragedy struck. Soon after the birth of their son, Gwenyth died. No one knew for certain, but young William said she gave her life to save her baby from the wicked Rowan. She had sent a servant with the baby to the cottage of a village woman. William surmised that in the process of sending the baby into hiding, she was trapped by Rowan, and he threw her from an upstairs window. Rowan had been heard to say that if he couldn't have Gwenyth, no one else would either.

"But others in the family thought Gwenyth had killed herself, because she'd been very nervous after her baby was born. Myself, I'd rather believe her husband, for she was a brave girl with a strong faith in God.

"After Gwenyth died, Owain quickly gained power and attacked Abergavenny and St. Mary's Priory there. He grew so powerful that Lord Westmoreland now feared him. To protect himself from Owain, Lord Westmoreland forced William to marry a wealthy English girl to form an alliance between their two families. Together the two families were strong enough to stand against Owain, and so they did. But the villagers who had loved Gwenyth understood that William never loved her.

"Once the danger from Owain was over, William took his son and fled to France. When his father died a few years later, he returned with his son to Whitestone. He refused to live with the Englishwoman and gave her a house of her own, which is still standing here in West-Holding. You know it as Brookside, now the home of Miss Blackwell. Despite his rejection of his English wife, some of the villagers still believed he murdered Gwenyth, saying that Gwenyth's ghost had returned to haunt him.

"Young Lord William Westmoreland built the first West-Holding School on this very ground. The original stone school building is now Gaylord Cottage next to our play yard."

Peggy walked to the blackboard and picked up a piece of chalk. "I read in Gwenyth's diary some of the prayers and poems she wrote. She prayed for peace in Wales. She even prayed for her enemy, the cruel Rowan from whom she had fled. She wasn't much older than you are when she hid in the hills on her way to Whitestone. Can you imagine what you would do if you lived then? This is her prayer for her enemy." She wrote on the blackboard, *Our Father, please, if Thou wilt, let Rowan hear Thy voice in the river's music. Let him inhale Thy presence in the perfume of wild honeysuckle. Surround him and engulf him with Thy Holy Truth, so that he at last may know you and be filled with the wonder of Thy love. Amen.*

"Now tell me, class, does this Gwenyth sound anything like the stories you've heard about ghosts?"

They all shook their heads.

"I'm going to leave her prayer here where we can read it all week. It will remind us to think about the real girl who was quite like you, and I hope it will help us each to be more forgiving."

With that, Peggy dismissed her class. She stood at the door and watched them go their separate directions. Peter Hilliard ran to the auto waiting for him. She thought again how he scarcely resembled his mother. Except for his black hair, he looked more like his mother's cousin, Laurie Barringer, who was sitting behind the wheel of the family car today.

Mrs. Hilliard's dark beauty suggested exotic tropical places, although her family had been in Britain for centuries. Someone in her past must've been Spanish or Portuguese, just as someone in the Hilliard ancestry must've been a fairer Saxon.

Annie, who had stayed after school to help decorate the room for the harvest festival, signed, *"Peter's mum . . . very beautiful."*

"Yes." Peggy signed. She wanted also to say, "But don't let her looks fool you." She suspected Mrs. Hilliard wasn't so lovely on the inside. The woman spoke as if she doted on Peter, yet never gave him her full attention. Her restless dark eyes were always searching elsewhere, as if she were in a hurry to be done with him. Maybe this was why Peter tried so hard to please his mother.

Since his mother had arrived at his grandmother's house, Peter had acted the young gentleman, treating Annie with awkward courtesy rather than his usual playful teasing. Annie had responded cautiously at first and then with passionate trust. Peggy couldn't help but worry for her. They were only children, but Annie was emotionally mature for her age. Peter or his mother would hurt her sooner or later. They lived in a totally different world than Annie's, not only because of her hearing loss, but because she was a commoner and they were gentry.

She'd seen the first danger in Mrs. Hilliard's eyes, when Peter introduced Annie to her the last time she picked him up from school. Annie had politely signed, *"Hello, I'm honored to meet you,"* and Peter translated.

Now as the Hilliard car drove away, Annie signed, *"May I hang the paintings in the window? Pretty for village people."*

Peggy hesitated, remembering Lady Westmoreland's last ultimatum: to stop wasting the children's time with arts and crafts or she'd lose her job. Annie's eagerness won out. After all, Lady W. was away, and as soon as the festival was over, they'd remove the window decorations. *"Excellent idea, Annie,"* she signed. Peggy showed her how to put a touch of paste on the corners of each paper and press it against the glass. *"Try on one window, then we'll go outside to look at it."* She wished she could sign faster. She'd needed little of it in the previous years when only watching Annie in the play yard. Even with the instruction she'd had during the summer from Annie's mother, she still didn't possess the skill to sign to the bright child all the things she wanted to say and to teach.

Peggy sat down at her desk to correct spelling papers, while Annie worked silently at the window nearest the door. A few minutes later Annie clapped her hands and signed, *"Teacher. Come see!"*

Peggy followed her outside to the sidewalk in front of the school. Annie had turned half the bright drawings toward the street and the other half toward the classroom. On the back of the ones facing the classroom she'd glued autumn colors of construction paper. The effect of alternating the solid colors with the pictures was striking, Peggy thought. Yet the construction paper was costly and in very limited supply. She started to say so, but then a glance at Annie's delighted face stopped her. She signed, *"Good idea! Beautiful."* She tried to sign, *"I would never have thought of it."*

Annie looked perplexed and then broke into a smile again. She indicated the back of the drawings facing the street and asked, *"Do these too? Pretty for class."*

"No, we must save on paper."

Annie nodded.

Annie followed her back into the classroom, and Peggy privately thanked God for the talent He'd placed in this one little girl and for the fact that Lady W. was away. She wasn't sure how far Lady W.'s power extended—whether or not she really had a say in the choice of curriculum—but she figured Annie's art exhibit for the harvest festival might be the last she'd be able to display.

Peggy had been very careful not to practice favoritism toward Annie in the classroom, but she intended to show the girl's artwork to someone of influence who might take a personal interest in her. She wondered about approaching Lord Westmoreland. He'd been generous about loaning the history books, always had a friendly smile, and from what she'd observed, he didn't hold as tightly to the ways of the gentry as his wife did.

On Wednesday Peggy accompanied Annie home to Brookside for tea with her mother and with Miss Blackwell, their landlady. After tea and chatting with both ladies in Miss Blackwell's pleasant parlor, Peggy asked Mrs. Nelson if she might see Annie's recent drawings and paintings.

Mrs. Nelson touched Annie's arm to get her attention and signed to her.

Annie smiled and beckoned, *"Come with me,"* and led the way to an upstairs bedroom at the back of the house.

Windows on two sides let in light. Besides a bed with a white crocheted bedspread, the room contained a desk, bookshelf, a small table with drawers, and an artist's easel. Pencils, a cup and cloth, and a handful of brushes lay on the table close to a watercolor tin. Peggy signed, *"Lovely room, and good light for painting."*

Annie beamed a wide grin. Then she brought a sheaf of papers and spread them on the bed where Peggy could view them.

Peggy studied the first picture, a watercolor of a garden with a woman and child kneeling, hands in the soil. Near them carrots peeped out of a basket. All had been rendered in soft tones of lavender, rose, pink, and several shades of green. The carrots were a light orange. The soil looked dark and rich in a natural shade of brown. The child's hair gleamed yellow in the sun, and the woman's face had been shaded with lavender-blue. The impressionistic effect reminded Peggy of paintings by Mary Cassatt.

Several times, Peggy signed, *"Very good, Annie. Excellent work."*

Peggy already had seen the child's natural sense of composition and fresh designs, but the quick works she'd done in school had never revealed the full scope of her talent. *"Annie, beautiful! You've done fine painting here. Thank you for showing me."*

Annie led her back downstairs and signed at length to her mother.

"She wants me to tell you she made her colors from plant leaves and blossoms and berries and even soil from the garden," Mrs. Nelson said.

"Wonderful! Can you show me how?"

"Yes. Now?"

"Sure, if you wish." So Peggy excused herself from the two women again and went with Annie to gather supplies from the garden.

Back in Annie's room, she watched and learned that red roses make purple, and other colors didn't turn out the way she'd expected either. The ingenuity Annie used in experimenting with color amazed Peggy.

As Annie tried to explain with signing, her shyness faded.

Watching this transformation, Peggy had the uncanny feeling she was suddenly conversing with an adult, despite the burden of signing.

In Annie's finished paintings, she had captured various village scenes, depicting cats, dogs, people, and gardens.

"Your paintings are so lovely. May I borrow one to show my friends? I'll be very careful with it."

Annie nodded and gestured for her to make a choice.

Peggy decided on the picture of the woman and child in the garden. She signed, *"Thank you. Shall we go back to your mother now?"*

Annie hopped to her feet, all little girl again. Peggy followed her downstairs, more determined than ever to continue art projects at school regardless of Lady W.'s orders. Annie wasn't the only child who blossomed when given an assignment that stirred creativity.

Nella found she had to snatch moments in the morning to work with Ember. Bryan was usually busy then, gathering the building materials for the festival. In the evenings, Thompkins instructed the Land Girls in the fundamentals of carpentry so they could help him and the older village boys construct the stage and the booths. These must be completed and in place before the harvesting began, and Bryan said that would be soon.

Just before sunset one day, while Nella was pounding together a small booth, her father's old auto chugged up the drive to the manor. She hadn't thought of a way to warn him not to come see her for a while. All she could do was pray that whoever had threatened her hadn't noticed and followed. "I have to go see my father," she called to Ruth, who was sawing a board.

Ruth nodded, not looking up from her work. The girl had a knack for working with wood.

Nella dropped her hammer and hurried up the hill. Surely Daddy would have brought Livie for a visit.

Nella had to slow down and walk the last half of the way. While catching her breath, she glanced up the hill at the chapel tucked into the forest. The sun had cast its tower in gold. Suddenly she caught a flicker of movement at the edge of the wood. A prickle of apprehension halted her. She felt as though concealed eyes were staring back at her.

She squinted, but charcoal shadows hid everything beyond the first line of trees. There! Again a movement—a man or woman—but it was too far away to be certain. The next instant she saw only the black trunks of trees. She drew in a shaky breath. Who was up there? Why did they disappear so quickly like that?

Had she simply seen the thing she feared most, as others turned indistinct shapes into ghosts? It was probably just an animal or a harmless villager. She decided not to add to the ghost stories surrounding Whitestone. She would keep what she'd just seen to herself and ask Bryan later what kinds of animals lived in the woods here.

By the time Nella reached the house, Livie was out of the car, hugging Ember, and her mother and father stood talking to Lord Westmoreland. Ember galloped to greet her, and Livie ran behind. "Mummy, Mummy!"

Nella snatched her up, kissed her, and held her close, inhaling the fragrance of her warm, soft skin. "I'm so happy to see you, love. How are you? What did you do today?"

"Angie made mud cakes. I help."

"What fun! I used to do that too." With Livie in her arms, Nella walked over to greet her parents and Lord Westmoreland.

"I was telling your father," Lord Westmoreland said, "that you've worked a miracle with my dog. He says you've always had a way with animals and want to own your own farm someday."

"Well, yes." She wished her father wouldn't tell about her dream. She'd endured too many skeptical looks.

To her surprise, Lord Westmoreland only said, "You've got the skill." Then he went back to his conversation with Ian.

While the men chatted, her mum quietly said, "Giselle wants to return to France, and Jean and I are trying to persuade her to wait till things settle down more. Jean's Uncle Al at the embassy in London says it's too soon, what with food shortages and so much destruction."

"Surely Claude wishes her to remain here."

"That's what Jean told her. Jean is also very worried about her nurse friend Marge. I just can't understand why they'd move a nurse from the station hospital, while more and more wounded are arriving every day."

Her mother couldn't know the complications behind Jean's concern, but Nella wondered the same. She hoped Marge had been transferred because of military necessity. "I guess there's no figuring out all the reasons when it comes to the military." Nella said.

The front door of the mansion opened, and Bryan stepped out. He stopped when he saw Nella. If he thought she should be working until bedtime, then too bad. She hugged Livie closer.

Livie squirmed and said, "Play with doggie, Mummy?"

She set her down and turned her back to The Bryan to speak to her mother. "Tell Jean I hope she can come with you and Giselle and the girls to the harvest festival. Peggy has invited a singing group and has arranged a talent show and a dance band of sorts."

"I'll tell them. Maybe Jean will want to bring some of the patients."

Bryan's voice cut in from close behind Nella. "Tell her there's a road leading right to the shearing barn, and the ground is level enough for wheelchairs. We'll set up food tables down there."

Her mother smiled. "I'll do that. It'll make a nice outing for the boys who are well enough."

"Maybe some of the hospital personnel can check it out ahead of time and then give suggestions for making it more accessible for their patients."

"That's very nice. I'll tell her."

"Now if you'll excuse me," he said, "I must be heading down to the barn to see how the work's going."

As he strode away, Elizabeth murmured, "Such a thoughtful young man."

Nella nodded. Her mum wasn't usually taken in so easily, but she could hardly say anything contrary with Lord Westmoreland only a few steps away. And he obviously had captivated her father.

Just then her father turned toward her. "We're needing to go soon. Maybe you'd like to show us the project down at the shearing barn. If Livie gets tired, I'll carry her back up the hill."

Lord Westmoreland said, "I'll walk along. Been meaning to check it out myself."

Halfway down the hill, Nella remembered the sighting in the nearby woods. She glanced over at the chapel tower above the dark trees. Now it looked quite forbidding, like the gray turret of a small fortress. During a lull in the men's conversation, Nella spoke up. "I've been meaning to ask you, sir, if you have many deer in the woods up there."

Lord Westmoreland looked to where she pointed. "No. The deer were hunted to extinction in my grandfather's day. I've always regretted that."

"Do you think they could come back from the mountains beyond?"

He shook his head. "None in the mountains either, not for years. For a time I thought about doing something to bring them back, but then I realized they'd just be hunted down again."

Nella couldn't see his face clearly in the dusk, but he sounded a bit sad and wistful so she didn't say anything about seeing something up there. Man or beast, she'd find out for herself. At first opportunity, she'd get Edith to go with her up to the woods.

CHAPTER EIGHTEEN

Not a day too soon the volunteers finished construction work for the festival activities at the shearing barn. At supper Bryan came to the Whitestone's kitchen and announced, "Tomorrow we begin the harvest. As soon as you finish morning chores, you'll go to the fields. The schoolchildren and their teachers will already be working by the time you get there. Those of you who have been trained to drive the lorries, do the milking before you drive out to the fields."

He gestured toward Nella and the other two women who drove tractor. "You tractor drivers, go to the fields closest to the village at first light and start turning up the potatoes there. Thompkins will bring you hot food at seven o'clock so you can keep working ahead of the harvesters. I suggest you go to bed early. The first day will be the hardest."

After he left, Kitty, one of the city girls, said, "He didn't say what he'd be doing."

"Prob'ly leave the work to his poor ol' da while he goes off to wherever he goes all the time," remarked Shirley, a gum-chewing, bird-like girl who reminded Nella of a fledgling just beginning to grow feathers. No matter how much time she spent primping, she looked untidy. But she had bright eyes, a pretty face, and a quick mind.

"Hush up that kind of talk. Cook might hear you," said Madge, one of the dairy girls.

"So wha's ailing you?" Kitty demanded. "You made your bed with him, aye?"

Madge glared and clamped her teeth together.

"Kitty, don't you know he's got his eyes on his new tractor girl now?" Shirley said. The other girls tried to hush them and ended up talking all at once.

Nella's cheeks began to burn. They'd gone on like this before, talking about Bryan behind his back. But never before had they connected her with him. She couldn't imagine why they would do this. She wanted to stand up and yell at them to shut their mouths, to tell them she'd never look twice at any less of a man than Rob had been.

Edith laid a hand on her arm. "Pay them no mind. All the rest of us know those smart-mouths are put out by Bryan, because he wouldn't bend to their wiles. He may be a shirker, like some of the villagers say, but he's respectful of his workers."

"But why do you suppose they've tied me to him?"

"They've done the same with each of us at one time or another. Don't you worry about it."

"I hope I haven't done anything that made them think—"

" 'Course, you haven't. Forget the likes of them."

"Thanks, Edith." Nella determined to remain at the table only long enough to avoid giving the appearance of fleeing, but in truth she had to get out soon or she might blow up at those two.

Outside the kitchen door she took only a few steps toward Garden Cottage, when Bryan appeared and fell into step beside her. "Did Shirley and Kitty upset you?"

She gave him a sharp look but didn't stop walking. "You heard them?"

"With voices like fishmongers, who wouldn't?" He grinned. "Like to give them something real to talk about? I'll take you up the hill to the chapel, if you'd like."

She stopped. "You can't mean that."

"Why not?"

"The last thing I want to do is give them a reason to talk."

"All right. But you did say you wanted to see the cemetery and the chapel. And you mustn't wander up there alone."

She raised her chin to look him in the eyes. "Then I guess I won't see it, will I?" She made up her mind that instant, however, to go anyway at a time when he couldn't stop her.

As if he'd entered her thoughts, he narrowed his eyes and said firmly, "I mean it. Don't go up there alone." He turned abruptly and stomped away.

The harvest proceeded throughout the daylight hours every day, as the potatoes were gathered and carried to storage buildings where they were sorted and sacked according to size.

Despite the long hours, Nella kept track of the war news. Bryan had set up a wireless in the kitchen, where the women ate silently for when the news came on. Airborne British and American troops who had been dropped behind the German lines in the Netherlands were now fighting to reach a battalion at the Arnhem Bridge. Each day the situation grew more dangerous for the men at the north end of the bridge. Then one morning the announcer said the paratroopers had been driven away from the bridge and from the battalion awaiting their support.

When the news had signed off, the women around the table began to pick up their conversations, yet their voices remained subdued. Taking Belgium and the Netherlands had been one long fight, impeded by flooded land, canals, and bridges. One of the Land Girls had a brother and another a fiancé in the British Thirtieth Corps, who were fighting to link up with the airborne troops.

Edith said to the nearest of them, "They'll make it, Jenny. Don't you doubt it for a minute. And your Harold will soon be sending you a letter from Germany, though he won't be able to say so. Keep the faith, girl."

Jenny brightened. "That's so, Edith. Thanks."

Nella saw past Jenny's smile to the fear of fearing. This girl was afraid that if she doubted her boyfriend would make it, he might not. Nella had seen the same superstition among the RAF pilots and the women who loved them. Nella sighed, for believing or doubting made no difference, and they probably all knew it deep down.

Later, as Nella steered the tractor carefully between the rows of potatoes, she thought again of the faith of women whose men were fighting. Every one of them believed in something. What they said suggested they couldn't go on without believing in fate or luck or having faith in something.

Nella thought if she asked them, most would say they believed in God, and so did she. She wondered how many also felt a million miles away from God. *How many feel that their prayers are bouncing off a cloud up there somewhere, as if God is unreachable ... or uncaring?* She glanced up at the gray sky, feeling very much alone.

The festival had been planned for the first Saturday after the potatoes were in. It turned out that this gave the Land Girls two days to catch up on chores they had neglected.

The evening after the harvest was in, Nella met Peggy at the shearing barn to supervise placement of the booths, benches, and tables. Ruth, who had helped many evenings, came down as soon as she finished with the supper dishes. She remained shy and reticent around Peggy but worked quickly with her hands. Watching her, Nella realized that, regardless of their chats, she knew very little about this girl.

That night, for the first time since the harvest began, Nella wrote in her diary before going to bed.

Wednesday, 4 October 1944

I have to write a bit about the war. Someday Livie may want to know what was happening in the world while her mum was a Land Girl. Our men are still fighting in the Netherlands, and the Americans have crossed the Siegfried Line. They say the Germans counterattacked today, but the Americans were able to hold their ground. The Russians are pushing toward Belgrade, and our forces are moving to take Greece. At the same time, the Nazis have crushed 200,000 patriots in Warsaw, and Hitler has ordered the city to be razed to the ground. Livie, dear, we went to war to save our country, but also to stop this cruel dictator who wants to destroy everyone who is not German.

As for the harvest here in West-Holding, the potatoes are in the barns. The work is a lot different from when I was a child. I see the farmer's side now, the long hours, the machines breaking down or workers getting hurt or the bad weather. Bryan says it's a good crop this year. He sounded honestly proud and very much the responsible farmer. But then it is to his advantage to have a fine crop. Money in his pocket. I don't know what to think about him. Maybe I can get a transfer to another farm if I don't hear soon from Corporal Peterson.

Having written the latter, she realized immediately that she didn't want to transfer. Such a troubling thought. Changing meant learning the ways of another farmer, having to make new friends. Besides, Peggy wouldn't be so close.

She thought about what Livie might think someday if she read that last sentence. So she wrote a bit more.

Livie, there's a lot I can't write that would help you understand why I had to go away and leave you with Mamgu and Dad-cu. I might never be able to explain it all, but I want you to know, in case you remember being left, that it was the hardest thing I've ever had to do. I never wanted to do it.

The next morning Bryan gave Nella the day off so she could help Peggy and her class decorate the barn and the bandstand with branches of autumn leaves they'd cut from the woods. They finished by noon, and Peggy took the children back to their classroom.

Nella headed up the hill to the manor for her lunch. As she followed the long path, she suddenly realized this was a perfect time to check out the cemetery and chapel. Everyone else was already eating, and the cook had promised to save food for her if she came late. Even though she would be venturing into the woods alone, it was full daylight. What could happen in the middle of the day? She needed to lay to rest her earlier fears by knowing exactly what it was like up there. And maybe she'd see evidence of deer for Lord Westmoreland.

With a burst of renewed energy, Nella carefully took her bearings by fixing in her mind the angle she'd have to walk to reach the partially hidden chapel. Then she climbed straight up the hill and entered the woods.

The thought flitted through her mind that Bryan was actually right—though he wouldn't know why—that she shouldn't go off alone. In this case, however, the woods were far removed from the public eye. Her greatest danger was to be seen in West-Holding by her enemy. So far she felt sure no stranger driving through the village had seen her.

When Peggy and her pupils got back to the school building, she saw a car was parked at the curb in front of her classroom. Inside the car Lady Westmoreland sat staring at the decorated windows.

Oh no. I'm in for it, Peggy thought. *Better just face it now and get it over with.* She told the children to go inside and take their seats and then she went over to the car where Lady W. glowered out the open window.

"Good afternoon, Lady Westmoreland. I didn't know you'd be back for the festival."

"I can see that, Miss Jones. I won't ruin the festival fun for the children by discussing your frivolous use of teaching materials now. I will review this with you on Monday after school."

Peggy returned her gaze and nodded respectfully. "Yes, ma'am.

Now if you will excuse me, I must get back to my pupils."

As she paused outside the door to take in a calming breath before facing the children, she heard the car drive away. *God help me, I really despise that woman.*

Nella's footsteps crunched over the thick carpet of leaves in the hardwood forest as she worked her way up the hill. The wild trees and bushes made a jungle, and the musky aroma of leaf mold filled the air. She glanced back to make sure she could still see the open hillside below. Above her head, a crow sent up a warning cry and flapped away. She stopped and the quiet hung around her like deep winter snow. The woods were cool. She shivered and rubbed her arms, thinking she'd better walk faster.

Continuing to follow her predetermined direction, Nella climbed until she was panting. Suddenly she came to a trail that appeared well traveled, a human footpath rather than a narrow animal trail. Well, now, this was better. It made sense that there would be a path to the chapel and especially to the cemetery, for family members would want to visit from time to time. Probably this path began near the house, if only she'd known where to look. She chose the direction that sloped upward toward her destination. Her feet fell silently on the packed earth, so that now she could hear the birds and the whisperings of the wildwood.

Between the trees below, she could barely make out the sunlight as it touched the meadow. Up the hill she could see only trees and more trees. Then the trail branched into two. She'd have to decide which way to proceed. Having come this far, she decided to go a bit more. She scratched a deep X on the path to follow when she returned and again climbed upward.

She almost walked right past the cemetery without seeing it. Lichen and moss camouflaged the stone fence posts, and the old wrought-iron fencing faded into the shadows. The moment she spied it, she left the path and tromped again on the crunchy forest duff. When she reached the fence and leaned against it to look inside, a crash nearby in the brush echoed like a shot. Her heart jumped and went to racing. She whirled around toward the noise. Nothing moved. She waited, frozen at attention for several minutes, holding her breath half the time to listen. Maybe she should leave right now.

When everything remained quiet, she began to relax. The forest was like an old house, making noises of its own. Finally, she felt safe enough to turn her attention toward getting into the cemetery.

After a moment she noticed a gate. It looked exactly like the fence except for an extra set of crossbars. Moving toward the gate, she caught a flash of brown in her peripheral vision. Something had streaked off among the trees. The crashes of its flight sounded definitely like a frightened deer. Lord Westmoreland would be pleased to know if the graceful animals were coming back. She rushed after the sound, hoping for a glimpse, but all she accomplished was to make it run faster.

Disappointed, Nella searched the area and found a trampled spot where the animal must've rested. When she had more time she would search along the trail for hoofprints or droppings. She didn't want to say anything to Lord Westmoreland until she knew for sure.

Returning to the cemetery, she tried to open the gate. To her surprise, the latch lifted easily, and the gate swung inward without complaint. Someone in the family must keep it in shape. Inside the enclosure, she went from marker to marker yet couldn't make out the names and dates on most of them. The few marble headstones had weathered away to indecipherable concavities where names had been. The granite markers fared better, but lichen had so filled the carvings that even these were difficult to read.

In the back of the plot stood a small mausoleum of age-blackened stone. Given the wet climate in Wales, a building like this was the way to preserve memorials. It was a wonder that the Westmorelands hadn't constructed more than one such building. From what she'd heard, they must have had the means. She tried the door, but it wouldn't budge. However, the walk in front of it looked as clean as the steps of the manor house. Only a few recently fallen leaves dotted the stones. Someone must come here often.

Cemeteries always had stirred Nella's imagination. They gave her a sense of the history of a place, as shown by individual lives. Reluctantly she made her way back to the gate. She would come again when she had more time. Out on the path she walked onward toward the chapel. With this good trail she wouldn't lose her sense of direction. Suddenly, around a bend the chapel loomed up in front of her.

Trees crowded against two walls of the old stone building, but the side with the entrance lay directly before her. The tower hovered above the weathered wooden doors. Even up close, it resembled more a Norman castle tower than a church steeple. She tried the door, but found it was either locked or rusted shut. She scouted slowly around the building. Deeply set apertures framed stained-glass windows. The chapel must be lovely from within, the kind of thing that would set Peggy to painting. Maybe she could persuade Lord Westmoreland to bring her and Peggy up here for a tour. He probably would know whose names were on the tombstones and which one belonged to the Welsh bride.

That's what she'd do—ask Lord Westmoreland. He had been quite approachable after he saw how she'd trained Ember. He might even spot a deer for himself. Pleased at the thought, she tromped back to the path that she'd followed from the cemetery. When she turned her back to the chapel, an eerie feeling came over her and made her squeamish, as if the chapel had eyes and they were boring into her back. She throttled the urge to run.

Turning around, she walked a few paces backward and studied the area around the chapel. Nothing moved anywhere. No deer, no hint of a living critter of any sort. A whisper of breeze chilled her cheek, which caused her to think of a ghost story she'd heard as a child. She started walking faster, and by the time she'd made her way back to the cemetery fence, she conquered her nerves and laughed at herself. She must've heard too many wild tales about the Welsh bride. The only thing she had to fear was a real person.

Then she saw him. A thin man, partly hidden among the trees and standing still. He appeared to be watching her. The man abruptly started toward her, crashing through the undergrowth. Terror welled into her throat and came out as a scream. Nella took off running down the hill. Just as she was about to collapse from exhaustion and fear, she rounded a bend in the path and saw that someone else was racing toward her!

She came close to fainting, but then her shocked senses returned when she realized the person coming at her was Ruth, her arms outstretched. Nella fell into them and hung on for an instant. Panting, she gasped, "I saw a man up there. I was afraid—"

"Come. Let's get out of this spooky place, and then you can tell me about it." Ruth kept an arm around her and led her swiftly down a trail to the meadow.

They exited the woods just above the manor and the kitchen garden.

Ruth paused. "You want to sit and rest here awhile?"

Nella shook her head, so they walked on across the grass.

"What did ye see, one of them ghosts the girls talked about?"

"No. I saw a real person, a man. I think he was spying on me. Then he started after me—" It dawned on her in retrospect that he had moved noisily but not with any speed. She must've panicked and now couldn't be sure what she'd seen. "He surprised me and I ran," she said. "I thought he was chasing me, but now I don't know . . . I feel foolish."

"You did the right thing to run. Nothing foolish about that. You never know a man's intentions, that's a fact."

"Anyway, I was glad you were up there, Ruth. How did you happen to be in the woods at this hour?"

"Well, if you won't be telling, Mrs. Harrison sent me out to pull the last of the beets while the girls was eating. I figured I had time for a walk. I do enjoy the woods when the leaves turn color. Then I heard you scream. Scared me to a frazzle for a minute there. I thought to myself, it's one of the Land Girls seeing the ghosts again, so I came running."

"Thank you," Nella said. "I was never so glad to see a friend in my whole life."

"It's nothing. You go on to the kitchen for your lunch, and I'll go get the beets."

Nella walked into the kitchen just as the others were heading back to work. Mrs. Harrison filled her plate, and as she ate hot stew and home-baked soda bread, Bryan stepped in.

"When you've finished, Nella, meet me down at the shearing barn. I found some extra lanterns, and I want you to show Thompkins and me where to hang them. We're neither one that good about decorating, and I'd hate to ruin what you and Peggy have done. It's really looking festive." He sounded genuinely pleased.

A second glance at his face startled her. His smile and his brown eyes radiated happy satisfaction. In fact, his whole face took on an engaging, congenial appearance. What had happened to The Bryan? Intrigued, she replied, "All right. I'll be down in a few minutes."

He saluted and left the kitchen.

Later when Nella entered the shearing barn, she found no sign of Bryan or Thompkins. She looked around in the shady interior of the large building and called. A muffled voice came from behind the band platform. So she walked across the wide floor and around to where she supposed Bryan and Thompkins were working. A cracking, rasping sound came from above and stopped her in midstride. She glanced up. The whole back portion of the temporary bandstand was falling toward her. She tried to leap out of the way. At the same time she threw her arms over her face. Something struck the back of her head.

CHAPTER NINETEEN

"Nella! Nella! Wake up!" a voice called urgently.

What? Startled, she opened her eyes. *Where am I?* Bryan's face was close to hers. She was lying flat on her back, and his fingers were biting into her shoulders. Confused and frightened, she struggled to break free.

"Hold still," he said. "You might hurt yourself more."

Then she saw the stage looming beside them, the high rafters overhead, and remembered. She searched his face for an answer. "I was looking for you. . . ."

"I heard a crash just as I opened the door. It took me a minute to see what happened. That whole section of the stage fell on you. I was afraid . . . where do you hurt?"

"My head."

He gently ran his fingers across her forehead, over her temples, and above her ears. "Where exactly?"

"Right side. Toward the back. Almost feels as if it's cut." She raised her hand to point.

He touched the area.

"Ouch!"

"Sorry. You have a knot there . . . and you're bleeding." He pulled out his handkerchief, folded it, and placed it in her hand. "Can you hold this against it?"

"Yes." Her hair felt wet and slippery with blood.

"Don't move until I check you." He held her other hand and, like a doctor, asked her to squeeze his fingers. Then he grasped each of her feet and checked her ability to move them. "You're sure you don't hurt anywhere else?"

"I'm sure."

He let go of her foot and straightened. "I'm going for help to carry you outside where I can see better."

"I can walk." She started to sit up.

"No!" He grabbed her shoulders and held her still. "Don't move. Stay down while I get Thompkins." He stood up. "I'll be back in a minute. Do not try to sit up."

"All right."

He hurried away.

She felt silly lying there on the dirty floor of the shearing barn when she knew she could just get up and follow him. But her head did hurt, and she didn't want to risk falling if she got to her feet and went dizzy or something.

She heard footsteps approaching, light and quick, not Bryan's. The next minute Ruth was kneeling beside her. "Glory, what happened? Are you all right?"

"I got a blow to my head, but I'm sure it's nothing serious. Bryan went to get Thompkins and told me not to move."

"Aye. He saw me first and sent me to sit with you. What an awful thing to have that piece of stage topple onto you. You must be shaking from the shock." She gripped Nella's hand. "Just try to rest easy till Master Bryan comes. He'll see you to the doctor."

It was a comfort not to lie here alone. "I'm glad Bryan saw you," Nella said. She had long since given up the idea prevalent among the other Land Girls that Ruth was flighty and lazy. She seemed to get her work done to the satisfaction of Mrs. Harrison, and her wanderings about the estate suggested a bright and curious mind.

The outer door banged open. Bryan had returned. Thompkins hurried behind him and exclaimed, "Oh, miss. What have they done building so flimsy a stage that it could fall on you like that!"

Bryan laid an old door beside her. They knelt and carefully lifted her onto it. Again she felt foolish. "Really, I'm all right now. I can walk."

"You just lie quiet and let us move you," Thompkins said.

Ruth, who had moved out the way, said, "He's right, you know."

The men situated her on the makeshift stretcher, and in moments she was outside in the fresh air and daylight.

"Thompkins, drive the car down here," Bryan said. "I'll take her to the hospital in town."

"No! I don't need to go to the hospital," Nella exclaimed. "Really. I am all right. I just need to clean up." She mustn't be seen with him in Abergavenny—in case her enemy was watching.

Bryan's mouth tightened. "You need stitches and a tetanus shot."

"They gave me a tetanus shot when I enlisted."

"Good, but a doctor must still examine you. I have my responsibilities as your employer."

She hadn't thought of that and so gave up resisting.

Ruth left with Thompkins.

Again Bryan checked her for bruises and other injuries. Then he allowed her to sit up with his arm supporting her. "Light-headed?" he asked while her head rested against his shoulder.

"No," she lied. She was sure her natural steadiness would return after a moment of being upright.

Still he held onto her. "I hear the car. Just lean on me until it gets here."

As he spoke his breath warmed her cheek. Suddenly she was aware of the warmth of his body coming through his shirt and hers. The hard muscles of his arm pressed around her shoulders. *Crazy,* she told herself. *Here I am with a blazing headache, and I respond to the first man to touch me in three years. This must be the reason widows can be tempted to marry rogues. Well, not me.* She turned her face away from his and thought about the things Peggy had said against the son of the lord. *The Bryan,* she thought. *I have to remember this is The Bryan who managed to save his own skin by avoiding military service, despite his being able-bodied.*

Thompkins drove the car close to her and parked. Bryan eased her to an upright sitting position. "Still okay?" he asked.

"Yes. I'm fine."

Before she could move to stand up, Bryan rose to his feet, picked her up, and carried her to the car. She wanted to scramble out of his arms and walk on her own, but he was holding her too firmly. His mouth set in a grim line, he carefully placed her on the seat and then climbed in the other side. To Thompkins he said, "Tell my father where I've gone, then take a look at that bandstand to see what went wrong with it. I want you to rebuild it yourself. No more village schoolboys working on it."

"Yes, sir. I'll see to it right away."

As they drove away, Nella said, "He's pretty old to set that up all by himself."

He glanced at her. "Thompkins is still worth any two younger men. If he does need a hand, he'll have one or two of the Land Girls help him. He doesn't need me to tell him that."

Nella said no more.

After some time had passed, he asked, "How do you feel—dizzy or anything?"

"No, I'm not dizzy." She was still holding his handkerchief against the cut, but the bleeding seemed to have stopped.

"That's good. So did you hear anything ... or see anything before that contraption fell on you?"

She froze for an instant. She hadn't thought of foul play, but he obviously was wondering about it. Her heart jumped in fear. She didn't want him to know, of course, that she'd come here on orders from a killer. "No," she said cautiously. "I didn't see or hear anything...." Even while she said this, she remembered voices coming from behind the stage and that she'd thought Bryan was there ahead of her.

"You're sure?" he asked again.

Was he there first and wanting to hide the fact? "Yes, I'm sure," she said. Good thing she wasn't Pinocchio or her nose would be a meter long by now. Glancing at him, she saw the pucker of anxiety on his forehead smooth into an expression of relief. Then, as if in response to her steady gaze, he quickly frowned at the road ahead. Why? What was he hiding?

To Peggy's low opinion of him, Nella added her own: A person couldn't count on him. Right now he could be acting a part, just as she herself had been doing. His solicitous attitude didn't fit at all with the way he'd been barking commands earlier, heedless of common courtesy.

At hospital emergency, an elderly doctor, who probably would be retired if the war hadn't conscripted all the younger physicians, examined her thoroughly. Finally he said her symptoms and the appearance of the wound suggested she'd received a glancing blow and was lucky. He instructed a nurse to give her a careful shampoo and to trim her hair away from the wound. Then he sutured the cut and ordered her to remain inactive for the rest of the day.

During the drive back to Whitestone, Bryan remained silent, occupied with his own thoughts as he glowered ahead at the road. *Probably resenting the time he's lost today because of me,* Nella decided. *But who could know for certain with The Bryan.*

Back at Garden Cottage, he ordered her to stay in bed. After she'd settled in, Edith came in from work early and announced she had been appointed to stay with her. At suppertime Edith fetched a tray of food for them both.

That night, as Nella was about to fall asleep, she realized with a shock that she hadn't thought of Rob at all when she'd suppressed her physical response to Bryan. Her memory of Rob was her protection. No one could ever take his place. This time apparently her practice in acting a part had helped her to react accordingly, and she had failed to include Rob in the background of her pretend character. This was a mistake she must rectify.

She imagined Rob's arms around her. When she finally fell asleep, she dreamed of him—one of the good dreams.

Festival day dawned crisp and clear. Nella's head was sore but not aching. She dressed for her before-breakfast chores and carefully combed her hair over the cut. Inspecting the result, she figured no one would notice if they didn't know the wound was there.

The girls already had the wireless turned on and were listening to the morning news. The BBC reporter was telling how the fierce fighting and flooded lowlands had halted the Canadians in Belgium, and the Americans were meeting strong resistance in Luxembourg.

Nella grimaced. "What a happy way to start the day."

"Never you mind. It can reverse by evening. Want me to turn it off?"

"Fine with me," Dora said as the news ended and music came on, appropriately the American song, "The Tulips Are Talking Tonight."

Nella agreed. "I'd like to forget the war for one day." She cooled her tea with a lot of milk so she could drink it fast and hurried out with Dora to help with chores.

When they approached the dairy barn, Ember woofed and ran to greet Nella. She bent to scratch the dog's ears. At the sound of heavy footsteps on the gravel, she straightened.

Bryan stood there studying her. "Good morning, ladies. Nella, how's your head today?"

"Sore, but fine."

"Good, but I want you to forget the chores this morning."

"That's not fair to Dora—"

"Oh, I can do your part," Dora said.

Bryan intervened. "I'm sending Kitty to help. Nella, go to the kitchen and get your breakfast, then go lie down."

One thing Nella hated and that was to be ordered about as if she were brainless or a slave. Who did he think he was? But she could see that arguing would accomplish nothing, so she gave in. "Yes, sir. Thank you, sir."

He gave her a raised-eyebrow look and then marched off toward the stable.

A few minutes later, from the manor kitchen she saw him on his favorite horse riding away toward the harvested potato fields. He was a puzzling man, but she wasn't about to try to solve the puzzle.

After a breakfast of porridge and cup of black coffee, she went back to Garden Cottage, changed into her Land Army uniform, and headed down the hill to the shearing barn. Peggy would be there early.

The clear, bright morning reminded Peggy of October days in her childhood. She had loved to go into Mr. Edwards' orchard and pick crisp apples for her mum to make sauce for poor Mrs. Edwards. Then after she moved to the manse, she'd loved to hike to the river on days like this with Nella and Charles. She used to throw her cares to the wind with the rocks she cast into the clear water. The last good days of autumn had always made her eager to soak in enough of the sun's warmth and light to last through the dark winter. With exuberance she aimed to do that today.

She quickly ate her breakfast and then marched up the village street toward the lane leading to Whitestone and the shearing barn. Most all of the festival activities would take place there, though Whitestone's gardens were to be open for the people also. A few mothers who had volunteered to work at the food tables were already out in their dooryards. They waved and assured her they'd be along soon.

Peggy greeted them and walked on, filled with happy anticipation. She knew folks were going to be having fun, and it pleased her to think she'd helped arrange the good time.

When she got to the shearing barn, she saw a tall man striding down the path from Whitestone. Seeing it was Laurie Barringer, Peggy almost turned back to the village to join some of the other women so she wouldn't have to be alone with him. But it was too late. He'd seen her and was hailing her. He met her at the door of the barn.

"I commend you on the decorating," he called. "It's wonderful. Did you design all this?" He gestured toward the booths and the garlands of ivy and autumn leaves festooning them.

"I made suggestions, but my pupils did most of the work. I have several who are very artistic. Nearly all have a good sense of design and color. They made sketches first, and then I let them supervise the process when they weren't strong enough to do the actual work."

He looked surprised. "You mean to tell me your students designed these festive arrangements? How old did you say they are?"

"Most are eleven or twelve. One girl is so talented I've been wanting to show her work to someone . . . hoping to find her a mentor."

"At age twelve? Must be a child prodigy."

"Actually I think she is."

"What does she do?"

"She draws and paints, mostly watercolors."

"Well, I'd like to see her work sometime."

Peggy wondered if he was just being polite. What connections would he have if he was serious? But not wanting to miss the chance, she continued. "I have a sample of her work. Maybe you could come to the school some day next week after the children have gone home."

"I'll plan on that."

"Hello!" Nella's voice interrupted them.

Peggy waved back at her and said to Laurie, "Come any day after Monday. Lady Westmoreland wants to talk to me on Monday."

"Bad news?" he asked.

Peggy shrugged. "Could be." Turning to Nella, she called, "You're early! I thought you'd have chores to do first."

Nella grinned. She made a pretty sight. Her Land Army uniform colors enhanced her reddish blond hair to a burnished gold. Walking over to Peggy's side, she said, "I was excused. Like you, I wanted to get here before the others. Hello, Laurie. I didn't expect you this early."

He laughed and bowed. "All-around handyman at your service, ma'am. Believe it or not, with an auto. I've saved petrol coupons for today. Anything you might need, just let me know. And look, here come your workers, so it turns out none of us are very early." He gestured toward the group of women, elderly men, and children coming up the road from the village. They would be managing the booths, serving food, and overseeing the children's games. Laurie looked around. "You ladies certainly have organized this day well."

"Peggy did the organizing," Nella said. "I helped with planning. Most of the musical groups, the bands and folk dancers, will be performing in the afternoon. There'll be bagpipers and morris dancers. In the evening we'll have three groups of singers, followed by professional fiddlers so that everyone may dance."

Laurie laughed. "Everyone who *can*, you mean to say. I was born with two left feet."

"So are most of us, but it should be fun to watch," Peggy said. "Nella does a smashing Highland fling."

"Oh, I haven't danced in ages. I'd be an ox."

"Then you'd better practice in private somewhere. I've told my students you'll show them how tonight."

"You haven't!"

"Absolutely. Oh, here comes Bryan. It's about time for the Young Lord of the Manor to be showing." Peggy glanced at her watch. "The public will be arriving at nine, and it's past eight already."

When Bryan joined them, the first thing he said was, "Nella, how are you feeling?"

Nella turned pink and said she was fine.

He nodded but kept his eyes on her overlong before he said, "Laurie, come along and help me move the benches and chairs for the servicemen. I think they should be closer to the food booths as well as to the road to save them from having to walk too far."

When the men were out of earshot, Peggy whispered, "What was all that about? You look very uncomfortable . . . or are you falling for The Bryan?"

"I'm definitely not falling for him!" She grew pinker now, the kind of blush, Peggy decided, that went with a burst of temper. "He was asking about me because I hurt my head yesterday, and he had to take me into town for a few stitches."

"Stitches! Let me see! Where?"

Nella lifted her hair slightly on the right side. "There. Can you see?"

"My word, you've got a long gash and a lump too. Nella, what happened?" She gently smoothed Nella's hair back in place.

"Part of the band stage toppled onto me."

"It just up and fell down on you? Were you working on it? I thought the carpentry was all finished."

"Supposedly it was. It fell over when I walked behind the stage. Bryan had wanted me to help him hang some more lanterns."

"So he was with you."

"Well, no. He came later. After the stage fell . . ."

"I think you'd better tell me exactly what happened."

Nella calmly told her about the accident, which all sounded a little bizarre after she'd explained it.

"How could the backdrop just fall down? I watched the older boys build it, and Thompkins checked it later. It looked solid to me."

"I don't know how."

The unanswered question worried Peggy. What if Nella's injury wasn't an accident? After all, someone had tried to kill her before, and she'd left her home thinking to save her family from the assailant. Yet Nella acted unruffled by this recent mishap. Suddenly there was no more privacy for talking. The people from the village were arriving by twos and threes and beginning to stock their booths with foods and the prizes for children's games.

Peggy made a quick decision. "If you're up to it, come with me while I help the folks get their concessions going." She hoped to keep Nella close beside her all day. Later, they'd have a serious talk.

CHAPTER TWENTY

As noon approached, clusters of people surrounded the shearing barn, laughing and calling to neighbors and friends. Beyond the crowd, children chased one another around the trees. Cheerful music and the fragrance of hardwood smoke and beef turning on a spit filled the balmy air. Looking about at the happy faces, Nella felt like dancing. Clearly the festival was giving people a bit of reprieve from the war. Nella reflected on how much Rob would have loved this, but somehow she could let go of him as never before. Her demanding heart quieted.

People came from nearby villages as well as from Abergavenny. Jean and Mary brought ambulatory patients from the military hospitals. Giselle and her girls arrived with Nella's mother, father, and Livie. Jacquie and Angie quickly joined the children playing games at the edge of the crowd. Giselle watched over them from nearby and chatted with the servicemen sitting on the grass. She, too, looked more relaxed and happy.

Nella hungrily gathered her baby into her arms. For today she was Mum again. Of course, after a big hug, Livie wanted down to run and play. Nella led her by the hand to the animal pens, set up so the younger children could pet rabbits, lambs, sheep-dog pups, and kittens. Her heart filled with joy over the simple pleasure. After the war, this was the way it would be for her and Livie. Somehow they'd find a bit of land and a small cottage just for the two of them, and they'd have all kinds of animals.

At the small animal enclosure, Nella brought Livie first to the box of toddling kittens. Livie stretched over the side of the box, barely reaching the soft fur of one. "They're still tiny babies, so touch them easy," Nella warned.

"Let her hold one," Bryan said. He'd been standing close by. He bent over and scooped up a fluffy orange kitten. Kneeling beside Livie, he offered her the kitten. "Hold out your arms."

Wide-eyed, Livie extended both arms and carefully cradled the kitten, which looked at her for a second and then snuggled quietly.

Bryan stood up, watching. "She's a lovely child. You must be very proud."

"And you no doubt are wondering how I could join the Land Army and leave her," Nella retorted. When his eyes met hers, she wished she'd kept her pain to herself, for his face registered both surprise and hurt.

He shook his head. "No. Anyone could see you'd never leave her without good reason." He lowered his voice so it reached only her. "Don't torture yourself now that you're here doing what you decided was best. Just enjoy every minute of days like today."

To Nella's dismay, tears rushed to her eyes. She bit her lip and nodded, unable to speak. Bryan touched her shoulder lightly and said, "I need to go help carve the beef." To Livie, he said, "Have you seen the puppies yet? No? Well, if we put the kitty back, your mother will show you."

Livie cheerfully gave up the kitten and smiled up at Nella. "Puppies, Mummy."

Bryan walked away, and Nella quickly composed herself. At the puppy pen, she laughed with Livie over two pups playing tug-of-war with an old shoe. Then her mind drifted to thinking about the sensitivity Bryan had just shown for Livie's feelings and hers. His surprising behavior unsettled her. It seemed out of character, but then she had to admit she didn't really know his character.

The mouth-watering smell of roast beef filled the air. A calf had been turning on a spit over a pit of hot coals since hours before daylight. It had been months since Nella had tasted good beef. At Whitestone they enjoyed occasional pheasants and wild hares as well as mutton, and had plenty of honey and butter and cheese, but beef went to the military. Even the Westmorelands had endured their share of American tinned pork.

For the festival, however, they had slaughtered the fatted calf and provided mountains of produce from the kitchen garden and orchard. Now Lord Westmoreland and his son helped Thompkins and Mrs. Harrison carve and serve the meat, while Lady Westmoreland walked through the crowd, smiling beatifically to the guests, charming many by calling their children by their first names. As Nella watched, this, too, surprised her. Lady Westmoreland's behavior didn't fit the dragon image Peggy had described.

Nella had never seen so much food in one small area. Large bowls brimming over with baked beans, roasted potatoes, Yorkshire pudding, and gravy from the beef drippings. Sweet corn and baskets of fresh bread, together with dishes of butter, pitchers of honey, currant preserves, and shining apples. The guests walked in a long line by the trestle tables and filled their plates to overflowing. For the men there were mugs of ale; for the children and women, cups of a fizzy fruit juice.

Ruth and Thompkins, assisted by Laurie and his car, kept the food tables replenished.

Along with the autumn leaves the children had fastened everywhere for decoration, old banners bearing the Westmoreland crest fluttered gaily at every booth. Bryan had hung them at the last minute. To Nella the scene looked like paintings she'd seen of festivals of the Middle Ages.

Nella led Livie to where her parents had spread a blanket on the grass, and they took turns filling their plates.

Livie was so excited she only ate a few bites and then wanted to play with Jacquie and Angie.

"We'll take her home for her nap pretty soon," Elizabeth said. "Maybe Giselle and the girls can ride back to town with Jean's group."

Nella couldn't stand having to let Livie go, but had to agree that she needed a nap in a quiet place. "I'll speak to Jean." She left Livie with her mamgu and went in search of Jean. She found her sitting in the shade, surrounded by her group of soldiers. Bryan was there too, lounging on the grass next to the servicemen. They were all laughing as if at someone's joke. Nella hesitated, wishing she could catch Jean alone. Then Bryan looked up, smiled, and beckoned for her to join them.

"Nella! Come sit with us!" Jean urged.

So she dropped down beside Jean. "Mum and Daddy need to take Livie home for her nap. They're wondering if Giselle and the girls can ride back to town with you in the personnel carrier. Is that permissible?"

"Of course. We can make room. I'm making two runs actually. I'll take some of the men back after a while. And I'll return for those who are up to staying on for the evening."

"Laurie could take your friend into Abergavenny any time she wishes," Bryan said. "That's the sort of thing he volunteered for."

"Oh... I forgot about that," Nella said. "I guess it's because I haven't seen him in a while."

"He drove down to the village with Peggy. He said she had forgotten something."

"Well, then, I guess one way or the other Giselle will be able to get a ride," Nella said. "I'll go let Mum know."

Peggy hurried to her room at Gatekeep, while Laurie waited in his car to take her back to the shearing barn. The cottage was unusually quiet with Mrs. Lewis gone to the festival. She searched through the papers on her desk and pulled out Annie's painting. Laurie had asked if he might see it today instead of next week. He said he was leaving for London Sunday afternoon, and if the painting was good enough, then he'd show it to a friend who was on the board of directors at the Art Institute—the school Peggy had hoped to attend before she turned to teaching.

Peggy held the watercolor at arm's length, trying to see it from an objective viewpoint. Was Annie as gifted as she believed? Or had her affection for the girl distorted her judgment? She squinted critically at the small painting. Yes, a trained eye would see unique talent here. Satisfied, Peggy hurried back to the car.

She climbed in and handed the painting to Laurie.

He studied it silently. Finally he said, "You're sure the girl did this by herself?"

"Positive." Then she laughed with relief at the expression on his thin face. He was as impressed as she'd been. "No one in the village or even in Abergavenny has the ability to help her. That's why I felt so strongly about finding her a mentor. Her talent for art shouldn't be wasted." Peggy didn't think it wise to tell him about Annie's deafness, not until he had the painting evaluated. People could be funny about such things. So she only said, "Her parents love her, but I know they can't afford a place like the Art Institute or for her to study abroad if that's an option after the war."

Laurie turned in the car seat to face her, draping his arm along the back of the seat as he listened.

Looking at him now, Peggy realized she'd been avoiding direct eye contact in a futile effort to keep him at a distance. The truth was she liked this man, no matter who his father was. She said, "I can't bear to think of Annie going back to London without hope of moving forward with her art. Her family thinks that painting is fit only for recreation. They have little understanding of her talent. If it's up to them alone, she'll probably never have the opportunities she deserves."

Laurie didn't say anything but looked from her to the painting and back again. Yet his silence didn't make Peggy uncomfortable.

Finally, without reservation, he said, "You're right about her talent. May I borrow this painting for a week or so? If my friend is as impressed as you and I, I think he will want to ensure this girl's future in the art world. And he's wealthy enough to sponsor her."

"Oh . . ." Peggy was at a loss for words. Could it be that easy? "Thank you, no matter how it turns out. Thanks so much!"

Laurie nodded and smiled. "You're very welcome. Now, as much as I wish we were going off on an outing alone, I think I should drive you back to the festival."

Peggy laughed and hoped that her treating his remark as a joke would keep him at a distance. If she made a list of things she never wanted to do, being on a date with Laurence Barringer the Fourth would be number one, even though he was nice.

By evening Nella was very tired and glad that Livie had gone home to the manse. Her neck and shoulders ached, probably the result of yesterday's accident. She thought of sneaking up the hill and going to bed early, but she had agreed to teach the villagers the steps of the Highland fling. She'd learned the old Scottish dance from her grandmother in Scotland and had danced with a group one summer before the war. She was sadly out of practice and never would've volunteered, but Peggy had cornered her.

Her demonstration would no doubt be an embarrassment to Grandmum, if the old woman could see her.

When the children gathered around the bagpipers, Nella marched resolutely to her place in front of them. She explained each step and movement, demonstrating first without music. The children copied her, and some did very well. Finally, she signaled to the pipers to play and led the dancers through the entire piece.

One by one her pupils fell out of the action, and before long, Nella was left dancing alone. Without a break the pipers moved into a faster tempo, and the music lifted her into a surge of new energy and joy.

Her feet knew the way after all and led her in a marvelous flight to the lilting tune. When at last Nella stopped, she found she'd attracted a large audience, which then burst into applause. Laughing, she bowed twice and then skipped out of the limelight.

Dora, Edith, and Maureen met her with enthusiastic laughter, clapping her on the back and saying, "Well done!"

"You never once let on you danced!" Dora exclaimed.

Over Dora's shoulder Nella saw Shirley sneering, looking like she'd just eaten a pickle. Before she could glance away, Shirley called, "That what ye use to get the young lord into tune? Quite invitin' for a goody-goody like yourself."

Standing beside her was Kitty, who laughed uproariously, then said, "Come on, Shirl. Don't waste your wit on the likes of her, when there's all these handsome soldiers waitin' to be entertained."

Before Nella could respond, drums rolled and the pipers struck up a fighting tune and began to march. Everyone retreated to the sides of the huge room to give them space. Nella edged her way to the outer perimeter of the crowd as she searched for Peggy.

Bryan intercepted her. "That was wonderful. No one told me you're a dancer. We could have planned more, using you as instructor."

She dismissed the idea with a laugh. "No one told you because I'm *not* a dancer."

"But Peggy said that you traveled with a Celtic dance group one summer."

"I was only fifteen then and just an amateur, but it was fun."

"You're a lady full of surprises. Prizewinning dog trainer, Celtic dancer—what other interesting things have you done?"

He was standing close to her, and because of the crowd, she couldn't back away. So she answered coolly, "Nothing else. If you'll excuse me, I want to tell Peggy I'm going to retire for the evening." Nella started to leave, but he caught hold of her arm.

"I'll walk you up the hill and tell her when I come back."

"Thank you, but I can walk alone. I don't need an escort."

"You mean you don't need *me*," he corrected. "Sorry, but I'm still the boss. Come along." He kept hold of her arm.

As he guided her toward the door, she saw Shirley and Kitty watching. Kitty was smirking as usual, but Shirley flashed her a look of pure hatred.

Nella yanked her arm free of Bryan's grip. "Please let go of me. I won't run away."

He took in the other girls at a glance and murmured, "You care what they think?"

"I have to live with them. And I want them to know the truth, that I'm not involved with you and never will be."

He frowned and placed his hand under her elbow. "Of course, but please act like a lady and allow me to lead you through this crowd without having to push you in front of me or stomp ahead of you like a boor."

Nella was too tired to blush. In fact, all the fight went out of her. She only wanted to get to her room and lie down. When they stepped outside into the fresh evening air, he paused and looked down at her in the dim light. "You feel limp as a rag. Is your head aching again?"

"No. But my neck and shoulders are, and I'm really tired."

"I'm driving you up then. Laurie gave me the keys to his car."

"I can walk—"

"You never give up, do you?"

"I hope not."

"Well, I have the say here, and you're riding." Then he escorted her past the long barn to the small parking area at the side of the road and opened the car door for her. She climbed in, and in a few minutes he parked beside the mansion. She let herself out before he could walk around the car to open the door for her, but then he appeared next to her just seconds later.

Taking her arm again, he said, "There's no one to see now, and you look as though you're about to drop. I'm only protecting myself as your employer. The woman who supervises my Land Girls is a warhorse, if you'll excuse the term. She'll make my life difficult if any of you come to harm. If you're going to faint, I'll be right here to protect my interests." He walked her toward Garden Cottage.

By the time they reached the door, she wondered if he was going to see her inside too, but he stopped and let go of her.

"I don't want you here alone. When you go inside, lock the door and keep it locked until Edith comes. I'd send Ruth, but she's still carrying food for Mrs. Harrison."

"Oh, please don't bother Edith. I'm not ill, and I'm not dizzy or anything. I'm just tired."

Bryan stared at her as if undecided and then said, "Both my father and Thompkins thought that heavy panel that toppled on you had been tampered with. So promise me you'll stay inside and keep the door locked until Edith comes."

"You think someone wanted to hurt me?" Nella asked.

"I don't know. Do you think that's possible?"

She almost answered *yes*. Just in time she caught herself. "No. Of course not."

Nodding, he said, "Good. I mean, it's good that you're not worried. Even so, I'm responsible for your safety, so lock the doors as I said."

As she moved to obey, he added, "No chores tomorrow, so don't bother getting up early."

Leaning against the closed, locked door, Nella reconsidered his earlier remark. *Good that I'm not worried? If he didn't want me to worry, why then did he tell me the accident might not have been an accident?*

The obvious answer was he did want her to worry. Well, he needn't have made an issue of it. She would have thought about the possibility of foul play once the rush of festival activities was over. She shrugged, went to the bedroom she shared with Dora and Edith, and turned down the coverlet on her cot. She was so tired, she sat down to undress and get into her nightgown. Slipping her feet into her worn slippers, she trudged to the bathroom to brush her teeth and wash her face. Then she saw the mail still lying in a pile on the lamp table by the front door. Someone had brought it in, but with the festival going on, no one had opened it.

She thought of leaving it until tomorrow, but then on impulse, tired as she was, she walked over and thumbed through the envelopes. One was for her. Someone had addressed it properly, yet there was no stamp and no return address. She'd hoped it might be from Corporal Peterson. Servicemen didn't have to use stamps. Then she noticed the writing. Her senses quickened, and she ripped open the envelope. Unforgettable black printing jumped off the page at her. *IF YOU TALK, THE NEXT ACCIDENT WILL BE FATAL.*

So her enemy knew where she was staying. Then the awfulness hit her—the killer must've come to the festival, watched her, and somehow learned where she was quartered at Whitestone. Then he'd devised a way to have this note delivered with today's mail. For that matter, Garden Cottage doors hadn't been locked. He could have walked right in. He'd been close enough to grab her . . . or Livie!

"Dear God," Nella whispered, "I'm so frightened. What if this person thinks I have talked? How will they know I haven't?"

Then the thought came to her that as long as the authorities refused to investigate, the killer would be biding his time. But when would this all end? Why would the killer be in this area? What was at stake? None of it made sense to her.

It was obvious now that she mustn't ask for a transfer from Whitestone or do anything that would suggest she wasn't cooperating. Nella stepped over to the fireplace and burned the note and its envelope. She checked all three doors again to make sure they were securely locked. As she went through the cottage and pulled down the blackout shades, she fastened all the window latches. From now on, she must assume someone was watching her.

Should she write to Captain Evers now instead of waiting for a letter from Corporal Peterson? Surely he would see a pattern now. Or would he? What if he just turned the matter over to Constable Burns? Or what if some assistant opened the letter and read it? No. She couldn't take the chance. Not yet.

She felt so alone. For a moment she wondered if she should confide in Peggy. But no, Peggy would be safer if she knew nothing.

In the end Nella accepted the obvious: She must not involve anyone else. She decided that she'd have to be extra watchful now. Slipping into bed, she lay back wide-eyed and waited for Edith's knock on the locked door.

Chapter Twenty-One

Sunday morning Nella attended church in the village, and after dinner, while all the Land Girls enjoyed a rare afternoon rest, she called for Ember. She wanted to stretch her legs and, with the dog for company, felt she could safely walk the open path down the hill to the shearing barn.

She found the booths still standing, but the leaves on the decorative branches had dried and shriveled, and the brightly colored Westmoreland banners had been removed. Despite some preliminary cleanup, bits of litter spattered the trampled grass.

Nella strolled toward the pit where the beef had roasted. As she passed the door of the shearing barn, she knew what had brought her down the hill to the barn instead of to the meadows on the other side of the manor.

"Ember, heel." The dog fell in step at her side, and together they entered the cavernous building and crossed the broad floor over to the stage. Nella climbed onto the stage and went to inspect the back section that had fallen on her. A metal panel of lights and amplifying speakers had added weight to the heavy panel. It looked like the section had been constructed to be all one piece, so it must've come down as a single huge chunk. A few splinters showed where it had pulled away from the floor planks. Thompkins had repaired the panel by bracing it with angle iron, fastened securely with screws. Nella couldn't picture how it could've fallen to hit her in the manner she remembered.

She walked behind the stage. The light from the small windows didn't penetrate the gloom back there. Since she couldn't see well, she felt her way along the ends of the planking until she located the same splintered area she'd seen before. Her fingers told her less than her eyes had, so she gave up and headed back outside.

When Nella stepped out the door, she almost collided with a huge man. She jumped back. "Oh!"

Ember gave a bark, then wagged her tail.

The man kept his large pale eyes fixed on her. Dressed in shabby overalls and shirt, a crumpled old cap, and farmer's high-top shoes, he looked out of place on the Westmoreland Estate. She'd seen his likes in the London slums when she'd been to the city.

"I'm sorry. You startled me," she explained.

The man made no response. He just kept staring at her.

"Did you come to the festival yesterday?" He looked as if he'd slept in the woods all night. Bits of lichen clung to his shirt sleeves and were caught in his long graying hair.

He raised his hands and pointed to his mouth, then his ears, and shook his head.

Sign language? Deaf? And was he mute too? Suddenly his behavior made sense. Nella wondered if he could lip-read. She touched the corner of her mouth with one finger and asked slowly, "Can you tell what I am saying?"

He grunted and hesitantly nodded.

"Very good. I'm glad. Do you live in the village?" She gestured toward West-Holding. She found she had to make gestures to get across her message. Too bad Peggy wasn't around to help out.

The man shook his head and said, "A-argh," as he pointed toward the woods.

"Oh, I understand. Over the hill there."

He nodded, watching intensely for her next words. She didn't know what else to say. She patted Ember's head and turned her face again to him. "She's not my dog. She lives at the big house."

He nodded and pointed to the manor.

"Do you like dogs?" she asked.

He gave a short grunt and then reached down to pet Ember.

"Good thing Ember knows him. She doesn't take to strange men," Bryan interjected.

Nella jumped, surprised to hear him so close without any sound of warning. She was instantly angry, both at him for coming up behind her like that and at herself for not being alert. She snapped, "Where did you come from? I didn't hear a thing!"

He shrugged. "You were too busy talking. I see you've met our neighbor from over the hill." He raised his hand in greeting to the man. "Hello, Albert."

The big man touched the brim of his battered cap as a gesture of respect and smiled.

"Tell your mother I've got the hen and chicks she asked about." Bryan made a few awkward gestures to go with his words.

"Aargh," Albert answered, bowing his head slightly in assent. Then he raised his right hand in an awkward good-bye salute and shuffled toward the woods behind the barn.

Looking after him, Nella said, "He surprised me too. I came out of the barn and nearly bounced off his chest. It took me a minute to figure out he couldn't hear me and couldn't speak either."

"He's harmless, but you shouldn't be down here alone after what happened the other night," Bryan said in a curt tone. "What were you doing in the barn, anyway?"

"I wanted to see if I could find evidence against it being an accident."

He gave a frustrated sigh. "Have you always been foolish, or is this a recent decline of good sense?"

"You're the one who suggested it could've been foul play. I think it makes very good sense to try to find out if that may be true," she shot back.

"Leave that to me. I thought I made it clear that you should not be wandering around by yourself." In contrast to her rising volume, Bryan kept his voice low, which only served to irritate her more.

"I'm not alone! I brought Ember."

"That idiot dog is compulsive and unpredictable."

Nella glared at him. "That's not so. Heel, Ember." She walked swiftly away and headed up the hill toward the manor. Ember trotted smoothly at her side.

To the dog she muttered, "That man is the most infuriating person I've ever had to put up with. You know that?"

Ember looked up and answered with a woof.

At Whitestone she sent the dog to the barn and retreated to Garden Cottage.

There she found the other girls quietly doing their hair and fingernails, writing letters home, and listening to records on Edith's gramophone.

Dora stopped combing her wet hair and said, "Nella, you really should try to avoid being alone with Bryan. It does give the gossips an excuse."

Before she could respond, Edith countered, "That's what she's been doing. I can vouch for that. But it won't matter what she does. They'll still smear her. I say she should forget them and do as she wishes."

That morning at breakfast Shirley and Kitty had made crude remarks about her "private" evening with the young lord of the manor Saturday night. Nella wanted desperately to stay away from the man, but lately he just showed up without warning, as he'd done down at the shearing barn. "You're both right. I can't keep away from Bryan all the time. This is his farm, and he's my boss after all. But I do try. Still, I can't be thinking all the time about what Shirley and Kitty will think, now, can I?"

Nella pulled up a chair to her bedside table and took out her diary. Before she forgot, she wanted to jot down the details of the festival—the food, decorations, games, entertainment, and a word picture of Livie playing with the animals. It had been a lovely day in spite of Bryan and the gossip that came from his insistence on driving her back up the hill.

She thought about the morning of the festival day and how he'd pierced her defenses with sympathy.

He was sympathetic, and appeared sincere this time. Bryan sincere? This fits that new word I learned—oxymoron. As far as Peggy is concerned, the name Bryan means the opposite of sincere. He is for sure unpredictable. I think at that moment, though, he meant what he said. It broke me up to have anyone show such understanding. It didn't matter that it was Bryan. Until he made me cry, I thought I was doing well enough all by myself. But alone is not good. I don't know what I'd do without Peggy here close by. It always sets me right, just to talk with her.

The afternoon of rest passed all too fast. Following supper Nella returned to chores with Dora, feeding and watering the animals and helping with the evening milking. By bedtime the cheerful ambience left by the festival had faded. Nella climbed into bed early but couldn't get to sleep. In the midst of her tossing, she heard a scratching noise outside their bedroom window. She held her breath and listened. At first she thought about the barn cats. Was it an animal?

A furtive scraping at the window persuaded her it was not. She crept out of bed and tiptoed to the window. Pulling back the edge of the blackout shade, she peeked out. A man was trying to break in! She clamped her teeth against a scream and hurried to Edith's bed.

Touching her shoulder, she whispered, "Edith, wake up! Someone's trying to break in through our window."

"What?" Edith sat up.

"Quiet. Listen."

The scraping persisted. Edith said, "What'll we do?"

"Go wake up Dora and keep her quiet. I'll wake Maureen and the others in the other room. Then we'd all better get out of here."

They went from bed to bed until all the girls were alert, and then all six crept silently out the front door and ran barefoot to the mansion. A sleepy-eyed Thompkins answered their knock at the kitchen door. He had pulled on his trousers to come to the door and, half-dressed, went to get up Ruth to ask her to rouse the rest of the household. Then he took off running to waylay the intruder.

The women huddled in the kitchen in their nightgowns until Mrs. Harrison came in and gave them shawls and comforters to wrap up in. Bryan hurried into the kitchen with Ruth at his heels and then ran out toward the cottage. Next came Lord Westmoreland.

Nella told him what she'd heard and seen, and he rushed out too.

"Shouldn't someone call the constable?" Dora asked.

"Master Bryan said to wait till he's had a look," Ruth said.

The women all lapsed into silence.

"I'll heat water for tea," Mrs. Harrison said. "You don't want to be chilling, the way you ran out in your bare feet and all." She poked the coals in the giant cooking range and put on water.

Nella was sipping tea with her housemates by the time the men returned. Obviously they'd failed to capture the intruder.

Lord Westmoreland's scowl expressed their frustration. "We'll have the constable out here as soon as possible. You girls go on back to bed and get your rest. The culprit won't be trying anything more tonight. Be sure to lock your windows and doors."

"I'll walk you to the cottage and look around one more time," Bryan said.

So barefoot but bundled in borrowed wraps, the women walked back to Garden Cottage. Bryan stood at the door, watching them safely indoors.

"Thank you. Good night," they said, one by one.

But when Nella passed him, she asked, "Did you see any signs at all of the attempt to get in?"

"Oh yes. The bedroom window frame was scraped up. And someone trampled the plants outside. We'll have the constable take a look. I doubt there's any danger at the moment, but I'll stay here and watch until the constable comes. Now try to get some sleep."

"Thanks. I'll try." Nella ducked inside, closed the old door, and locked it. She wished she could believe that the intruder had chosen her bedroom window purely by chance.

For Peggy the hours passed swiftly Monday. Suddenly it was time to dismiss her class and time for her appointment with Lady Westmoreland. Peggy hated conflict, and Lady W. had a talent for making her fighting mad.

She made sure all of the children headed for home. She didn't want any after-school helpers today. The paintings Annie had hung so painstakingly in the windows were still there, as if fuel to get Lady W. started. Peggy wondered if the woman would dismiss her. Probably not. Because of the war, it wasn't easy to find teachers right now.

A car door slammed outside. Peggy sat down at her desk and posed herself to look like she was busy correcting papers.

After a long moment there was a tap on the door, and without waiting for an answer, Lady Westmoreland marched in. "Good afternoon, Miss Jones." She glanced around the empty room and nodded approvingly. "I was sure you'd remember our appointment and make it private."

Peggy stood up. "Good afternoon, Lady Westmoreland. Please come and be seated." She gestured to the only adult-sized chair in the room besides her own, which was placed next to her desk.

Lady W. looked at the chair but said, "I prefer to stand, thank you. This won't take long." She came forward and stood before the desk.

Peggy didn't want to sit and have to look up to her, so she remained standing also.

They eyed each other across the old, worn teacher's desk as if it were a battle line, Peggy thought as she waited for her supervisor to speak.

"Miss Jones, I'm disappointed that you seem to have no thought for the other teachers and students. Your class has used far more than its share of paper and colors. I don't know why you have chosen to disobey my orders this way, but let me be very clear. You must stop what you call creative art projects and for the next three months confine your use of school supplies to ruled paper and paste."

Peggy felt her careful control beginning to slip. She pressed her lips together. *I won't let her get me going*, she vowed to herself. *That's probably just what she wants.*

Lady W. went on. "For the rest of the year, remember that the paints and colored pencils are for making maps and for the little children to learn their colors and words. Nothing else. Because you are a good teacher and well liked by the parents of the village, I'm willing to overlook your uncooperative attitude this time. But I warn you, if you continue to defy my wishes and the needs of the other teachers, I may have no recourse but to dismiss you. And a dismissal on your record will make it very difficult to obtain a new position as a teacher or governess somewhere else."

She made a precise half-turn toward the door and waved her gloved hand at the windows. "And please remove those drawings before you go home today. Good evening, Miss Jones." She then turned her back and left.

Peggy heard her car drive away. She got up, stomped to the window, and with clenched teeth began removing the paintings. If it weren't for the children, she would have ripped them down and torn them to pieces. Instead, she carefully peeled them off the glass and laid them in a neat pile on her desk. If she didn't quit her teaching job before bedtime, she'd give them to the children in the morning to hang in their homes.

That evening Nella raced her bicycle down a country lane behind Peggy, watching her friend with concern. Peggy had said she needed to talk, but she also apparently needed to work off some of her anger at Lady Westmoreland.

When Peggy finally slowed down, and they rode side by side again, Nella asked her, "Would she really dismiss you for such a small thing? I don't see how she could if the parents all wanted you, and I know they do."

"That's not my problem," Peggy said. "Right now I just want to quit. I want to walk away and let the war-horse struggle trying to find another teacher. I'm so angry!"

"I don't blame you one bit. It's unfair."

"This is only the most recent of her dozens of restrictive demands." Peggy took off again, pedaling furiously. Nella followed as fast as she could until she began to feel winded. Her sore shoulder muscles ached. She called to Peggy, "Let's stop to rest by that tree up ahead next to Willow-wythy Creek."

"Fine."

They coasted to a stop, leaned their bicycles against the tree, and dropped down on the grassy creek bank in the early evening sun.

Peggy huffed a noisy sigh as if to expel her frustration all in one breath. "I'm glad you could come with me. I felt I was going to explode if I didn't do something to work off my anger."

"Feeling better now?"

"A little. I don't think I'll resign."

"Good. The children need you."

"It's only for them that I'm willing to stay."

"Good for you. I don't know if I could do the same."

"Sure you could. I've seen you win plenty of battles with your patience and your strength." Peggy leaned back on her elbows and looked up at the sky where white puffs of clouds drifted southward. "You know, when I take the time to look up at the sky, day or night, I can usually get myself back into proper perspective. It's just that Lady W. makes me feel like I did when I first came to the manse. She makes me forget that God loves me, no matter where I was born. My dear mum never was able to get that into me. It took Father Mac and your brother Charles to do that."

"Not me too?" Nella teased.

"You were such a little girl, I thought. Not worth listening to." She turned and smiled softly. "I was so wrong back then, Nell. You and your certainty about God sustained me many times. You always had a solid inner calm no matter how impulsively you leaped from one project to another. I miss that . . ." The soft look in her eyes changed to concern.

When she paused, Nella knew what was coming next.

"How are you doing now?"

Nella shook her head. "I can't make myself believe something just because I want to. It's as if . . . all that I counted on turned out to be wrong. I was a naïve little child. It's not that I don't believe in God. I just don't know *what* to believe about Him."

Peggy studied her anxiously for a while. "I wish I could help you, but you know me. I have my own questions. Too many who claim to be Christians act like the devil. Money and position are their real gods, even for some in your father's congregation."

"So we are the blind leading the blind," Nella said with a laugh. But Peggy didn't laugh. She looked gloomy again. "Are you thinking about Lady Westmoreland again?" Nella asked gently.

"Waste of time and energy, isn't it?" Peggy acknowledged. "So . . ." She sat up and stretched. "Do you have more work to do when you get back to the manor?"

"No. Bryan hasn't put me back on evening chores yet. He thinks he has to pamper me a bit after the accident."

Peggy sat up abruptly. "I was so angry, I almost forgot! Does your head feel all right? Maybe you shouldn't have come bicycling."

"My head is fine. As the doctor said, I am lucky. I went to the barn yesterday to look at that stage piece that fell on me and saw that I could've been hurt a lot worse."

Peggy sat up, looking tense again. "Did Edith go with you?"

"No. I took Ember for a walk and ended up down there, so decided to have a look."

Peggy was quiet for a moment. "Maybe you should stay away from the shearing barn. When I went in there alone, it felt spooky. The place is so big and isolated."

"Are you thinking about the old ghost stories?" Nella teased.

"No, I'm thinking about real flesh-and-blood evil. What if the murderer has found out where you are? You need to act as if he were watching you. Don't go off alone like that."

It was all Nella could do to keep from telling Peggy about the two notes, especially since last night's intruder at Whitestone. With determination, she put on her most cheerful, innocent smile. "You sound just like The Bryan."

Peggy gave her a look of surprise and distaste.

Nella forced a chuckle. "With a little effort you could learn to glare like he does."

"Nella! How can you joke about this? You left home because you believed someone wanted to kill you. Have you changed your mind?"

Nella sobered. The stark fear that the second note had triggered struck her again. She put on a smile and tossed her head in what she hoped was a breezy manner. "Of course not. I'm on my guard all the time. It's just that I find it funny that you and The Bryan agree on something."

"You're good at acting," Peggy said, "but you're still the world's worst liar, especially with the people you love. Has something happened that you aren't telling me?"

"Of course not. We've always shared our secrets. That hasn't changed. . . ." She picked up a pebble and tossed it into the smoothly flowing stream.

"You're scared. I can see it on your face. Now, what's happened?" Peggy insisted.

"Nothing has happened . . . I'm just a bit headachy."

"You may have a headache, but I can recognize fear when I see it."

Nella relented. "Okay, I admit I'm scared. Last night a man tried to break into Garden Cottage through my bedroom window."

"Oh no! So what happened? Was he caught?"

Nella recounted the frightening incident, and before she knew it, she was telling Peggy about the two threatening notes.

When she finished, Peggy's horrified expression settled into resolve. "I'm so glad you've finally told me. Look, don't you remember all the times we've had to help each other out? I'm your partner in this. Together we'll outsmart whoever wrote those notes."

"I wanted to keep you out of it," Nella said softly, "but it's such a relief to have you know."

Peggy wrapped an arm around her shoulders. "You and I can do whatever has to be done."

Nella gulped at the lump in her throat. "It's so dangerous. I'm afraid for you."

"I think we may both be the safer, now that I know. Now that the harvesting is over, why don't you leave Whitestone? Ask for a transfer to some other farm. That way for a while the killer wouldn't know your whereabouts."

"No! I'm afraid the killer would think I was going away to set someone on his trail. I mustn't make that kind of a change. I have to keep everything the way it is and hold to this course. And it's important that no one suspects I'm scared or that I'm looking to leave Whitestone."

Peggy sat staring at the sky. Then she said, "You know, what you're going through reminds me of the Welsh bride. She also came to Whitestone to hide from an enemy. I've finished reading her diary. It's pretty inspirational. When we get back to Gatekeep, I'll give it to you to read."

"Thanks, I've been looking forward to it." Nella glanced at the sun low in the west. "I think we'd better head back now."

They mounted their bicycles and rode side by side down the quiet lane toward the village. At Gatekeep, Peggy gave Nella the leather-bound book, carefully wrapped and inside a cloth carrier, which Nella slung over her shoulder.

As Nella left, she murmured, "It's such a comfort having you know the truth. Now you be very careful."

"Aye. And you too," Peggy whispered back.

They hugged each other good-night, and then Nella began her race with the lengthening shadows. On the steep part of the hill, she pushed her bicycle upward, more aware than ever that because of her lack of foresight, she was alone again in the woods at sunset. When she was nearly out of the woods, she heard footsteps crunching through the leaves. It took all her self-control to halt and look around. Just as she thought she'd heard an animal, she saw the shape of the man—the same small man she'd spied in the woods up by the chapel. He was half hidden and far enough away that she could run up toward Whitestone rather than back through the woods. She dropped her bicycle and ran.

CHAPTER TWENTY-TWO

As Nella raced up the gravel drive toward the front of the mansion, the sun was almost set. She started up the steps to bang on the heavy door of the main entrance.

Then Bryan came out of the stable and hailed her. She spun around and rushed down the slope to him and gasped out what she'd seen.

"I'll go have a look," he said and hurried back into the stable. In a few moments he appeared again, this time sitting bareback on his horse. "Go to Garden Cottage," he ordered, "and don't come out. Tell the rest of the girls to stay indoors too, until I return." He kicked the horse into a run.

At the cottage mentioning a stalker set the other women in such turmoil that they all talked at once.

"Did you get a good look at him?"

"Did he look like the intruder?"

"Did he come after you?"

Nella tried to answer each one. "I left my bicycle and ran and didn't look back. But I think he looked the same build as the man at our window."

"Downright scary, this is," Dora said. "It freezes my blood to think of going out in the dark for morning chores."

They paced the floor and peeked out the window as they waited for Bryan to return.

Finally, the servant girl, Ruth, came trotting from the big house and knocked on the door. When they opened, she said, "Master Bryan, he rang up from down in the village and said to stay inside. He's called the constable again. Constable Burns, he'll be sending a man to look about and keep watch tonight." She looked around nervously. "And me, I'm going right back inside too." She turned and sprinted back to the mansion.

Nella sighed. "So here we are, prisoners again. I just hate this." She wondered if the intruder was after only her.

Next morning everyone went about the chores as usual, but Bryan and the constable's man hung about and kept an eye out.

After Nella finished in the barn, she headed for the kitchen with Dora and met Bryan coming from the house.

"Nella, hold up a minute. I want to talk to you," he said.

Dora took the hint and walked on to breakfast.

"You feel all right this morning?"

"Yes, fine."

"Last night just before you came home, I was about to send someone looking for you."

"Why should you do that?"

"That nasty bump on your head. The doctor said you should be quiet and resting."

"That was two days ago. I'm all right now."

Suddenly right there in plain sight of anyone in the mansion or the outbuildings, he reached out and took her hand. With his other hand he gently folded her fingers over, forming a handclasp between them.

His strong, warm hand stirred feelings she didn't welcome, like wanting him to take her in his arms. She tried to free her hand but didn't want to make a scene.

Then he let go of her and said softly, "Nella, please don't be so careless. Surely you must see that my cautions are justified. Don't go off alone until we catch the man who tried to break into the cottage. Ruth told me you were up in the woods and saw someone there too. You should have told me. I'm beginning to wonder if someone is specifically after you."

"And why would that be?" she countered swiftly. He mustn't get the constable stirred up about her, not now.

"Some deranged person might be attracted to your natural beauty."

"That's nonsense!"

"Nevertheless, you must never wander out alone."

"How do I get my work done or go to the village?"

"I'll have everyone work by twos. As far as going to the village, don't right now. Not until the man has been caught."

"All right. I just hope that's soon."

"Good." He stood smiling down at her. She thought he might touch her again, but he didn't. Stepping back, he said, "I've a bit more to do in the stable. Go on in and have your breakfast. I'll be along soon to give out the work orders." With that, Bryan turned and walked away.

Nella felt conspicuous standing there by herself on the gravel drive. No doubt Shirley was somewhere watching, and she was in no mood to listen to Shirley right now. In a confusion of emotion, Nella made herself move toward the kitchen.

Bryan organized work teams of two. The way he stated it, no one could imagine he thought maybe someone was after only Nella. The day went smoothly, and after evening chores, Nella gratefully retired to the bedroom to read and take her mind off stalkers and murderers. She carried the Welsh bride's diary to the writing desk and opened it. Hopefully the book would distract her from her own problems, at least for a few minutes. She longed to forget having to act a part; she longed to forget how easily Bryan Westmoreland had awakened a desire to be in a man's arms.

Edith, Dora, and the other girls were getting ready for bed. Edith asked, "How's the head feel, Nella?"

"It's still sore but on the mend now." It occurred to Nella that she might have said the same thing about her heart. Why else would she have wanted Bryan to hold her? She silently chastised herself for letting physical attraction confuse her. Her body had simply betrayed her. She could never love someone like Bryan Westmoreland.

"I hope you don't mind if I read a bit before I go to bed," she said to Edith.

"Not at all."

She unwrapped and opened the diary. As Peggy had remarked, the girl was a devout Christian. The first page she turned to began with a prayer.

15 April, in the year of our Lord, 1403

    O Christ, Thou who knoweth the hearts of men, protect me through the night. Please send angels to watch-care over me. For I am not wise in the ways of the world or the ways of the English. I need Thee now more than ever. Amen. Gwenyth of Nantyllaithdy.

Nella read on to discover that Gwenyth had just fallen in love with William, the eldest son of Lord William Hastings Westmoreland. She was frightened, for William loved her and their two nations were at war. The chieftains of Wales had rallied around Owain Glyndwr, who led them against the English to found a sovereign Welsh state. Owain was Gwenyth's father's cousin, as was a man called Rowan. Gwenyth feared that Rowan would kill William if he learned of their love, because Rowan, a violent man, was determined to marry her himself. Terrified, she hid at Whitestone.

> *If any of Glyndwr's men learn my whereabouts, I am lost, and so will be my beloved. O dear Lord God! Thou hast taken my father to be with Thee. Now Thou art my only Father. Save us from Rowan. Thou art our only hope....*

Peggy was right. Nella identified immediately with this girl's fear and with the fact that they both had fled to Whitestone seeking safety. Their big difference was that Nella still had her earthly father, who couldn't protect her. And she had lost touch with the heavenly Father....

"I say, Nella, when are you going to turn out the light? Morning's coming fast," Dora complained.

"Oh, sorry!" Nella switched off the light. Gwenyth's diary had gripped her. She hated to put it down.

Lying in the dark, Nella tried to remember how Gwenyth looked in the oil painting she'd seen hanging in the Whitestone library. The girl's desperate prayer to be saved from Rowan could as well have been her own, except that Gwenyth knew her enemy, and she did not. *But whether I feel like it or not, I do have the same heavenly Father, even though He seems a million miles away.* Spontaneous prayer didn't come easily, so she silently prayed the prayer Jesus taught his disciples. *Our Father which art in heaven, hallowed be thy name. Thy kingdom come. Thy will... be done in earth, as it is in heaven....* When she finished, she felt no peace or comfort but decided the prayer was a beginning, an act of obedience insofar as she could give it.

The next day after lunch a cool wind was rising, so Nella stopped in at Garden Cottage to get her cap before going to the field. The cottage was empty. Curious about the latest news, she took a moment to switch on the wireless.

The timing was just right. A BBC announcer reported: "...U.S. First Division has entered Aachen and is engaged in bitter street fighting. Today the Germans turned their V–1 and V–2 rockets on Antwerp. In Italy our British 46th Division has taken Carpeneta; however, the fighting continues south of Bologna. On the Eastern Front, the Russians have broken through the defenses around Riga. . . ." The announcer continued, giving details of the battle in Greece, where British and Greek forces had landed near Piraeus. The newsman signed off, and then strains of "The White Cliffs of Dover" came on.

Nella turned the knob to Off. Would it never end? Some Germans had tried to kill Hitler, yet he went on and on. Maybe the war wouldn't end because of his death, but she couldn't help but feel it might.

Since Nella was alone, she decided to steal a few quiet minutes. Gwenyth's book on her bedside table drew her. She picked it up and opened to her bookmark. Contrary to the old style poetry she'd read in school, Gwenyth's verses were unrhymed, maybe because of the translation.

> *In The Beginning*
> *Baby*
> *Flesh of our flesh,*
> *Bone of our bone,*
> *But separate, thou art*
> *On heaven's loom.*
> *Still face to face*
> *With thy Weaver,*
> *Sing Him a song*
> *Of praise for me.*
> *By Gwenyth Westmoreland, 19 March 1404*

The words, written so long ago, captivated Nella. She read on, stirred by the young woman's awe while expecting her first child. With every word Nella remembered her own joy when she anticipated the arrival of Livie. The miracle of Rob's love and their baby growing within her had made every day seem like heaven. The more the baby grew in her womb, the further the war receded. All that mattered was Rob and the baby.

Nella read the poem over again. Tears blinded her. Gwenyth had died. Rob had died. So many now were dying. So much for any heaven on earth, she thought, and closed the book. While she dried her eyes, she wondered how Gwenyth, a person of such bright happiness and faith, could have fallen into despair and killed herself as some of the family had said. It seemed more likely that her death had been an accident ... or murder.

Laughing voices announced the arrival of the other girls. Nella slipped Gwenyth's diary back into its wrapping and laid it in her clothing drawer. She went out to meet her working partner. Edith was going to work on hedgerows, while she drove tractor in the same field.

That afternoon as Nella prepared the field for winter, her thoughts returned to the Welsh bride's writings and the girl's faith, strong in the face of danger. She wished that she could visit the girl's grave sometime. Since Bryan had loaned Peggy and her the book, he might be willing to take her there. From the little she'd read of the diary, she felt a kinship with Gwenyth, who also had endured tremendous fear.

Peggy was glad for the time and effort she'd put into the harvest festival. The brief festivities seemed to have created a lasting positive effect on her pupils. They had settled down in the classroom quickly and kept their minds on their work.

Now at the end of the day, they lined up at the door to leave without much scuffling. Standing beside the door, she smiled down the quieting line. Although they came from a mix of backgrounds, they were beginning to accept one another's differences. Each year she strived to guide her classes toward feeling like a caring family. Usually she succeeded. Getting the village boys to accept Peter, who came from a landed family, was her big challenge this year. Right now his mother waited for him in her car. He was the only pupil whose parents owned a car. Happily, some of the boys had made Peter their friend.

Three of them whispered with him, most likely planning something that Peter's mother wouldn't allow.

"Please do not run as you leave," Peggy announced and opened the door.

As they marched past her, most gave her a respectful "Good-bye, Miss Jones."

After acknowledging each farewell, she watched them to the road. Out there the scuffling broke loose, but as far as she could tell it was all done in goodwill.

She noticed Annie, with papers in her hand, following Peter to his mother's car. As usual, Mrs. Hilliard, who looked glamorous despite the privations of war, made Peggy feel uncomfortable. She watched uneasily as Peter addressed his mother and then signed to Annie. She could see Mrs. Hilliard motion impatiently with her hand. Peter wasn't looking at his mother or at Annie, but had frozen as if a statue with his head down.

Peter's two buddies paused nearby. Several girls stopped and looked back at Mrs. Hilliard with startled frowns. Annie's sisters arrived and stood beside her.

What was going on? Not caring what Mrs. Hilliard might think, Peggy went out to see. As she approached the car, the woman's voice cut through the chatter and the shouts of other children heading for their homes. ". . . and I can't imagine what's come over you, Peter, to even think of entertaining a friendship with a . . . an evacuee. As for her, no matter where she came from, she ought to know enough to say no to such an invitation!"

Annie's sister Emma said, "Ma'am, she can't hear you, and I hope she can't read your lips!" She pulled at Annie's arm, but Annie resisted, watching Mrs. Hilliard with the intense gaze of a deaf person, trying not to miss anything.

Mrs. Hilliard's expression grew angrier.

Peggy rushed forward and came to a halt between Peter and Annie. "I beg your pardon, Mrs. Hilliard, but—"

The woman's dark eyes stabbed her direction. "Miss Jones, I've been against Peter attending a public school from the beginning, and this proves me right. But I had assumed you would at least include some basic instruction on social skills."

Peggy's temper flared. "Madam, these children surpass your social skills by so far you can't look high enough to see them. They've learned that before God there are no commoners. They've learned to be kind. Now I'll thank you to leave this school yard!" She put her arm around Annie's thin shoulders and drew her close. She wanted to do the same for Peter but knew better than to embarrass him before his friends or aggravate his vicious mother any further.

Mrs. Hilliard's beautiful face twisted in contempt. "You will regret this impertinence!" She reached for the ignition key. "Get in the car, Peter!"

Instead, Peter bolted, running full tilt down the road and into a side lane. His friends charged after him. Mrs. Hilliard raced the car engine, backed up and turned around until she faced the direction he had fled, then roared after him.

Peggy hugged Annie close. "Come back inside with me," she said to Emma and Frances. She signed to Annie. To the other girls who had remained transfixed by the scene, she said gently, "Go along home, girls. We'll talk about this tomorrow."

Annie walked stiffly at her side until the classroom door closed behind them. Then she burst into broken sobs. She obviously had understood Mrs. Hilliard's meaning, if not the words. Emma's face flushed with anger, but Frances cried with Annie.

Peggy held Annie close again, her own heart breaking that this sensitive, gifted child should suffer such abuse. She was so enraged, she wanted to attack and pound that woman into the ground. Thinking back, she was glad none of the other teachers had been outside yet. Some of them might've agreed with Peter's mother. Worse yet, she might not have had the nerve to order the woman off the school grounds.

Finally Annie stopped sobbing, and Frances quieted.

Peggy signed, *"Come and sit with me for a few minutes."* To Emma and Frances she said, "You don't want to walk home so upset."

Annie sniffed and nodded.

Peggy guided them to the chairs at the craft table and sat on one herself. Leaning forward, she said, "Frances, can you tell me what happened? What did Peter say that made his mother so angry?"

"He only asked her if Annie could come to dinner at their house, so she could see some of the paintings they have—"

Annie signed frantically, *"I didn't know . . . wrong! Peter, nice to me. I thought his mum . . . nice . . ."* Her mouth trembled, and, dropping her face to her hands, she wept again.

Peggy patted her shoulder, feeling that Annie's pain was partly her fault. Mrs. Hilliard had been right about one thing. She hadn't taught the children traditional "manners." She'd failed to prepare them—as her mother had failed to prepare her—for this sort of thing. She figured their parents had done enough of that.

When Annie quieted down, Peggy said and signed, "I'm so sorry. I know you feel very hurt, but that unkind woman isn't worth a tear! I told her the truth. Before God there's no such thing as gentry or commoner. It may take a long time, but I believe this evil in our country will disappear, and we shall all be the better for it. You girls may be some of the very people to help build a new way."

Annie rubbed her eyes but looked doubtful. So did her sisters.

Peggy handed her a handkerchief. *"When I was very young, someone treated me like Mrs. Hilliard treated Annie today."*

"They did?" Emma gasped in surprise.

Annie watched intently as Peggy spoke and signed the best she could. She told them about the time in Blaenavon, about how terrified she'd been, and how ugly she'd felt when the strange man shook her and called her names. *"It took me a long time, but I finally decided some good came out of that. Little as I was, it made me decide to make something of myself. Annie, I hope you will try to forget Mrs. Hilliard's meanness and concentrate on being your own sweet, beautiful self. No one can make you a less worthy person unless you believe their mean words. And as I said to Mrs. Hilliard, God didn't make commoners and gentry."*

The red spots were fading from Annie's cheeks, leaving her face pale and tense looking. She signed, *"I can't imagine anyone talking to you . . . the way she talked to me."*

"Well, I never imagined Mrs. Hilliard would do what she did today. There's no accounting for the likes of such people."

"Poor Peter," Frances said in a tight voice. "What will she do to him?"

"Yes. Poor Peter. Say a little prayer for him. He'll be needing it," Peggy said.

Annie's eyes flashed from one to the other of them. Then she glanced at the clock on the wall. *"Time to go home,"* she signed.

"Yes." Peggy stood up and walked to the door with them. "Emma, it might be best not to tell your mother what happened until I can talk with her. . . ." Suddenly she realized other children may have told their parents already, and Mrs. Nelson may know. "If she's heard about it from someone else, tell her I'll be along soon to explain."

Peggy watched Annie as she walked down the street between her sisters, looking somehow smaller than when she came to school that morning. Her chin was down, and her arms hung rigid against her sides. If only Peggy's words could have eased the child's pain. She was still so angry she couldn't think of adequate words to express her outrage. She hoped the bitter woman wouldn't influence Laurie against helping Annie with her art. He hadn't come back yet from London. It would probably be to Annie's advantage if he didn't return until Mrs. Hilliard had time to calm down, if that was possible.

She sat down at her desk and tried to compose herself, but the scene with Mrs. Hilliard played over and over in her mind. She thought about what she'd said to Annie, Emma, and Frances in the classroom. Then she saw herself in a new and unpleasant light. She had put great effort into teaching the children that God hadn't created commoners or gentry, that one must be kind to all people. Yet when had she ever entertained kind thoughts toward the gentry?

She never thought about Laurie's father being a child of God. Theoretically she always knew he was, but it was like thinking of Hitler as a child of God. Near to impossible. Laurie's father and her own mother had taught her to fear and to despise the gentry. Now she was a hypocrite, teaching the children one thing and she herself doing the opposite. She knew now what Nella had meant when she said she couldn't make herself believe. Peggy could not make herself think kindly toward those people of the gentry.

Slowly she gathered her students' papers to bring home, straightened her desk, and walked down the lane toward Brookside. In her present state, she wasn't sure how she would explain things to Mrs. Nelson.

CHAPTER TWENTY-THREE

Peggy rang up Whitestone during what she guessed was the supper hour and asked to speak to Nella. She desperately needed to talk to the one person who would understand her turmoil. The girl servant answered, and finally Nella's voice came on.

"Hello. Peggy?"

"Nella. I'm so glad I caught you. I . . . I had a bad day at school." She told Nella about the set-to with Mrs. Hilliard. "I'm sure Lady W. will hear all about this, and I can guess what she may do."

"Oh, Peggy, you did the right thing. How could a grown woman treat a little girl, and her being deaf, like that?"

"I'm afraid that being deaf and dumb made Annie subhuman in m'lady's estimation. Some people think because a person can't hear and speak, that they must be slow too. And if they're slow, they must be depraved."

"How awful! But it's true I didn't know what to expect when I met Albert—I mean, about how much he could understand. If I hadn't known about Annie and how bright she is, I may have thought he was simple."

"Aye. Well, it's an easy mistake. But even if he were, you'd not think the less of him. Mrs. Hilliard is just plain mean and self-centered. Thanks for listening to me rant. I needed a sympathetic ear. I tried not to let go in front of Annie's mother or Mrs. Lewis. I think it nearly broke Mrs. Nelson's heart to hear what happened. She brought Annie here to protect her, and now she's been so hurt."

"Is there anything I can do for Mrs. Nelson or her girls?"

"I don't think so. I wondered about asking Father Mac to come out and talk to them, and then I thought maybe I should leave that decision to Mrs. Nelson. I'll try to think of something to bring back Annie's happy spirit."

"Surely the other teachers at school can help, especially those who had her for her earlier classes."

"I hope so. I'm not sure where they may stand on the way I treated Mrs. Hilliard. I do try to avoid conflict, but that woman was so abusive. . . . Oh, Nella, do you think we'll ever break away from this class system that has held back children for so long?"

"I think we will, but it will take a long time."

"Aye. But enough of my complaints. What about you? How are you doing, if you can say?"

"After I left you Sunday night, I had another scare."

To Peggy's horror, Nella said a man had stalked her in the woods, the constable had left a man to keep watch, and Bryan ordered the women to work in pairs.

"What a terrible thing!" Peggy cried. "Here I went on about my troubles and someone was after you. Do you think . . . he could be the murderer?"

"I just don't know."

"I'm so frightened for you. I wish you could stay here with me."

"Even if I could, how would that help? At least Bryan is trying to provide protection here."

"Nella, you have to admit he hasn't been inclined to be so helpful in the past. Do you suppose he's taking an interest in you?"

"He's looking out for all the women here."

"You're sounding a bit defensive."

"Look, he's unpredictable, but he takes the responsibility of our safety seriously. A few times he's acted as if he were personally concerned about me, but basically he treats all of us Land Girls alike. Being thoughtful isn't totally out of character. He was tender with Livie at the festival and respectful and caring toward Albert, the deaf-mute man. Bryan has his faults, but maybe no worse than the rest of us."

"You can't go too much by that, Nella. I've read that Adolf Hitler loves children and is very kind to them. And look what he spawned. Look at Giselle's experience in France and how the Nazis treated the Jewish children."

"Aye, talking to Giselle made me realize we've got to win this war, not just for the British Empire, but for the whole world. That's what Rob believed too."

Peggy recognized an old trick of Nella's. She used to evade anything she didn't want to talk about by pulling the conversation off into a different subject. "Let's get back to the problem at hand. How can Bryan guarantee your safety?"

"I'm not sure, but I believe him when he says he can. Please trust my judgment about this, Peggy."

"Are you falling for this guy?" The minute the words were out, she knew she'd made a mistake.

"No!" Nella spat out. "Never!"

She sounded too angry, considering the circumstances. So Peggy quickly dropped the subject. "Forgive me, please. I shouldn't have said that. I know how you treasure your memories of Rob and want the best for Livie." She didn't need to say the obvious, that certainly Bryan was *not* the best.

Nella accepted her apology and rang off with affection.

Peggy hung up the receiver and walked pensively to her room. Now she felt even more concerned for Nella. An evil man was after her, and persistent by the sound of it. On top of that, if Nella *were* attracted to Bryan, she likely would trust him sometime when she shouldn't. And he had no idea of the real danger she faced.

Peggy felt glad all over again that Nella had told the whole truth to her, hard as it was to bear. Together they would fight and win this secret war.

Following evening chores, Nella met Lord Westmoreland coming through the garden with Ember at his heels. The dog woofed and bounded to her side. Her master shook his head in mock despair. "You've stolen her affection from me. I never dreamed she'd be so disloyal."

"Ah, it's only that she has a weakness for admirers." Nella knelt and looked into Ember's amazing blue eyes. As always, she felt the gaze concealed an almost human intelligence. "She's one in a million, sir."

"I've always thought so." He leaned on the cane he was carrying. "You've done a marvelous job with her training. She's performing as well as I believed she could. If it would not be an offense to old Will, I'd have you watching the sheep instead of him."

"If ever I can help without making him feel bad, I'd love to do that, sir."

"I'll remember that. I'd have him take Ember and work her now, but he doesn't like her. He says she has evil eyes. The dog senses that and so doesn't obey him with the spirit she shows when you command her."

"One thing that some men don't like about Ember is that she thinks for herself. She's smart about figuring out things, and she does her very best if you trust her and give her a little leeway to herd her own way."

"That right? I can see how that would disconcert Will. He's always been partial to dogs that are utterly predictable. Likes to know he's in control. I admit I like that too." Bemused, he started to stroll away, then stopped and poked his cane into the soil at the base of a rosebush. "Tell me, did you ever see a sign of deer in our forest?"

"No, sir." Regardless of Peggy's warning not to trust anyone, she knew Lord Westmoreland was not a threat. Throwing caution to the heavens, she blurted, "I've wanted to go up there and really investigate, but Bryan said I shouldn't go alone. I wonder ... would you walk up there with me sometime?"

He raised an eyebrow. For a moment she thought he wasn't going to answer her audacious request. Then he smiled. "I should think that could be arranged. Are you finished with your work now?"

His quick decision caught her unawares. She stammered, "Yes ... yes, I am."

"Come along then." He gestured with his cane and set off across the garden at a pace that proved the cane was a walking stick, not a crutch.

With Ember at his side, Lord Westmoreland led Nella up the hill behind the manor and across the grassy slope. Soon they were walking the trail through the trees that she'd used when running to safety with Ruth.

He slowed. "If there should be deer, this is a good time of day to see them. Walk quietly now. Ember, heel." The dog obeyed, and so did Nella.

He marched along at a steady pace, pausing only occasionally to probe with his cane the carpet of moldering leaves alongside the path. She was warm and breathing hard by the time they reached the branch in the trail where one way led down to the shearing barn and the other up to the cemetery and mausoleum.

He halted. "It's as I thought. There's no sign of deer. But then that's no surprise. But it was worth checking," he said, obviously pleased with himself and his surroundings.

"It's lovely here. You must have enjoyed these woods when you were a boy."

He nodded and looked around with an affectionate smile. "I spent many an hour here when I was home from school."

"Did you ever wonder about your ancestors down through the generations, how it was for them?"

"Oh yes. I felt I knew them, of course, because of their portraits in the house. And then at an early age I was brought up the hill to see where they were buried. By the time I was born, the family had ceased to have worship services in the chapel, but as a schoolboy I loved to go in there and sit quietly, especially on a sunny day when the light brought the stained-glass windows to life." He turned toward her. "Would you like to see the inside of the chapel?"

"Could I?"

He nodded and said, "We're nearly there, and I'd like to go in again myself."

She and Ember followed him toward the chapel. Nella wished he'd tell her more about his childhood, but he walked on, silent and sober.

At the cemetery he paused. "There lies our family history. I suppose we ought to care for it better, but we're so short of hands now. Can't use you Land Girls for our private needs. Still, it's important to remember and respect the past. That's what makes Britain strong, you know, preserving the old ways that have served us well." Then he frowned. "You're Welsh. Maybe you find English traditions offensive."

"No. I'm British at heart. Actually, my father and mother are of Scottish descent."

He didn't respond to that. Instead, he said, "You've heard of the Welsh bride—the one who is supposed to haunt the mansion and who has been seen up here from time to time?"

"Yes, but I don't believe in ghosts, sir."

"Good. I thought you'd have your head on straight."

"Actually, I would like very much to see where the Welsh bride was buried, if I might. Bryan is letting me read her diary, and I've come to feel I almost know her."

He looked at her with a frown. She thought he was angry until he spoke in his usual cool, courteous tone. "So you're reading the diary. Well, I can't show you where they buried her. Back in those days, suicide was considered a mortal sin, and her body wasn't allowed in the family cemetery. My ancestor, the aunt of long ago who had her poems translated and made into a book, placed a memorial plaque for her in the old mausoleum. But no one knows where her body was buried."

"How sad!" Nella exclaimed, not stopping to think whether or not he was in agreement with the attitude of his forebears.

In a noncommittal tone, he grunted and then said, "Well, come along. I'll show you the chapel and the plaque too, since you're interested."

He marched on to the chapel. Beside the door he pulled back overhanging branches, lifted a stone from a space in the stone framing, and removed a large iron key. When he turned it in the lock, it moved smoothly. Dropping the key into his jacket pocket, he opened the heavy oak door. Inside, though the sun was low in the west and not reaching the windows with direct light, the tall windows glowed with color. Nella stepped in behind him. The air was cold but not as dank as might be expected in a long-closed building. She guessed Lord Westmoreland still made pilgrimages here.

He waved his hand in an encompassing gesture and became a tour guide. "On the left you see Moses and Elijah and King David. Up front are all the apostles, of course, and the Christ with his mother, Mary. On the right there's Jesus walking on water, healing a blind man, raising Lazarus from the grave. In the Lazarus window, you see the second Lord Westmoreland in the foreground, watching this miracle of the Lord."

"It's all beautiful, sir. What a treasure to have in your family."

"Yes. I think it is, though I may be the last Westmoreland to appreciate it."

She wanted to ask if Bryan cared about it, but the closed look on his face forbade her. Sensing he didn't want reassuring remarks, she kept quiet. It was a place where silence was comfortable. She wished she could stay awhile, but already he was moving toward the door.

Nella waited outside while he locked up and put the key back in its niche, apparently unconcerned that she now knew its hiding place.

Without comment he led her back to the cemetery. The small mausoleum, probably holding no more than a half dozen crypts, had a stone façade that appeared rough with age and black from the lichen. She waited eagerly as he opened a small door in the stone wall.

This time he muttered, "Now who hasn't replaced the key?" He stirred the rotted leaves below with the tip of his cane. Then, just to be sure, he tried the latch without the key. "It's locked, all right. I'll have to ask Bryan about this. I hope Albert hasn't been here and carried off the key. It's difficult to tell whether the man is simple or not.

Have you met the deaf-mute who lives over the hill?"

"Yes. Down by the shearing barn Sunday afternoon, I almost walked right into him." She saw again that the step into the mausoleum was brushed clean. Lord Westmoreland appeared not to notice. Maybe he came here often.

"Well, big as Albert is, he's harmless. But it's just as well the Land Girls are afraid to come up here because of the ghost story. Now that you've been here, I suggest you don't come back alone. One never knows . . ."

"Yes, sir. So Albert lives just over this hill?"

"That's right. In our old woodcutter's cottage. I wasn't eager to let it to him and his mother, but Bryan vouched for them. Seems he knew of them from some school friend. It's true they've been no problem. They pay their lease on time, and we seldom see either of them."

He led Nella back down the hill, not bothering to talk anymore. She felt disappointed over not getting to see Gwenyth's memorial plaque. She told herself it didn't matter, but the nagging desire to get into the mausoleum stayed with her. Maybe she could come again when the key turned up.

———— ✦ ————

That night Nella read another of Gwenyth's poems before she went to bed. By this time the others knew about the diary, and several of the women had read a bit and then laid it aside. The Welsh bride didn't interest them beyond the possibility that she was a ghostly presence on the estate.

Nella savored each poem, reading many of them again and again. She decided to copy her favorites into her own journal before returning the book to the Westmoreland library. Then Em, the only professional writer she knew, could read them someday.

Tonight she turned to a poem titled "William."

> My people call you enemy—
> I call you friend.
> They wish you dead—
> I live for your embrace.
> On their lips your name's a curse—
> I lawfully wear it with joy.
> And yet I live in sin
> From loving you too much.
> "Thou shalt have no other gods

Before Me!" the Lord God said.
My forbidden love,
Whereto can we flee?

Nella placed the book back in her drawer. For the first time she felt at odds with the young poet. Her love for Rob had blossomed so joyfully, partly because she knew when she first met him that her mother and father would accept and love him. And they did. He'd been like family even before they married. How would it feel to be entwined in a forbidden love? She couldn't even guess.

CHAPTER TWENTY-FOUR

Neither Peter nor Annie was at school the next morning. Peggy suspected that Peter's mother had persuaded his grandmother that the boy belonged in a private school, war or not, money shortage or not. Yet from what Peggy had seen, the old lady could hold her own with a determined daughter-in-law if she wished. The question was what did she want? Peggy knew that underneath the elder Mrs. Hilliard's friendly exterior traditions held sway.

When the children asked about Peter and Annie, Peggy reassured them that all was well and they'd be back in class soon. Peter's mother merely had a misunderstanding with Peter. They accepted her brief explanation, but those who had been standing close enough to hear Mrs. Hilliard wore troubled expressions.

She'd always been honest with her pupils, so now they must be wondering. "Boys and girls, about what happened after school yesterday, I should've said that I don't know if Peter will be back. His mother was very angry with me. As for Annie, I'm sure she's fine at home with her mother. When she—and Peter—do return, we must be sure to welcome them but not ask questions. If they want to talk about it, they will in their own time. Otherwise, what happened is over and best forgotten. Will you help them that way?"

The room echoed with yes, righto, and aye.

"Good!" she said. "Now let's get to the spelling list. Who can spell 'informative' and use it in a sentence for me?"

A hand went up, and the day's work proceeded, but Peggy had a difficult time keeping her mind off Annie and Peter.

At last the school day ended. The class filed out of the building, and just as Peggy was about to close the door, the Hilliard family car drove up and parked at the edge of the school yard. Peggy got ready to do battle, but then Laurie stepped out, alone.

She swung the door open again and waited to see what his face would reveal. Was he an emissary of bad news or good?

He smiled and walked toward her with a little less limp, she thought. Was his lameness then something that would heal? No one had ever told her, and she certainly wouldn't ask.

"Hello," he said easily. His eyes smiled as well as his mouth. Thin as he was, he still was very handsome. She wished he weren't. She didn't want to think about him that way. For that matter, she didn't want to think of any man that way. She planned to give herself fully to art school and to painting, once the war was over.

"Hello," she answered. "Please come in."

He chuckled. "I'm surprised. I thought because of everything that happened with my cousin, you might feel the same about the whole family."

Did this mean he wasn't going to let her treatment of Peter's mother stand in the way of helping Annie? She shook her head, smiled, and led him inside. "Please sit and tell me if your art friend in London had a chance to see Annie's painting."

He sat but wasn't ready to discuss his trip to London. "Adrienne is still fuming. I think I should warn you that she'll do whatever she can to have you removed from West-Holding School."

"Well, then, that makes two of them."

"Two?"

"Lady Westmoreland. The difference is she's in a position to do something about it."

"Miss Jones . . . may I please call you Peggy? I'd like to be friends."

She'd heard that before from the likes of him, but in a flash she knew he really meant it—even if he didn't live up to the kind of friendship that first names implied. And after all, she needed a friend among the gentry. "I'd like that," she finally replied.

He grinned. "Splendid. That being taken care of, I want to assure you that I'm on your side. I know how vicious Adrienne's mouth can be. I regretted it when my cousin Chester married her, and she hasn't improved with age. I don't doubt a bit you were justified. Furthermore, Peter privately told me what happened. Poor boy. His father can't be here to stand up for him, and I suspect his mother may prevail and get him sent to a private school."

"I'm sorry. He's doing very well here and has made good friends."

Laurie nodded. "So he says. He thinks highly of you. I must say I'm glad. Because of being separated from his mother so much, he slavishly worships her. It hurts now, but seeing her true colors may be his salvation. I had to go through the same with my father. A shock can be for the good if it comes from understanding the truth. . . ."

She wanted to ask how it had been good for him, but instead she nodded and said nothing.

He went on. "Now, about my trip to London. I showed little Annie's painting to my friend, and he took them to another friend, and . . ." He stopped, gave her a sober look, and cleared his throat. "I'm afraid I have bad news."

Peggy's heart sank. "They don't think she has talent?"

"They both agree that the painting shows incredible talent, but they don't believe a child could have done it."

"But . . . then why do they think I sent it?"

He sighed and cleared his throat again. "They proposed that you had done the painting yourself in an effort to help Annie."

"That's insane! Would any of them consider coming here to meet Annie and see her in the process of painting?"

"I suggested that, but they dismissed the whole idea. I think the fact that the Art Institute is closed for the duration makes them less receptive. Maybe after the war . . ."

"You said they thought I did it. Do you mean Annie's teacher did it, or do they know my name?"

"I told them your name and that you had been offered a scholarship yourself. That was my way of getting them to look at Annie's painting."

"And they believe I would cheat like that! My reputation with them is destroyed unless they come and see Annie for themselves."

"If that's a problem, your integrity will be reestablished. After the war I'll plague them to come and meet Annie and talk with her."

"Laurie," Peggy said slowly, "did Peter tell you Annie is deaf and can't speak yet?"

His mouth fell open. "No. No, he didn't. And Adrienne . . . what a rotten thing for her to do. But why didn't Peter tell me?"

"Maybe he thinks it's not important," Peggy mused. "You know, he is a remarkable boy." For the first time since her confrontation with Mrs. Hilliard, Peggy felt at peace inside. Peter hadn't been so accepting of differences at the beginning of the school term. Her efforts at making the classroom into a kind of family must've led Peter to take on this rightful attitude. Now if only Annie's pain could be healed, she wouldn't worry so much if she did lose her position. She stood up. "Thank you for telling me this, and thanks for trying to help Annie."

He rose to his feet, towering over her. "Your happiness is thanks enough," he said. "You're a fine teacher, Peggy." Suddenly he bent and kissed her lightly on the lips. Then he left without looking back.

Pressing her fingers against her lips, she stared after him in shock. She should be angry with him for taking advantage of her moment of gratitude, but she wasn't. She hurried to the window in time to see the car pull away. Laurie didn't look back. Maybe he was as sorry for his impulsiveness as she was pleasured. That probably would be a good thing, but she hoped he wasn't regretful.

She walked slowly back to her desk and sat down. Laurie didn't fit her image of the gentry at all. Why was she so surprised to find he was a thoughtful and humble man? Once again, she had to face her own prejudice. She'd worked hard and evidently had succeeded in helping the children to accept one another. How had she remained so blind to her own prejudice?

Peggy thought back to the day in the manse when she had confessed her faith in Christ to Father Mac. Back then for a long while she loved everyone indiscriminately. Then Charles's highborn school friend, Joseph Winthrop, had pursued her, and after winning her heart, he'd dropped her unceremoniously for a girl of his own social class. At fourteen she thought she'd never get over it. Now she couldn't even remember how Joseph looked. But she remembered the pain, the same feeling of uncleanness as when she was five years old.

When Laurie kissed her, she hadn't wanted to run away. She hoped this was a good sign. She wanted to practice what she preached to her students, but having to deal with someone like Adrienne Hilliard made old feelings die hard.

Suddenly aware of the time, she gathered up papers and closed up the classroom. She headed for Brookside to see how Annie was faring.

Annie's sister Emma answered the door. Right behind her came Miss Blackwell and Mrs. Nelson.

"Hello, Emma ... Miss Blackwell, Mrs. Nelson. I was concerned about Annie. I hope she's not ill...."

"She went out to the meadow a while ago," Emma said. "She's been sad all day."

"Emma, take Frances and go tell Annie that Miss Jones is here," Mrs. Nelson said.

"Tell her I'm making splits and jam for tea," Miss Blackwell added.

Emma and Frances left, arguing about who would get to tell Annie that her teacher had come.

Peggy smiled and followed the two older women to the kitchen. "The girls do watch out for Annie and for each other, don't they?"

"Yes, but Annie's the little mother when they're all together, even though she's disabled," Mrs. Nelson said.

"I think they all take after you," Peggy said. "You've done marvelously for them, especially regarding Annie."

Miss Blackwell set the water to boil and placed the splits and jam on a lovely china platter. She said, "That is so. She's a wonder with Annie, and the young ones never feel left out either."

"Thank you, but I just love them all, and they know it," Mrs. Nelson said. "It was their father who gave them the good start, and we still miss him." Mr. Nelson had died in the blitz soon after his family had come to West-Holding. This was one reason Mrs. Nelson had chosen to stay on. Now she put on a smile and asked, "May I take the cups to the table?"

Miss Blackwell nodded. "These are the girls' favorites, the ones with yellow and blue primroses."

The girls' mother set the cups on the nearby table.

"Tell me, how is Annie?" Peggy asked. "Have you been able to help her feel better?"

Mrs. Nelson's forehead puckered with concern. "I did what I could, but you know this sort of thing leaves a lasting impression."

Miss Blackwell nodded. "She did well and even tried to help Annie be sorry for people like that Hilliard woman. But it was all I could do to keep from walking out to the Hilliard Estate and giving her a raking up one side and down the other. Never in my day would a mother talk that way to a child. Say what you may about the high and mighty landlords of the old days, still most took care not to hurt children, even their servants' and tenants' children. I don't know what has happened to simple decency."

Peggy had no answer to this, since she had no respect for the way things used to be any more than for the way things were now. She didn't want to offend kindhearted Miss Blackwell, so she said, "I wonder what's taking the girls so long. Shouldn't they all be back here by now?" She glanced at Miss Blackwell's kitchen clock. Half an hour had passed since the girls had gone to call Annie.

Mrs. Nelson said slowly, "I should think so, unless Annie has wandered farther than her usual haunts." She stood up. "Let us go look for them. I abhor shouting, and I know the place." She put on a jacket, and they went out through the garden to a back gate that opened to the meadow.

She followed a small trail all the way to Shearing Creek, which meandered its way to the Usk River. They crossed the shallow water on boards resting on rocks, then Mrs. Nelson pointed ahead. "That thicket of trees is where Annie likes to sit and sketch. The children may have become distracted and are playing ... although it isn't like them. It's been a long time since they disobeyed in that way. They know that I worry about Annie being out here alone." She glanced at Peggy as if needing to defend her position. "She does need as much freedom as possible, you know."

"Of course," Peggy quickly answered back, yet at the moment she felt more than anxiety for Annie. Suddenly she was scared. "Do you mind if I run ahead?" she asked hesitantly, not wanting to offend or frighten Mrs. Nelson.

"Miss Jones, I would appreciate it. I'm sure you can move much faster than I."

"You just take your time or go back to the house, if you like. I'll hurry them up ... or come tell you if I don't see them right away."

"Thank you. I think I'll go back to the house in case they come home a different way."

Peggy made record time to the stand of trees. "Emma! Frances! Where are you?"

A child called from a distance. Peggy turned toward the sound. Back near the house, Miss Blackwell stood with the children. They were waving at her and their mother. But there were only two girls. They hadn't found Annie yet. With a pounding heart, Peggy started back.

When she reached the creek and Annie's bridge again, she heard a distant shout. Downstream toward the river she saw a boy, a girl, and a man. Even from a distance she recognized Annie's silver-blond hair and Peter's sturdy build. She set off at a jog, as they walked toward her.

"Miss Jones," Peter called, "Were you looking for Annie?"

She reached them before answering. "Peter, wherever have you been? Annie's mother is worried." She then signed the last to Annie.

"Annie was feeling bad so I brought her a treat, and Aimes—he's Grandmother's butler—he came along. He likes to keep me out of trouble." He grinned up at the gray-haired man who huffed along behind the children.

"It's a fact, miss," he said. "Master Peter needs an advocate now and again, so it seemed best for me to come along on his mission of mercy."

Annie watched each speaker in turn, then she held out her hand to show Peggy. From somewhere Peter had found lemon stick candy and given Annie a stick for herself and one for each of her sisters.

"That's very special, Peter. Now I have to get Annie home. Her mother is worried. Didn't you hear Emma and Frances calling for her?"

"No, ma'am."

"It's the truth," the butler said. "We must have been too far away."

Peggy made a hasty good-bye and led Annie home. She didn't try to communicate with her along the way.

As soon as they came into view of Brookside, Mrs. Nelson ran to meet them, hugged Annie, and signed to her so rapidly that Peggy couldn't follow the conversation. Annie nodded soberly. *She must be getting a good scolding,* Peggy thought.

In Brookside's kitchen they had tea together, and by the time Peggy left, Annie was laughing and teasing her sisters. Watching her, Peggy had the feeling Annie was resilient enough to surmount the hurdles that lay in her future. Somehow, someday, an art critic must see this child at work with her paintbrushes, not to clear Peggy's name but to place Annie where her skills might grow to the measure of her talent.

Later that night when Peggy was alone in her own room, she let herself think about Laurie. Now that the shock had worn off and Annie was safe and feeling better, she remembered how she'd wanted Laurie to stay, to hold her in his arms and kiss her again. Her heart bounced at the memory of his startling, gentle kiss. She'd never cared enough for a man to welcome his kiss; for to her, a kiss meant too much to be given or accepted lightly. Sometimes her distaste for casual intimacy made her wonder if God had meant for her to be married to her art. Her response to Laurie's touch blew away that theory.

Surprisingly she'd liked Laurie from the beginning, though she hadn't wanted to. Adding physical attraction to the friendship could possibly mean love. *Now what, Peggy Jones? You've knocked yourself right into heartbreak for sure.* Laurence Barringer the Fourth would never see her as a woman to love. And even if he did, they couldn't have a life together, seeing as who his father was.

She turned off the light, opened the drapes and blackout shade, and collapsed onto the upholstered chair beside her window to stare at the dark garden and the night sky. She couldn't act a part—not like Nella could—but somehow she must conceal her true feelings. For several reasons she must stay free of any attachment to Laurie—the first being she didn't want to be hurt.

CHAPTER TWENTY-FIVE

Nella made a final furrow along the field and lifted the plow blades. She waved to Edith, who was weaving saplings into a weak spot in the hedgerow, and steered the lumbering machine down the side of the field to pick her up. Edith piled her ax and nippers into the carrier boot, climbed aboard, and squatted beside the seat for the ride back to the manor.

Ember had followed them this afternoon, a sure sign that Lord Westmoreland wasn't home. Nella waved her hand at the dog, pointing to where she was going, and Ember loped ahead of the tractor until they reached the road where Nella could drive faster. She motioned Ember to stay to the back, and again the dog obeyed.

Opening the throttle, Nella began heading toward the house. But when she glanced back, Ember wasn't following. She was streaking up the hill to a wooded area. Good grief! What was she after? It wasn't like her to chase animals.

Nella turned off the engine and shouted to the dog, but she had disappeared into the trees. "I'd better go fetch her. You can stay here, if you like."

"Not on your life," Edith said. So they both climbed down and ran after the dog.

Where Ember had disappeared there was no trail. Nella called, and the dog barked in answer from somewhere off to the left. She and Edith rushed toward the dog's bark. Nella called again and listened. Then she heard running feet, which she hoped belonged to the dog. They did.

Kneeling down, Nella said, "Good girl, Ember. Now, why did you run off like that?" Ember laid her ears back in submission and then turned to peer behind her. Someone was in the woods, approaching. Nella stood up and waited.

"Who do you suppose that is?" Edith whispered.

"We'll see in a minute. At least he's not a stranger to Ember."

A giant figure appeared and came steadily on—Albert. He stopped in front of them and lifted his hand in greeting.

"Hello," Nella said, then caught herself. She copied his hand signal. "Edith, this is Albert. He can't hear us. Or have you met him before?"

"Yes, I've seen him around," Edith said.

He smiled and beckoned for them to follow.

Albert led them to a small clearing in the trees, and there on the moss lay three dead rabbits. He made gestures that indicated he had killed them, with what she couldn't see. He showed he meant to take them home to eat and offered one to them.

Nella smiled and shook her head. How could she say thanks, she wondered.

At that moment, he pointed at himself, then at her. He put his hand over his heart and bowed slightly. Maybe this was how. She copied his movements, and he smiled with childlike delight. Then he picked up his rabbits and gestured good-bye.

Nella waved back and said, "Ember, heel."

Back on the tractor, she decided to drive slower this time to force Ember to stay ahead where she could see her.

Soon they pulled up to the barn. Bryan was there and came to meet them. Nella started to tell him about Albert offering them a rabbit, but the look on his face stopped her.

"Your mother called," he said. "Your little girl is ill and wanting you. I'll drive you in."

"Oh, Nella!" Edith exclaimed and laid her hand protectively on her arm.

"What's wrong with her?" Nella asked. Her voice slipped out of control, rising higher with every word.

"A bad sore throat. When they asked if you could come, of course I said yes." He glanced at her boots and soiled overalls. "Do you want to change first?"

She shook her head. "I want to go right away if you can take me."

Edith said, "I'll tell the others. Want me to take your oilskins to the cottage?"

"Aye, please do."

"The lorry's ready." Bryan walked over and opened the door for her.

In a few seconds they were on their way down the hill to the village. Nella's stomach churned. Mum would never call unless Livie was seriously ill. She wished Bryan would go faster.

On the ride to Abergavenny, she sat braced against the seat of the lorry in a cold sweat and wondered how this return to the manse would look to her enemies. She could only pray they wouldn't know. *Please, dear God, make them blind to this,* she begged. *Keep us safe . . . please!* If anything should happen to Livie, she'd die herself. She never should have left her, even for the sake of trying to protect her. She should've looked for a way for both of them to leave Abergavenny. But where could she have gone? And it would be terrible to have Livie ill while staying with strangers.

Bryan's voice broke into her silent agonizing. "Surely she'll be all right. They've had the doctor over."

"I pray you're right! It's just that with little ones things can get serious quick, and I feel terrible for not being there with her in the first place." She bit her lip. She'd said too much.

It was too late. "Why did you decide to join up, Nella, when you so obviously would rather be with your girl?"

"Any mother hates to leave her baby, but all over Britain mothers are doing it," she hedged. "When Livie's father was killed, I vowed to do what I could to help win the war and build a better world for our child. It's been three years since his plane went down . . . but I can't forget. I had to do something."

"I see."

She knew he didn't. Even though what she said was true, her words sounded shallow to her own ears. She stared ahead at the narrow road. "Can't we go faster?"

"Sorry. I'm limited by how far these blacked-out head lamps shine."

She didn't answer and was glad he said no more.

At last they reached Abergavenny. At the manse she jumped down from the lorry and called back, "Thanks! I'll call in the morning to let you know . . . how she is." She didn't wait to hear his answer.

With her heart racing and her stomach in a queasy knot, she let herself into the front hallway. "Mum, I'm home!"

Her mother appeared at the other end of the hall and hurried to greet her. "Nella. Oh, she'll be so glad to see you." She caught Nella in a hug and held onto her longer than usual.

"What's she got, Mum? What did the doctor say?" Nella asked before pulling away.

"He's not sure yet. It's maybe her tonsils or flu. But he's ruled out scarlet fever. It's just she's so miserable, I thought you should be here."

"It's all right for me to come. Bryan was understanding. Is she awake now?"

"No. You'd hear her if she was."

"I'll go have a look." Nella went to Livie's bedside. She looked so tiny in the big bed she had graduated to when Nella moved out. Nella wanted to gather her up in her arms and rock her. Instead, she sat in the old rocking chair next to the bed and watched her. Prayer came instinctively. *O heavenly Father, please make my Livie well. I never wanted to leave her. Please make her well.*

Her mother tiptoed in with a cup of tea. Nella took it gratefully and whispered her thanks. She couldn't tear herself away from Livie's bedside, even to wash and put on clean clothes.

That night Nella slept in Livie's room, rocking her when she awoke, bathing her when the fever flared up, and coaxing her to take as many swallows of water as she could.

It took three days for the fever to disappear. Each day Bryan called. Her mother talked to him and relayed his messages. He said she was to stay as long as she felt it necessary.

Jean called daily from Govilon too. Speaking to her was the only time that Nella left Livie in her mother's care. The third day Jean asked, "Are you going to switch to part time and stay at the manse, now that your month is up?"

"I don't know. Do you think the situation has changed?" she asked, choosing her words carefully in case her mother could hear.

"Well, there's not been a peep about Rufe's lost letter. And no one has heard a word from Marge. The nurses are still wondering why she was singled out and sent to France, while the rest of her group remains in Gilwern. It's peculiar, but when I asked Uncle Al at the Embassy, he said maybe someone was able to have her transferred for her own safety."

Nella thought the battlefront was an odd place to send someone for safekeeping, but she couldn't say so with her mother within earshot. "I'll keep that in mind. I don't know how soon I can begin staying here regularly at night."

After she rang off, her mother came from Livie's room. "I'm afraid I'm coming down with whatever Livie's had."

Nella's heart sank. Her mother definitely looked flushed. "I'll call the doctor. Maybe he can stop by after lunch. You go lie down."

"I'm so sorry, dear. Surely I'll be fine after a rest."

"Yes. Don't worry. Just lie down, and let me take care of things."

The doctor's visit confirmed that Elizabeth's throat looked as bad as Livie's had. He wrote two prescriptions and handed them to Nella. "Get these filled right away, and maybe she can throw it off faster than the baby has."

Nella nodded. After the doctor left, she realized she'd have to go to the chemist's herself. Giselle was at Govilon for volunteer work at the hospital, and her father had gone to visit an elderly parishioner who was dying. She couldn't take Livie out and hated to leave her, but her mother said, "I'll take her to my room to lie down with me. At least she can't catch what I've got."

So Nella carried Livie to the other bedroom and filled a pitcher with fresh water for them.

Then she heard the front door open and close. *Ah,* she thought, *it must be Daddy, back early.* She hurried out to look. "Peggy! What a happy surprise! How did you get here?"

"Bryan brought me. It being Saturday, I figured you could use some extra hands for a couple of days."

"Oh, can I! Right now I need someone to run to the chemist's shop. Mum is ill now and needs a prescription."

"Well, give me an umbrella, and I'm on my way. But first I have some really good news for you. Bryan said to tell you they caught the intruder-stalker!"

"Are they sure?"

"Positive. She confessed."

"She?"

"One of the Land Girls, the one called Shirley."

"Shirley! What will they do to her? Will she be put in jail?"

"Bryan says that's up to you. He will prefer charges if you want. Otherwise he'll just have her sent elsewhere to work."

Nella was angry enough to want her arrested. "She ought to be locked up for what she put us through! Don't the others want her in jail, for pete's sake?"

"I guess you'll find that out when you go back to Whitestone. She's confined to quarters until you return."

"Why me? Why don't they decide?"

"Bryan says she was after you, wanting to scare you so you'd leave. She was jealous of you. She's turned sorry now, so he'll hold her for you to decide. The others think that's fair."

Nella groaned. "Well, mad as I am at her, I'm glad to know we won't all have to creep about the place, feeling like someone is about to grab us."

"You'll still need to take care, though," Peggy said quietly.

Nella sighed and nodded. "I know, but still, this is a relief."

Peggy hurried to the chemist's shop. With her head down, using her umbrella for a shield, she splashed along the familiar street.

Once inside, the medicinal odors reminded her of all the winter colds she'd ever had. Treatments apparently hadn't changed. She had no desire to linger. As soon as she had Mother Mac's medicine in hand, she walked out and decided to take a shortcut. A heavy shower struck as she darted into an old narrow alley that she and Nella had discovered one day when they were nearly late for school. The area was so cluttered with dustbins and rubbish that most people avoided going this way.

Holding her umbrella tightly, she ran down the alley and around the corner of a building and collided with a solid body. "Oh!" she cried out in shock. Her nerves made her voice sharp. Below the edge of her umbrella she saw the rain-drenched shoes and trouser legs of a man. She raised her umbrella.

"Sorry!" She exclaimed. "I didn't expect—" To her surprise, Bryan was staring back at her in shock, as were three other men hunched in the soaking downpour. The others were strangers to Peggy. One, a pudgy-looking man, peered at her through glasses so thick they magnified his eyes. Behind the bottle glass, he exhibited the forthright gaze of a child. As rain-spattered as the lenses were, she wondered how he could see anything. His graying hair dripped where it straggled from under his wet cap. The taller man stared back at her with eyes as opaque and black as a chunk of Blaenavon coal. The third was a huge, fleshy man with blue eyes. A knit cap covered his ears. He was dressed poorly, like some old hermit. His face reminded her of a codfish.

"I'm so sorry. I wasn't looking where I was going," she stammered. "I didn't expect anyone to be here. . . ."

"It's no problem at all," Bryan said briskly. "We should have realized we were blocking the way. Excuse us, please." He stepped back and gestured for her to proceed. The huge man smiled and gave her a little salute.

Flustered, Peggy hurried on without responding. Then she felt guilty. She should've acknowledged the man's greeting. But it had all happened so fast. She just did what Bryan seemed to want, which was for her to be on her way. What a strange place to be standing and talking, surrounded by dustbins and trash from stores. There was no accounting for men when they got onto something they wanted to discuss.

She hurried on to the manse and told Nella about her surprise meeting with Bryan. Nella laughed and agreed that when men got to talking, they could be worse than women about losing track of what's going on around them.

By Sunday evening Livie felt much better, and Mother Mac began to show some improvement. So Peggy returned to West-Holding, preparing herself for an inevitable meeting with Lady Westmoreland. The fact that Lady W. hadn't appeared immediately after Peggy had ordered Peter's mother to leave the school yard didn't mean she would not.

During the week that Nella remained at the manse, it rained incessantly. The last hint of summer fled, and even when the sun came out, the air remained cool. She wondered who finished the tilling she'd begun at the Westmoreland Estate. She would soon find out, for her mum insisted she could take over caring for Livie again, and Livie had become her usual cheerful self.

Bryan had ceased calling every day once Livie got better, so Nella called Whitestone to ask if he could come get her. The farm had more petrol for the lorries than her father could obtain for his old auto. Bryan agreed to come that evening.

It was dark by the time he arrived. He came in briefly to greet Nella's parents, and then Nella followed him out to the lorry. She was glad for the cover of darkness that hid her from prying eyes. She hoped that returning to the manor at night would keep her visit to the manse a secret from her enemies.

As they drove through town, Bryan commented, "Peggy gave me a shock the other day. Did she tell you she crashed into me in that alley?"

"As a matter of fact she did. She was as surprised as you, but allowed that when men get to talking they pay no attention to weather or location."

He laughed lightly. "I would say that fits women more than men."

Then in a more sober tone, he said, "She's as bad as you for dashing into lonely places."

"That alley is one of our regular shortcuts. We've never considered it a lonely place. By the time I entered school, every shopkeeper along there knew me and watched out for me. I guess that's what comes of having a gregarious father who's also a minister. And when Peggy moved to the manse, I took her all around to show off my new sister."

In the dim light Nella saw him cast a quick look her way and face the road again. "Times have changed. You're no longer a child. Would you let your daughter do what you did when you were a girl?"

She thought for a moment. "No. But then, I'm more of a worrier than my father was."

"Abergavenny is not the quiet market town it used to be." He shifted down to turn a sharp corner. "You really need to update your outlook. Young women like you and Peggy ought not to be wandering alone into solitary places." Anger edged his voice.

She stiffened. How dare he take that tone with her? He was being The Bryan again. "I know quite well how to take care of myself. So does Peggy."

He said no more. As they neared West-Holding, he broke the silence. "Did Peggy tell you Shirley confessed to trying to frighten you? That she was the stalker?"

"Yes, and I'm sorry to hear it was Shirley but glad we don't have to worry anymore."

"She wants to talk to you tonight. Her future is in your hands, you know."

"So Peggy told me."

"It would be a kindness to settle it right away. I'll bring her to the kitchen, if you aren't too tired."

"I'm not too tired."

"Good."

"Did she have anything to do with the accident in the barn?"

"She says she didn't."

"And you believe her?"

"Yes."

She turned and looked out the window at the dark landscape, and he made no effort to break the ensuing silence.

A few minutes later, they made their way up the hill to the manor, and Bryan pulled to a stop by the kitchen entrance. "I'll bring her along in a minute," he said.

Nella went inside and sat down at the long table. Mrs. Harrison and Ruth evidently had retired for the night. The great house was quiet.

Soon Bryan came in, holding Shirley by the arm.

Nella needed very little imagination to see that, if Shirley wore men's clothing, she'd look like the thin and scraggly man she had seen in the woods.

Bryan let go of her. "Go ahead, Shirley. Tell her what you told me."

"I was wanting to play a prank. I didn't mean to hurt nobody," Shirley stated, her eyes looking at the floor.

"That's not quite the whole of it," Bryan prodded.

"Well, I did mean to scare you. From the beginning I wanted to send you packing. I took it in my heart to dislike you. I wanted to scare you so bad you'd run for home. Twice I tried to make you think I was a ghost in the woods. When that didn't work, I thought to scare you right in your room." She stopped as if unable to say another word.

"Tell her the rest," Bryan said.

"I'm sorry and I won't do it again," she blurted like a child who has been thoroughly coached. "If you'll forgive me, Bryan says I can stay in the Land Army and work some other farm."

Shirley looked so trapped and utterly defeated that Nella felt sorry for her. Without effort she said, "I accept your apology, Shirley. I wouldn't want you arrested. But tell me for sure, was it you I ran from that day in the upper woods?" She had to be certain.

Shirley nodded miserably. "It was me."

Nella nodded, glad this mystery had been resolved. She wished the rest of her fears could be banished as easily.

Bryan escorted Shirley back to the dorm in the stable, and Nella headed for Garden Cottage.

The girls in the cottage were in bed already, so she undressed as quietly as she could in the dark. Morning would come all too soon, but it would be a relief to work without always needing a buddy. Much as she liked Edith, she preferred working alone.

Next morning after breakfast Nella headed for the tractor. Bryan had said to finish the field where she'd been turning new sod for wintering.

Suddenly someone hailed her. Lord Westmoreland came with Ember at his side. "You're to come with me out to the south pasture. Old Will has come down with a bad fever, and Bryan took him to hospital. You and Ember can see to the flocks until Will returns."

She wanted to ask if Bryan really wanted her to work in the distant pastures alone, but couldn't bring herself to question the lord. Anyway, Shirley had been apprehended so it seemed quite safe today.

"Do you ride?" Lord Westmoreland asked.

"A little," she replied.

"Well, come along. You can take one of the ponies. They're more to your size anyway."

The farm kept several Welsh ponies, sturdy small horses. But to horsemen like the Westmorelands, they were ponies for women and children.

He showed her how to saddle the pony and place the bit in its mouth. Mounting up, she followed him along the road to the south pasture. It took more than half an hour to reach the old sheepherder's fieldstone hut and barn. The pasture extended upward to the tree line, over the side slope, and out of sight. No farms or houses could be seen.

She thought about Bryan's warning to avoid solitary places. He must've finally admitted that there were times when the work had to be done, no matter what. She dismounted. Ember ran to greet the three dogs that lay by the gate of the sheep pen. Wooly bodies inside the fence crowded so closely to one another that the dogs could've walked across the entire large enclosure on the sheep's backs.

"You can leave the pony in that small paddock by the barn there. Then you'd best have the dogs take the sheep up the hill. They need pasture. Oh, and take the oilskins from the back of the saddle. It could rain before Bryan comes back."

Nella fumbled with unsaddling the pony and then turned her into the paddock he'd pointed out.

Lord Westmoreland stayed to watch her begin moving the sheep. Ember showed her best and took the lead, and the other dogs let her. This was unusual, but Nella thankfully accepted the ease with which they worked together. As they started up the hill, Lord Westmoreland called, "I'll have someone bring you lunch. By then we should know whether or not you need to stay the night."

Nella's mouth fell open. She didn't want to be out here alone at night. Then she quieted herself with the thought that Bryan no doubt would find some old herder to work for him if Will were too ill to come back. He had such an aversion to women being out alone.

CHAPTER TWENTY-SIX

In the meadow near the shepherd's hut, Nella turned her attention to the task of driving several hundred sheep toward good pasture. The dogs responded well to her signals. She waved good-bye to Lord Westmoreland, who sat on his horse like a general. Then she followed the flock as it moved up the hill.

The morning went by fast. Nella was starved by the time Ruth showed up with a cozy-wrapped jug of hot tea and thick cheese sandwiches.

"It's sure a long ways out here. You'll be careful, won't you?" Ruth said.

"I'll be fine now that Shirley's escapades have ended. Besides, I have the dogs. They'll watch out for me as well as for the sheep."

"Still, you're out here all alone. Don't turn an ankle or any such thing."

Nella smiled. Ever since the episode in the woods, Ruth had taken a personal interest in mothering her, which was laughable coming from one so small and probably younger. "Ruth, when the war's over, what do you plan to do?"

Ruth turned and gazed out over the hills and woods. "Me, I'd like to stay on at Whitestone. Mrs. Harrison takes to me. I'd like to see the great house come back to life with enough servants to care for the whole of it. I'm hoping I might be considered for housekeeper. That'd please me to no end."

"But don't you want to marry and have a home of your own?"

"Aye. My boyfriend, he talks about settling in South Wales. I fancy we could live in Garden Cottage, and he could be Whitestone's gardener. That'd be fine." She grinned and stood up. "Now I got to be ambling along. Mrs. Harrison will want me to help with tea. It'll be Thompkins coming out next, if you're still here."

"Tell him no need. I'll fix my own tea at Will's hut. Tell Mrs. Harrison I'll do my own supper too. For sure Will has a store of food."

"I'll tell her. Like as not Master Bryan will find someone else to watch the sheep come nightfall."

"Bye, then, and thanks for the lunch and tea."

Ruth waved and walked briskly down the grassy hillside toward the road that led back to the manor.

Nella finished her sandwich and then directed the sheep around the brow of the hill and down to a meadow where she spied a little creek that tumbled from the forest above. While the flock drank, she downed the last of her tea. Then as the sheep settled down for a rest, Nella set the dogs to watch around the perimeters of the flock. She stationed Ember on the far side, because Ember knew her best and therefore was more attentive to her hand signals.

The sun came out and looked to stay for a while, so Nella pulled off her wool jumper and sat on a hummock to soak in the unexpected warmth.

Suddenly a dog barked. Nella sprang to her feet. She saw Ember taking off away from the flock, running and barking toward a thicket. "Ember!" She whistled to turn her back, but the dog ignored her. Nella commanded the other dogs to hold the sheep in order and ran to where Ember had disappeared. She was no longer barking. Had the dog fulfilled Bryan's predictions and chased off after a rabbit or something?

At the edge of a dense growth of hazelnut shrubs, Nella stopped to listen, then called, "Ember, come!"

A plaintive whine came from straight ahead but didn't sound like a whimper of pain. Why didn't the dog obey? She called again. Still Ember whined. Slowly Nella parted the bushes and worked her way toward the whining sound. At last she reached an open area on the other side of the bushes and saw the mottled gray coat of the dog. Ember was crouched down next to some rocks. "Ember, come here!" she ordered, half-angry and half-frightened. What held the dog? She could be excitable but not openly disobedient.

Ember turned to face her and barked. When Nella came closer, she discovered why the dog hadn't come. Ember was guarding the prostrate body of a man.

Nella's breath caught in her throat. Staring at the body sprawled at the base of the rocks, she wanted to run but couldn't get her feet to respond.

Wide-eyed, she peered in all directions to make sure she was alone. Then she realized Ember would've let her know if any stranger lurked nearby. But the dog focused only on the man lying on the ground, stretching her nose toward him and sniffing. With pricked ears, she gazed up at Nella as she wagged her stump of a tail.

Nella crept forward and knelt beside the man. Was he alive? She gingerly touched the skin of his cheek and found it warm. Slipping her fingers under his coat collar, she searched for a pulse in his neck. She pressed in several places and felt no trace of a heartbeat. But then he was fleshy. Maybe she wasn't pressing hard enough, so she tried once more. His head turned slightly. He opened his eyes.

No. They hadn't opened. They were fixed and not seeing anything! The man was dead. Then she saw his glasses, thick as bottle glass, lying unbroken under his cheek.

Nella rose to her feet and glanced fearfully in all directions again. Silently she motioned with her hand for Ember to heel. She pushed her way through the bushes back toward the grazing sheep, feeling eyes boring into her back. Then something grabbed her jacket! She cried out and spun around. It was only a branch. Yanking herself free, Nella plunged ahead and escaped the thicket.

When she got back to the flock, she sent the dogs to circle the sheep and herd them near the hut. She needed a telephone, but as she approached the hut she noticed there were no wires of any sort going into it. Should she try to saddle the pony? She wasn't sure she remembered how and she certainly couldn't ride bareback. She put the sheep inside the pen. While the other dogs lay down by the sheepfold, Ember followed her to the barn, watching her every move.

Nella halted and studied the dog. Would she run for help? *It's worth a try. Ember can cover ground faster than I can on the pony,* she thought.

As she'd hoped, the door of the hut was unlocked. Inside she searched for a piece of paper. Finding an old envelope, Nella wrote on it: *Lord Westmoreland, Bryan, Please come quickly to the sheepherder's hut. Ember has found a dead man. Nella.* She located one of Will's colored handkerchiefs, made a pouch of it by knotting the corners together, and tied the pouch around Ember's neck using a bootlace from one of Will's leather boots. She adjusted the pouch so it would be immediately noticeable but wouldn't hang down for Ember to try to pull it off.

She knelt in front of the dog. "Ember, this is your chance to show your skill. Please don't let me down." She hugged the silky neck and then stood up. Pointing down the road to the manor, Nella ordered firmly, "Go home. Go find your master. Go home!"

Ember backed away and then suddenly stopped. With one forepaw raised, her blue eyes searched Nella's face.

Nella waved her hand. "Go!" She kept her arm extended, pointing to the road. Ember laid back her ears and took off running down the road.

Nella watched her disappear, praying the dog would attract the attention of someone at the manor. Now that she was gone, Nella felt utterly unprotected.

She sprinted to the barn, took the bridle from its peg, and went to call the pony. The small mare just stared at her from across the paddock and refused to come. When she approached, at least the pony didn't run nor fight accepting the bit. Nella patted and praised her mount and led her over to the barn.

But the pony didn't want anything to do with the saddle. It was difficult to see clearly inside the barn, so Nella led her out into the daylight and looped the reins around a post. She lugged the saddle and saddle blanket outside too. With the blanket in place, the pony tossed her head and pulled back as if frightened of the saddle. Nella dropped everything and reached for the reins. "Whoa!" she said. "Steady!" In the next instant little mare reared, broke free of the hitching post, and bolted.

Nella's hopes collapsed. She watched her mount disappear down the road without her and so she headed for the hut again. If no one came within an hour, she'd start walking.

Nothing could have prepared Peggy for the letter the headmistress of the school handed her after she dismissed the children. It was purportedly from the village parents but had been signed by Lady W.

Dear Miss Jones:

It has come to our attention that you have repeatedly refused to follow guidelines to which you subscribed when you first came to West-Holding School. Against specific orders to focus on basic education, you have wasted time and materials on frivolous subjects. Now we learn that you have insulted a parent and ordered her from the school property.

In view of this, we regret that we have no recourse but to dismiss you. A new teacher will take your class on Monday next. Please have your students prepared for this change and your desk cleared by Friday evening.

Lady Clementina Pryor Westmoreland, on behalf of West-Holding School parents.

Peggy crumpled the letter and threw it into the dustbin beside her desk.

Then she marched to the office of the headmistress. "Do you know what was in that letter?"

Laura Brownlee flushed. "Lady Westmoreland told me they were replacing you."

"You know what she's like. And you know how well my pupils have done in the basic tests. Did you tell her?"

"She never gave me a chance! I had no warning until this afternoon, when she told me a new teacher will be arriving Monday." Laura tapped her pencil nervously. "Peggy, there are other things you can do for the war effort. After I thought about it awhile, I felt you'd probably be happier not having to deal with Lady Westmoreland anymore. You and she have been at odds from the beginning."

"But didn't you give any thought to my pupils and how they will do with this sudden change? They . . . they're just beginning to take off and fly."

"Peggy, this is one of your problems, your penchant for trying to make school a thrilling game. The parents don't care whether their children become more excited about school than they were when they attended. That's not what they count as important. All they want are the basics. They got by, and they figure their children will too."

"So the parents were consulted about dismissing me?"

Laura couldn't meet her eyes. "I was told they were."

"Well, I'm not going to give up without a fight. It's the principle of the thing." Peggy stamped out, grabbed her coat, and marched home.

Nella found some tea in a can and set about starting a fire in the little stove of the sheepherder's hut. As she poked at it and blew, suddenly the front door flew open. She jumped up and spun around. Ember bounded in, barking and dancing around in front of her. "Oh, Ember, I told you to go home—"

Before she could say any more, a heavy boot hit the porch, and Bryan burst into the room. In the next instant he was holding her in his arms.

After the initial shock had worn off, she right away thought of Rob and wanted to push Bryan away. But then she relaxed against him, feeling strangely as if she'd come home.

He released her and peered into her face. "I was so afraid something had happened to you! Are you all right?"

"I'm fine." Her voice trembled despite her effort to sound calm. She was not all right. It should never be that she could respond so instantly to the embrace of a man she scarcely knew.

He glowered at her. "You scared the sense out of me. What does that note on Ember mean?"

"Then Ember did find you—"

"That idiot dog. You were taking a chance sending her. What's this about a dead man?"

"Ember discovered a body beyond the upper pasture. I couldn't think what to do."

"You should have left the sheep and come yourself." He turned away from her and looked out the small window toward the barn. "I told you not to go off alone. The minute my back was turned, you trot up here with my father."

"You told me I should obey him and talk to you later," she countered. "I didn't know what else to do. But how did you get here so fast?"

"I was coming to take you back to the manor where you belong. Halfway here that fool dog met me. She circled me and my horse and wouldn't stop barking. Finally I saw the kerchief you'd tied on her neck." He ran his hand through his hair, a gesture she was beginning to associate with his fits of irritation. "I guess you'd better show me the body, and then I'll take you back to the house and call the constable."

"Aye. It's off over the hill to the south."

Outside he insisted that they ride. So she had to tell him she'd lost the pony.

His eyebrows went up, and his mouth tightened.

In defense she said, "I'm good with sheep. I never said I was any good with horses."

He mounted up and hoisted her to sit behind the saddle. "Hold onto me. It's a mite farther to the ground than from the back of a pony."

She gripped the back of his jacket.

"I said hold on. Put your arms around me."

Gingerly she obeyed and pointed the way. He kicked his horse into a canter, and she tightened her grip on him. Ember ran beside them. When they reached the thicket, Bryan jumped to the ground and reached up to help her down. She ignored his hand, slid off, and nearly lost her footing. He caught her arm, steadying her.

Nella pulled away. "Let me go first."

But the dog went first. She seemed to know exactly why they'd come. When Nella reached the point where she could glimpse the body, she stopped and pointed. "Over there beside those rocks," she said.

Bryan's face turned into an expressionless mask. He pushed past her. "You stay here," he said.

She could see him drop to his knees beside the body and search for a pulse, just as she had. Then he reached into the man's coat pockets. He pulled out a wallet, glanced through it, and put it back. Then he searched other pockets. Finally he rose to his feet and stood with his head bowed, looking down at the body for a moment as if he were a mourner. Then he straightened and came back. A bit of white paper flashed in his hand as he put it into his own jacket pocket.

Silently he led the way back toward the meadow.

"Was he a friend?" she asked in sympathy.

"No." He kept walking without looking at her.

"Do you think he . . . just died . . . of natural causes?"

He shook his head. "I don't know. A coroner will have to decide that. I didn't want to disturb the body until the constable can look over the situation."

"But you put something in your pocket. Did that suggest a reason for his death?"

He stopped and turned slowly to face her. "Nella, I need to ask a favor, and I can't explain why. Could you . . . just trust me?" The frozen mask was gone. His gaze met hers with such intensity, she stared back in surprise.

She had the strongest, most illogical feeling that she could trust him—even with her life, if the need arose. Before she thought, she answered. "Yes. What is it?"

"Don't tell anyone you saw me take anything from that man's body. It's a matter of life or death."

"Why? And why would anyone ask?"

"They won't likely. Just don't tell anyone. Please."

She nodded. "But I don't understand."

"I must have your promise."

She sighed. "All right. I promise." She'd given her word. Now what had she gotten herself into?

"Good girl. Someday you'll know why, and you won't regret it." He mounted up and reached down to help her. As they rode back to the herder's house, Nella's emotions ran the gamut from puzzlement to anger when she finally had to admit to herself that she'd probably agreed to lie for the worst possible reason. She was seriously attracted to Bryan.

Without telling Mrs. Lewis why, Peggy said she was going up to the manor and not to worry about keeping her supper hot. She aimed to speak to Lord Westmoreland about her dismissal. Peggy had heard he was fair-minded, and she desperately needed justice right now. So did Annie, who had been cruelly mistreated.

When she reached the front of the mansion, she was surprised to see Bryan ride in from the hills with Nella seated behind him. He guided the horse to where Peggy stood, dismounted, and helped Nella down. Then he handed the horse to Thompkins who came jogging around the corner from the garden. Without saying more than hello, he hurried into the mansion.

He wasn't usually quite so rude. Peggy wondered if his mother had told him about her dismissal. Then a closer look at Nella's face took her mind off of her own problem. "What's wrong? Why were you riding with The Bryan? And what's got his dander up?"

Nella gave her a dazed look, half-scared and half-sick. "I found a dead man . . . up in the hills where I was tending the sheep."

"Oh no! Anyone you know?"

Nella shook her head. "No. Never saw him before."

"Well, are you all right? What were you doing out in a place like that?"

Nella's mouth opened but no words came out.

Peggy dropped her bicycle where she stood and put an arm around her. "Come on. Let me take you to your room."

"I think I should stay here. The constable may want to talk to me."

"Well, sure, and Bryan won't know where to look for you. Come on." Peggy had been to the Garden Cottage several times, so she led Nella around the mansion to the little house and walked her in. All the other girls apparently were still out working. "You sit yourself down, and I'll make us some tea," she told Nella.

When she brought the teakettle a few minutes later, Nella came to life, reached for a cup, and said, "What brought you up here this time of day?"

Peggy sat in a chair beside her. "I nearly forgot. Old Lady W. had me dismissed. I was so angry, I was going to put up a fight over it. I thought I could appeal to Lord Westmoreland. Now they'll be occupied with the constable and the dead man. I guess fate is against me, or maybe God is closing a door, as Father Mac would say."

"She's dismissed you! How can she do that?"

"Same way all the lords and ladies get what they want. She just did it. Though I never really believed she could . . . or would."

"Well, once they calm down from finding a dead man on the estate, you can surely get some justice from Lord Westmoreland. He's a good deal kinder than she."

"She's already hired my replacement. I've got to be packed and gone Friday night."

"That's not fair! She's never been fair with you."

"Well, I may have given her just cause now. I probably should've handled Mrs. Hilliard in a more respectful manner."

Color returned to Nella's cheeks. "From what you say, I think you did what any decent person would have done."

"Thanks, little sister. I'm afraid you're biased, but it's nice to have you for me."

"So you won't be contesting your dismissal?"

"I'll see how I feel tomorrow. I'm sure I'll handle it more rationally after I sleep on it—" A sharp rap on the door interrupted her.

Nella went to answer. A girl's voice said, "The master wants you to come talk to the constable now."

"Thank you. Tell him I'll be right along. Where will I find them?"

"In the kitchen," came the answer in a bit of a flippant tone.

When Nella returned for her coat, Peggy said, "Who was that?"

"The house servant. She's very young."

"Sounds it. She ought to be in school. She needs more time to grow up."

"That's what Bryan says."

Peggy stared. Was Nella blushing? This had been Peggy's first concern, that Nella might lose her head over The Bryan. Surely she hadn't, not sweet, sensible Nella. "Would you like me to come along with you? When you talk to the constable, I mean. You still don't look yourself."

Nella laughed. "No, Mummy. I can do it myself."

"Yes, Livie," Peggy tossed back. She walked with Nella as far as the kitchen side entrance. "Look, let me come with you. I'll leave if they insist, but I think this whole thing is more of a shock than you're willing to admit."

"You're wrong there. I'm very willing to admit it's a big shock. Okay, come then. I hope they'll let you stay."

So they entered the kitchen together. Only the cook was there.

"Oh, dear," Mrs. Harrison said, "they've gone to the library now. Can you find your way?"

"Yes, thanks," Nella replied.

Nella led Peggy out and down a long dark hallway that looked as if part of a museum. When she knocked on a door near the front entry, Bryan opened it and, after a startled glance at Peggy, ushered them both in. "Please be seated." He gestured to a couple of chairs and took another for himself, obviously intending to stay and listen, just as Peggy had decided to do.

At the constable's request, Nella told how she'd found the body and what she'd noticed. Then the constable asked questions. Routine, Peggy decided, but at one point she noticed something odd.

When he asked Nella if she had seen anything at all unusual, Nella answered with a gush of words. Peggy doubted anyone else would notice who didn't know her very well, but Nella had gone on like that whenever she and Peggy had kept a secret from Father and Mother Mac.

Peggy listened, growing more and more uneasy. What was Nella working to conceal?

CHAPTER TWENTY-SEVEN

As the constable's inquiry dragged on, Peggy's thoughts strayed to her own worries. She'd have to come back later if she wanted to fight for her teaching position, which in her mind amounted to fighting for the sake of the children.

At last the constable ended his questioning and left with Bryan. Peggy followed Nella back toward the kitchen. They'd only moved a few steps when Lord Westmoreland came down the wide staircase beside them.

"A sorry business, that!" he exclaimed, looking from Nella to Peggy and back again. "I'm not sure whether Ember passed a test or failed. She ought not to have left the sheep for any reason."

Peggy had heard about the wonders of his dog and how he loved it. However, he should be showing concern for Nella rather than Ember.

Good thing Nella spoke first. "I've told you, sir, she thinks for herself when it's important. That's not so bad. I'll wager nothing could have drawn her away from the flock if a predator had been within a kilometer."

"Yes. Well, Bryan is now positive she can't be trusted with the flocks. He thinks you've wasted your time on her." He strolled closer until he stood looking down at them, taller than Peggy had realized. For all his gray-haired age, he was still handsome.

Peggy had never trusted extremely good-looking men, not since her school days when she'd had that crush on Joseph Winthrop and he dropped her in a minute at the sight of Mary Ellen Archer. A handsome face, she realized, was one thing she held against Bryan. So here, like a centipede under a rock, was another of her prejudices. With conflicted feelings she gazed up at his father.

"Lord Westmoreland," said Nella, "this is my friend, Miss Jones. She's really more my sister than my friend. She lived with us while attending school in Abergavenny."

He nodded courteously. "Ah, I believe you are one of the village schoolteachers. A better task for a young woman than trying to do a man's work out here, wouldn't you say? This war has turned our values upside down."

"Sir, Peggy has her problems too," Nella said. "Did you know that due to a misunderstanding, she is being let go from the school?"

Peggy wanted to hush her up. This was not a good time. But of course it was too late.

He said amiably enough, "Lady Westmoreland works for the school, you know. She's always loved to tend the needs of the villagers. I'm glad to leave that to her." He smiled, and Peggy could see why Nella thought of him as more kind than his wife. "Miss Jones, I'm sorry if you've had a problem with the school committee. Do give a call and make an appointment with Lady Westmoreland. She's a great one for taking on causes."

As calmly as she could, Peggy said, "Thank you, sir. I'm afraid... Lady Westmoreland is my problem. If you'll excuse me now, I think I'd best go home."

He stepped back, gave them both a piercing look from his eagle eyes, and said, "Young lady, if you came to do battle with her, I should warn you that she can be a hard adversary. Good day to you." He nodded and strode into the library, closing the door behind him.

"So much for the kindly Lord Westmoreland," Peggy muttered.

"I'm sorry! I thought he might speak to his wife for you."

Peggy sighed. "That old curmudgeon has you hoodwinked. You were naïve, but I doubt you ruined anything for me. I had little hope she'd change her mind. Now that I think about it, I just wanted to tell her what I thought of her. You've no doubt saved me from making a fool of myself."

"You mean you're just going to give in? You're not going to fight for a fair hearing before the parents?"

"Maybe I'll see it differently tomorrow, but right now I just want to go home and lick my wounds. Nella, will you be all right staying here after finding that body and everything?"

"As all right as possible." She lowered her voice to a whisper. "Are you thinking I'm in more danger because someone else has been found dead?"

"I don't know what to think. Ever since that poor soldier boy drowned, ugly things have been happening. Sometimes I wish you and Livie had moved far away from Abergavenny."

"Come on. We mustn't be talking this way here in the hall where someone might hear." Nella led the way quickly back to the kitchen and out the side door to the drive. Then she continued in a low tone. "Sometimes I wish I had moved far away too, but I can't see any other way I could've handled it. There seems to be no good answer. Though if I had to for Livie's safety, I'd out and out disappear."

Her desperate words sent a chill through Peggy. "Don't say that! Don't even think it!"

"Don't worry. I'm not getting hysterical."

On impulse Peggy asked, "If you confided in Bryan, do you think he'd be a help? I've seen him looking at you as if . . . he's concerned for you, more than just a little. You've got to admit, he's shown some personal interest—taking you to hospital and taking you home to be with Livie."

Nella didn't react, didn't even look to be breathing for a moment. Her voice when she spoke was rushed and tight. "He would have done that for any of the Land Girls. Besides, Bryan is the last person I'd ever confide in for any reason. Good grief, you're the one who told me how much he's all wrapped up in himself. How could you think of him as . . . as someone I could trust?"

"Put that way, it was an idiot idea. I don't know what possessed me." And truth to tell she didn't. Maybe it was something about how intently he'd been watching Nella while the constable questioned her. Then she remembered Nella's odd reaction at one point in the questioning. "For some reason, Nella, I felt you weren't quite on the up and up with the constable."

"But I answered all his questions."

"Yes, but when he asked if you noticed anything unusual, you acted as if you didn't want to say. You can fool other people, but not me—"

"Peggy!"

A point of fear flashed through Peggy. Nella looked stricken, all right. "What is it?" Peggy whispered. "What have you gotten yourself into now?"

"Nothing. You've got to believe me. I promised."

"Promised who?" Peggy hissed.

Nella silently shook her head. "Please don't ask or mention this again. I'm not in danger, I swear."

Peggy knew she'd get nothing more from Nella now. "All right, but you will tell me if you get a hunch about anything going wrong. Swear you'll tell me if you don't feel safe about this secret."

"I'll let you know."

The other Land Girls were coming up the drive in twos and threes to go in for supper. Although Peggy knew several of them, she didn't want to talk to anyone else tonight. "Look, if you'll be okay, I need to go."

"I'm fine."

"If you talk on the phone to Mother or Father Mac, don't mention my dismissal, right? I'll call them myself after I calm down a little."

"Sure. I won't say a word. They'll probably phone me when they read about it in the paper, but I'll let you deliver your own news."

"Thanks. Bye then." Peggy picked up her bicycle and pushed it toward the front of the manor. The constable's men were lifting the dead man onto a stretcher. As they turned to angle it into the back of the coroner's wagon, the sheet slid off the victim's face. He was a portly looking man with thinning gray hair. Then she saw the glasses, thick and heavy, taped beside him on the stretcher. She caught her breath. She knew this man. She had seen him with Bryan that rainy day in Abergavenny.

The constable's men glanced at her and quickly covered the man's face again.

She hesitated. Nella hadn't mentioned the fact that Bryan knew the victim. Had he not told her? Had he told anyone? The constable's questions never suggested that he knew the deceased. What were the implications if Bryan had denied knowing the man, and Nella was covering up for him? No, she wouldn't do that, would she?

Peggy had to know. She turned back toward the kitchen entrance where she'd left Nella.

Nella was nowhere in sight. Chancing she may have gone to clean up before supper, Peggy hurried across the grass to Garden Cottage and knocked.

Nella opened the door. "Peggy! I thought you'd be almost to the village by now." She stepped outside and closed the door. "What's wrong? You're pale as a sheet."

"Can we talk privately inside?" Peggy whispered.

"No," Nella murmured. "Come along to the back where we have an outdoor bench."

When they were seated, Nella asked, "So what is it? Did you meet Lady Westmoreland after all?"

"No, I saw the dead man. Do they know whether he was killed or died of natural causes?"

"Bryan said the coroner would know."

"Then he wasn't bleeding from a wound or anything?"

"I didn't see any blood."

"But the coroner asked a lot of questions for a possible death from natural causes."

"Routine, I suppose. We'll know more in a day or two. Why has this upset you so? You've seen dead people before."

"Did Bryan tell you he knew that man?"

Nella's lips parted, then closed. "No . . . h-he didn't say anything about recognizing the man. Why?"

"Don't you lie to me, Nella Killian!" Peggy warned, keeping her voice low. "You've already admitted to keeping some kind of a secret. Is that it?"

"No! I swear. He said nothing to me about knowing the man." She paused and then whispered as if to herself, "He actually said he didn't know him."

Peggy took a deep breath and started over. "So just suppose . . . if the man was murdered, and Bryan recognized him but wanted to keep it a secret, where would that put you?"

Nella's hand flew to her mouth. "I don't know," she gasped.

Peggy took a long breath and reached out, gripping Nella's arm. "I just saw the dead man's face when they were lifting the body into the coroner's wagon. He was one of the men with Bryan that day I ran into him in the alley at Abergavenny. I remember the man well because of his thick glasses and sparse gray hair. Bryan definitely knows him, Nella."

Nella huddled with her fingers pressed against her mouth. She looked about to faint.

Peggy gave her a little shake. "Listen, you may be in terrible danger here at Whitestone. Come down to Gatekeep and stay with me tonight. Then we'll go home to the manse in the morning, and you can tell the authorities all that you know."

"I can't!" Nella cried softly. "If I do they may kill us all! Have you forgotten? I came here to show I would cooperate and not tell anyone—" She stopped. A horrified expression twisted her face.

Peggy thought for a moment that Nella was going to scream. Instead, she sat mute. Peggy persisted. "How can you be sure that staying here will be understood the way you say?"

"The note said so, Peggy! They will be watching me. This won't go on forever. I'll be getting a letter from Corporal Peterson any day now, and then maybe we'll see a way to get help from the authorities."

Peggy sighed, reflecting that her idea contained as much risk as Nella's. "All right. You keep on playing your part. You've done superbly so far, I guess."

Nella gave her a hug. "My big sister," she whispered. "Thanks."

"You should probably go to supper as usual, and I should go home as usual."

Nella gave her a confident smile. "Aye, aye." They stood up and strolled to the front of Garden Cottage.

On parting, Nella said in a stage whisper, "If the dead man died of natural causes, we won't have a worry about Bryan."

"I hope so. Let me know as soon as you hear."

"And you let me know tomorrow how you feel about contesting your dismissal."

"I can let you know now. I'm going to pack my things and leave peacefully on Friday. I'll tell the children I have to go for personal reasons. There's no point in making a fuss that could upset them."

Nella nodded. "I think that's wise, even if it isn't fair."

With that they parted, and Peggy rode her bicycle back down to the village. The truth was, after recognizing the dead man and knowing that Bryan had lied about knowing him, the quarrel with Lady W. faded in importance. The children would get along, and she would stay in touch with Annie. But until Nella was safe, Peggy had to be free to concentrate on helping her. She wished she knew how.

Nella anticipated her parents' call all the next day, yet it never came. For some strange reason, news of the man found dead on the Westmoreland Estate did not appear in the paper in Abergavenny. Nella decided not to mention it to them till the death became public knowledge.

During the next two days, the Land Girls speculated about the mysterious dead man, but the Westmorelands acted as if nothing unusual had happened. Then following Friday's lunch, as Nella was about to leave to work on ditching the newly turned field, she met Bryan coming up from the stable.

She seized this first opportunity in three days to speak to him alone. "What's happening in the investigation? Anything discovered to explain that man's death?"

"Oh, I meant to tell you. The coroner has ruled it as death from natural causes. Apparently he had a heart condition and went into heart failure when he was out there climbing the hills. Sad case. People don't seem to realize they need a hiking buddy, even in our lower hills."

"Good. I mean I'm glad it wasn't a murder."

He nodded. "It's still important to keep mum about seeing me take that paper from him. You understand that, don't you?"

She had to be honest. "I don't understand."

"I can't explain, but I assure you it's important. For now . . . you must trust me and keep silent. You must!" His sudden passion and his troubled expression held her transfixed, just as it had when she'd first agreed to keep his secret.

Suddenly he whispered, "I love you, Nella. I'd lay down my life to keep you out of this. No matter what happens, please believe me."

His brief look of anguish sent her heart thudding against her ribs. His startling declaration ignited such turmoil within her that she whirled away and rushed to the barn. She grabbed her tools and hurried back out to go to work. When she glanced toward the stable, Bryan was nowhere in sight.

She tromped out to the field and set to work with a fury. Dot and Edith had trenched the first marked area and now paused to rest and have a drink of water.

"So what does Bryan say about that dead man?" Dora called. "We saw you confabbin' with him over by the stable."

"The coroner says the man had a heart seizure," Nella replied.

"I must say I'm relieved the poor man died of a natural cause. But it's too bad he was out there alone," Dot said, wiping her perspiring face with her kerchief. "It looks to rain. I hope it does. My back's pure done in."

Edith laughed. "What makes you think you get to quit just because it rains?" She'd no more than ceased laughing when the first large drops spattered on Nella's face.

The other two grabbed their mattocks and shovels and started for shelter. "Lucky you," Dora called. "You get to stop before you start."

Nella shook her head. "I'm still going to work on awhile."

"Come on along. You'll make us look bad!"

"Don't worry. I'll be in soon."

Nella could hear them laughing as they fled under heavier rain now. Throwing herself into the job, she chopped with the mattock and lifted with the shovel, glad for the effort it took to pit her body against the weight and toughness of the earth. She reeled from Bryan's last words, her emotions spinning a hundred directions. She felt she had to do something vigorous just to keep from running and never coming back. Maybe she had misunderstood. He was whispering after all. If Peggy was right in thinking he loved her... it just wouldn't do at all. She was attracted to him, but if he left her alone, she'd get over it.

Heavy, cold rain soaked through her work clothes. Her hands slid up and down the wet handles of the tools. Finally her booted foot slipped off the shovel, and losing her balance, she fell flat out in the mud. In frustration she dropped her head to her wet arm and gave in to a good cry. *Oh, Rob, I never wanted there to be anyone but you... Livie and me and you—*

She stopped crying when she realized she wasn't denying, as she'd meant to do, but that she'd begun to love Bryan. Slowly she picked herself up, gathered her tools, and trudged back to the barn.

Everyone else had cleaned up already, so Nella used the last of the hot water and took time to soak in the metal bathtub. She toweled herself dry just in time for supper.

Most everyone was seated when she arrived at the manor. They passed her the serving dishes but went on with their own conversations. As soon as she could, Nella hurried to the barn to help with the last of the evening chores and then retreated to go to bed early. Before the others came into the cottage, she took out Gwenyth's book and flipped to the bookmark she'd left in place.

> *Lambing Time...*
> *Storming night...*
> *Spring lambs huddle close to ewes,*
> *Blessed tended lambs.*
> *Stalking wolves...*
> *I huddle by side of my own dear lamb.*
> *My poor wee lambkin,*
> *And I a lamb myself—*
> *Good Shepherd tend us both!*

Nella closed her eyes, sorry that she'd read this plaintive poem tonight when she was so troubled herself. It about broke her heart to think of the young girl with her new baby, trapped by that long-ago war. This, too, she had in common with Gwenyth. Yet Gwenyth had met everything with the naïve faith of childhood, her being so close to those innocent girlhood days.

Nella opened her eyes and turned the page. To her astonishment, the written words answered her thoughts as if she'd been heard across the many years.

My dear son,

If I could, I'd spare thee disbelief. Seeing the cruelty of my uncle, I cursed God for allowing him to live when my father had to die. Then I found a way to escape. I fled through the forests alone, trying to reach Whitestone before Rowan could catch me. With hope nearly gone, I prayed despite my doubts. When I reached the safety of your father's home, I vowed I'd never forget the mercy and goodness of God, and I haven't. God saved me, I know right well. Alas, I cannot give thee my faith. I can only keep on praying for thee.

Nella slowly closed the book. So the girl's faith had been through a fire. She reached for her journal. She couldn't put on paper the secrets she bore, yet had to write down one thought: *I don't know what to do or how this will all end, but if anything happens to me, Mum, Daddy, Livie, Peggy—I love you ever so much.*

And then in spite of her doubting, she wrote a prayer: *Dear Lord Jesus, watch over my little lamb and my mum and dad and Peggy. Good Shepherd, help me find my way. Amen.*

She put both books in her clothing drawer and climbed into bed, wishing for sleep to come quickly before the others girls came trooping in and wanting to talk.

Chapter Twenty-Eight

The classroom door swung open Friday after school, and Peggy looked up from her desk, hoping it wasn't one of the children. Good-byes today had been more painful than she anticipated, even though she'd tried to prepare herself.

She let out a shaky breath at seeing a tall silhouette against the afternoon light.

"Hello," Laurie Barringer said. Without waiting for an invitation, he came and sat beside her desk. "I just heard. I'm so sorry. There are times when I despise my cousin Adrienne. She's upset Aunt Eunice to the point of illness and has broken Peter's heart. What will you do now?"

"I don't know. I need a few days to think, so I'll move back to my old room at the manse tomorrow."

"I'll bring the car by to take your things to Abergavenny. What time should I come?"

"Oh, you don't need to do that! Father Mac can drive out—"

"I want to." He leaned forward, elbows on knees, and studied his clasped hands for a moment before looking up. "I'd like to stay in touch, wherever you go. Would that be all right?"

Her spirits lifted. "Yes. I'd like that. And I want you to meet Annie."

He smiled. "I shall be pleased to meet her. Maybe you can teach me a bit of the sign language."

"I'll try, but Annie is the best teacher. You'll love her—" She stopped. How presuming to think she knew what he'd love.

He filled in immediately. "I'm sure I will. I like children, you know.

I've been thinking that after the war ... I'm not wealthy—my father dissipated everything that might have come to me—but I'd like to help her in some way."

"That's very kind of you, but maybe you should meet her first."

"Certainly. However, I decided the minute I saw Annie's paintings that I wanted to help her. I'm not that canny about art, so I enlisted Meredith Kinney, a wealthy widow who knows fine talent when she sees it. She's also my mother's best friend. She was willing to take my word that Annie created the painting by herself."

"But why didn't you tell me you wanted to help Annie?"

He shrugged. "I don't much like to be thought of as a philanthropist. My father always made a show of giving to causes, but he was such a hypocrite. I've never wanted to be like him."

"Was? Is your father not alive then?"

"He died a couple of years ago. I hate to say I'm glad he's gone, but he made Mother's life miserable for so many years. I could escape, and when I went off to college, I finally did. But poor Mother ..." He stared again at his hands. "Well, she's blossoming now, though she wouldn't like to admit it. Dishonoring the dead and all that."

"I'm sorry you had that kind of father," she said quietly, remembering the harsh man who had thrown her to the ground and the wistful look on the face of his son as he shoved him into their auto all those years ago.

Laurie looked up, startled. "You sound as if ... did you have such a father too?"

"No. My father was kind and gentle. It's just that I've known people like your father."

"Parents of your pupils?" he asked.

She nodded. "Peter's mother is a female version."

"I hadn't thought about that, but you're right. Even though she's never laid a hand on him. My father had a heavy hand. When he was in his cups, I learned early to disappear. Because of his drinking, he lost the family stock in the mines and almost lost us the glass factory, all of which put Mother deep into debt. She held on to the land and paid off much of his liabilities. For my sake, she says. I don't look on myself as landed gentry. My father destroyed any leanings I might've had in that direction, but if Mother wants to save the place, I may go back and become a gentleman farmer."

Peggy couldn't picture him as a gentleman farmer. Right now she was still seeing him as a tragic little boy being shoved into a big black car by his meanspirited father.

"If you didn't become a gentleman farmer, what would you like to be?" asked Peggy.

"A physician," he said without hesitation. "I'd be a country doctor who made house calls and knew all his patients by first name."

"Then why don't you? Surely your mother wouldn't stand in the way of a dream like that."

He smiled and raised his eyebrows. "You have a way of clearing out excuses. As you say, Mother would even embrace my dream. However, she needs me to get the rest of Father's debts cleared up first."

"You said she's already paid off a lot. Have you helped her so far?"

He stared at her in mild surprise. "Well, no. I've been tied up, what with the war and all.... You know, she has done admirably well on her own."

Peggy laughed. "So there you have it. If you want to become a physician, tell her. See what she says."

"I say, I came by to cheer you up, and you end up cheering me. I didn't know I'd fallen into such a rut."

"It always pays to talk things over with someone."

"I haven't had much experience at that."

"Then it's time you learn."

He straightened. "I shall. Miss Jones," he said with mock formality, "what about you? What are you going to do now that you've been dealt with so unfairly?"

"I don't know. I'm not likely to get a teaching position soon. Maybe I'll enlist in one of the services."

"I can't picture you in the service."

"Are you one of those men who think women only belong in the home?"

"Not exactly. I see you somewhere doing your own painting and maybe teaching art to a few gifted children."

She cocked her head sideways and pursed her lips. A tightness inside her melted. "That's a lovely thought, Laurie. I'd like that."

"So we each have our dreams," he said. "We need to stay in touch to encourage each other."

"I'd like that too," she said and smiled. "I already said that, didn't I?"

He laughed. He had a merry laugh for a man. "It's worth repeating, just so I can believe you mean it. About your father. You said he was kind. Have you lost him, then?"

"He was a miner. He'd worked underground since he was ten. He died of black lung when I was eight. He was good to us five children, but a miner doesn't have anything to leave his widow. Mum managed to find work as a housekeeper to a farmer, and all of us children worked too. The farmer's wife was ill in bed, so I helped her a lot."

She thought for a moment about how kind Mrs. Edwards had been and her so weak and in such pain. "Before she died, she made her husband promise to send me to school in town. That's how I came to Abergavenny to live at the manse. My mother married Mr. Edwards, and she's still there on the farm, worked to the bone. Mr. Edwards isn't a cruel man, just hardened from the life. Mum says she's happy. I don't see her much, what with travel being so difficult now."

"And what about sisters and brothers? Do you have both?"

"Aye, two sisters and two brothers. The girls are married to dirt poor farmers, and the boys are in the army."

"I always wished I had a brother or sister."

"They're a comfort, but with me being sent away, we're not close anymore. Maybe after the war we can be a family again. Nella is my sister now too." She glanced out the classroom window. "I'm sorry to break off this conversation, but I think I'd better be leaving. I'd hate for Lady W. to come by and think I was dallying."

He glanced at the carton of personal items she'd gathered from her desk. "I'll help you get these things to Gatekeep. May I carry this to the car now?"

She'd lost all inclination to argue. Knowing how he felt about his father removed one of the barriers she'd erected to keep him at a distance. "Thanks. Let me empty this last drawer, and I'm ready to go." Peggy had been dreading her final walk home from school, uncertain as she was about how many people knew she was leaving and why. It was a great relief to have a ride with Laurie.

At Gatekeep Mrs. Lewis insisted that Laurie stay for tea. Shortly after he left, Annie came with her sisters and mother for a last good-bye. Then several other parents came to say they were sorry to see her go. They didn't know the real reason she was leaving, and she didn't enlighten them.

Mrs. Lewis stayed silent on the matter of Peggy's dismissal as Peggy had requested, but after they were gone she exploded. "Why didn't you tell them what that woman did to you?"

"Because they have to live here and go on with Lady Westmoreland. It will be easier for them not to know."

"Mayhap it would be easier to have better leadership than her ladyship," Mrs. Lewis sputtered.

Peggy laughed. "You almost made a poem." She felt good to be able to chuckle.

"I s'pose you want to be leaving the village now. Well, I'm not taking in anyone else. Your room will be here for you whenever you want to stop by, like if you want to visit your friend Nella or Annie or"—she gave a sly wink—"even that Mr. Barringer."

"That would be wonderful. But don't you need the money? I wouldn't be paying full time anymore."

"You won't be paying anything at all. You'll be my invited guest, young lady."

"Why, thank you! That will be wonderful. I'd like to keep on helping Annie with her artwork."

Mrs. Lewis nodded. "The room is yours, same as if you were family coming back home." She looked a bit flustered over her show of emotion and asked, "Would you like more hot water for tea?"

"Yes, please. And thank you!" The prospect of a room for staying over when she came to West-Holding to visit seemed a godsend. Father Mac would say, of course, that it truly was.

———✦———

Nella had Sunday off from farm chores and wished she could visit Livie, which of course she couldn't. So instead, she rang up the manse to talk with her. Her parents finally had heard about the dead man. She reiterated that the man had died of natural causes, just as the paper had said. They didn't question her beyond that. The fact that they weren't worried about her gave Nella a modicum of comfort.

She talked with Livie awhile and then asked her to call Aunt Peggy to the phone. When Peggy came on, Nella asked, "How are you doing? Was your last day horrible?"

"Not bad, to both questions."

"Good. I wish you were still here, today especially. I have the day off and really need to talk over some things."

"I'll come, then."

"Bicycle?"

"What else?"

"You're not too tired, and you won't mind? I mean with Lady W. being here and all."

"Not as long as you need me, and that's where you are."

"Oh, Peggy, you're an angel. How soon can you come?"

"Be there by two o'clock."

"Meet me down by the shearing barn. Then you won't have to risk coming upon the master or mistress of the manor by accident."

"Sure thing. See you soon."

Nella changed into slacks, a warm jacket, and her old walking shoes and, about quarter of two, stepped outside.

Ruth appeared in the kitchen doorway with a garden basket in her hand and waved. "You off to enjoy the sun?" she called.

"Yes. Meeting Peggy down at the shearing barn."

"Aye. Well, this is a day to be out. Lucky you!" She grinned and trotted the other way toward the kitchen garden.

Nella tromped down the hill to the shearing barn and found Peggy already seated on a stump in the gentle sunshine. Peggy immediately asked, "Everything all right?"

"Fine," Nella responded. "Nothing's really changed. Now that we know the dead man wasn't murdered, I feel a bit safer."

"Nella, don't let down your guard . . . ever. You mustn't, promise me."

"Sure, and I promise. Peggy, it does ease me to be able to talk with you about this. I just pray we can maintain the usual so that whoever's watching me won't be alarmed."

"Well, for starters, let's go for a hike. That's normal. And we can be singing, laughing, and teasing as we always do. Let's put on a good show."

"Aye-aye. Are you game for a climb? I've wanted you to see the Westmoreland chapel windows. They're really old, maybe eleventh century, but still glorious."

"Out here at the end of nowhere? I'd love to if the family doesn't mind."

"If there comes a problem, I'll make it plain it was my idea."

Nella led Peggy to the trail's beginning beyond the barn. "I hope I can make the key work," Nella remarked as they ascended the steep hill. "I'm sure no one minds. Lord Westmoreland himself took me inside. He says he's about the only one in the family to care about it now."

"You think it's safe?" Peggy lowered her voice. "I mean, going off like this into such a wilderness?"

Nella laughed. "Look around. Do these woods look like a wilderness?" Through the trees, the valley below gleamed in the soft sunlight, and all around the same light shone on the forest floor where fallen leaves reflected back their autumn colors. Open sunny glades spread around them on all sides. "Don't worry," she whispered. "This is what we would normally do, and I know the way."

"Lead on, then. I'd love to see the windows if we can get in."

They walked briskly and soon were breathing hard from the climb.

Peggy exclaimed, "This reminds me of the time we went walking after Joseph couldn't take his eyes from that highborn new girl who was visiting the Flint family. How could I ever have thought that boy loved me? Live and learn, they say. . . . Anyway, I felt a lot better after we climbed the mountains. Remember what you said?"

Nella paused to think. "I guess I don't."

"I said I'd never love another man as long as I lived, and you said, 'Oh, Peg, you don't want to die that young!' "

Nella giggled. "I don't remember that at all!"

"It was perfect. Made me laugh." Peggy leaned over and picked up a walking stick. "You said you needed to talk to me. What about?"

Nella, caught off guard, blurted out, "I think I'm falling in love with Bryan."

Peggy halted, gave her a sideways glance, and swung her cane at an offending briar that hung into the trail. "I was afraid you were. I wish I could make you laugh and forget about him."

"So do I. I hate how this makes me feel."

"What do you mean?"

"Mixed up. Wanting to marry him, while at the same time I don't!"

"Oh, Nella. You mustn't! He . . . I don't trust him. He's hiding something, even if that poor man wasn't murdered. Good grief, even if he doesn't pose a danger for you, the minute he suspects your feelings, he'll try to take advantage of you."

"But I won't let him," Nella declared. Gwenyth's diary entries, written after the birth of her baby, had awakened Nella's most tender memories of her own beautiful baby and her commitment always to think of Livie first in every decision. Livie was her defense. She simply needed to keep her baby in her thoughts. She'd never get into a relationship that wasn't the best for Livie. And certainly Bryan and his family were not the best. "It appears Bryan *is* hiding something, but I'm sure he'd never harm me. And I doubt that he'd try to take advantage of me. Anyway, I can certainly take care of myself in that kind of a situation."

Peggy swung around and studied her with a worried frown. "I didn't mean physically. I meant he'd try to use you in whatever shady thing he's up to." She paused in the middle of the path and faced Nella squarely. "Other than that, did you ever stop to think that maybe . . . maybe this attraction is only a sign that you're healed from your long grief over Rob? Have you considered that?"

Nella pondered the idea. Slowly she let the idea sink in. The more she thought about it, the more sense it made. "I think you've hit it straight on. Why didn't I think of that? I'm getting back to normal. I'm attracted to Bryan simply because he's there, the only young man around." She clapped Peggy on the shoulder. "I knew you'd help me see things more clearly."

They came to the old cemetery. At the lichen-covered fence, Nella stopped and said, "Unfortunately a lot of the markers aren't readable anymore. I asked Lord Westmoreland about the Welsh bride, and he said she wasn't buried here because the family believed she committed suicide. He doesn't know where her gravesite is. In the beginning, as I've read her diary, I couldn't imagine her killing herself. Then last night one poem may suggest she became blue and anxious after the birth of her baby."

Peggy moved out onto the trail again. "I remember that feeling too, but her prayers showed such faith—"

Dead leaves crackled.

Peggy whispered, "What's that noise?"

"I don't know."

"Well, let's forget the chapel and get out of here."

Nella was about to agree when a giant shape rounded the turn in the trail that led to the chapel. "It's Albert!" Nella exclaimed. "He's that man who can't hear. Come and meet him." She raised her hand to wave, and he smiled and gave her his version of a salute.

She led Peggy closer and by means of gestures tried to explain that Peggy was her sister. She couldn't keep from talking at the same time. Albert watched her intently and finally with a big grin, nodded.

While they greeted Albert, a gray-haired woman walked slowly around the bend. "He can't hear you at all, miss," she called. "Nor can he speak."

"I know. We've met before. I just talk out of habit."

The woman came to stand beside Albert. She must be his mother, yet her face looked remarkably youthful. Over her arm she carried a basket brimming with edible mushrooms.

"How do you do? I'm Nella Killian, and this is Peggy Jones. I was trying to tell Albert we are sisters."

The woman tapped Albert's arm, and when he faced her, she gestured and said slowly, "Sisters." He nodded and bowed to them.

"Does he lip-read?" Peggy asked.

"A few words," the mother replied.

More footsteps approached. Nella turned toward the sound. Bryan strode into sight from down the hill. He walked fast but was breathing easy. "Hello. I see I'm not the only one wanting one last breath of fall before the dark days of winter come. Hello, Mrs. Miller, Nella, Peggy, Albert." He nodded to each in turn. As if they'd asked, he explained, "I had a yen to visit the old cemetery and maybe sit in the chapel a bit. Any of you want to join me?"

"Yes," Nella answered. "I've wanted Peggy to see the stained-glass windows ever since Lord Westmoreland showed them to me."

"I thank you kindly, sir," Albert's mother said, "but me and Albert need to be getting home, if you'll excuse us."

He nodded. "Certainly. Is there anything needs fixing on Dabney Cottage before winter? Shall I send Thompkins over to have a look?"

"Everything's fine. Thank you, sir." She bobbed her head in old-fashioned courtesy and touched Albert's arm. He turned to her. "Come along, son. Home."

He tugged at his forelock in a farewell salute and nodded, first to Nella, then to Peggy.

"Hasn't anyone ever tried to teach that man standard sign language?" Peggy asked.

Bryan glanced at the retreating backs of the couple. "I guess not. I don't think Mrs. Miller knows much about it."

"That's tragic. It leaves him so isolated," Peggy said.

Nella suspected Peggy was already scheming on how she might teach Albert and his mother sign language, but Peggy didn't pursue the subject.

"This way, ladies, to the family chapel," Bryan said. He made a play of gallantly escorting them to the door.

As he reached the key, Peggy said, "The building looks like an old Celtic shrine. Could it ever have been?"

"Family history says it was always Christian. But I agree, it has a mysterious appearance. I used to come up here with my cousins. We'd be knights, fighting evil forces of the forest. Sometime we scared ourselves."

Bryan unlocked the tall old door and escorted them inside. The afternoon sun lit up one side, casting streams of ruby, azure, amber, and emerald across the old pews. He sat down and leaned back. "The pews are a recent addition, only about a hundred and fifty years old. The windows were designed and constructed in Venice when one of my ancestors stayed on there after the Crusades. We've been fortunate that all of the original panes remain unbroken." He told about each window just as his father had told Nella, and listening, she wondered why Lord Westmoreland thought he was the only one who cared about the old chapel. Bryan's affection for the place was unmistakable. What a strange family that they knew so little about one another.

Nella studied the windows, trying to imagine what life was like when the chapel was new. As she listened to Bryan and Peggy talk, she could almost see him as a boy facing forest dragons with his friends.

Suddenly Peggy said, "Nella, we're ready to go now."

She jumped. They had been walking from window to window, and she'd lost track of their conversation. She arose quickly and followed them out. Passing Bryan as he held the door for her, she glanced up. He smiled, and for an unguarded moment his face softened with pleasure.

Feeling her cheeks burn, she looked away quickly. "Thanks for taking us inside," she said lightly and moved swiftly toward the path while he locked the door. To Peggy she said, "We'd better be going, so you can get back to town before dark."

"Can you ladies find your way out of the forest by yourselves? I want to take a look at Dabney Cottage, despite what Mrs. Miller says."

"Of course we can," Nella replied.

Peggy thanked him again, and they turned down the hill. When Nella glanced back, he was standing watching them. He raised his hand but made no move to go his way until they went theirs.

When they reached the trail back to the shearing barn, Peggy said, "Your face is a dead giveaway. You blush too easily. You'd better keep your distance from The Bryan."

Nella sighed. "I'll try." *I forgot to keep Livie at the forefront of my mind,* she thought all too late. "It breaks my heart to be away from Livie so long, but I'm going to stay out here full time for another month."

"In view of your instructions, I suppose that's wise. But, Nella, how are you going to get out of this? You can't go on forever stuck here, living in fear."

"I know. We must come up with some kind of plan . . . especially if we don't hear from Corporal Peterson. I keep thinking he might reveal something definite that I could send to Captain Evers. Surely we can think of some way to put a safe ending on the situation."

"Can you manage a whole month more if it should take that long? You admitted that being with Bryan all the time led to your mixed feelings."

"I'll be all right, now that I understand. Until we find a safe way for me to leave Whitestone, remaining here protects the family."

"Dear God, I hope so. And that's a prayer."

"Then I say, amen!" Nella sighed. "So far, staying here has kept them safe."

Peggy nodded. "Good point."

Up ahead the shearing barn came into view. Nella stopped and hugged Peggy. "I don't know what I'd do without you. Take care of yourself."

"You know I will." As Peggy mounted her bicycle, she said, "Oh, I forgot to tell you! Mrs. Lewis is saving my room for me. Whenever I want to come, I can stay at Gatekeep. So I don't always have to be rushing back now that the days are growing shorter and the weather harsher. I want to keep in touch with Annie, work with her on her art. And after meeting Albert, I'd like him to meet Annie so he can see how signing might help him. I suspect with Annie's help I could teach Mrs. Miller the rudiments. I think it would make Annie feel good to be doing for someone, don't you?"

"Aye! That's a marvelous idea. Once you find your way to Dabney Cottage, you wouldn't need to count on me having to take time off to go along."

"Yes, but it would give me an excuse to be with you more often."

Nella gave Peggy another hug. "It will be wonderful. Let's do this as soon as you can get Mrs. Nelson's consent to bring Annie."

They parted on this happy note. All the way up the hill to Whitestone, Nella tried to think of a way to escape from her strange imprisonment at Whitestone. She came up with no possible solutions. But hopefully, now with Peggy to help, they'd devise a good plan for Nella to leave Whitestone and Abergavenny soon.

CHAPTER TWENTY-NINE

Early in the day before chores, Nella picked up Gwenyth's diary. She was nearly finished reading it and beginning to feel guilty over keeping the book so long. She carried her tea to her bedroom, sat down, and turned to where she'd stuck her bookmark. The page revealed Gwenyth's thoughts in short prose.

So many things are out of my control, out of my hands. I fret, and then I remember how God saved me and brought me to White-stone. I remember how even when I doubted, God protected me. There are those who say if one doubts he has no faith. I say faith without doubts is weak-kneed faith.

Nella copied the words into her own journal, attributed them to the author, then read them back to herself again. She had heard her father say much the same thing. However, it hadn't made sense to her till now, written in the words of the Welsh bride.

"Nella, you going to sit there all day? I'm off for the barn now," Dora called from the doorway.

So Nella closed the diary and followed her out.

Later in the morning, while Nella drove tractor, the gray sky descended to the hilltops, and gusts of wind chilled her ears right through her knit cap. Her feet inside her boots were stiff with cold. She'd soon be treated to a soaking rain. However, if she quit tilling the northernmost new field, the rest of it might have to wait until spring.

She doggedly circled the field, ignoring the purple-black ceiling of thunderheads that had cast a false twilight over the Usk Valley.

When the first lightning flashed, followed by an explosion of thunder, she decided to stop the tractor and pull on her oilskins. One more sweep to the far end of the field and back and she could leave feeling it wouldn't matter so much if winter took over the hillside. Keeping her eyes on her goal, she guided the machine.

Suddenly lightning struck a tree standing at the upper edge of the field, directly where she was heading. The deafening blast came instantly. She braked the tractor and jumped to the ground, realizing she'd made a foolish choice in continuing to work. This was no ordinary storm. Moving away from the tractor, she threw herself flat into an untilled swale. Then as lightning flashed nearby again, she knew she still wasn't far enough away from the tractor. On hands and knees, as her brother Charles once had told her to do, she kept close to the ground and moved toward the field's edge. She sought shelter beneath an arch of brambles still holding on to most of their leaves. But they offered no real protection.

When the rain came, it gushed like a giant waterfall and poured into every opening of her oilskins—down her neck, into the front, and up the sleeves. The other girls were probably back at the barn by now and drying off.

Around her lightning continued to flash, and thunder banged and rumbled away over the Brecon Beacon mountains. Nella couldn't help but think about the soldiers out in all kinds of weather. Whatever did they do to keep their guns dry in storms like this?

She considered running for the barn the minute the lightning eased up. No one would mind if she left the tractor out until the storm blew over. Then she changed her mind. It was much too far to walk. A bit longer and she could drive back. Shivering, she hunched down. The wind blew steadily now, driving the rain sideways.

Then she saw someone on a horse, head down to the wind, approach the abandoned tractor. She couldn't tell, but it must be Bryan. He circled the tractor as if searching for her. She'd better get his attention. She struggled to her feet, more clumsy and stiff than she realized. She called, but the wind carried her voice away. Waving her arms, she stumbled out toward the tractor. He finally caught sight of her and set the horse cantering to meet her.

"What are you doing still out here?" Bryan yelled down at her. "Climb up." He kicked his foot free of a stirrup for her and reached a hand down.

His hand proved too wet and slippery, and she found she was so stiff from the cold, she couldn't hoist herself up anyway. "I'll walk," Nella said. "Or drive the tractor."

"You'll do nothing of the sort," Bryan snapped. He dismounted and lifted her bodily into the saddle. Then he hopped on behind her and reached around to control the horse. He guided the horse to the edge of the woods. At first she thought he was taking a shortcut home, but then he halted, dismounted, and helped her down. "There's a cave over here where we can wait out the storm. I barely got across Shearing Creek when I rode up. The bridge is under water, and if this doesn't let up, its moorings will wash out."

Bryan led the way into a cave just high enough to permit the horse to enter also. The passage opened into a wide cavern, too dark to see beyond a few meters. Looping the horse's reins over a jagged outcropping of rock, he said matter-of-factly, "That should hold him. He doesn't like coming in here."

She looked around, still shivering. "I don't blame him. Do you by any chance have an electric torch with you?"

"Sorry. I came unprepared for going in a cave."

"Why did you come? I would've driven back as soon as the lightning quit."

"When I saw the creek, I knew you couldn't make it. And I was afraid you'd try. You're a stubborn woman, Nella."

"I-I'm used to farming. I t-told you that when I first c-came h-here." She shook so much now her voice betrayed her boast.

In the dim light she saw him reach toward her. He touched her cheek with the back of his hand and felt her sopping jacket collar where the rain had poured in. "You're soaked and freezing. Even your neck is cold. Come on, you've got to move to warm up." He tucked his arm under hers and made her walk beside him farther into the cave and then back. Her legs moved as if not under her control at all. Gradually her vision adjusted to the dark. He walked her in a large circle around the cave's perimeter.

Nella stumbled. "My feet are numb. It feels like I'm walking on stumps."

Holding her up, he said, "You'll get your feeling back when you've walked long enough. Come on."

Her legs didn't want to move to her command nor his. She staggered, but he kept pulling her along.

Finally she gasped, "I'm so tired . . . let me rest."

"That is exactly what you may not do. Pick them up and put them down." He kept her walking and began to talk at the same time. "This is one of those caves where my cousins and I fought dragons when we were boys. Of course, we didn't come inside like this. We fancied the very opening breathed out sulfur. I learned to associate its natural dank odor with dragon breath and so wouldn't come near the place without my cousins nearby for moral support. Together we were daring enough to hurl stick spears inside. Then when I was thirteen, I came home on school vacation and decided I must put childish fears behind me. I came up here alone. My self-imposed coming-of-age test would be to stay in the cave all night."

"D-did you s-spend the n-night, then?" she asked.

"Yes, though at one point I nearly gave it up. An animal dashed in, chasing something. Sounded like a bear ... or a dragon. Luckily I had my electric torch in hand and could see right away it was just a fox."

"M-may I rest a b-bit?" Nella was panting now.

He clasped her hand. "You still aren't warmed up, but I'll give you a couple of minutes to rest. Then we'll move again." He didn't let go of her hand. "If you're such a good farmer, what possessed you to stay out there in the field when you saw that sky? You should've known this was no ordinary storm."

"I g-gambled that it would only hit the m-mountains."

"You're right you gambled. You could have been blasted off that tractor." He sounded angry, which was more like him.

"But I w-wasn't, was I?" she said.

"Come on. Let's walk again." He dragged her around and around the cave.

After a while, she said, "My feet have come back."

"Good," he said, but he kept on walking her.

The horse nickered from its post near the entrance. Bryan stopped. "Listen. I think it's stopped raining."

He led her to the opening. Sure enough, the wind had quieted, and the rain had turned into a normal shower.

He looked down at her. "I think the worst is over. Do you think you can walk back to Whitestone? I'll walk alongside you. I'm afraid you'll chill again if you ride. I once saw a grown man just lie down and die when he got chilled in a rain like this. I tried to keep him on his feet, but in the end, I couldn't."

She saw the lines at the corners of his eyes scrunch up before he turned away from her. "Was he a friend?" she asked.

"More or less," he said in a tight voice. He let go of her arm and reached out to pat the horse. "Poor Sir William, you need a warm-up too. We'll get you out of here and back to the barn in short order."

The horse blew through its nose and, like a big dog, rubbed its face against Bryan's chest.

Nella walked over. "He's a fine horse." She touched his wet velvet nose. "You should've maybe spent part of your energy on walking him."

"I knew he'd be all right. I wasn't so sure about you." Without warning he leaned over and kissed Nella's lips.

She froze. His gentle touch created an instantaneous desire to be in his arms. She backed away. "I wish you hadn't done that."

"Do you really?" he murmured. "Your kiss said differently."

"I didn't kiss you!"

"Ah, but you did. It's even better if you did it unconsciously," he teased. Before she could answer, he turned his back and walked out of the cave. From outside he called back, "I think we can go now. We'll climb the hill to a place where we can more safely cross the creek." He returned and picked up the reins of the horse. He didn't ask how she felt.

It was a long walk. At one point the sun broke through the thick clouds. The brief warmth penetrated Nella's soggy clothing, giving life to her limbs. When they finally came to the creek, he stopped and studied it. "Sir William can manage the current better than we can, and there's no point in getting cold again by wading through it. We'll ride across."

He hoisted her into the saddle again and sat behind her. His breath was warm on her cheek as he gripped the reins and urged the horse across. On the other side he slid down and assisted her to the ground. Though she stood steady, he still held onto her and then drew her into his arms, holding her firmly against his chest. "Nella, I'm sorry I chose a scary place like a dark cave to steal that kiss. It was stupid of me. And I guess I should have asked. I'd ask now, but I'm afraid you'll say no."

When she glanced up, his arms tightened around her, then he kissed her solidly as he held her close.

She felt herself slipping into a dreamlike euphoria. After she came to herself and pulled back, he instantly released her.

He studied her face and tenderly brushed a stream of rain away from her eyes with one hand. "I really do love you. Could you ever care about me, Nella?"

She almost said she never kissed people she didn't care about but caught herself in time. She meant to say no, but it came out, "I don't know." She stepped away from him.

He studied her face silently. "So . . . on to Garden Cottage where you can get into dry clothes and warm up."

She didn't tell him she was warm already. Her heart was pounding up its own storm. Whatever was she to do, if she did love this man who had remained safe at home while Rob and most other young men had enlisted and risked their lives to turn back the enemy? She said, "I am cold. Which way now?"

Without saying anything he led her at a fast walk through the dripping forest and across soggy meadows she'd never before seen until they came to a muddy road. At first sight this, too, looked unfamiliar and then she realized it was a road she'd traveled on the tractor several times before.

At last they reached the barn. He halted in the rain, turned, and said, "I meant what I said out there, Nella. It's not a passing fancy with me, even though you are the most beautiful girl I've ever met." Then he led Sir William into the stable.

Nella hurried to Garden Cottage. The windows were steaming from all the wet coats draped around the stove.

"I was so worried about you!" Edith exclaimed. "I couldn't imagine why you didn't come running in like the rest of us when that storm hit. You must be nearly frozen. We've got water hot, so you can have yourself a bath. Here, give me your dripping clothes." She moved around like a mother hen. The other girls laughed and pitched in too. They were all dry except their hair.

Nella laughed. "It smells like a flock of wet sheep in here!"

Dora threw a wet sock at her, and Heather hit her with a pillow.

While Nella was soaking in the tub, Edith tapped on the door. "Bryan left some old-fashioned bed warmers. Says to heat them in the oven, then wrap up and put them on our feet. Can you figure that? He's a slave driver one minute and a magnanimous papa the next. Maybe that's why Shirley was so besotted with him. She said that she'd never had a da."

Edith backed out of the small room where they'd set the washtub beside a glowing hot coal stove and closed the door, leaving Nella alone with her uncomfortable feelings about Bryan. She needed to talk to Peggy again to get some balance.

With everyone warmed and dry, the Land Girls bundled up and went out again to tend to the animals' needs.

That night when Nella finally slipped into bed, she was almost too tired to sleep. "Mind if I read a bit before turning off the light?" she asked her roommates.

"Go ahead," Edith said. Dora didn't answer. She was already asleep.

Nella lifted Gwenyth's diary from her drawer. She was near the end now and hated to give up the book. From the beginning she'd felt close to this girl of long ago—all except for her faith. Then this morning she discovered Gwenyth didn't believe without having doubts. In spite of losing her father and fearing for the lives of her husband and baby, she seemed able to trust in God's care. This steady faith, tested by Gwenyth's own times with the war and a brutal man trying to find her, had impressed Nella deeply.

Tonight the book fell open at the dedication page. Nella had noticed the faded handwriting before but hadn't taken time to try to decipher it. With the strokes so faded, she'd supposed it was useless to try. Now she looked again more intently. Once she realized the wording was very formal and old style, she made some progress in understanding it.

> *I have cause . . . make . . . this book, for the . . . exoneration of an. . . . honorable young . . . woman, my ancestor of Welsh descent. May her true . . . words find . . . home in honest . . . hearts. May her memory be . . . sanctified, and the . . . sins of our fathers cleansed. Herewith I set my hand, Cecile Anne-Marie Westmoreland, sister of Lord Henry James Westmoreland.*

An added line read, *Today found . . . Gwenyth's grave . . . took flowers. C. A. W.*

Nella almost cried aloud in her surprise. She wondered where the grave might be and how Cecile had recognized it. Did the present Lord Westmoreland know the grave had once been discovered?

Nella turned to her bookmark where she'd stopped from before and started reading.

> *Remember,*
> *My child, If you find me gone,*
> *Don't grieve my too soon death.*
> *He who counts hairs on heads and*
> *Marks sparrow's secret fall*
> *Shall keep my heart with thine.*
> *You shall know me when we meet*
> *Beyond the edge of time,*
> *And if He wills, I shall not be*
> *Ever far from thee.*
> *And neither shall He.*

As usual Gwenyth's poems gave her a lump in her throat. Knowing the young mother's fears had come true, that her baby never got to know her, now grieved Nella as if this had happened only yesterday to a close friend. The Welsh bride had feared for her life. Therefore, it seemed highly unlikely she would've committed suicide.

Nella shuddered as she thought of the attempt on her own life. The knowledge that Gwenyth had died when she so wanted to live for her child's sake made Nella want to rush back to the manse and hold Livie in her arms, to sleep beside her and never come back to Whitestone. There must be a way. As Peggy had said, she couldn't go on indefinitely like this.

She turned the page and read some more.

In the final say, my days and nights are in God's hands. If this seems fearful, I am not looking far enough to see His love. His will for me is good. If His will contains a Calvary, it also contains an open tomb and resurrection life. . . .

Nella wished for this kind of confidence and peace of mind. She wished she could write such a statement of trust. She could not, but she copied it into her journal anyway. Then she wrote, *Bryan said he loved me, and regardless of my vow to stay sensible, I feel drawn to him. Yet until I know why he asked me to lie, I dare not trust him. I must keep my distance. He is too attractive to me. . . .* She stopped, looked at what she had written, and blacked it out since she couldn't erase the ink. It bothered her to think her family might read such a confession if she were to die young, as Gwenyth had.

She placed her journal under the clothes in her drawer and laid the bride's diary out where she would be reminded to return it in the morning. Then she went to bed, tossing and fretting her blankets into knots. She began to wish she'd never read the bride's diary. For despite Gwenyth's faith, her suffering was enough to give anyone nightmares.

After breakfast Bryan assigned everyone to shoring up the main bridge over Shearing Creek. The flooding had indeed washed away the fill at each end, leaving the span stranded as an island. He called to Nella, "I'll take you back over the hill to get the tractor. That machine has the power to move boulders, and we're going to have to reconstruct the bank as well as do some filling. Put on your oilskins and gum boots and come to the stable. I'll have a pony saddled for you."

She nodded, curtly she hoped. "I can go alone. I know the way."

"Then who would bring back your pony?" he asked with an irritating quirk to his eyebrow.

If he meant to make her feel foolish, he'd succeeded. A disgusting blush heated her cheeks. "I'll be ready in a few minutes. I'd like to return the book you loaned me. May I take it in to the library?"

"Of course. You've finished reading it, then?"

"Yes."

"Did you enjoy getting to know Gwenyth?"

Nella found she couldn't lie to him. "Yes, I came to like her very much."

"I thought you would. In some ways, you remind me of her. I'd like to hear your thoughts on her as we ride."

She swallowed. "You may not like some of them."

"You may be surprised." He had a serious expression on his face now.

Turning away, Nella said, "I'll meet you shortly at the stable."

CHAPTER THIRTY

Nella moved quickly through Whitestone's long silent hallway. Lord and Lady Westmoreland must be still in bed. She felt like an intruder even though she had permission from Bryan to go to the library. Leaving Gwenyth's diary on a table in the dark formal room, she hurried back to the kitchen and then out to Garden Cottage.

The wireless was reporting that the battle for Aachen and the Scheldt estuary continued with no progress. The Americans in northern France had begun an offensive against Epinal.

"It looks to be a long bitter winter for our troops," Nella remarked.

"Aye. Getting colder already," Dora said.

Edith groaned as she pulled on her boots over thick wool socks. "Days like this I wish I'd signed on at a factory. At least then I'd stay warm and dry."

"Are you sure of that?" Nella teased. "I doubt the factories are all that warm in the winter."

"Righto, Nell," Dora said. "I chanced to visit my mother at work, and I'd take this over what she's doing. Mud washes off, but grease has to wear off. Her nails and hands are a sight worse than mine."

"Do ye think we're getting a mite cocky?" Maureen said. "Remember how we'd do anything to help out in the beginning?"

Edith sighed. "You do have a way of pulling me back to real, Maur. 'Course you're right. Did you hear the latest? Hitler has ordered every male, sixteen to sixty, to join up and fight to the finish. Can you imagine? Children and old men! I guess he wants every German dead with him and as many of our men as he can take out. I wish someone could assassinate him."

"Well, maybe they'll try again and succeed," said Nella. "For our part, I'll be seeing you at the bridge, ladies. I'm to bring the tractor for moving rocks." Nella ducked out before they deduced that she was riding out with Bryan.

As she headed for the stable, her heart lifted like a girl going on a date. She chided herself, tightening her mouth against an urge to smile when she saw Bryan holding Sir William and the pony she'd ridden before.

Without greeting Bryan, she took the reins, mounted the small horse, and kicked her forward up the road. Rain steadily spattered against her face. After the storm, this ordinary shower seemed mild.

Bryan rode alongside and paced the taller horse to the pony's speed. "We can take the road. It'll be easier to cross the creek now, and I want to tell the others what to do till we return."

Oh, fine, she thought. *Even with Shirley gone, Kitty and her friends will make something of this, sooner or later.* She rode stolidly as they approached the washed-out bridge and waited impatiently while he directed three of the girls who had arrived with axes.

"You ladies take down those two trees," he said, pointing. "Fell them over there and limb them. We'll need to lay them as a bed for new planking. The rest of you, clear out the brush and debris that's damming up the flow. Nella will be back shortly with the tractor to lever rocks into a new roadbed at each end of the bridge."

The women groaned and made smart remarks, but Nella noticed they already were picking up their tools.

Bryan urged his horse into the stream, and Nella nudged the pony to follow. Once across, Bryan set off at a trot. As before, Nella held back her pony until she had to lope to catch up. When she came even with Sir William, Bryan slowed him to a walk. Except for the patter of rain on the remaining leaves, they rode on in silence. Not even a crow cawed.

After a while Nella stole a look at Bryan. With a fisherman's knit cap pulled snug and his oilskin spread out over the horse's rump as far as it would stretch, he rode as if he were part of the horse. *A centaur,* she thought. *Peggy would have a better simile, no doubt.* She suppressed a grin.

He turned the second she glanced his way. "So what did you think?"

Nella jumped and couldn't find a quick word to cover for her staring at him.

He smiled. "Of Gwenyth and her poems, I mean. Do you think she had talent?"

For an instant, she'd been afraid he was going to get personal again. She relaxed now.

Under brooding clouds and dripping branches, the woods, so bright with autumn leaves a week ago, now slumped dismal and dark beneath a wintering sky. Riding in the rain on a muddy road seemed an odd time to discuss poetry, but Nella's interest immediately rose to the task. "I'm no judge, but anyone who makes me feel what she feels by putting words on paper surely must possess talent."

"I think so too. I was captivated when I first discovered Gwenyth's poems on a high shelf in the library . . . albeit I was a romantic fifteen then, and she seemed like a princess to me. For a long time I searched for her grave."

Startled, Nella took her eyes off the road to look at him. "You did! Did you find it?"

"No." He slapped the ends of the reins against his thigh, as if still frustrated about it. "I suppose the marker, whatever it was made of, crumbled and fell into the moss long ago."

She sighed. "It's sad. After reading her journal, I feel as though I knew her. I can understand why your long-ago aunt had them translated and preserved. I'd want to do the same. It's such a pity that Gwenyth died so young. . . . Do you think she could have killed herself?" She turned to watch his face.

His expression gave her no clue to his feelings. "It never made sense to me. She seemed so in love with her husband, her baby, and with life."

"And she had such faith in God's love that I can't see her choosing her own way to die."

"That too," he said. "It goes against everything we know about her to say she took her own life."

"Peggy says that in the family history book her husband insisted she had given her life to save her baby."

Brian nodded. "That's what he wrote."

"You don't believe it?"

"There's no way to know the truth. He probably believed she did."

"I wonder why your whole family insisted she killed herself."

"Probably to save their own necks. If Rowan killed her, they wouldn't have dared to oppose him or Owain. They weren't strong enough to protect themselves until they formed the alliance with William's second marriage."

"What if a Westmoreland murdered the Welsh bride so that alliance could be made?"

He turned to her with eyes narrowed, and frowned. "You think to save their own necks they killed her and married off William to a powerful family?"

Nella realized she'd gone too far in her speculations. She was surprised at the hurt in his voice. "I'm sorry. I got carried away. As you said, it doesn't matter now...."

The sucking mud under the horses' hoofs punctuated the silence now between them. Irritated, she glanced at him. He hadn't even acknowledged her apology.

As they rode on, she reflected on what she'd read last night. It seemed to her that Gwenyth had voiced more than worry about the dangers of childbirth. "It's sad that people should think a courageous woman gave up and killed herself. I wish—"

He gave her a sharp look. "So you want to play detective at this late date?"

"No, of course not—"

"Good. No point now." He turned his attention to the road, but even his profile looked stern. "There are times when curiosity is a dangerous trait. I suspect that's the way it was back then with Owain's rebellion in full swing."

She let that remark hang between them for a while, then said, "Why did you loan Peggy and me a book about a life that ends in tragedy and possibly casts a bad light on your family?"

He looked at her sharply. "I never saw the story that way. I loaned the book to Peggy to help her students see the truth about all this ghost story claptrap. As for you ... maybe I wanted a Welsh girl such as yourself to know that the Welsh bride was loved and cherished by her English husband."

"I'm not Welsh."

"Perhaps neither are you forgiving."

His brown eyes challenged her, and then the odd concealing look came over him again. "In the days of Gwenyth and William, one murder justified another, creating feuds that lasted for generations. Maybe one Westmoreland preferred to practice Christian forgiveness rather than enter into a long history of bloodshed." Without a change in tone or pace, he said, "When we get back with the tractor, you'll have to work fast to get a good bed of rock laid before the end of the day. The longer the stream washes at the new bank, the more difficult it will be to repair."

So much for his wish to discuss the diary of the Welsh bride. She sighed and clamped her mouth shut, wishing herself to the tractor as soon as possible.

———— ★ ————

In Abergavenny, after the rain had let up, Peggy bicycled out to West-Holding with an overnight carrier strapped to the back of her bike. As she passed by the post office, a man stepped out the door. For a minute she thought she knew him and almost called hello. Then when she came closer she saw he wasn't the villager she'd expected, yet he did look familiar. He glanced up at her. The narrowed eyes and grim mouth tripped up her speculating. This man had been with Bryan that day in the alley, along with the man now dead and the one resembling a codfish. He had a cruel look and seemed to see through her, making her want to hurry away. What on earth was he doing in West-Holding? Here to see Bryan maybe?

Peggy passed him in a second and then pedaled on toward Gatekeep. Looking back, she noticed the man walking down the street behind her. The minute he saw that she was staring at him, he stopped and turned into the pub.

At Gatekeep she parked her bicycle and hurried in to greet Mrs. Lewis. A few minutes later from her front bedroom window, she saw the same strange man walking by. He glanced quickly at the cottage as he strode past. He looked furtive. All the risky business surrounding Nella made her jumpy and suspicious, but Peggy truly felt the man had followed her and marked where she was staying.

No point in guessing or worrying Nella about the man. Nevertheless, she'd keep her eyes open in case he showed up again.

After she settled into her room, she walked down to Brookside and presented her idea to Mrs. Nelson about helping Annie with her art education. Once the idea had been happily received, she asked permission to take Annie to meet Albert.

Returning to Gatekeep, she rang up Whitestone and left a message to let Nella know she was in the village.

At the end of the school day Annie came to Gatekeep, and Peggy laid out pastels for them both to draw portraits of each other. Then after a knock at the door, Mrs. Lewis ushered Laurie into the kitchen where Peggy and Annie were drawing.

"Hello," he said. "Our all-seeing, all-knowing postman told me you were in town, Peggy. Mind if I sit in on the art lesson?"

Peggy signed to Annie, *"This is my friend."* She leaned over and wrote his name on a piece of scrap paper.

Annie nodded and smiled. Her hands flew as she signed, *"I'm pleased to meet Mr. Barringer. Will he let us draw him?"*

Peggy laughed and translated to Laurie.

He put his hand on his flat waist, bowed exaggeratedly, and said, "I would consider it an honor."

Annie giggled, and when Peggy relayed his words, she clapped her hands and signed, *"Tell him first he must learn my signs."*

So for a few minutes Annie taught Laurie the signs for *hello, how are you, I'm fine, please,* and *thank you,* while Peggy served as the translator.

Then Laurie sat near the window and turned his head at Annie's command until she was satisfied with his pose. Taking care not to move his head while Annie drew, he said to Peggy, "She's remarkable. I can see why you're so taken with her. Bright as a new shilling in the summer sun."

Annie kept her eyes on him, sketching vigorously, seemingly undisturbed that she was missing the conversation.

"Wait till you see what she produces," Peggy said, holding up Annie's first sketch of herself.

"Great Johnny Hopkins! She did that?"

"She sure did."

"I can't wait to see what she does of me."

Mrs. Lewis set a teapot in a cozy and cups on the table for all of them. Annie kept working, so Laurie continued to sit like a statue.

Finally, Annie signed to Peggy, *"All done. I want my tea cake now."*

Peggy laughed. *"Go ahead. May I show him what you did?"*

Annie nodded, smiling.

Peggy passed the drawing to Laurie. He studied it and said softly, "I don't know what to say. She's so good. What can anyone show her?"

"That's my problem. What kind of assistance can I give her that won't interfere with her natural style?"

"I really must show this one to Meredith. Ask Annie if I may."

Peggy asked the question, and Annie signed back, *"I did it for him to keep."*

When Laurie understood, he awkwardly motioned, *"Thank you."*

"You're welcome," signed Annie.

Laurie guessed the meaning and then nodded with a smile.

Watching him with Annie only made Peggy more captivated by this tall, kind man. It was her misfortune that he'd been born into the gentry. While she liked him, she knew she'd never fit in his life. Their ways were too incongruent. Still, they could be friends. . . .

Mrs. Lewis joined them for tea, and afterward Peggy and Laurie walked Annie home where Laurie met her family. Peggy could see that he'd been a hit with all of them and was glad.

The work on the bridge progressed very smoothly with Bryan overseeing the steps of reconstruction. However, it turned into an extra long day. When Nella parked the tractor in the shed, it was all she could do to make herself eat supper before falling into bed. Then just before undressing, she realized she'd left her wet rain gear rolled up and strapped behind the tractor seat. The rain had stopped before they'd quit, and all she'd been able to focus on was the prospect of rest. Now she had no choice but to go back to the barn and get it, or she would spend a miserable day tomorrow in cold, soggy clothing.

So she grabbed her coat and tromped out again. The wind had died down now, and stars gleamed through breaks in the clouds. The cloud-draped moon gave off a little light. As she crossed the drive and marched toward the barn, Ember suddenly nosed her hand. "Hello, good dog." She scratched Ember's neck. Her undercoat had remained soft and dry, but her outer fur suggested a recent trek in the rain. She usually stayed under cover in a heavy rain. "Where have you been? Don't you know it's bedtime?"

Ember danced foolishly, woofed, and with ears at alert, stared behind Nella.

Nella jumped. There Bryan stood not three meters away. "Oh! You scared me. What are you doing out here?" she asked him.

He laughed. "If that dog could talk, she might ask you the same thing. I thought you'd be so tired, you'd be asleep by now."

"I left my oilskins rolled up on the tractor. I need to hang them up to dry." She started walking toward the tractor shed.

He matched her pace. "I'm going that way too. I want to fill the tank with petrol for tomorrow."

So much for getting away from him, she thought. Against her will her heart speeded up. "Do you think it will rain again tomorrow?" she said, for the sake of saying something impersonal.

"Weather report says no, but who knows." He inhaled deeply. "I've always liked the smell of autumn, especially after the first rains."

"You sound like a farmer at heart," she said, her voice betraying her surprise.

"At heart," he repeated with amusement. "The word comes easily to your lips, for a young woman who seems sometimes heart-less."

She stopped. "What on earth do you mean by that?"

Bryan paused beside her. She wished she could see his face clearer, but it was too dark.

"What I mean is that you haven't forgiven me for my clumsy, presumptuous behavior," he said.

She caught her breath, glad he couldn't see her face. "All right. If that's an apology, I accept it, and I forgive you." *Walk away*, an inner voice warned, but a conflicting thought compelled her to stand her ground and face him. Once and for all she must look straight at this man and see him for what he was, the pampered son of a lord, who somehow had managed to avoid military service when his country most needed him. Rob had enlisted in Canada and crossed an ocean to fight for English land. From what she'd heard, Bryan had continued his easy life at Oxford as long as he could and then simply came home to Wales. She concentrated on this, imagining him ensconced in the manor like a schoolboy, home for a holiday.

"I wish I could believe you meant that," he said quietly.

"Of course I meant it." It was time to put an end to this conversation. She turned and headed toward the tractor shed. She could hear his steps crunching on the gravel behind her, but he didn't speak.

In the shed he turned on an electric torch and began to tinker with the tractor. She realized she should've brought her own torch. She had supposed she could feel her way around enough to grasp her rain gear and unlash it from the tractor seat. Now, although she found her oilskins easily enough, she couldn't unfasten the wet straps that held them. She worked and worked at it, hearing him rattle metal against metal, then the sound of petrol gurgling. The odor of the fumes drifted toward her. He'd propped his torch so he could see, and it cast black shadows on her own project. The gurgling stopped, and she heard him replace the cap on the tank.

Light beams swung around her when he picked up his torch and moved. The shadows reflected his pause. Conscientiously she kept her eyes on her task. Surely he'd offer her the light and maybe even work the wet knots loose. In the next instant the light moved, and she heard him walk away. He was going to leave her here in the dark. Of all the arrogant ingrates. "Bryan!"

He returned. "Yes?"

"The torch. May I use your torch?" She was so angry she said it like a command rather than a question.

"Certainly. I thought you'd never ask." His light tone made her angrier. He didn't hand her the light but instead stood shining it onto the knotted lashing.

Nella struggled harder, and suddenly her hand slipped. "Ouch!" she gasped. Hunching over, she clamped her other hand tightly over the sudden pain.

"What happened? What did you do?"

"Nothing. Just a scrape," she said through clenched teeth.

He reached for her hand. "Let me see."

She slowly unfolded her fingers, and he held the torch close. "Oh!" he exclaimed. Her hand was sticky and smeared red. A ragged tear ran from the heel of her hand into her palm. "Whatever did you hit?" He pulled a handkerchief from his coat pocket and wrapped it around her hand. "Hold that in place. Come along to the house. You need that cleaned and bandaged properly."

"No, it'll be all right—"

"Come along," he ordered. With a firm grip on her arm, he led her to the manor kitchen.

At the sight of Nella holding the handkerchief around her hand, Mrs. Harrison turned into a fussing mama. She seated Nella near the heat of the huge old cooking range and fetched the medical box she kept on hand for tending minor injuries. Bryan lingered, watching while she bathed Nella's hand, dried it, applied iodine, and bandaged it. "Had she better have a tetanus shot?" Mrs. Harrison asked Bryan.

"I had one when I enlisted and another when I hit my head," Nella volunteered.

"I'll ring up the doctor in the morning and ask," Bryan said. "You all right for now? I'll see you to the cottage."

"Yes." No point in making more fuss than she'd already created.

After breakfast the next morning, Bryan called her aside as the women were leaving for their work assignments. "You need to keep your hand clean and dry for today at least. Put on some warmer clothing. I want you to ride out with me to take our new sheep to Will. Father says Ember can probably manage them adequately if you go along. Meet me at the stable in fifteen minutes."

"All right." In spite of her good intentions to dampen her feelings toward him, the thought of spending the next several hours with him stirred a happy tingle in her chest.

When she reached the stable, he had the horses saddled and was busy strapping a bundle behind Sir William's saddle. "Lunch," he said. "Is that your rain gear?"

"Yes. Still a bit wet, but usable."

"Good." He took the oilskins from her and strapped them behind her pony's saddle.

It took only a few more minutes to open the sheepfold and get Ember to bunch the small flock of sheep and start them moving toward the far pastures. The rain of the previous days had moved out over the sea now, leaving every branch and leaf glistening in the sun.

Nella kept her attention on the dog and the sheep. Bryan rode beside her in silence.

Ember performed flawlessly. Nella began to relax and enjoy the quiet work with the animals. Working with a good dog gave her both peace and joy. If she were to tell Bryan how she felt, she'd probably say something like the overused phrase, "God's in His heaven, all's right with the world." But how stupid that would be, with the war and all, especially with her here and Livie in town with her grandparents. She sighed and unconsciously kicked the sides of her small mount, and willingly broke into a trot. Reining her in, she glanced at Bryan. "Sorry. I got to thinking about the war."

"Easy to do, what with the fighting grinding on and on."

"Do you think it will be a long struggle to get to Berlin?"

"No doubt about that. The Germans will be as desperate to protect their homeland as us. There'll be a lot of bloodshed, some of it civilian. It's too bad it has to come to this."

His conciliatory attitude grated on her. "But the Germans have brought it on themselves. They put Hitler in power."

"No doubt about that. But I had some good friends who were German. They were entrapped. Once they saw the truth, they couldn't escape."

"I wish those men had managed to assassinate Hitler when they tried."

"That may not have been a solution."

She turned in her saddle to try to read his face, but he had that closed, unreadable expression again. "You sound unusually sorry for the enemy," she challenged.

He flicked a glance at her, then watching the sheep ahead of them, he replied, "They are people who hurt like we do, Nella." He kicked his horse and moved around the left flank of the sheep and into the lead. The sudden movement of the horse scattered a few ewes.

Ember ran to gather them into the flock again.

Nella watched Bryan up ahead of her. All the questions he provoked spun around in her mind. His remarks were too ambiguous. What did this man really think and believe?

CHAPTER THIRTY-ONE

By the time Nella and Bryan arrived at the sheepherder's hut, it was so close to lunchtime that Bryan accepted Will's offer of tea and spread out the lunch he'd brought on the rustic kitchen table.

Ember had been allowed inside now that Will's sheep dogs were watching over the new sheep. Nella sneaked bites of her pasty to the gray dog while the men discussed a stray ewe that had been injured by some kind of a predator.

"I'll be watching 'em closer now," Will said, visibly distressed.

"These things happen, no matter how closely we watch. It's part of the business," Bryan said. "Did you see any tracks?"

"Aye. It looked like several dogs. One a good deal bigger than my dogs. Probably untrained pets of villagers or of some small holder."

Bryan sighed. "Probably. I'll keep an eye out. They could still be around."

Will nodded. "No doubt they'll come back. Hard to break them of chasing sheep once they start."

Bryan pushed a thick pasty toward the old man. "Mrs. Harrison sent these especially for you, remembering how you like lots of onions."

Will bit into the thick crust, chewed lustily, and then wiped his mouth with the back of his hand. "She'd make some lucky man a fine wife if she was willing to marry again. She's wasting her talent on folk that don't even like a good pasty."

"Her talent isn't wasted on me," said Bryan. "But my mother and father prize her for her Yorkshire puddings and lemon curd."

Nella surreptitiously slipped Ember another bite of the crust from her pasty.

Will gave her a sideways glance and smiled. "You're right fond of that lass, I see."

Nella grinned. "She's a gem. Whenever you decide to use her, you'll find she's learned her lessons well."

"Aye, no doubt. The lord himself has bragged on how you've brought her into line. One day I'll give her a try again."

Bryan stretched. "Well, it's time to go back. The way Nella is feeding Ember, she'll need a good run."

While Bryan gave a few final instructions about the new sheep, Nella went out and led the horses from the small barn where they'd been tethered and mounted her own. Ember followed as she rode to meet Bryan. Although Ember greeted Bryan as part of her family, she definitely preferred Nella's company. This made Nella smile secretly. The dog simply knew who liked her best.

On the road home the sunlight remained dazzling. Ember ranged into the woods beside the road and out again, following her nose now that she had no sheep to guard. They hadn't ridden for more than fifteen minutes when Ember, out of sight in the woods, began barking furiously—her bark of alarm.

Nella yanked her horse to a halt. "She's cornered something."

"Or something has cornered her." Bryan leaped to the ground, dropped his reins over a bush, and ran toward the barking. By the time Nella got her horse tethered, furious growls and yips came from the woods. The deep bark of a very large dog joined the chaos of snarls and yips. The pack of dogs that Will had mentioned—Ember must've confronted them! Or they'd become serious predators and attacked her. She could be killed.

With her stomach curled into a knot of panic, Nella ran toward the chaos. Through the trees she spied a melee of snarling dogs, one a huge German shepherd. A flash of white and gray told her they had Ember down. Bryan, crouching beside the lunging bodies, snatched up a broken tree limb. He wielded it as a club, yelling commands and knocking dogs to the left and right. Gradually the pack backed away and then fled en masse. Ember lay on the ground not moving. Beside her lay the remains of a yearling lamb.

Nella ran to Ember. The dog was bleeding from a dozen wounds. She cried Ember's name and reached for her. Opening her eyes, Ember whined and then licked Nella's hand.

Nella's eyes filled with tears. "Oh, Ember! Good dog. Good dog."

Bryan knelt beside her. "Let me check her."

Nella moved back, keeping her hand on Ember's silky head. She watched as Bryan gently inspected the sources of bleeding. Finally he turned to Nella. "She's going to be all right, but we have to get her to the vet. Can you get my coat from my saddle? I want to wrap her to carry her."

The look on his face, one of both pain and tenderness, drove straight to her heart. For all of his complaining about Ember, he loved her!

She ran back to the horses and returned quickly with his weatherproof jacket. He tucked the coat around Ember and gently turned her over until he could get a good grip on her. His unguarded look of compassion told Nella more about him than all of his words to date. Peggy was wrong. Whatever else Bryan Westmoreland was, Nella felt sure he wasn't irresponsible, as Peggy had said. He'd said he loved her, and now she had a glimpse of how caring and gentle he could be.

All the way back to the manor, Bryan carefully cradled Ember in front of him across the saddle, as they rode at a fast walk. Nella watched as he adjusted his supporting grip on the dog to ease her through every movement of the horse. Ember lay with her head against his thigh, eyes open, but glazed from pain.

They arrived at Whitestone in less than half the time it had taken to deliver the sheep to Will. At the stable Bryan dismounted and carefully placed Ember on clean straw in an unused stall.

"Stay with her," he said to Nella. "I'll go call the vet and tell Father."

In minutes Lord Westmoreland appeared and took Nella's place beside the dog. As she stood up to leave, she said, "What will be done about the pack of dogs?"

His face hardened. "Bryan will take care of them. They could become a danger to people as well as livestock."

Because of it being near suppertime, Bryan didn't assign her more work. So Nella headed for Garden Cottage while he and his father took Ember into town to the vet. As she watched them leave in the farm lorry with the dog on Lord Westmoreland's lap, she realized she had irrevocably fallen in love with Bryan. In fact, maybe she'd loved him for a long time and his behavior today simply made her admit it.

She cleaned up and lay down on her cot to rest, but her mind and emotions were moving like a speeding train. She reached for her journal. When she couldn't talk to Peggy, writing helped her to think more clearly. *I never thought this could happen.* To her great surprise, it was possible to still love Rob and at the same time love Bryan in a different way. *Have I failed Livie? There's still so much I don't know about*

Bryan. I shall have to remind myself that nothing has changed except how I feel....

———⭐———

Saturday morning Peggy rang up Whitestone and asked for Nella.

A few minutes later, Nella called back. "I'm so glad you're at Gatekeep! Maybe we can get together later today."

"I was hoping you'd walk with me over the hill to look for the home of the deaf man. If he and his mother agree, I'd like to teach them sign language. I thought we could take Annie with us."

"It might be a long walk."

"She's up to it. Her mum thinks it would be a good experience for her."

"Why don't we locate the cottage this afternoon, and then if Albert and his mother are interested, we can take Annie another time?"

"Good idea. I'll tell her mother. Shall I meet you at the shearing barn, then? What time?"

"I think I can get away right after lunch, so about two o'clock again."

After Nella rang off, Peggy put on her coat and walked to Brookside, thinking she'd at least talk to Annie about teaching Albert sign language.

Mrs. Nelson welcomed her without her usual cheery hello and invited her inside.

"Has something happened?" Peggy asked. "What's wrong?"

"It's Annie. She's very upset and won't tell me why."

Annie sat hunched in an upholstered chair, staring out the window toward the hills beyond her special hideaway. She hadn't yet noticed Peggy's presence.

"The girls have tried to get her to go out and play with them, but she refused. She just sits there. I'm sure something terrible has happened!"

"Do you mind if I try to talk with her?"

Mrs. Nelson shook her head. "Please do."

Peggy went and touched Annie's shoulder. Annie turned slowly, saw her, and then turned away.

Peggy knelt beside her chair. *How do I communicate with a deaf person who won't look at me?* she wondered. She decided to pull up a chair and simply sit there with Annie.

They sat silently for several minutes until finally the child turned and began to speak with her hands. They flew much too fast for Peggy to follow.

Fortunately Mrs. Nelson was watching. "She says she doesn't want to go to school here anymore. She wants to go back to the city—to her old school."

Peggy signed, *"Why? What happened?"*

Annie, with her lips pressed tight, signed carefully, *"I want to go to my old school."*

"But what has happened to make you feel this way? Can you tell me?"

The child lowered her chin and bit her lip, but Peggy could see the tears pooling in her eyes. Peggy looked to Mrs. Nelson for help.

Mrs. Nelson shook her head and said quietly, "Try again."

Peggy leaned forward. *"Would you come for a walk with me so we can talk?"*

Annie vigorously shook her head.

The girl's vehement expression took Peggy by complete surprise. She signed, *"I'm sorry if I've offended you. Very sorry."*

Annie signed, *"I don't need you or anybody. I never wanted to come here."*

Mrs. Nelson started forward, looking embarrassed over her daughter's behavior.

"It's all right," Peggy said. "Let's let her talk." Then she turned to Annie. *"I care about you. I hated leaving West-Holding School, mostly because of you."*

"Then why did you go? It's all your fault. Lady West... more... land said so."

Peggy gasped.

With a look of pure desperation, Annie looked at her mother and signed, *"I don't want to talk anymore."* She began to sob.

Her mother gathered her in her arms and, over the child's head, said to Peggy, "Maybe it's best you go now, but thank you. At least you got her talking. I'll let you know when I learn more about what happened."

Peggy walked back to Gatekeep, heartsick over the sudden unhappy change in Annie. The trusting, outgoing child had actually turned bitter. Surely Lady Westmoreland wouldn't have intentionally hurt a child. Despite her authoritarian ways, she did care about the children.

There was no way to know, however, if Annie refused to tell. If Mrs. Nelson had learned nothing by the time Peggy planned to meet

Nella, she would go up to Whitestone and ask to speak with Lady Westmoreland.

She hated the thought, yet she had to learn the truth. She wouldn't back down to anyone when it came to Annie. Her future, as well as her present happiness, could be at stake.

After a quick lunch with Mrs. Lewis, Peggy went back to Brookside. Mrs. Nelson invited her in but said Annie hadn't revealed any details and finally refused to talk about what had happened.

She led Peggy into the kitchen where the cooking range warmed the whole room. Emma and Frances sat at the table playing a board game. Annie was nowhere in sight. "Hello, girls. I see you've found a cozy spot to play."

"Hello, Miss Jones," Emma said. "Have you come to see Annie?"

"Well, yes. And to say hello to you too. How are you?"

"We want Annie to play with us, Miss Jones," Frances said. "Can you get her to come out of her room?"

"I'll bring her," Mrs. Nelson said.

"No, wait. Let me talk with the girls first." She sat down across the table from them. "Do either of you have any idea why Anne is so unhappy?"

Emma shook her head. "She just came home from school yesterday mad as anything and said she wasn't going back."

"So we said we wouldn't go back either," Frances exclaimed. "Then Annie got mad at us."

"And she never told you why she suddenly hated school?"

"She said she'd learned all she needed to know."

Peggy sighed. Annie could be very private, apparently even with her sisters.

"Shall I get Annie now?" Mrs. Nelson asked. "Would you like to try talking to her again?"

"What do you think? I don't want to press her if it'll just upset her."

"Maybe she'll talk to you now. Let me go get her."

In a few minutes she came back, shaking her head. "I'm sorry, but Annie says it's not Lady Westmoreland she's upset about. It's . . . it's you. She says she never should've believed anything you said. I . . . I'm sorry, but I feel you should know this. I can't imagine what has so changed her. She's always loved you." Mrs. Nelson slumped onto a chair beside her two younger girls. "I don't know what to do. This just isn't like her at all. . . ."

"I've got to find out what happened," Peggy said. "I have a hunch

Lady Westmoreland may be able to shed some light on this. I'm going up to Whitestone."

"Shouldn't you telephone first?"

"No. I think I'll take my chances. Anyway, I have a date with Nella, so I'll just go a bit early. If Lady Westmoreland won't see me, Nella might be able to learn something through Bryan. He seems to like her a lot." Peggy spoke with assurance, but she didn't feel confident at all. The minute she thought of approaching Lady W., she wanted to do battle. Yet for Annie's sake, she must behave peaceably, and she wasn't sure she could.

CHAPTER THIRTY-TWO

To Peggy's dismay, neither the lady nor the lord of the manor was at home. With travel so difficult and petrol severely rationed, she'd supposed they would be. But then, Laurie managed to drive about, and he didn't even have a farming allotment.

Nella had just finished lunch. "Give me a few minutes to change from my coveralls and boots, and then we can go. There's a trail here by the kitchen garden that will take us directly to the chapel and on over the hill. Come along while I change."

"Fine by me," Peggy said. As they crossed the deep green lawn between the great house and Garden Cottage, Peggy told her about Annie's distress.

"That's too bad," Nella murmured. "What about Peter Hilliard? You said they're good friends. Any chance he might know something?"

"I didn't think of that. Maybe I should call and ask for Laurie. I know I won't get through if Peter's mother answers. But could you speak to Bryan too? Ask him if he can find out anything?"

Nella's cheeks blossomed pink. "I guess I could."

"You know you could. He's smitten with you. Take advantage of the situation."

"Peggy!"

Peggy peered at her. Nella looked altogether too agitated. No doubt about it. She was more than attracted to Bryan. "You've really fallen for him, haven't you? For pete's sake, think, Nella. There's too much about Bryan that doesn't add up. Where is that instinct that you claim to have about people?"

Nella put a finger to her lips. "Don't let the others hear you."

As they entered Garden Cottage, Peggy glanced at the women chattering in the front room. "They're so busy talking, they can't hear anything but themselves." But she still lowered her voice to a whisper. "How can you love someone you can't trust?" The mintue she said this, she wanted to take it back.

Pain flashed across Nella's face, but she only said, "You mean *you* can't trust him."

Peggy followed her to her bedroom and sat on a cot while Nella put on clean clothes. "It's just that I'm so worried for you."

"I guess what hurts is you don't trust me."

"I do trust you, but... not your judgment right now. Does that make sense?"

"Your problem is that you think the world should make sense. A lot of life doesn't make sense. Why a woman loves one man and not another will never be logical. Surely you know that." Her smile softened her words.

Peggy grinned and threw up her hands in defeat. "You win. I will try to keep my mouth shut from now on." But she couldn't turn off her anxiety that easily. She felt more desperate than ever about figuring out a way for Nella to leave Whitestone.

"Okay, I'm ready," Nella announced as she finished tying her walking shoes and grabbed her jacket. "Let's go, only first I want to run down to the barn and look in on Ember."

"Oh yes. How is she?"

"Coming along all right, poor thing."

As they walked, Peggy returned to her concern for Annie. "Nella, you will try to find out what you can through Bryan, won't you... for Annie's sake?"

"Of course, if there's an opportunity to talk with him."

"You can make one."

Before Nella could answer, they passed near the stable, and there stood Bryan inside the open doorway talking to three men. The deaf man Albert stood to one side, staring at a horse in the paddock. His mother was nowhere in sight, so he must've wandered to the manor by himself. The other men acted as if he weren't even there. Peggy remembered the times she'd been treated that way and how it felt. Was Albert aware of the common slight? She couldn't tell.

Then she saw the face of one of the other men. It was the grim man, whom she thought had followed her to Gatekeep. Just looking at him set her nerves awry. Still, it wasn't fair to be judging him by his looks. Even if he did remind her of a medieval executioner, he probably was an agricultural agent or something.

Nella led Peggy on to the livestock barn where Ember lay on a mat of clean straw in a small stall of her own. While Nella was telling Peggy about the attack, Bryan came in.

"I was going to rub some more salve on her wounds," he said. "Hello, Peggy. Come to join the Land Army for a day?"

"Not on a bet," she answered.

Nella held her breath for fear Peggy would bring up uncomfortable questions about Lady Westmoreland and Annie. Nella couldn't picture Lady Westmoreland doing anything cruel to a child. She was set in her ways and domineering but not mean.

Peggy didn't pursue the subject. Instead, and almost as embarrassingly, she stood back, watching Nella, as if to say, "Get started."

Nella stammered, "Peggy is staying at Gatekeep this week . . . and we planned to go walking today. Would you like me to put the salve on Ember . . . before we leave?"

He grinned. "Since when have you begun to ask?" He handed her the medication and turned to Peggy. "Did she tell you about the dog's narrow escape?"

"Yes. Have you identified the rogue dogs?"

"Some of them. Their owners have the choice of putting them down or shipping them off to where there's no livestock."

Nella looked up from smoothing medicine over the shaved wound on Ember's shoulder. "It's sad. They're probably family pets."

Bryan looked at her with raised eyebrows. "I thought you wanted to be a farmer. You can't be sentimental about livestock predators."

She sighed. "I know. It's just that after the heat of the battle, it becomes a pretty cold-blooded deed."

Bryan narrowed his eyes and frowned as he stared down at Ember. "Kind of like war. Men do what they must, and then they look back and wonder if they might've had a different choice."

"That's true, I suppose," Peggy said, "but you'd better be careful who's listening when you say that. Sounds a bit soft on the Nazis."

"I meant it to be soft on all men." He slapped his work gloves against his thigh and said to Nella, "Leave the salve on that shelf, and I'll check her again at bedtime."

He left and when he was out of earshot, Nella said, "Do you see a change in him?"

Peggy stooped and patted Ember's head. "No. I still think he's a man playing both ends against the middle to get what he wants."

Nella burst out, "If you'd seen him when he rescued Ember and how he carried her home, then you'd agree with me. He was so compassionate. You mentioned my instincts. I do have this kind of inner sense that he's totally trustworthy. And this is absolutely separate from how I feel about him. Either we haven't really known him, or he's changed."

"I'll tell you how he's changed. He's changed in your eyes only. You've fallen for him, Nella, and therefore you're not in your right mind."

"That's not true. Well, at least I'm in my right mind. I think I've loved him quite a while but just couldn't admit it. For me, loving a man has to be all right for Livie and not disrespectful of her father's memory. I have to make sure of this . . . but I do love Bryan."

Peggy chewed her lip, obviously burning to offer more advice. In a careful manner she asked, "Does Bryan know?"

"Not yet."

"Then please don't tell him. Let's plan a way to get you safely away from here. Give yourself some time away from him. If you really love him, it won't hurt anything. If he loves you, he still will when it's safe for you to return. I don't like you being here where he's the boss—the British lord with his Welsh girl."

Anger consumed Nella's self-control. "Peggy," she sputtered, "keep out of what you cannot know!"

Peggy snapped back, "All right. Well, maybe I should just head back to Gatekeep. We can talk later." She turned and stomped to the door of the barn.

Nella hesitated, still angry, and then she ran after her. "No. Please don't go."

Peggy stopped and heaved a big sigh. "You were right. It's none of my business. I just don't like being wrong." She reached out for a hug.

Nella obliged, and together they returned to Ember's stall. Nella smiled. "I'm glad you care enough to want to protect me. Thanks."

Peggy chuckled. "You thank me for insulting your intelligence."

Nella knelt down, daubed some more salve on Ember's shoulder wound, and teased back, "Well, thanks for thinking I have any."

"So shall we climb the hill and look for Dabney Cottage as we planned? Did I tell you I found its location on an old map?"

"No, you didn't. I wonder if the cottage is the same woodcutter's cottage the Welsh bride mentioned in her diary. By the way, let's also look along the way for Gwenyth's grave."

"Her grave. Why?"

"No one knows where it is. You'll think this is silly, but I feel as if I knew her. Reading her diary reminded me of how I felt when I first fell in love with Rob, and of my joy when we were expecting Livie, and even this . . . this scary situation now with someone threatening my life. You have to agree there are parallels. I have this strange feeling . . . it's important for me to know where she was buried."

"I guess I mostly was impressed," Peggy said slowly, "with her un-wavering faith and the beauty of her written prayers. They're inspiring, coming from a girl so young."

"That too. I returned the book to the manor library, but I copied some of her poems and prayers. The last one I read convinced me she didn't kill herself. And yet Lord Westmoreland says she wasn't buried in the family cemetery due to her having committed suicide."

"Hmm. So the family ghost story may have started with someone who disagreed with the suicide theory."

"Could be. I wish Gwenyth could know that some of us still care about her today, that she's an inspiration when we're frightened."

"Father Mac would say that someday, when you get to heaven, you can tell her, or maybe she does know now."

"I hope so. I hope Rob knows that I still love him."

"Dear heart, if he doesn't, then it's because heaven is so wonderful he doesn't need to know." Peggy gave her another hug and then turned toward Ember who had remained on her straw bed. "Are you finished treating the dog?"

"Yes. We can go now. I know the general direction of the trail Albert takes to go home."

"I do hope he and his mother accept some lessons in sign lan-guage. It would make his life so much easier, and I think Annie might cheer up if she could help him."

They crossed the kitchen garden and took the trail upward through a sloping green pasture to the tree line. Most of the leaves had fallen now, allowing light into areas that had seemed dark and forbidding in the summer. Without stopping they passed the ceme-tery and chapel and followed the trail that Albert had taken the last time Nella saw him near the chapel. The route ran at a gentle slope down the opposite side of the hill from Whitestone.

As they walked, Nella glanced from left to right, searching for a hint of an ancient grave marker. At a branch in the trail, they stopped to rest.

"Which way now?" Peggy asked.

"I suppose the more worn trail is the one that leads to their cottage, but why don't we go explore the other a bit, just to see what's there?"

"You and your search for the grave," Peggy remarked.

"Yes, but I do just want to know what's there."

"Okay. Lead on."

After a while, Nella stopped. "Maybe we should go back now. We can come this way another day." Suddenly she spied an opening in the rocks above the trail, a small cave that would be hidden were the leaves on the trees. She was positive she only noticed the cave now because the light was hitting it just right. Maybe it really wasn't a cave. "Wait! I have to see what this is."

Nella climbed the jumble of rocks and stopped. She couldn't see any hint of a cave, only more rocks and bushes.

Still standing on the trail below, Peggy called, "What is it? Did you think you saw a gravestone?"

"No. I thought I saw the opening to a cave." She pushed at the thorny bushes. "Ouch!"

"Well, come on. It can't be worth going into a briar patch."

"Right." Nella went to back out, but a branch grabbed and held her shoelace. "Oops." She bent to pull her foot free, and then she saw it, dead ahead through the lower limbs of the bushes. "Peggy. Come on up. I found a cave."

By the time Peggy reached her side, she had separated the bushes enough to crawl to the opening. She led the way, pausing at the entry to look for animal tracks. There was no sign that any creature had entered. She crept in on all fours. The light from the opening faded quickly into almost total darkness. Looking back, Nella said, "Come on in. I think it's rather big."

Peggy crept in and squatted beside her. "I think you're right. Have you tried standing up yet?"

"I thought I'd wait till my eyes adjust. Listen. I hear running water. Maybe there's a stream in here."

They sat quietly and after a bit found they could see the dim shape of a cavern with several black openings, mouths of caves leading deeper into the hill.

Peggy said, "This doesn't look man-made, not like a mine, anyway. It's spooky. Let's get out of here."

"I wish we had an electric torch."

"Maybe we can come back with one later." Peggy started to crawl out.

Nella followed. When they stood up outside the thicket of bushes again and she looked back, the cave had become invisible again. "This would be an ideal hideaway. I wonder if Bryan and his cousins ever hunted dragons here." Peggy didn't say anything, probably wanting to avoid talking about Bryan. So for her sake, Nella changed the subject. "Let's backtrack now and see if we can find where Albert lives." The huge mute man had stirred her sympathy, and maybe Peggy's hand signing would help encourage him.

The other trail continued downward. After about fifteen minutes they came to a meadow. On the near edge stood a small stone cottage and a few outbuildings. A narrow drive angled between hedgerows to a still lower vale and more woods. Close to the cottage lay a tidy kitchen garden, and inside a fieldstone fence, three goats grazed in a stretch of pasture. In the dooryard a small flock of chickens scratched at the ground.

"You suppose this is it?" Peggy asked.

"I know how to find out."

As they approached, despite the presence of the animals, something about the cottage gave it the air of an abandoned house, an empty shell of a home that had once been filled with a family. She supposed this was because the building looked so very old, even though in good shape for its age. Nella went to the faded green door and knocked.

The gray-haired mother of Albert appeared, peeking out from the cracked-open door. "Oh, it's the Land Army miss. How ever did you find us?" Without waiting for an answer, she swung the door wide. "Do come in. We have so few guests up here that I forgot my manners. Come sit right down and let me bring you a cup of tea."

"Thank you, but we don't want to put you to all that work," said Nella. "My friend Peggy here is a schoolteacher, and when she met Albert, she became interested in teaching him sign language. I didn't know if he'd learned any, so we were wondering if you would want to try signing with him ... that is, if he doesn't already know. . . ." She felt more and more awkward, as Albert's mother appeared to be mystified by Nella's words.

The older woman smiled and patted her arm. "You just sit down now. I'll bring tea, and then you can explain those signs to me." She motioned to her small parlor.

"Thank you," Nella said. "Actually we'd love tea."

"I don't think she knows what you were talking about," Peggy whispered. "Do you suppose they've been isolated from help for all of Albert's life?"

"I don't know, but I'm glad you thought of doing this," Nella whispered back.

Soon Albert's mother returned with a teapot, a plate of scones, and black currant jelly. "I made the jelly from our own currant bushes, saved sugar for weeks to be able to do it. Albert so loves black currant jelly."

"Mmm. It looks good. Will Albert be joining us?" Peggy asked.

"He's out and about. Never can tell when he'll come home, but he's safe. He knows his way, and local folk know him." She poured their tea and handed them the cups. "That's fresh goat's milk for the tea. I hope you like goat's milk."

"Oh yes," Nella said quickly. She glanced at Peggy in time to see the corner of her mouth twitch. They both hated goat's milk. She reached over and poured a little in Peggy's cup and then more into her own, not daring to meet her eyes for fear she'd laugh.

When she sipped the tea, she was surprised to find the goat's milk tasted fine in tea. She smiled and watched Peggy. With her first sip a look of relief flashed over her face.

"Now please show me this hand language for the deaf," the woman said. "I've heard tell of it but never had any chance for Albert to learn it."

Peggy handed three pages of drawings to her and began to explain and demonstrate with her hands. Nella watched and listened. If Albert were to learn this, then she could practice with him and maybe even teach the rudiments to Bryan.

They became so engrossed that Nella jumped when the front door swung open and Albert stepped in.

His mother gestured for him to come have tea and a scone. She spoke with her gestures and explained, "Sometimes he seems to read my lips, but mostly I talk to hear myself. Might lose my voice if I don't use it." She laughed, and Albert, watching her, grinned and bobbed his head up and down in his quirky way that seemed to mean anything agreeable that he wished it to mean, including hello, good-bye, yes, and how-do-you-do.

Peggy glanced out the window. "I think we should be getting back to the manor. It gets dark so much earlier now. Will you try to explain to him about the signing?"

Albert's mother walked with them to the door. "I'll try to learn the signs from the drawings and then teach him."

"Just go slowly," Peggy said. "I'd like him to meet a young friend of mine, a deaf girl. I think it would inspire him to see how well she communicates."

"It's nice of you to offer, but we don't want to put you out none. I'm sure we can manage."

Albert appeared behind his mother, watching and bobbing his head.

With a final wave good-bye, Peggy and Nella set off up the hill and into the woods.

"I don't know, Peggy. It looks like a big job to teach Albert."

"Well, I'll bring Annie once and see how it goes."

The way back seemed much shorter. When they'd made their way to the summit and passed the chapel, Peggy stopped and said, "You won't forget to speak to Bryan about Annie, will you?"

"I'll watch for an opportunity tonight. He often comes to the kitchen at suppertime to outline tomorrow's work. Occasionally he eats with us when Lord and Lady Westmoreland are gone."

"He does? That seems odd for the lord of the manor."

"He's never acted like the high and mighty master. I've tried to tell you that."

"Okay. So maybe he's a natural to obtain help for Annie."

"I'm sure he will if he can." Nella's thoughts went to Bryan and lodged there. Her desire to be near him nagged like hunger pangs. She wasn't aware of her own silence until Peggy called it to her attention with a question.

"You must be a million kilometers away," she teased. "I said, will you be coming to church tomorrow?"

"Yes. We always get time off for church."

"Do you have to work after church?"

Nella nodded. "We take turns caring for the animals on Sunday, and tomorrow will be my turn. That's why I had today off."

Back at the manor they parted, and Nella decided to check on Ember before washing up for supper. To her surprise, Bryan was in the barn, hand-feeding the dog from a bowl he'd obviously brought from the kitchen.

CHAPTER THIRTY-THREE

Bryan, sitting beside Ember, looked up and smiled. "She's got her appetite back. Mrs. Harrison gave me some liver scraps for her."

Nella crossed the straw-strewn floor and knelt on the other side of the dog. She gently smoothed the fur on her back and scratched behind her ear on the side that hadn't been wounded. "She's coming along fine, isn't she? I was afraid of infection."

"Doctor Llewellyn was here today and said she's safely past that. In time she'll be good as new."

"I'm so glad. Your father's really fond of her."

"He's outright foolish about her." He gave Ember the last bit of liver and, when she'd swallowed it, scratched her under the chin. Ember looked up at him with devotion written all over her speckled gray face. She folded back her ears and half-closed her blue eyes in what Nella had learned to interpret as a dog smile.

"She's really taken to you too. I hope your father won't be jealous," Nella said with a teasing laugh to cover the warmth she felt at seeing his obvious affection for the dog. "Have you changed your mind about her being stupid and unreliable?"

His eyes met hers quizzically. "Need you ask? I don't mind admitting I was wrong about her."

She felt herself melting under his glance, not wanting to pull her gaze from his face, which seemed at the moment to be glowing from an inner light. Suddenly he rose to his knees and leaned toward her across the dog. She knew what he was about to do and couldn't make herself retreat. Without touching her with his hands, he kissed her lips gently, tenderly.

Then he sat down again on his side of Ember, watching her. "You didn't run away. Does that mean you may be admitting you were wrong about me?"

"Yes," she whispered.

"What?" He was on his knees again.

She found her voice. "Yes," she said firmly.

He stood up and held out his arms. She rose to her feet and stepped into his embrace. She returned his kiss fervently until he stopped and simply held her close. Then he said in a low voice, "Your friend Peggy was right about one thing. I am a manipulator. I've loved you since the first moment I saw you. I did everything I could think of to see you again and to get you assigned to our estate." He pulled away and held her at arm's length. "I even loaned you the Welsh bride's diary, hoping you might think more highly of me if you admired my many-greats grandmother. I had no idea you might decide that one of my ancestors may have been a murderer. Lately, I began to fear you'd never trust me or even like me."

She slowly shook her head. "I've been trying not to love you almost since I first met you. I don't know how you did it, but I'm so glad you managed to bring me here." She leaned forward, and they kissed again.

This time when he let her go, he said, "I meant it when I said I was serious about loving you. I want to marry you and help you take care of Livie. I'll care for her as if she were my own."

A flock of butterflies took off in her chest at the thought of marrying him. Then a small inner voice whispered, *He asked you to lie for him*. She backed away. "I . . . everything is going too fast. Please. I need time . . . to get used to the idea of marrying again."

"Of course you do. I should have waited. I just wanted you to know I have honorable intentions." He picked up her hand and held it against his cheek. "Only one thing . . . please tell me as soon as you are sure?"

"I will."

He kissed her again, then holding her hand he led her to the door. "I think it wouldn't do for any of the Land Girls to happen in and find us like this. Shall we keep our love a secret for now?"

Nella smiled. "That's a good idea. At least until I change to part-time work and return to the manse. Some of the girls here have designs on you."

He nodded. "Kitty and her cohorts. It's been difficult not to send them packing right along with Shirley. If they weren't such good workers, I would have." At the open door he halted. "You go ahead. I'll stay here awhile. I should see to the horses anyway." He drew her aside, away from public view again, and held her in his arms. Over the top of her head, he said, "I can't believe you love me. Me! The worthless son of the lord."

"Bryan!" she scolded.

"Isn't that what Peggy and most of the villagers call me?"

She didn't answer.

"Come on. You know it is."

"It doesn't matter. They don't know you."

"You're right there, but thanks for believing in me."

"I love you," she said. She stretched upward and kissed him one more time, then pulled away and hurried out, not waiting for his answer.

As Nella entered Garden Cottage and faced her roommates, she felt as if they could see the imprint of Bryan's kisses still warm on her lips. Surely she didn't look like the same person who had left the cottage that morning. It would be a challenge to conceal her love for Bryan, yet she heartily agreed with him that she should.

Peggy couldn't get Annie off her mind. After church Sunday she happily accepted an invitation to lunch from Mrs. Nelson and Miss Blackwell and walked with them to Brookside.

Annie kept her distance and went to her room until her mother brought her out to the table to eat. Following lunch, Mrs. Nelson said, "Miss Jones, Annie wants to talk with you alone. She would like you to go to her room with her."

"Surely."

Annie closed her door, which struck Peggy as unusual, since whatever Annie said would be silent. Then she realized the closed door kept her sisters out.

Annie gestured to the chair at her desk and signed, *"Please sit with me."* Peggy sat down while Annie climbed onto her bed and let her feet dangle over the edge. *"I'm sorry for saying everything was your fault."*

Relief flooded through Peggy. Annie was coming back to her. *"It's all right,"* Peggy signed. *"I understand. You were angry and hurt."*

"Yes. My mother explained that you never wanted to go. Peter's mother said more bad things to me. I was angry about everything." She touched her ears and lips. *"I hated not hearing and not speaking more than ever."*

"*Can you tell me what she said?*"

Annie shook her head. "*I don't want to. I have no signs for it.*"

"*I understand. Try to remember how much we all love you. I want to help you with your art. I stayed at Gatekeep this week just so I could. I'll be coming often. Mrs. Lewis has invited me.*"

Annie smiled and nodded. "*I like for you to help me. You make me very happy.*"

Peggy smiled back and said, "*You make me very happy too.*" She decided now was a good time to see if Annie wanted to help Albert. She signed as best she could, "*Would you like to help a man who cannot hear? He doesn't know how to sign. He can't talk with anyone.*"

"*No signing? I could show him how.*"

"*It is a long walk to his house, but your mother said you could go.*"

"*Today?*"

"*We must ask her.*"

Annie hopped off her bed and hugged Peggy. Peggy held her close, wishing with all her heart that Annie could hear the "I love you" that came to her lips. She released the little girl and signed the words instead.

Annie responded, "*I love you!*"

Together they went to ask permission to visit the deaf man who didn't know how to sign.

Mrs. Nelson said, "*Yes, of course.*"

Emma and Frances asked to go too, and Annie said she'd like them to come. So Sunday afternoon Peggy went back to Dabney Cottage with the three children in tow.

They reached the dooryard before she stopped to think Albert might not be home. Hoping for the best, she knocked. After her second knock, Albert's mother opened the door. "Hello again," Peggy said. "I hoped my little deaf friend here might meet Albert today."

The woman slowly opened the door. "Why, yes. Come in. Albert is here." She beckoned to the girls. "Come in, children." They all stepped in and huddled together.

"Come, now, do sit down." The woman waved one hand at an old sofa.

Peggy sat beside them. "Let me introduce the girls. I'm sorry, I only know you as Albert's mother. . . ."

"Miller's our name, dear."

"I don't remember if I said before, I'm Peggy Jones. This is Frances, Emma, and Annie." Each girl stood up as she was named. Peggy signed to Annie, speaking aloud as she did so. "*Annie, please show Mrs.*

Miller how you sign 'I'm pleased to meet you.'"

Annie did so.

"So this is the deaf one? A pretty little thing, she is. They're all three lovely children. Are they kin of yours, Miss Jones?"

"No. I'd be pleased if they were. I was Annie's schoolteacher at the West-Holding School."

"Was?" Mrs. Miller said.

Her alert response surprised Peggy. At first the woman had given the impression of being a bit slow. "Actually I lost my position a couple of weeks ago. A matter of differing opinion with my supervisor."

"Aye, and I'll bet she was none other than the Lady Westmoreland."

"You would win that bet." Peggy glanced around. "You said Albert is home?"

"He's in his room. I'll go get him."

She left, and Peggy could hear her talking as if Albert could hear, just as she'd done the day before.

Then she brought Albert in, clutching his arm as she led him. He looked perplexed, and then at the sight of the children, he smiled. He bobbed his head to each one. Peggy was pleased to see them nod to him as they said hello. Annie stood up, and with hand gestures and body language, tried to let him know she couldn't hear or speak. Her signing seemed to bewilder him.

Mrs. Miller made some gestures of her own, and Peggy could see understanding begin to cross his features.

Albert pulled up a chair and sat directly in front of Annie. Annie walked over to a small table. She pointed to herself, then at the couch and the table. She signed, *"I walk to the table."* Again Albert agonized for a moment. Then he got up and went to the table, touched it, and came back and sat down. He tried to copy her hand signing.

Annie smiled, clapped her hands, and signed, *"Very good."* She repeated her first signing, but this time helped his large hands to form the phrase more accurately.

"My goodness, what a bright child she is," Mrs. Miller said.

"Yes. Very much so," Peggy agreed.

Annie went on to teach Albert how to sign *Hello, Thank you, Please,* and *May I have a drink of water?*.

As she worked with Albert, Emma and Frances, who had been very quiet up to now, finally began to fidget and become restless.

"I think it's time for us to go," Peggy said. "We didn't mean to stay very long. But it does appear Albert is enjoying this new way to communicate. I know Annie is having a good time showing him how."

"I think your little friend has made him want to work at it," said Mrs. Miller. "I can teach him myself now from the drawings you left for me. I'm sure we won't be needing more help."

"Well, if you do, you can send a message to Bryan Westmoreland at Whitestone. He'd let me know."

"That I will. Please tell Annie thank you for us."

Peggy touched Annie's arm to get her attention and then relayed the message.

Annie signed, *"You're welcome,"* and Peggy interpreted.

Albert watched, gave them his all-purpose head bob, and with a wide smile, followed them to the door. When Annie waved to him from the dooryard, he signed a successful *"Thank you"* and *"Good-bye."*

She clapped her hands and signed, *"Very good!"*

Annie's good spirits kept all four of them energized during the long hike back home. Peggy rejoiced privately that her plan had succeeded so well, even if Annie never worked with Albert again. Maybe Mrs. Miller would see she needed more help and change her mind.

As the shadows from the western hills changed the Usk Valley into a twilight monochrome, Peggy finally returned to Gatekeep.

Mrs. Lewis turned off the wireless the minute Peggy came in. "If you'd fancy a bite before you go to bed, I've our ration of cheese, some fresh baked pikelets, and stewed apples."

"Oh yes! That sounds lovely." Peggy gratefully sank down on a kitchen chair. "I'm so tired. Those girls stood the hike much better than I did."

"And did Annie take to the idea of helping the deaf man?"

"Like a duckling to the pond. She is so cheered up, I can hardly believe it."

"Did she ever tell you what made her feel so bad?"

"Not really. But we're friends again. Whatever it was, the crisis is over. I'll ask Laurie if he heard anything from Peter. I'd feel better knowing the whole of it."

"That sounds a good plan. I like that young Mr. Barringer. He's not one to grumble, and from what I heard about his father, he's had fair reason to."

"You're right. He's not a complainer at all. In fact, he works at making others comfortable."

"Aye, a pleasant man all around. You could do worse, young lady, even if he isn't in the service and fighting for his country. Whatever's wrong may not be all that harming."

"Oh, I don't think poorly of him," Peggy said quickly. She didn't need a matchmaker. "I think he was in the service and was mustered out after the wound that makes him limp."

"That right? Well, that fits. So he's as good a catch as any of the able-bodied soldiers."

"Mrs. Lewis, I know you're looking out for me, but I don't want a beau. At least not right now." To steer her to another subject, Peggy asked, "What's the latest news from the Front?"

"Them Communists, they've freed Belgrade. Our soldiers, they're still going for Antwerp. It looks to be a cold hard winter for our men. I had so hoped the war would be over by Christmas, like some people said. Would you like to listen to the wireless for yourself while I serve up your supper?"

"Please."

Peggy listened to the end of the news, then her thoughts returned to Albert and his mother. She wished they'd wanted Annie to come again. Peggy had her doubts about Mrs. Miller's ability to take Albert very far in his signing without help from someone like Annie who really knew. The woman had been hospitable and grateful, yet Peggy came away feeling she'd been an imposition. Well, it stood to reason anyone living so far from any neighbors probably got used to having privacy all the time.

It was too bad, though, for Albert wouldn't have the opportunities available to many deaf people.

On Monday, when Annie didn't come to Gatekeep at the appointed time after school, Peggy waited awhile and then walked to school to meet her. It would save Emma and Frances the extra walk to Gatekeep.

At the school Peggy saw no activity behind the classroom windows, and no children lingered in the school yard. She hesitated at asking the new teacher about Annie. Her continued presence in West-Holding and her friendship with Annie might be awkward for the woman.

So Peggy walked briskly on to Brookside.

"Oh, I thought Annie had told you," said Mrs. Nelson. "She wanted to gather some wild rose hips and other pickings for a still-life arrangement. She went to her hideaway in the meadow. I did expect she'd be back by now. Oh dear, Emma and Frances went off to play with their friends at the other end of the village. I'll go for Annie—"

"It's all right, Mrs. Nelson. I'll go myself," Peggy said. "I can help her carry the bits and pieces, and I shall enjoy the walk."

"I did want a word with you, long as she isn't back yet."

Peggy stood by the kitchen door where she could see if Annie decided to cut across the meadow to go directly to Gatekeep. "What is it? Is Annie all right?"

"Oh, right as rain, as they say. She had a wonderful time yesterday and can talk of nothing but going again to help that poor man. It's something else. Maybe you've noticed, but I thought I should mention that I've seen a gradual change in Annie. Little things in the past weeks that made me think she's feeling the first stirrings of womanhood. I've come to the conclusion that her extreme reaction may not be that sudden. And it well may be part of growing pains coming on."

"You're probably right. She won't tell me what Mrs. Hilliard said to her. But that, too, could've cut more deeply because she's leaving childhood behind."

"Yes, and I've tried to think for a long time how to help her, her being deaf. I know it pains her now, where when she was a wee girl, she simply accepted her condition as a normal part of her life. I'm telling you this so you can help her too, understanding that she's experiencing some womanly feelings now."

"I will do all I can, Mrs. Nelson."

"Thank you. She's so fortunate to have you."

"I've come to love her very much," Peggy said. "You've done so well with her. I think you've prepared her for whatever life may bring."

"Thank you, Miss Jones. Now I won't keep you. I am a bit concerned that she has taken so long, especially after I lectured her about this very behavior the other day."

"I'll bring her back this way so you can talk to her again about that."

Peggy slipped out the door and strode out the gate of Brookside's back garden. The meadow lay in a green carpet all the way before her to Annie's thicket.

Peggy crossed the broad meadow swiftly. Shearing Creek was a bit high from the recent rain, but she crossed easily on the stepping-stones Annie had arranged as the water had risen with the fall rains.

When she'd reached the thicket, she hesitated, looking for the path to Annie's private sanctuary. Spying it, she bent over and scrambled through the barrier of hazelnut, hawthorn, wild roses, and vines of wild honeysuckle.

She slowly advanced till she reached a clearing overarched by branches of the surrounding trees. Standing up, she looked in every direction. Annie wasn't in sight. This must've been the center of her secret place. All was quiet. She wished Annie could hear; she'd never before had to search for someone who couldn't.

A mossy stone stood at one edge and beside it a log. Peggy walked over to the stone and ran her hand over the smooth area where Annie probably sat, using the stone for a natural desk. A crumpled bit of paper lay behind the stone. She picked it up and smoothed it. Annie had discarded a colored pencil sketch of marsh marigold.

Peggy studied the sensitive drawing for a moment, then carefully folded the picture and stuck it in her pocket. She didn't know where else to look for Annie. The thicket continued onward for a short distance, but no other trail opened a way through the thorny brambles. Might as well go back to Brookside and wait. Annie would have to come home on her own. Maybe she was already there. Even as she thought this, a tendril of doubt twisted into her mind. She glanced around the clearing again.

Then Peggy saw the bit of torn fabric hanging from a hawthorn branch. She hurried to the far edge of the little glen and studied the piece of fabric. She'd seen the same cotton print on Annie. How long had it been hanging here? The ground below the snagged cloth looked tumbled, as if an animal had dug or scuffled on the spot.

She caught her breath. To one side lay a scattered bunch of freshly picked rose hips and a few curling willow twigs. The torn cloth must've caught there recently. She bent close to the ground and saw a trail of sorts, a narrow trail such as wild animals make. In the scuffed, damp soil Peggy thought she detected indentations left by a large man's boot. It looked as though Annie hadn't walked out of the thicket alone. Someone had taken her, possibly by force.

Breathless with fear, Peggy squeezed through the brush and followed the animal trail to its end. There she found another strip of meadow separating Annie's thicket from the forest that went on uphill toward the source of Shearing Creek, far above the Westmoreland shearing barn. Annie was nowhere to be seen.

Peggy turned and rushed back toward Brookside, all the way praying that Annie would be there waiting for her like every other day, safe and signing a happy *hello*.

CHAPTER THIRTY-FOUR

At suppertime Nella walked down the slope to the barn to check on Ember before going to Garden Cottage to wash up. With Bryan in Newport, the dog, still confined to a clean stall, might need water.

When Nella passed the stable, she noticed the door stood ajar. Men's voices came from inside. Bryan must be back home and talking to Mr. Thompkins. She paused, wanting to say hello. Then she heard an unfamiliar and angry voice say, "We have waited long enough!"

Bryan said something in a low tone. He sounded angry too. Something was wrong. She wondered what sort of trouble he was facing. Curious as she was, she didn't believe in eavesdropping. He would tell her later anything he wished her to know. As she started to tiptoe away, Bryan raised his voice.

This time she heard his words clearly. "I tell you, Nella will not be a problem. You've seen how compliant she is. And now she believes I love her and plan to marry her. I have her in the palm of my hand. Anyway, it will all be over by tomorrow night!"

Nella froze. She didn't want to believe what she'd just heard. She must not have heard correctly.

"Leave her to me," Bryan said loudly. "She'll do anything I say."

Bryan's words and meaning left no more room for doubt. He didn't really love her. Peggy had been right all along. It had all been an act to use her for his own purposes, whatever they were. This was what she'd walked into when she agreed to lie for him. The constricting pain in her chest made Nella queasy. She slowly backed away from the stable.

What a fool she'd been! She wanted to run, but then a wave of rage swept through her. Of all the arrogant gall! She'd show him what kind of problem she could be. She marched back to the stable door and pulled it open. Three men stood off to the side near Sir William's stall. They turned toward her as if the three were one.

But Nella looked only at Bryan. For a fraction of a second, she thought she saw fear flash in his eyes. Then he stepped forward with his hand outstretched. "Nella!" His fingers closed over hers, and he pulled her closer to the two men.

Watching him, she suddenly thought of the Welsh bride and how she'd married a Westmoreland for love and then lost her life. Maybe there was a fatal flaw in this family that led them to deceive others without conscience, even to kill if need be.

Bryan spoke. "Nella, I'd like you to meet Mr. Hostetler and Mr. Beech, both manufacturers of uniforms for our servicemen. I brought them up here from Newport to look over our sheep and to advise me on what breed to add to our flock for next spring." He turned to the men. "Mrs. Killian is as canny with our sheep and sheep dogs as our old herdsman. She trained my father's dog when no one else could."

The men greeted her politely, and she acknowledged them in the same manner. Even if she hadn't overheard Bryan, she would've felt the strange coldness from the two men. One had a face like a fish; the other had an aggressive gaze that reminded her of a wolf. She felt he was capable of anything. Fear sharpened Nella's senses.

She decided to play along with Bryan's charade. As warmly as she could, without sounding false, Nella said, "I'm pleased to meet you, gentlemen."

Smiling up at Bryan, who was still holding her hand, she thought of what a gifted liar he was. She subtly leaned into him, as if unable to keep a physical distance from him. Her responsive stance took very little acting, for her body had remembered how. She said the first thing that came to mind. "Bryan, I want you to come and take a look at Ember. She's stopped eating suddenly."

He turned on the charming smile that had so disarmed her only hours before. "I'll get her something from the kitchen. Don't you worry."

"I can't help but worry. Please. She's so quiet. Surely these gentlemen would excuse you for just a few minutes."

Without hardly moving a muscle, Bryan's face changed into the emotionless mask that had irritated and puzzled her and had also made her distrust him. How could she have ignored this studied deceptive look?

He said firmly, "Run along, Nella. I'll see to Ember, and we'll . . . talk later." He lowered his voice and squeezed her hand when he spoke the last words.

What a showman. Now she wanted to slap his face and tell him what she'd overheard, but the other two were watching her. Bryan's comeuppance would be sweeter later, hopefully in front of the other Land Girls. So smiling affectionately, Nella replied, "Of course. Whatever you say."

Bryan let go of her hand. She nodded to the two hard-faced men. "So glad to have met you." Then she left, not waiting for their response. Outside, her throat knotted up nearly choking her. She felt so demeaned, and yet she'd walked right into his arms so eagerly. Her face burned just thinking about it.

Obviously he was up to no good. At that thought, Nella recalled Bryan's odd reaction when he'd seen the dead man with the thick glasses, how he slipped something from the man's pocket to his own. And later when the constable had come. Was it in fact a death from natural causes or part of some plot to hide the truth, as in the case of Rufe's death? What if that man was murdered? What if Bryan . . . No, he was far away at the time. Or was he?

Again Peggy was right. Nothing made sense about Bryan.

Suddenly Nella wondered if the two deaths were linked in some way. She'd tried so hard to obey the threatening notes. Was she in more danger now at Whitestone than she would've been had she stayed at the manse? Bryan's words, *"I have her in the palm of my hand,"* suggested something dreadful. The hairs on the back of her neck prickled at the thought of the three men probably watching her walk back up to the cottage. The wolfish one could be plotting her death this very minute! How could she have been so stupid?

Nella fought the urge to run. In case they were watching her, she must continue with the act of sweet compliance and walk casually to the cottage. Once there, she could escape Whitestone and hide in the forested hills. Then she'd have to find a safe route to Abergavenny across the valley farms and country lanes to the manse. She would tell her parents everything and send for the constable right away. Hopefully he could do something to protect all of them.

Thinking of Livie, Nella's eyes filled with tears. *I never wanted to leave you, love, but I thought I had to. Dear Lord, help me this night. Deliver us all from evil!* She wiped her eyes and willed them to stay dry. She needed all the self-control she could muster.

At Garden Cottage she found herself alone. In the unusual silence she stuffed some leftover biscuits and a canteen of water into a muslin carrier, along with a rolled-up warm jumper. As an afterthought, she grabbed matches, an electric torch, and Edith's Swiss army knife. She scribbled a note to Edith, saying she would return the knife as soon as she could.

Slipping into her all-weather work coat and cap, Nella let herself out the back door and fled through the rear gate of the kitchen garden. The sun would be down in less than an hour. She hoped she could cross the hills and reach a safe route into town before dark. Breathing hard, she hurried to the trailhead.

Just before entering the woods, she glanced back and saw Bryan. He moved with his familiar swinging walk as he crossed the gravel drive toward the manor's front entrance. At the same time Ruth came out the back door.

Nella darted into the long shadows of the trees for fear the girl would hail her.

But Ruth didn't call or wave. Instead, she tossed some water on the plants growing by the steps and then went back inside.

Hitching her bag higher on her shoulder, Nella hurried on up the hill toward the chapel. The only path that she knew to the other side of the hill was the one that passed by Albert's house. As long as no one was missing her yet, she could take the path. It would be much faster than to search her way through the undergrowth.

Nella had no idea how far Dabney Cottage was from a public road. She tried not to dwell on the fact that she could still be walking in the forest after dark.

She paused at the chapel to catch her breath. Just a little farther and the trail would lead downhill, but she had to rest a minute. Then she heard him. Bryan, from somewhere on the hillside below, was calling her name. Had he seen her enter the woods? She ran on past the chapel and up the hill until, collapsing against a tree, she stopped to regain her breath again.

He called again, sounding closer now. He was following her! Was he alone or were those other men with him? Nella forced herself to continue running. Her breath came in dry sobs, and her heart hammered as if it would burst out of her chest. At last the trail leveled and then began its gradual descent toward Dabney Cottage. She wished she could cut straight down the hill but had no idea where she'd end up. Bryan knew this forest as well as he knew his way around the manor. He'd find her for sure.

She remembered the hidden cave she and Peggy had discovered

yet doubted whether she could find it again. Her best hope was in reaching Dabney Cottage. She'd ask Mrs. Miller to help hide her. She seemed to be a kindly woman. Or maybe she ought to hide in their small barn without their knowing. If Bryan did find her there, surely he wouldn't kill her in front of witnesses.

Nella ran on as quietly as she could, pausing momentarily for gulps of breath and to listen for her pursuer. He was still coming. By now he should be approaching the chapel.

At last she could see the narrow valley that surrounded Dabney Cottage. A pale column of smoke curled from the chimney. The fact that Albert and his mother were home was a relief and gave her renewed energy. By the time Nella got to the meadow and started toward the cottage, she was staggering from fatigue. She had no opportunity to hide in the barn, for Mrs. Miller had stepped out the door and seen her. She darted back into the cottage, and then Albert lumbered out and across the wet grass to meet her.

When the big man reached Nella, she tried frantically to sign to him that she was being chased and needed to hide. She couldn't tell if he understood, but he abruptly leaned toward her and picked her up like a child, then carried her to the cottage. As he brought her inside and set her down on the sofa in the little parlor, Nella started getting her breath back, though she was still terrified.

Mrs. Miller came in from the kitchen with a wet towel in her hand. "My, you must've taken a fright. You just lean back and let me put this cool cloth on your forehead. It will make you feel better."

"But I need—"

"Don't be trying to talk yet. Just lay your head back and rest a bit. You're safe now that you're here."

She had to talk. "Don't let anybody... know I'm here... not even... Master Bryan..."

"Don't you worry. After you, is he? Well, I'll take care of the young lord if he shows himself."

Nella began to relax under the older woman's ministrations. Once she had rested a few minutes, she would leave and find a place to hide that wouldn't involve these folks.

Suddenly she heard Bryan calling. "Hello, Millers! Are you home?"

She sat up and yanked the wet towel from her face. "He's here! I've got to hide!"

"Stay quiet. I'll go talk to him. Don't worry, I won't let him in."

Albert had disappeared, so Mrs. Miller went out alone to greet Bryan.

Nella sprang up from the sofa. She must get out of sight in case Bryan came walking in. She hurried to a closed door she assumed would be a bedroom. Given the furnishings, she decided it was probably Mrs. Miller's room. She halted at the sight of a half-open armoire. On a shelf sat an odd-looking wireless. During her WAAF training, Nella had seen wireless sets of different sorts. This one was definitely for sending as well as receiving. No ordinary British citizen would own such an apparatus. Obviously Mrs. Miller wasn't a simple farm mother. The account of the women spies at Crickhowell flew into Nella's mind. Could Mrs. Miller be a spy?

What better cover than to be an aging woman with a disabled son? She might even be connected with the two arrested at Crickhowell.

Nella clapped her hand over her mouth as she fought for self-control. She must appear ignorant of this dangerous knowledge when the woman returned. She spun around to hurry back to the sofa, but the sound of men talking outside the bedroom window caught her up short. Bryan hadn't come alone!

She stepped over to the old window frame and leaned close, taking care not to disturb the curtain. Through the dusty lace, she saw only Bryan and Albert and Mrs. Miller. But she'd heard two men speaking; she was sure of it.

Then she saw and *heard*. Albert was speaking. Of course. If Mrs. Miller wasn't a simple farm mother, then it stood to reason her son wouldn't be deaf and unable to speak.

Albert's voice came out harsh and angry. "I had to bring the child! She saw me talking to Hanson and would've let the whole village know. We could've just left her here tied up, but then you go and chase this woman up here. Now we'll have to kill them both. We'll be far away before anyone finds the bodies, but we've got to move fast. Horace can tell Wilhelm to signal the U-boat for tonight."

"You're playing the fool," Bryan snapped. "We need Nella and the child as hostages until we're safely out to sea. When we're through with them, then we can kill them—"

"If you want the woman, take her now," Albert said. "I listened to you once about no more killing, and now look what we have to deal with. There'll be no more compromises!"

"If I'd wanted her, I could've taken her anytime," Bryan said and with such contempt that Nella seethed with rage. She almost forgot her own danger as she leaned closer to the window.

"Has Brighton made contact with Du Plessis? And how are we going to get the man here by tonight?" asked Bryan.

"Relax, they're on their way," Mrs. Miller said. "I took the precaution of ordering his capture a day early . . . just in case."

An instant of silence preceded Bryan's response. "Good. If we succeed, you'll receive the honor you've long deserved."

"As will you," she said. "Heil, Hitler!"

"Heil, Hitler!" Bryan answered.

Nella began to tremble. *Bryan, a Nazi? O dear God in heaven. Please help me get out of here safely.* Then she remembered Albert had mentioned a child. Had he kidnapped a child? Had he kidnapped Livie? But he said the child could tell the villagers. Must be one of the village children, then. One who knew Albert as a deaf person and then discovered him talking to someone.

Nella felt like the room was spinning. She gulped in deep breaths till her vision cleared and then ran back to the parlor. She couldn't escape without trying to save the child too.

She had no more than made it to the parlor when the front door swung open. Mrs. Miller stepped in along with Albert. Following close behind was Bryan.

Bryan's eyes met Nella's sharply, searchingly. The contempt she felt for him must have showed on her face. His expression hardened. He made no effort to pretend any longer. The need for playacting was over for both of them.

Without preamble, Bryan said, "Why did you run from me, Nella? Now that you've rushed in where you don't belong, we must make sure you don't disrupt our plans."

He turned to Albert. "Where did you put the child?"

"In the goat barn. The feed room is small but secure."

"Good. Get me some rope for Nella. We'll put her there too, until we're ready to move out."

"I'm warning you, Westmoreland," Albert growled, "we're not going to let her or the child jeopardize the mission!"

"And let me remind you that you've nearly exposed us three times. I won't let you risk everything again. The woman and child are both more valuable to us alive."

Nella looked at Bryan's cold face and wondered how she could've been so deceived. He was a consummate actor, but she should have believed in her first reservations about him. And she should have listened to Peggy.

CHAPTER THIRTY-FIVE

At Brookside Peggy rang up the constable in Abergavenny. Unable to keep her voice from shaking, she said, "We have a missing child out here in West-Holding. She's deaf and has to use sign language. I . . . I'm afraid there's been foul play." She told him what she'd noticed in the thicket.

"How long since she come up missing?"

"About an hour."

"Well, she probably just walked off a bit and got lost, especially if she went up the hill into the woods."

"Annie is twelve years old. She's lived here near to five years, since the first evacuation of children from London. She wouldn't get lost." Peggy's voice went up, out of control.

"All right. Just stay calm, miss. You say her mother's home? Let me speak to her, please."

Peggy handed the receiver to Mrs. Nelson, who looked pale enough to faint.

Mrs. Nelson said hello and then fell silent, listening. At last she said, "But it's not like her at all. . . . Yes, sir . . . we will. All right . . . thank you . . . good-bye." She looked dazed.

Peggy took the receiver from her hand and hung it up for her. "What did he say? Is he coming right away?"

"He said he'd come as soon as he could gather his men, and we're not to tell the villagers until he can look over Annie's hideaway. He says a bevy of people would destroy any trail she may have left. We're to wait here in the house with Miss Blackwell. He thinks Annie may still come home on her own, as that's what usually happens in these cases. I'm to call him immediately if she does."

Peggy was shaking, but seeing Emma and Frances sitting on the edge of the sofa, watching her with wide, frightened eyes, she tried to steady herself. "Maybe he's right." She wanted to reassure them more, yet the words wouldn't come.

Miss Blackwell came to the rescue. "Now, girls, you go to your room and play. You know how Annie loves to be alone. She most certainly will come home soon. She's just gone for a longer walk than she planned, that's all."

Frances perked up. "Maybe she's gone off with Peter. She's been meeting him at Shearing Creek where she made the stepping-stone bridge. Peter helped her move the bigger rocks."

Peggy said, "I had supposed by now that Peter had been sent away to school."

"Not yet. He's still at home. He was real mad about his grand-mother getting a governess. Said he hated governesses, that only ba-bies have one. What's a governess?"

"A governess is a teacher who also lives with a family," Miss Black-well said. "It's unusual for a boy Peter's age to have one. Before the war, boys from families like his were sent away to school at age eight."

Peggy hardly heard the conversation after the mention of Peter. Maybe Peter knew where Annie was. "I'll go out to the Hilliards. Maybe Annie is there with Peter right now. She could have walked across the meadow in their direction."

"If Peter's mother is home, you'll get a bad reception and probably not get to see him," Miss Blackwell said. "Why don't you use the tele-phone?"

Peggy straightened on her chair. The decision to do something brought back her waning confidence. "You're right. I'll call. I won't say who I am if Peter's mother answers. I'll just ask for Laurie. And if he's not in, then I'll ask for Peter's grandmother."

When the call went through, a woman answered.

"May I speak to Laurence Barringer, please?" Peggy asked.

"Whom may I say is calling?"

Peggy recognized the elder Mrs. Hilliard's voice. She said in a rush, "This is Peggy Jones, Mrs. Hilliard. I really need to speak with Laurie."

With only the slightest hesitation, the older woman said, "I shall call him. One moment, please." Her tone sounded as friendly as ever. Maybe she hadn't been soured against the terrible Miss Jones by her daughter-in-law.

Soon Laurie's warm voice came on. "Hello, Peggy. Good of you to call."

"Oh, Laurie, we have a problem. Annie has been gone for a while, and we can't find her. We were wondering if she might be with Peter or if Peter might know where to look for her."

"She's missing! What happened?"

Peggy told him in broken sentences, the facts coming out in a jumble. "I just learned from Frances that Annie has been meeting Peter regularly, and I thought . . . is Peter there? If so, maybe he saw her this afternoon and could shed some light on where she might be."

"He's here. I'll question him, and then I'll be right over." Laurie's words became suddenly clipped and decisive. For the first time, she could imagine him in a military uniform, giving orders to his men. "You said you're at Brookside?" he asked.

"Yes."

"I'll be there shortly. I'll want you to show me Annie's hideaway."

He rang off, and Peggy hung up with rising hope. His obvious concern was a relief after the impersonal treatment by the constable. Perhaps Laurie could help find Annie before the constable arrived.

When Laurie got to Brookside, Peggy led him out across the meadow to the thicket. On the way, she described the piece of torn cloth she found, the rose hips that had been cast aside, and the evidence of a scuffle.

His face took on a stern expression, but he said, "Isn't it possible that she simply wandered away on a long walk, perhaps searching for better materials for her still-life project?"

"That's what Constable Burns says, but it's so unlike her. Wait until you see where she was."

He nodded and walked faster. Peggy had to jog to keep up with his long strides. They arrived at the thicket with Peggy puffing and panting, but then she took the lead to show him into Annie's small glen. There he silently searched the area, finally crouching down beside the scuffed-up moss and the bit of torn cloth that still hung from the hawthorn bush. Seeing it again, Peggy felt certain that Annie hadn't just wandered away and lost track of time.

Laurie rose to his feet and faced her. "She could've roughed up the ground just pulling her dress free. I'm inclined to agree with the constable. Let's keep this quiet till he can look for himself."

She stared at him openmouthed, unable for a moment to believe her ears. He wasn't worried after all? Finding her voice, Peggy gasped, "But I thought you'd help me search for her. How can we just wait around when she might've been kidnapped?" She remembered all too well how Giselle's little girls had been taken from right in front of the manse.

His gaze softened as he moved toward her. "I think you have let your affection for Annie take you beyond reason."

She took a step backward, not wanting him to touch her. "Beyond reason! Good grief, Laurie! We're talking about a missing child here. A deaf missing child. How can you presume she is safe?"

He pursed his lips. "From what Peter told me, Annie has been very angry and upset. His mother caught them playing together when Peter brought her to the estate to show her his pony. Well, Adrienne blistered Annie with invectives that would be more fitting coming from the mouth of a sailor than a so-called lady. Peter says Annie seemed to understand his mother's intent if not her words. And then Lady Westmoreland showed up for a visit at that moment. When she tried to soothe Adrienne, she apparently hurt Annie's feelings even more."

"That's because Annie can lip-read a little," Peggy said. "From what she said to me, she must've understood some words."

"She told you?"

"Yes. She said Peter's mother had said things she wanted to forget."

He shoved his hands in his pockets and strolled back toward the path they'd used to enter the thicket. "If I had known, I'd have told you. Maybe she was hurt enough to run away."

"Laurie, she's deaf. She's too smart to think she could get along all by herself. Besides, she'd gotten over the initial hurt." She followed him but stopped short of leaving the clearing. "Aren't you even going to look along that other path, the one she or someone else chose for leaving?"

"We should leave that to the constable. When he arrives, I'll come back here with him."

Peggy wanted to argue, to make him as worried about Annie as she was, but she could tell her effort would be wasted. In frustration she pushed ahead of him out of the thicket and hurried back to Brookside. If she only knew where to start looking, she'd search alone for Annie. Then she thought of Nella and the dog Ember. She didn't know whether a sheep dog could track a person, but she decided instantly to ring up the manor and ask Nella.

Bryan roughly lashed Nella's wrists together behind her back and pushed her ahead of himself out the door of the cottage.

Mrs. Miller followed him. She called back to Albert, "Send a message to Hanson immediately. We will move tonight. Tell him to take Du Plessis straight to the rendezvous at Newport. He and Du Plessis must leave on the U-boat, whether or not we get there."

Albert responded with a curt "yes," and Nella heard the cottage door close behind her.

Then the woman spoke to Bryan. "Here. Tie this over her mouth. If you want her alive, you'll have to keep her quiet."

Bryan yanked Nella to a halt, took a rag from Mrs. Miller, and tied it tightly over her mouth. Then he faced her and glared into her eyes. "You heard her. Any noise and you and the child will die. Now move along." He broke off and gave her a shove that made her stumble.

Then he grabbed her arm, and his fingers bit into her skin. He kept a tight grip, as if he thought she was stupid enough to try to run, bound up as she was. Nella pulled away, glowered at him, and with her chin up, marched toward the goat shed. He left her free and paced beside her. From the corner of her eye, she saw him watching and ready to grab her if she made a wrong move. She stepped over to the door of the shed and waited for him to open it.

Mrs. Miller moved forward and unlocked the door. "I see you're smart enough to understand your options," she said.

Nella stared straight ahead, not acknowledging that she heard. She sensed that if she were to die, it would probably be at the hands of this woman. From the moment Mrs. Miller no longer needed to be Albert's mother, she'd become steely eyed and obviously younger than the role she'd been playing.

Bryan pushed Nella into the shed, walked her into a small storage room, and shoved her down onto a heap of hay. Then he turned her over onto her stomach and tied her feet together. She felt his fingers at the ropes around her wrists, tugging them tight. Apparently satisfied, he rolled her back to her side and stood up. "That will hold her," he said.

"You go take care of explaining her absence and of concealing your own when we leave," the woman said. "I'll send a message from the hilltop and then keep watch over these two."

"You're incredible, Gerda. You're about to become a national heroine, and you're so calm about it." He spoke in the same admiring tone he'd used once with Nella. "Taking Du Plessis as well as his blueprints seemed impossible, and now it's coming together like one of the Fuehrer's own plans."

"Don't try your charm on me, Bryan. It doesn't matter about me or you or Albert. The only thing that matters is the Third Reich. Once

Du Plessis is safely under our control and cooperating, the tide of the war will turn. His guidance system on the next family of V rockets will put an end to the Allied advance and to their resistance. And when England crumbles, the Fuehrer will not make the mistake again of being merciful to the British people. He'll be in Buckingham Palace as soon as his troops secure London."

Nella blinked in disbelief. She didn't know who Du Plessis was, but this woman sounded out of touch with reality. The Allies had had control of the air since D day, despite the buzz bombs and V–2 rockets the Germans had launched at England. The Allies were poised to move into Germany on several fronts. But then Nella had to admit she didn't know what this guidance system they spoke of could do.

Nella heard her captors lock the storeroom door. As they moved away, Bryan's voice still carried well enough for her to understand a few words. She didn't like what she heard. Something like "By midnight... no one will miss... a fast drive will still take..." Then she heard the outer door slam shut and cut off the sound of their voices.

Back at Garden Cottage, no one would miss her until bedtime, and Bryan could just tell the other Land Girls that she was staying the night with Livie in Abergavenny. They'd accept anything he said. So she couldn't expect help from anyone. She had to free herself. She strained against the ropes imprisoning her hands and feet. But they were tight with no give for working them loose. She'd have to find a way to cut them. Though the sun must be dropping down, it hadn't been dark outside yet. In the storeroom, however, it was very dark.

She looked around for a metal object with an edge to it, a broken tool, an iron hook, or a spike protruding from the timbers that formed the walls of the storeroom. There must be something. She did some experimenting and found she could move by rolling, even though the ropes cut deeply into her wrists with each effort. When she turned onto her back, she could put her weight on her head and heels and inch blindly in the direction her head was aimed.

Her laborious effort took her toward the bolted door. Suddenly her head banged against something hard and solid on the floor. "Ouch!" she cried out, more from shock than the pain.

Then Nella heard a rustling nearby. The child? She tried to call in a reassuring tone. She hoped her gagged voice came out like a greeting or question. There was no answer. She wriggled around to try to see what she'd come up against. She mumbled a call again, but still no sound came in response. Maybe the noise had been from a rat.

The constable finally arrived at Brookside. Peggy didn't go with him and Laurie to Annie's hideaway; instead, she phoned Whitestone and asked the servant girl Ruth to tell Nella to call her.

After she rang off, she decided not to trust Ruth about promptly delivering her message. The sun was down, and soon it would be dark. She couldn't sit around and wait for Nella to call. She'd go ahead and walk up to the manor.

She told Mrs. Nelson and Miss Blackwell her plan and asked for a garment Annie had worn recently. "The dog Nella has trained will do most anything for her. Maybe she can help find Annie. I can't just sit here doing nothing while those men make excuses about Annie being so upset that she ran away."

Mrs. Nelson hurried to Annie's room and came back with her nightie. "I'll get you a carrier for it," she said and did so.

As Peggy went out the door, she turned and said, "If Mr. Barringer returns, tell him what I'm doing. Ask him to drive up and bring us back down in his auto. The dog should start her tracking from Annie's hideaway."

Peggy set off through the village, praying none of the villagers would hail her. She'd have a hard time obeying the constable and not telling them about Annie. In a few minutes she left the village behind and hurried up the narrow lane to the manor.

At best it took twenty minutes to walk up the hill. By the time she reached the manor, the only light came from the sky still pale in the west. To the east the stars pierced the descending edge of night. Peggy thanked God that no clouds had formed. At least Annie wouldn't get wet. Just as Peggy arrived at the front of the mansion, Bryan appeared. He looked unkempt as if he'd been digging ditches or something.

He gave her a raised eyebrow look. "Hello. I'm afraid you've missed Nella. She's off on a walkabout. You know how she is."

Peggy wanted to sit down right there in the drive and cry. "I wanted her to help look for Annie," she said. She wanted to tell him why, but suddenly she couldn't get a word out without crying.

He took her arm. "I say. You look done in. Come into the house and sit while I get the car. I'll drive you back to West-Holding."

"Thanks," she said, gulping hard to get control of her voice. "But I don't need to rest. I'll come with you to get the car."

He didn't argue. "Come along, then."

As he was backing the car from the garage, Laurie pulled up and parked behind them. Bryan switched off the ignition and went out to talk to him. In a minute he came back. "Laurie says he'll drive you down and wherever you want to go. He says the constable is organizing a search team and the villagers have been alerted."

He walked her to Laurie's car and opened the door for her. To Laurie he said, "Sorry I can't help. An emergency came up with the sheep. When I've put down the crisis here, I'll get in touch to see if you still need help." Then he looked at Peggy and said, "Try not to worry. Most likely she's just fine. I'm sure they'll find her quickly."

Peggy suddenly remembered the dog. "Do you think Ember would take to tracking at all?"

A troubled look crossed Bryan's face, but then his smile erased it. "She might if she had her strength back. She was so badly chewed by a dog pack that she's not up on her feet yet."

"I was hoping she was well by now."

He shook his head. "We nearly lost her."

"Well, good-bye then," Peggy said. She couldn't waste time talking when the search was on. It was growing quite dark now, and her heart shrank into a hard lump of fear over Annie's being out at night.

As they drove down the village main street, Peggy was surprised to see Bryan in his old sports roadster speed past them after he'd said he had to stay at the manor. He didn't even glance at them as he passed. She hadn't seen him drive that car in months.

As if reading her thoughts, Laurie said, "He must be going for the vet or something. Look, there's a group forming to help the constable. We'll get in on it."

He pulled up in front of Brookside. Peggy climbed out, started around the car, and halted with a gasp.

Laurie, coming around to meet her, looked at her and then in the direction of her stare. "What's wrong?"

"That man over there. Do you know who he is?"

Laurie shrugged. "I supposed he was a villager. But if you don't know him, then he must not be. Probably one of the constable's men. Come on. Let's go listen to the constable's instructions."

Peggy knew who the man was. He was the one with the evil-looking face, the one she'd seen with Bryan. She had hoped Laurie would know him and say something to wipe away the dread she felt in seeing him. With Annie out there someplace, she didn't want that man finding her. But what could she say? She hurried after Laurie to join the organized search.

CHAPTER THIRTY-SIX

In her struggle to find a way to free herself, Nella came smack up against a partition. They must've not only bound and gagged the child, but dumped her into a different room. Then in the dim light she detected a shape that suggested she hadn't hit a wall but rather the side of a trough or storage chest. She turned sideways and thumped her feet against it to let the child know she was there.

Still no response. Why was the child so quiet? Maybe she was unconscious.

It was growing darker now. In a few minutes she wouldn't be able to see anything. Then it would take forever to find a way to cut through the ropes. And if Gerda came and found her gone from where they'd left her, she would not hesitate to kill her.

Terror threatened to shatter Nella's ability to think clearly. If she failed to break free and hide herself and the child, she had signed their death warrants by trying. If only she hadn't barged into the stable back at Whitestone to confront Bryan. She could've escaped to Abergavenny, told the constable, and held Livie in her arms again, never to let her go.

But no! She hadn't known what Bryan was then.

In the midst of the panic, she remembered her father saying that nothing happens by chance. *Oh, Daddy, are you sure? Was God in control when Rob went down? Was God in control when Charles died? Am I here because God wants me here?* Her father's kind face appeared before the eyes of her mind, and she remembered he'd never lied to her. Suddenly her heart ached with love and thanksgiving for her father and for the God he loved and honored.

As she thought of God, her mind began to clear. The child needed her. Without hesitating, she silently cried, *Dear Father in heaven, please help me now. Help me to save this poor little girl!*

A calmness surrounded and filled Nella, leaving her steady and clearheaded. She drew in a deep breath, feeling physically different. For a moment she simply rested in the clarity of this new peace. She recalled Gwenyth's writing that said faith without doubting was weak. The young girl had known. She must've experienced this revealing light that burned away doubt and left faith stronger than ever before.

Nella knew that whatever happened, God would turn it to good. In the meantime, she prayed again, *Lord, help me save this child!* Then methodically she began to scan the walls, the posts, the doors, and the floor inch by inch looking for anything to use to break her bonds.

After minutes of searching, as the tiny room grew darker, Nella discovered an old iron spike protruding from a board on the base of the partition. The large bent head had a sharp, rough edge. Her hopes soared. She maneuvered close and, after working at it awhile, got her wrist ropes in position to use the spike head as a saw. She scraped her binding against it and prayed. *Please, Lord, keep Gerda and Albert from coming.* The effort to cut through the ropes with such an inefficient object rubbed her skin raw, and she couldn't tell whether the rope was wearing. Finally, overcome by the pain, she stopped to rest. It seemed impossible. How could she ever get free before Gerda returned?

While resting her arms, she decided to try to work off the gag. If she could talk, then at least she could whisper some encouragement to the child. She rolled to her other side and wriggled till her face was close to the spike. Soon she had the metal hooked under the edge of the rag where it passed over her ear. Bracing herself, she arched her back and pushed with her heels against the floor. After several attempts, she succeeded in pulling the rag down around her neck without gouging her skin in the process.

Quietly Nella said, "I have my mouth free. I found a big nail, and now I'm trying to saw through my ropes with it. Try to rest easy until I can untie us both." Then she rolled over again and worked feverishly on her wrist bindings. The burning pain on her wrists turned sharper. It was all she could do to keep on and not cry out loud. She gritted her teeth and prayed and kept sawing. It was difficult to see anything now. The spike had to work. She couldn't see to search for any better tool.

Nella scraped the rope over the iron spike again and again, hoping she was hitting the same place as when she'd started. Finally something gave. She caught her breath and tried to separate her hands. Yes. Everything was loosening! In seconds her hands were free.

She whispered the good news that she was free, but the girl didn't respond. Was she all right? Had she fallen asleep? Or was she not here?

She pried loose the knots in the rope tied around her ankles. Kicking free, she stood up and grabbed hold of the edge of the stall to catch her balance. Then she reached down inside the feedbox to feel for the girl. When her hand encountered a warm little body, the girl jumped and thrashed around, obviously terrified.

Nella whispered, "I've come to help."

Still the girl struggled like a wild animal. Nella caught hold of her arm, held tight, and managed to pat her back. The girl grew rigid, so Nella fumbled for her gag to remove it. At last she had it off.

"Stay quiet," she said, pressing a finger to the child's lips. She could just make out the pale oval of her face. She patted her cheek and smoothed her hair. Then she started to work on the rope around her wrists.

Once Nella freed the girl's hands, she sat up and worked at the rope around her ankles. When her feet were unbound, Nella helped her to stand. The girl caught hold of her hand and placed it on her own. Nella couldn't figure out what she was doing until suddenly she realized she was hand signing. She grabbed the girl's face in both hands and pulled her close. It was Annie! It made sense. Peggy must've taken Annie to meet Albert as she'd planned. Certainly Annie would be shocked to see the man, whom she believed couldn't talk, all of a sudden talking normally to someone.

Nella gave her a big hug. Holding her close, she wondered how she could get them both out of here. Escape would be difficult enough with a hearing child. Once more she pressed a finger against Annie's lips in a shushing gesture. She felt Annie nod her head.

Nella helped Annie out of the feedbox and kept hold of one of her hands. She dreaded losing physical touch, their only means of communication in the dark.

To her surprise, Annie pulled her a few paces forward, stopped, and put Nella's hand on an upright beam. Annie managed to convey she wanted to climb it, so Nella let her. Keeping one hand lightly on her, she felt Annie make her way up the beam until only her foot was in reach of Nella's hand. There was a grating and a creaking sound and then Annie's foot flew upward. She'd found a way to escape through the ceiling.

Nella ran her hand up the beam and found a thick cross board near her own eye level. She climbed up onto it and slowly stood. When she straightened, her head bumped the ceiling. Exploring above her head with one hand, she felt the edge of an open trapdoor. Annie must've seen this while it was still daylight.

Nella felt the shape of the opening, then cautiously hoisted herself onto the rough plank floor of a loft. She reached out and, to her relief, her hand touched Annie's shoulder. Carefully Annie placed her hand on the trapdoor, and she and Nella quietly closed it.

Now they must find an exit to the outside. It was pitch-black in the loft. Holding hands, they felt their way until Nella bumped her head on the rafters. Then she fumbled along the sloping rafters around the loft's perimeter. There must be a door of some kind where they put in the hay.

When they came to the gabled end, Nella discovered a window of some kind. The glass had been replaced with canvas, which was nailed over the opening. She pulled till the canvas tore away from the nails. Peeking outside, Nella saw that it wasn't completely dark yet. They were above the goat pen. Off to the left, splinters of light glowed at the edges of the blackout curtains on the cottage windows.

Nella guessed she was about three meters from the ground. She couldn't go first and leave the deaf child alone inside, so she quickly pulled Annie close and had her look out. She took Annie's hand and pointed her index finger to the ground, then placed both of Annie's hands on the sill of the window and pretended to lift her out. *Please, God, help her understand what she must do.*

She felt Annie nod her head. Helping her up and hugging her, Nella eased her feetfirst out the window. Then holding Annie by the arms, Nella leaned down as far as she could safely stretch.

Oh, Lord, help her not to be hurt!

She let go. She heard the child land and then silence. She simply had to trust that Annie was okay and had moved out of the way. With a fast-beating heart, Nella scrambled out, lowered herself to the length of her arms, and let go. When she dropped, she lost her footing and rolled onto her back, but wasn't hurt. She jumped to her feet and immediately felt Annie's hand on her arm.

They ran to the gate of the pen. One of the goats began to bleat. Nella grabbed Annie's hand and pulled her through the gate and then quickly closed it. Together they dodged behind the fieldstone fence and sprinted toward the nearby woods.

They made it to the woods just as the door of the cottage below opened. Nella's chest was heaving as she pulled Annie into the cover of trees.

She heard Gerda call, "Come along. Something has stirred up the goats. We can't risk keeping those two alive any longer."

Swiftly Nella guided Annie farther into the darkness of the woods. *Please hide us, Father.* She stood still, once again pressing her finger against Annie's lips. Then she bent over and patted the girl's feet. Again she touched her lips. They had to move fast, but she wanted Annie to step quietly. Annie nodded.

Thank God she was quick to understand. They hurriedly crept away from Dabney Cottage. Nella could hear Albert and Gerda talking, excited and then angry, though she couldn't understand their words. She focused on getting as far away as they could, as fast as they could.

After climbing upward until her legs burned with fatigue, Nella moved along the side of the hill, following its contours. They had to stay in the woods yet not pass over the hill toward Whitestone or West-Holding. Annie stayed close to Nella the whole time, moving as quietly as a small forest creature.

They stopped to rest for a moment, and Nella heard a stream. Then as they continued on, her feet detected the downward slope into one of the tiny gorges made by streams that flowed down the hillsides. By the sound of it, this stream tumbled over rocks.

Behind them, Nella could no longer hear the voices of Albert and Gerda. She slumped to the ground to catch her breath and pulled Annie close beside her. Annie leaned heavily against her. Without being able to hear or see, the girl must feel isolated, yet she'd responded to everything with steady courage. Nella gave her a hug and got a hug in return.

Suddenly in the distance a gunshot cracked the air. Nella grasped Annie's hand and leaped to her feet, pulling Annie with her. They headed up the gully, not knowing where they'd come out. But surely the thickest part of the woods would be safer than where they were. Another shot rang out and then several more in rapid succession. She slipped her arm around Annie and tried to pull her faster. Every so often a rock rattled under their feet. Then Nella lost her footing, and they both went down. She held her breath. Although Annie could have cried out, she didn't.

Instantly they were on their feet again. Even with it being dark, Nella began to see better now. She could discern shades of black and make out the shape of Annie's face. She patted the child's cheek to reassure her and smoothed her hair.

The girl clung to her, and together they climbed upward. A rush of noise and pale vertical column warned Nella they'd reached a small waterfall. The only route onward was to go back to where they could scale the bank and come out above the falls.

As they were leaving the gully, Nella heard distant shouts. The killers were searching for them. But they couldn't afford to chase them forever, could they? For they said they had to be in Newport sometime tonight. If only she could find a good hiding place. Nella thought of the hidden cave she and Peggy had discovered. She'd have to find the path that led there.

She stopped and peered into the darkness. She'd only been there once and didn't have any idea where she was now.

Annie clung to her hand in silent trust. Nella stood still and tried to picture where they might be in relation to Dabney Cottage. The goat pen was near the woods that led up to the chapel. She had angled to the right of that trail. When she and Peggy were coming from the opposite direction, they had found the cave off this way. But how far? She decided they might be close to the cave. They hadn't come upon any other stream. Maybe this stream was the one she'd heard when they were in the cave.

It was worth a try. Besides, Annie must be near exhaustion. They had to find a place to hide and rest. She followed the bank of the stream upward. As they climbed, she heard distant shouts from time to time but couldn't understand any words. No need to know what they were saying. They were looking for their escaped prisoners. Nella pulled Annie onward, feeling the weight of the child's weariness slowing them more and more.

Then she felt smooth-packed turf under her feet and stopped. A path. Then she remembered she and Peggy hadn't crossed a creek to reach the cave. So she and Annie must remain on this side of the creek. Leaving the trail, they continued upward. Hand in hand they walked, keeping close to the sound of the tumbling water. Nella tried to remember if she'd heard the creek before she had entered the cave, but she couldn't be certain.

Far below she heard a call now and then, but no more shots. Soon they were confronted by a large solid blackness straight ahead instead of the scattered dark verticals of tree trunks. She proceeded toward the mass of black with her free hand outstretched. Her toe struck a rock. She pitched forward and hit her head against the stone barrier and then crashed to the ground, yanking Annie down with her. They both cried out in shock. Nella froze and listened. All was quiet. She sat up and groped for Annie. Finding her, Nella patted her, and together they stood up.

Nella moved to the left, stepping carefully, touching the rock wall from time to time. When she stumbled into some thick bushes, she stopped. From down the hill she heard voices again, and they were growing louder. Once she thought she heard her name. If this were not the area of the cave, they could never get away now. Annie was near the point of collapsing. For that matter, so was she. She pushed her way along, squeezing between the rock wall and the bushes.

Maybe they could just hide in the bushes until dawn. As the way grew more constricting, she realized the bushes would be their best hope. No way could she find a hidden cave in this darkness. As soon as she could tell where the bushes and the cliff screened out the stars, she halted and sank to the ground, pulling Annie with her. Nella drew her close and wrapped her jacket around the both of them. Sitting on the damp ground would be cold, but it was a relief to rest.

As she held Annie close in the thicket, hoping they were hidden from view, Nella was reminded of a Bible verse she'd learned in Sunday school about being sheltered under God's wings. When a child, she'd always pictured baby chicks hiding under their mother's wings, and the image had made her feel cozy and safe. *That's what we need now, Lord. Shelter us under your wings.*

After a little while, a male voice came from directly below them. "She must not have come this way. We would've overtaken her if she had."

Nella jumped and almost gasped aloud. Fortunately Annie was asleep. Nella could see light from an electric torch, flickering on the lower branches of the thick stand of trees below. She held her breath and poised herself to put a finger on Annie's lips if she awakened.

"I say we go back and try again come daylight," a man said.

"Right. Can't be doing much more now," another man answered. Their voices carried as clearly as if they were only a few meters away. They sounded English, but then so had Gerda.

Soon Nella could tell they were moving away. When they spoke again and their words were no longer discernable, she huddled against Annie and tried to stop trembling.

Sometime later Nella awoke in moonlight, stiff and shivering. After their long flight through the woods, her clothes were damp with perspiration. Now the cold earth was sapping her body heat. Despite her chill, the rope burns on her wrists felt like they were on fire.

Annie slept soundly against her. Nella wondered if she should awaken her and try in the dim moonlight to find the cave. Uncertain, she made herself relax. Finally she dozed off.

CHAPTER THIRTY-SEVEN

The constable's men and the villagers searched for Annie until near midnight. Peggy would have gone on all night, but the constable called a halt, saying it was fruitless when they couldn't see and the child couldn't hear them call.

One good thing, Peggy thought, was that the man with the evil-looking face left right away in an auto that looked to be going in the direction of Abergavenny.

Peggy obeyed the constable's order to return home and get some rest only because she had a plan of her own. She said good-bye to Laurie at Gatekeep and went inside as if to retire. Tiptoeing to the kitchen, she put a kettle on to boil.

Mrs. Lewis appeared in the doorway. "I finally just got me to sleep." She studied Peggy's face for a moment. "No sign of her then?"

Peggy shook her head. "Not a glimpse of anything. But I'm not giving up. I can't bear to think of her out there alone or in the hands of someone horrible. I just came for food and a jug of tea and maybe a heavier jacket."

"Let me help. I'll pack you cheese and biscuits. You be about finding proper clothes."

So Peggy went to her room and rolled up a thick fisherman's knit jumper to take along. She also grabbed the nightie Mrs. Nelson had given her when she went to ask Nella about using Ember for tracking. When she returned Mrs. Lewis handed her a small knapsack.

"Don't be forgetting your electric torch," Mrs. Lewis said.

"Aye." Peggy took it all and strapped the whole bundle over her shoulder with a leather belt. As she went out the door, she said, "Just as well keep mum about me going out again. The way the constable was acting, he might try to make me stay indoors."

Mrs. Lewis nodded. "He'll get no word from me."

Peggy said good-bye and closed the door. The village was pitch dark, what with blackout curtains and people already in their beds. With renewed energy, she set out at a fast walk toward Whitestone.

She made her way up to the mansion, but decided not to awaken Nella. Doing so would mean also waking up the rest of the women in Garden Cottage, maybe Bryan and his family too. She didn't want any interference from them. Skirting the edge of the gravel, she furtively hurried to the livestock barn, hoping Ember would recognize her and not bark. The large door had been left open. She tiptoed in and called softly, "Ember! Here, Ember!"

The dog yipped and whined, but she didn't come. Of course. She must be tied or shut in a stall. Peggy risked a bit of light from her torch to help locate the dog. Ember welcomed her as an old friend. After petting her, Peggy searched and found a rope that would serve as a leash. She tied it to the dog's collar and led her out.

Ember seemed strong enough, certainly in better shape than Bryan had suggested. The dog tugged at the leash, glad to be out of the barn, no doubt. Peggy led her away, down through the fields to the side of the village and Annie's hideaway. Then she put Annie's nightie to Ember's nose. "Go find her, Ember. Go find!" she commanded as she patted the ground. Ember sniffed, then raised her head and barked at Peggy.

Peggy held out the nightie again. Ember sniffed and just stood there. Feeling desperate, Peggy kept trying to get Ember to track. At one point the dog seemed to understand, but then simply went in a circle and stopped. Finally Peggy realized Annie's scent must be lost in all the odors left by the searchers. She slumped down to rest. Ember came close and sat beside her. She put an arm around the dog and gave in to tears. "Oh, Ember, what shall we do?"

The dog whined and leaned against her. After a while, Ember stood up and, with her ears pricked forward, stared intently at the woods. Peggy watched the dog's gray form in the dark as she moved to the end of her leash. She wanted to go to the woods. Peggy rose to her feet and let the dog lead her.

When they reached the trees, the dog began moving confidently up the hillside, yet not putting her nose to the ground at all. She could be after anything, Peggy realized, but decided to let her go and follow along. She kept her torch turned off so her eyes wouldn't have to readjust to the dark. They walked on, and underbrush slapped Peggy in the face so hard she almost let go of Ember.

Then farther on she lost her footing and fell flat. The dog stopped and came back to her side. "Oh, Ember," she groaned. "Do you really know where you're going?" She held out Annie's nightie again. The dog obediently sniffed it and waited for her to stand up.

Before long Peggy was totally exhausted. Just when she was about to give up and go back toward the village, she felt the smooth surface of a trail underfoot. Ember tugged eagerly at the rope. Well, she might be wanting to go home, but Peggy was ready to give up anyway. She'd never find her way out of the woods without the dog. Again she let Ember lead. They were going downhill now. At last they reached the edge of the wood, where Ember stopped and whined. Peggy struggled to figure out where they were until it suddenly came clear. Below them was Dabney Cottage. Ember pulled at the rope, as if wanting to go to the cottage.

"No, Ember. We don't want to wake anyone."

Ember returned to her, whined, and struck out to the end of her rope again, facing the cottage. Could Annie have wandered this far, and they'd taken her in?

"All right. Let's go, Ember."

At the cottage door Peggy hesitated. She hated to wake them if Annie wasn't here. Then Ember solved her dilemma by pulling her away from the door and heading for the little barn. Peggy followed only because she hated to bother the Millers. From the goat pen, Ember led Peggy across the meadow and into the woods again. Peggy would've stopped her and pulled her back to the walking path, but now the dog was excited and seemed determined. So Peggy followed.

Nella dreamed about Ember and then awoke with a jolt. To her surprise the dog was really there, licking her face and whining.

An electric torch shined on her. Peggy's voice exclaimed, "Nella! Good grief! And Annie! Oh, thank God. I hoped Ember knew where she was going, and she did!" Peggy pushed the bushes aside and dropped beside Annie. Annie jumped and tried to get up and run.

Peggy quickly shined her light on her own face.

Annie gave a happy little cry and grabbed her around the neck.

"It's been so hard for her," Nella said, "not being able to sign to me."

Peggy hugged Annie. "How did you find her? And why are you sitting out here in the woods at night? Couldn't you find your way back in the dark?"

"Oh, Peggy, keep your voice down. Did you see or hear anyone else in the woods?"

"No. Everyone gave up the search hours ago. Why be quiet? We ought to be shouting that we found her."

"Peggy, I couldn't bring her back. They wanted to kill both of us. Maybe they're still waiting to catch us in the morning." She quickly explained the truth about Gerda and Albert and Bryan.

When she'd finished, Peggy sat stunned. "Bryan is a Nazi agent? Mrs. Miller and Albert too?"

"Look," Nella said, "the best I can think to do is to find that cave you and I discovered and hide there until we can determine if it's safe to come out. They were to meet a submarine tonight, but some of them might still be around here."

Peggy agreed and signed to Annie so she would understand the plan. Until dawn they'd stay where they were. Peggy placed Annie's nightie under Annie for protection from the cold ground and pulled the large bulky jumper over her head and down over her other clothes. Then they huddled close for warmth. Ember curled up beside Nella. After a few moments, Annie's even breathing indicated she was asleep again.

Nella whispered, "The fact that you didn't see any movement at Dabney Cottage doesn't prove that Albert and Gerda are really gone. We can stay here for another day, if need be, and then after dark sneak down to the village—"

"But the villagers will be out at dawn, looking for Annie. Her poor mother. I wish we could let her know Annie's all right."

"I know. But we can't. Not until we can all go out. I'm wondering how we'll convince the authorities that Bryan is a traitor."

Peggy murmured, "Well, you said he was leaving on a submarine. Him being gone, that should say something. What a shock for Lord Westmoreland. I can't believe I actually feel sorry for Lady W.! And what will Laurie think of his longtime friend?"

"I . . . still find it difficult to believe. It's just so . . . preposterous. You think I'm a good actress. You should've seen him when he proposed to me."

"He asked you to marry him? Oh, Nella. What did you say?"

"Fortunately I put him off. It makes me feel sick to think how I fell for him, and to him it was all a big act."

"Just be glad you had the good sense to put him off. That shows he didn't completely deceive you."

"I suppose." *But he did,* her heart cried. *I truly loved the man I thought he was.* Aloud, she admitted, "I loved a lie, Peggy, and I'm so ashamed."

Peggy reached over Annie and gave her shoulder a squeeze. "It's not the end of the world, little sister. It happens to all of us, and too many times people marry the lie before they find out."

The excitement of having Peggy find them kept Nella awake, but Peggy grew quiet and finally Nella could tell she'd fallen asleep.

Nella stared into the night and waited for the darkness to fade. Finally the forest turned gray with the coming dawn. She sat up and wriggled her toes. Ember raised her head and sat up too, but Annie didn't stir.

"Peggy," Nella whispered.

Peggy moved and then sat up abruptly.

"We need to look for that cave before complete daylight."

Peggy struggled to her feet and helped Annie to stand up.

Nella rose and staggered. She could scarcely feel her feet.

Annie's teeth were chattering with the cold.

"We've got to warm her up," Nella said. "Let's get moving." Once more Nella pushed her way between the rock wall and the thick bushes.

It was near to full light when she came to a rugged jumble of rocks. She considered taking to the trail to get around the barricade, but then above her in the tall shrubs she spied a crevice. She whispered to Peggy, "Stay here while I go and look." Then Nella climbed eagerly upward. A moment later and she'd found it! She beckoned for Peggy and Annie to come, and soon they were all three inside the cave.

This time they had an electric torch. Peggy beamed it around the cavern. As before, no animals were about.

And as Nella had remembered, she could hear water tumbling and splashing somewhere. "First we find a drink of water," she whispered.

"Wait! I have tea," Peggy said.

She poured the tea, still warm from its careful wrapping, and gave Annie the first cupful. Then she insisted on Nella drinking the next, and she finished the last. "We can look for the water after we eat. Voilà!" Peggy pulled out her bundle and produced chunks of yellow cheese and chocolate biscuits.

After they ate, Nella said, "It's wonderful how food makes the world look better. If you think your torch will last, I'd like to explore the cave a bit, and we need to walk Annie until she warms up."

"Sure thing. Do you think I'd come without extra batteries? Lead on." She switched on the light and signed their intention to Annie. Then she handed the torch to Nella.

The cave made several sharp turns, as if an ancient earth tremor had fractured the walls and created the many crevices. Peggy's light struck the glitter of a glassy pool. A tiny waterfall splashed into it, and water obviously exited under rocks at one side. Although the cave continued on the other side of the pool, the water blocked going that direction.

Nella knelt, scooped up water in her hand, and tasted it. "It's sweet. At least we won't go thirsty. Let's go back to the main chamber and take the other tunnel. It may lead to another way out."

When they'd found their way back to the main chamber, Nella led them into the other branch of the cave. Feeling had returned to her feet now, and though she wasn't warm, at least she wasn't freezing. She remembered how Bryan had walked her around in the cave to keep her warm. Turning to Peggy, she asked, "Are you warmer now? Is Annie warmer?"

Peggy paused. "Shine the light on me, so she can see." She signed to Annie, and the girl responded. "She says she's better now."

"Good. We've got to keep moving and not get so chilled again. Follow me, then." She kept the light shining where their feet would step. The cave made two turns and then widened.

Annie suddenly gasped. Nella turned the light on her and then to where she was pointing.

Peggy exclaimed, "The wall, it sparkles like jewels!"

Nella raised her light when she saw the glitter, supposing the shine was from the water. But it wasn't. Crystals of some kind sparkled from the rock wall on one side. She moved close and touched them.

"Do you suppose they're real gems?" Peggy asked.

"I don't know. But I imagine they're not, or someone would've mined them long ago." She moved the torch light over the wall and noticed a rectangular shadow, something hand-hewn? She went to investigate. Someone had carved out a small alcove, and there was a vase of some kind in it. She picked up a very old, corroded metal urn.

At her elbow Peggy asked, "What is it?"

"I have no idea. I wonder if this was an ancient place of worship or something." She gently replaced the container. For some reason the place didn't feel eerie, as she would've expected of a pagan place. Her father had taken her to Stonehenge before the war, and she had to leave quickly because of the sense of evil she'd felt there. But here there was none of that. When she lowered her light to the floor to lead Peggy and Annie onward, she saw why. Clearly carved in the cave floor was a Celtic cross and something more.

She stooped and brushed away the fine dust. Peggy joined her. Sure enough, there was carving on the floor of the cave, not unlike the memorial markers in many of the great cathedrals. Could it be the lost marker for the Welsh bride? The carved words finally took shape under their hands: *Gwenyth, Beloved Wife of William Westmoreland. A sweeter grace earth shall never see. Gone to be with the Lord on 18 April 1404.*

"We found it!" Nella exclaimed. "This is incredible!" Someone had created a lovely memorial for her, someone who truly loved her. Her English husband?

Annie signed to Peggy, and Peggy interpreted. "She remembers we talked in class about the Welsh bride."

"I wonder if she's actually buried here. Or is this just a memorial?"

Peggy said quietly, "I don't suppose we'll ever know for certain. I remember the family history said William found her grave desecrated. But it didn't say whether her remains had been stolen."

For an instant Nella thought, *I can't wait to tell Bryan.* Then she remembered again who he really was—a traitor and her enemy. He would have killed her if necessary, just like Gerda. If he was still at Whitestone, he would still kill her. "Let's go back and look in the other branches of the cave," she said.

They followed the other branches of the cave and found they all ended in closed crevices. Disappointed, Nella returned to the main cavern where morning light dimly shone in through the small entrance. Here, too, they could be trapped if Gerda and Albert were still in the vicinity. The way they'd talked, they couldn't search forever, and yet they'd said if they didn't get to the U-boat on time, it was to leave without them.

"I wish we knew whether Bryan and his associates are gone," Nella whispered.

"Well, we're probably safe here," Peggy said.

They sat down, backs to the wall, close enough to the entrance to not need the torch for signing to Annie.

Annie quietly leaned against Nella and, in the dim light, signed to Peggy.

Peggy translated. "She says she thought Mr. Albert was nice. She doesn't understand how he was so mean and she never knew it."

Nella sighed and said, "Tell her I thought Mr. Westmoreland was nice too. It really hurts to learn that someone has been lying to you all the time."

Peggy signed and Annie nodded.

Annie didn't answer, but after a while she signed again. "She wants to know if we really can get away without those bad men chasing us," Peggy said.

"I pray to God that we shall," Nella answered. "Tell her that. Tell her to pray with us." And then she heard distant voices calling. The men who had given up their search last night were returning.

CHAPTER THIRTY-EIGHT

The sound of the men's voices sent Nella straight to her feet. Every nerve in her body shrieked.

Peggy was instantly beside her.

Watching them, Annie's eyes went wide with fright.

"Peggy, take Annie to the jeweled cave. The entrance to it is hidden. I'll stay here. If it looks as if they're about to discover the cave, I'll sneak out onto the trail and mislead them."

"I can't let you do that! Come with us, and we'll wait it out together."

"No! Take Annie and go. Hurry! And take Ember too."

Peggy stopped arguing and grabbed Annie by the hand. They moved quickly out of sight.

"Ember, go," Nella said, pointing after them. The dog dropped her head and obeyed. Nella tiptoed to the narrow mouth of the cave and tried to see through the thicket. Silently she prayed, *Please help us, Lord.*

Although Giselle had never told her the graphic details of her treatment at the hands of the Gestapo, Nella knew from the extent of her surgery that they'd been brutal. Again she prayed silently. *Please, Lord, not Annie. Not Peggy . . . or me.*

The voices came closer now. "You think they could've come this far?" a man asked.

"I don't know," another one replied.

Ember suddenly brushed past her legs and barked. Rushing down the hillside through the brush, she kept barking. All was lost unless Nella could get to the trail and keep the dog from leading the men back up to the cave.

Below, through the branches, Nella glimpsed their booted feet moving. She scrambled out and over the rocks and came onto the trail well ahead of her pursuers. Ember broke through the brush and ran to her, barking the whole time. Then the dog dashed toward the men on the trail, but her bark turned to yipping as she danced around them. Nella's heart nearly stopped. Ember was greeting Bryan and Laurie.

Laurie must be one of them too. If Bryan hadn't left for Newport, then maybe Albert and Gerda were still here. Angry and terrified at the same time, she faced the two men. This probably would be her final act, and it had to be good so they wouldn't find Peggy and Annie.

Whirling around, she sprinted down the trail away from the cave. Ember bounded back to her and loped beside her.

"Nella!" Bryan called. His footsteps pounded after her. She knew she'd never outrun him, so she veered off the trail and crashed through the brush. She heard the waterfall almost at the same instant she stumbled to the edge of the ravine. She hesitated. In the next instant Bryan grabbed her, wrapped his arms around her, and held her in a viselike grip. Then he pressed his cheek against the top of her head as if showing affection.

Who was he acting for this time? Infuriated, Nella fought to break free. Her rope-burned wrists made her cry out in pain. His arms tightened around her again.

He was talking, but his words passed over her fury in a blur. Then gradually she began to hear him. "Nella, it's all over! You're safe now. We got them. Albert and Gerda were killed." His voice cracked. "I was so afraid! So afraid I'd lost you! Afraid they'd gotten to you first! You're safe."

What was he saying? Safe? Then she realized he was no longer restraining her. He was cradling her. She stopped fighting and looked up into his eyes. "What do you mean?" she demanded.

"I wasn't one of them, Nella. It nearly killed me to treat you the way I did, but I had to keep them believing I was on their side. I couldn't even loosen your bonds without them suspecting me and killing you."

His brown eyes gazed warmly into hers, the way they had when he'd said he loved her. His arms still surrounded her protectively. Could she risk believing him? "Are you some kind of secret agent?"

He nodded. "Yes. Laurie too. We had to try to keep you safe and at the same time play our parts as Nazi agents. At last it's over. We caught every one of them before they could take one of Britain's most brilliant research engineers and his latest design plans back to Germany."

"The man they called Du Plessis?"

"That's right. If they had succeeded, it would have prolonged the war. The Germans might've even turned back our assault."

Laurie called from the trail above them. "Where's Annie? Have you seen Peggy?"

Is this real? she thought. *Can I really trust these two after all I've been through?* She looked up again at Bryan, who still had his arms around her. He bent his head and kissed her gently on the lips. Then he let her go but kept a hand on her arm while they climbed back to the trail. Looking from Bryan to Laurie, she said, "Wait here. I'll go get them."

They waited. She realized, after the fact, that by asking them to wait, she'd unconsciously tested their motives one more time. They stood quietly waiting. Still, she climbed a circuitous route back to the cave, and when she brought Annie and Peggy out, she returned the same way.

When they reached the trail, Peggy walked slowly toward Laurie. He held out his hands, and she took them. "Are you all right?" he asked softly.

She nodded.

"And Annie too?" He let go of one of her hands and reached for Annie's. The girl smiled up at him and gestured to Peggy with her free hand.

Peggy said, "She wants to say something, but she needs both hands."

Laurie let go of her hand.

Peggy translated the girl's swift signings. "She says please can we go home. She's very hungry."

They all laughed, and the last wisp of doubt left Nella. This was real. Beside her stood the Bryan she'd grown to love. She shyly slipped her hand into his. "Do you suppose Mrs. Harrison could cook us up a bite?"

He laughed. "If she doesn't, I'll do it myself!"

Laurie and Peggy and Annie marched down the trail toward Whitestone. Nella walked hand in hand with Bryan, close behind them.

At Whitestone Peggy rang up Brookside to tell Mrs. Nelson that Annie was safe and Lord Westmoreland was bringing her home. Once Annie was on her way, she went to the kitchen of the great house, where Laurie, Nella, and Bryan waited.

While Mrs. Harrison, red-faced from the excitement, was serving up huge omelets and sausages with leftover tea scones, farm butter, and honey, Peggy took her place beside Laurie at the big table.

Bryan was holding Nella's hands, pushing back the cuffs of her wool jumper sleeves. He gasped. "Why didn't you tell me sooner? Ruth, fetch some warm water. She needs to soak her wrists."

Mrs. Harrison set down her pans and spatula and rushed to look. "I'll get the magnesium salts. Ruth, you take care of the food."

Peggy slumped onto a chair. "You never said a word. That must've been hurting you all night."

Nella's wrists looked as if someone had tried to saw off her hands. An inflamed wound encircled them like ghastly bracelets.

Bryan looked ill. "I'm so sorry! I can't bear to think that I put those ropes on you."

"You had to do it, Bryan," Laurie said. "They'd have killed her and you too, if they had found the ropes loose."

"I'm all right," Nella insisted. "It looks a good deal worse than it feels."

Mrs. Harrison returned with a basin of water, clean towels, and bandages. "You just ease your hands into that, dear, and let them rest there. Bryan, you feed her and get some tea into her. The rest of you eat while your food is hot."

Peggy couldn't keep from staring at the spectacle of The Bryan spooning eggs and sausage into Nella's mouth as solicitously as if she were a baby. He glanced at Peggy, and she shook her head in mock dismay. "I would never have thought to see the young lord spoon-feeding a poor damsel."

He grinned. "I'd even feed you, if you needed. You've earned every bit of being waited on. Nella told me that you knew all along about the threatening notes and the reason she felt she must stay here. If you had breathed a hint of your knowledge to anyone, more people might've been killed, and the Nazis would likely have escaped. You ladies both behaved superbly, I must say. I hated it that you became involved, but you handled yourselves like masters."

"Peggy kept me from panic more than once," Nella said. "Now if you've all had enough to eat, before I go collapse in bed, I'd like the answers to some questions, that is, if you two secret agents can give them."

The men looked at each other and back to Nella. "We'll tell you as much as we can," Bryan said.

Peggy said, "All right. Nella, let me go first. I can't wait to know. Bryan, was I right about you working secretly to get Nella out here to Whitestone?"

"Yes. It took some doing from our office in London, and for a while I was afraid the Land Army people wouldn't cooperate."

"Why did you want me out here?" Nella asked. "It seems to me I was in more danger here than if I'd gone a long way some other direction."

"Gerda was for killing you, Nella, after she learned that you had a letter from Private Rufe Johnson. She had one of her men working in the Gilwern hospital as an orderly, a man who had stolen the identity of a real orderly on his way to Gilwern from London. The Germans needed a network of people in this area to penetrate the secret defenses surrounding Doctor Du Plessis' laboratory up by Crickhowell. They recruited Rufe before he came to Gilwern. Then the false orderly used him to pass on messages to agents up the river. The two women who were arrested had visited Rufe regularly. Rufe got into it for the money they offered, but he also believed a tale that he was helping the British secret service. Somehow he caught on to the truth, so the orderly killed him.

"After Jean and Nella found Rufe's body, Gerda kept them under surveillance. She wasn't sure how much they had learned but couldn't take a chance on anything. Since Jean never saw Rufe's letter, Gerda ultimately focused on Nella.

"It was a case of bad luck when Nella met Rufe's friend at the USO. The orderly had learned about Corporal Peterson from reading Rufe's mail. One of Gerda's men had followed Peterson from London. Both the orderly and the London man overheard your conversation, Nella." He stopped and gazed soberly at her. "I hate to have to tell you, but Corporal Peterson never left Abergavenny alive."

Nella shuddered. "How awful! Then . . . I was responsible for Corporal Peterson's death!"

"No, you mustn't think that. They probably would've killed him anyway, as soon as he led them to Rufe's money. The misfortune I meant was the way you became their next target. I would've given anything to spare you what you've suffered."

Bryan looked so grieved for her that Peggy gave up her last reservation about whether Nella would be hurt by this man.

He slipped an arm around her shoulders and pulled Nella close. "I knew you'd blame yourself for Corporal Peterson's death. It was an unfortunate circumstance you couldn't really help. It's the way of war. Try not to blame yourself."

Nella bit her lip and nodded, but her eyes filled with tears.

"Nella," said Peggy, "try to think of how things have turned out. The whole spy ring has been broken. That's what Rufe and his friend would've wanted, now, wouldn't they? They're both heroes, and you can tell Rufe's mother how he stood up bravely against evil when he saw it."

A bit of relief came to Nella's face. "Aye. I can do that for certain. But poor Rufe. He was so very young. . . . What about my letters to Corporal Peterson?"

"Our people intercepted them," Bryan said. "Otherwise you would've been notified he was missing."

"Then . . . was Rufe's letter really lost?"

"No. We had that too."

"Did Captain Evers in Gilwern know?"

"Evers is a good man. He knew a little, but mostly he understood that he must meticulously obey orders from our London office. On our orders, he did have a man watching out for you until we got you out here to Whitestone."

"I never guessed," Nella said. "Well, my next question is, what about the dead man I found out on the hillside?"

"He was my partner, Ray Ellsworth. To the shock of all of us, he really did die of heart failure. His death put Albert on the spot with Gerda. At first, she didn't believe his claim of innocence. I'm not sure she ever did, but when there was no investigation, she focused on completing her mission. Albert stayed in line till he felt he had to apprehend Annie. Nella, what you saw me take from Ray's pockets was a paper that might have branded him as a German agent, at least until the truth could be revealed after the war. I couldn't let his family suffer that.

"But back to Gerda. Her man out at Gilwern tried to kill Nella, because she had read Rufe's letter. As far as he knew, the letter may have exposed Gerda's operation. When Nella escaped his hit-and-run attempt, and I found out about it, I persuaded Gerda that killing Nella would be more risky than keeping her under surveillance. Nevertheless, in the beginning, I didn't trust Gerda to let her live, so I took a calculated risk and had her sent here to Whitestone, where I hoped I could protect her."

"I don't understand how you persuaded them not to kill me," Nella said. "Gerda was vicious."

"I told her that your body would make one too many when she was within days of completing her mission and capturing Du Plessis. Unlike Corporal Peterson, you would be missed, and she couldn't be positive your body wouldn't be found. Obviously the local authorities would set up an intensive search and investigation. She could see it truly was too much of a risk with so much at stake. The same with Annie. Actually, to Albert's credit, he didn't really want to kill Annie, but he would have if it became necessary. I kept reminding them they didn't want to stir up the local authorities when they were so near the fulfillment of their mission."

"But how did you think you could stop them from killing me?" Nella asked.

"Let me start by saying that I fell for you the first minute I saw you in the chemist's shop. It knocked me for a spin when I thought you were married. But then when I found out you weren't married, it was easy to say that I'd make love to you, so you'd do anything I asked."

"You didn't!" Nella sputtered. "How could you think I'd submit to that?"

"It was another calculated risk, especially since you disliked me on first sight. But I hoped you'd respond to my real love for you."

"And she did," Peggy broke in. "I thought she was crazy and told her so."

"Peggy!" Nella cried.

Bryan laughed and put a piece of honey-covered scone in her mouth to silence her. After she swallowed, he asked, "Is there anything else I haven't explained?"

"Yes," Peggy volunteered. "Laurie, where do you fit in all this?"

"For one thing, it was my job last night to keep the searchers away from Dabney Cottage so our men could move in and take Albert and Gerda by surprise. When Peggy took off on her own, she outsmarted me, but fortunately our agents already had closed the noose tight. I also had to keep an eye on one of Gerda's men who showed up to 'help' with the search."

"That horrible man who looked like a cold-blooded executioner!" Peggy exclaimed. "I thought he followed me once."

"Gerda's people watched you as much as they watched Nella,"

Bryan said. "You were under their surveillance from the time Nella escaped the near hit-and-run, because you were close to Nella."

"The upshot of it," Laurie continued, "was we had to watch over the both of you. Last night, if 'the executioner' had seen the searchers get close to Dabney Cottage, he would've done something to mislead them, just as I would have. When the constable called off the search until morning, it freed him to rush to his other duties. Our men nabbed him in Newport, along with the others."

He leaned back and stretched, rubbing his neck. "You can't know what a satisfaction it was to see those Nazis lined up in restraints and to take Doctor Du Plessis back to his home and his work here in Wales. The past twenty-four hours have been long, but the plan to take in this spy ring has been in the making for many months. Ages ago, Bryan had to win the trust of the Germans so he wouldn't be under suspicion when he invited Gerda and Albert to live on the estate. I came in a little later. I'd been wounded in North Africa and judged unfit for active service, so I applied for volunteer duty. When they learned of my friendship with Bryan and my Hilliard relatives here, they assigned me to this mission."

"Did the Germans believe you were one of them, like Bryan?" Peggy asked.

"No. To them I was just his old school chum."

"That accident in the barn," Nella asked, "was it really an accident?"

"That accident actually increased your safety," Bryan said. "Albert set it up unbeknownst to Gerda. When he failed, she threatened his life if he ever again took things into his own hands. The mission had been assigned to her personally by Hitler. If any of us failed, she failed. After Albert's bungled accident, she made Nella my special responsibility."

"I suppose some of the times I thought I was seeing and hearing deer in the woods and up by the chapel, that it wasn't always Shirley," Nella said.

Bryan laughed. "Ruth, come here for a minute."

"I was just bringing more hot water for her to soak her wrists," the girl said.

Peggy noted that she'd suddenly dropped her subservient attitude.

Ruth poured a little water in the basin for Nella. "Are they feeling better yet?"

"I think so. Thanks."

"All right, Ruth," Bryan said, "now put down the kettle and sit with us. Nella, I want you to meet your personal bodyguard. Ruth is a talented special agent, and when you were not seeing Shirley or hearing clumsy Albert, you were seeing glimpses of Ruth. She's the one who observed your flight into the woods last night and let me know."

Nella looked flummoxed. "Ruth! I never would've guessed. Well . . . thank you!"

Ruth smiled and nodded formally. "My pleasure."

"I never guessed either," Peggy said. "She sure carried off the impression of a very young, and not too bright, serving maid."

Ruth laughed. "I went to a great house to learn the trade . . . and quick, you know. And it's not difficult for me to play 'not too bright.' I have to say, Nella, you were a bit of a challenge, always taking off somewhere."

"Wasn't she now," Peggy remarked. "You did have your work all lined out for you." She turned to Bryan. "What about the girls who quit because of seeing ghosts before Nella came?"

"The girls saw Gerda, Albert, or some other of the agents who stopped to plot with Gerda. It was to everyone's advantage that those girls believe they saw ghosts. I encouraged the idea, because Gerda had a powerful send-and-receive apparatus set up in the mausoleum. She didn't want anyone nosing around there. The wireless in the cottage reached only to her cohorts here in Britain. Of course, our intelligence service had intercepted her messages from the beginning."

Bryan paused and gazed apologetically at Nella. "There's one thing more, Nella. I wrote the threatening notes. I had to scare you enough to keep you in line."

"You sure succeeded in doing that."

"I hoped you'd react the way you did. I was terrified for you, and yet I had to play my Nazi part."

"I can see you did." She lifted her hands from the basin and accepted a towel Ruth handed her. "But what was your plan for me if I had gotten out of line and Gerda decided I must die?"

He became very still and glanced at Laurie. "I . . . I would have tried to think of something, but I had no other plan. We had to capture the spy ring before they committed their final desperate act. As Laurie said, we worked for months to set up the trap. Gerda's espionage would bring together six Nazi agents, the cream of Hitler's crop in Britain, whom they'd been trying to capture for three years. You weren't part of the plan, and when you stumbled in . . . The truth is, I might not have been able to save you. I prayed for you every day. . . ."

Nella reached for his hand. "I'm so glad you prayed. So did I." She glanced at Peggy. "We made it, Peg! We really did. I can't get used to the fact that we're safe. And I can go home and take care of my baby again."

Peggy smiled and nodded. "We made it all right." The words came out like a giant sigh. She was so tired she was losing track of the whole conversation.

"Nella, will you try to get out of the Land Army now?" Bryan asked.

"No. I'd still like to help part time as long as there's a need."

Mrs. Harrison appeared at Nella's side. "Let me put my special ointment on those wrists of yours and give them a moist wrapping whilst you get your nap." She proceeded to apply her medicine without waiting for Nella's consent.

Peggy's eyes became blurry with fatigue. She stretched and smothered a yawn. "I hate to end this fascinating discussion, but I can't think anymore. I could sleep a year. Laurie, would you please drive me down to Gatekeep?"

"Be my pleasure." They excused themselves and went out to his car.

Peggy leaned her head against the back of the seat and would've fallen asleep right there had it not been for her clear view of Laurie's profile. It pleasured her greatly just to look at him. How could she have thought he would be like his father? For that matter, how could she have assumed that all gentry were like his father? That childhood impression didn't fit Peter Hilliard's grandmother, not even Lord or Lady Westmoreland. Laurie's father was an aberration, and she'd let the beast affect her all these years. But no more. She gazed fondly at Laurie. He, so good and decent, more than made up for the ugliness of his father.

As they left the gates of Whitestone, Laurie glanced her way. "This is my last active assignment for the secret service. I'll hold down a desk job in London now."

"You're leaving West-Holding for the duration?"

"I'm afraid so." He drove slowly through the woods on the way down the hill to the village. "I'd like to stay in touch if I may."

"I'd like you to stay in touch," Peggy said quickly.

"Not just for Annie, you understand." He reached over and took her hand. "I don't know how you feel about having a duffer with a gimpy leg coming to court you, but that's what I want to do."

He reminded her of a schoolboy for all his shyness. "I would welcome your courting, Laurie," she said with a smile.

"You would?" He braked the car to an abrupt halt. "Peggy, may I kiss you?"

She answered directly, as was her nature. "Yes, Laurie."

He pulled her into his arms, and his kiss wasn't shy at all. She thought fleetingly of their first meeting at age five when she'd felt as if she were flying with him down that muddy road in Blaenavon. Now they were really flying.

Someday she would tell him about that time when she first loved him.

After soaking in a warm bath and taking a morning nap, Nella asked Bryan to walk with her back to where he'd found her hiding. She could hardly wait to show him the Welsh bride's memorial marker. She wanted to surprise him.

As they neared the cave, she said, "You said you prayed for me every day. Did you really believe God would keep me safe?"

He looked down at her, and his hand tightened on hers. "I can't tell you the agonies I went through worrying about you. I didn't have any great peace-giving faith, if that's what you mean. I was terrified for you, for Livie, for Peggy—your whole family. I kept praying but knowing that God would have the final say."

She nodded. "I know what you mean. Me too. But do you remember what Gwenyth wrote about faith? That she prayed even though she didn't have hope?"

"Yes. When I was a boy, that didn't mean much to me, but I've done a lot of that kind of praying lately. Gwenyth was an unusual young woman."

"Aye, but she was praying to a merciful God," Nella said thoughtfully. "I couldn't understand her faith a few days ago. I hated that she died so young and wondered where her God was then. Just like I hated it when Rob died. After I lost Rob, I sometimes prayed out of habit but figured it didn't count for much. And sometimes I prayed because I thought I should but didn't believe that counted either. Then when I was trying to save Annie and I knew I had no one but God to help me, it seemed like God reached down and said 'I'm here.' That was pure mercy.

"I didn't know if we'd make it, but that almost didn't matter as long as God was so real and close. Now I see that God was with me from the instant that jeep roared after me . . . and before. He's always been with me." She smiled up at him, trusting him as well as God. "Am I sounding like a typical minister's daughter?" she asked lightly.

He stopped and pulled her into his arms and held her close. "You sound only like yourself, the most beautiful woman in the world." He kissed her a long moment, then they walked on. "I've had my doubts too. Hard doubts. You know what helped me to believe again?" His arm around her tightened. "You. I've seen so much evil, so many warped, sadistic minds that revel in greed and torture and killing. As a double agent, I've had to lie, cheat, steal . . . and kill . . . until I wasn't sure that goodness and God really existed. Then I saw you. Nella, no matter how you felt about God before today, His goodness shone in your face that day I first saw you. I knew again what I was fighting for."

She turned to him, reached up, and ran her fingers down his cheek. "Oh, Bryan," she whispered, "I don't know what to say. I'm not good at all."

He caught her hand and kissed her fingers. Then he smiled and said lightly, "Your ignorance in that matter makes you all the nicer. Now, what about this surprise you have for me? Is it much farther?"

"No! We're nearly there."

A few minutes later she led him into the jeweled chamber and showed him the urn and the carved white stone that had been set into the floor.

"So you found Gwenyth's memorial," Bryan said softly. He brushed more of the fine soil away from the carving. "I think this white stone is a piece of the Cefn-gelli Stone, a large white monolith on this hill that was revered by the local people. It was white like marble, but hard like granite. Not native stone at all. Legend has it that the stone had been part of a Roman officer's home. Then when the Romans left, people hauled the beautiful stone to this hilltop to mark the burial place of a devout and holy man of God—the first person to tell the hill people here about Christ."

"What a lovely legend." Nella ran her finger in the grooves of the old letters. " 'Beloved Wife.' I'm so glad to know her husband really loved her."

He leaned back on his heels. "Didn't you read her entire diary?"

"I read the part that had been typeset. Then I decided I shouldn't be keeping it so long."

"I gave it to Peggy and to you for as long as you wished."

"I know, but I worried about what your mother and father might think."

"They might think I was smitten by my own modern-day Welsh bride."

"But I told you I'm not Welsh!" She laughed and realized she was still a bit giddy from fatigue and relief and happiness.

He rose to his knees and reached for her just as Ember imposed her presence between them. "That dog!" he exclaimed and leaned over to kiss her anyway. She met him halfway.

When Nella drew back for a breath, he said, "If you had read to the end of Gwenyth's book, you would've seen a poem my many-greats aunt copied by hand after the book was printed. I hoped you would take it someday as my declaration of love for you. It goes like this:

" '*Sweet breath of heaven,*
My reason for living.
No feud, no war, no incantation
Can annul our sacred vows;
And if I die, my love,
I still shall live eternally—
Loving thee.' "

"Gwenyth wrote that for her husband?"

"No. William wrote it for Gwenyth. It was signed by him, and he titled it simply, 'My Gwenyth.' According to family records, William's father forced him to marry for a political alliance, but William refused to consummate the marriage. As soon as the importance of the alliance faded, he took his and Gwenyth's son to France and didn't come back to Whitestone until his father died. It was when William left that his father destroyed the Cefn-gelli Stone, as if it had meant something special to Gwenyth and William.

"When William returned to Whitestone, he set up a separate household for his English wife and supported her but never lived with her. While he was in France, someone, perhaps the murderer, had desecrated Gwenyth's grave and removed the casket. So William made his own memorial to her, but he never revealed its location."

"What a tragic romance!"

"His love for her never ceased. For me that removes the sting." He took her hand. "Nella, right now I would be asking you to marry me if I followed my heart. But I have another assignment waiting for me as soon as I can leave Whitestone. I can't ask you to wait for me, but when the war is over, if I make it back and you're not married—"

She pressed her finger across his lips as she'd done to Annie such a short time ago. "Don't talk like that. You will come back. I'll be praying for you every moment. I will wait for you . . . or I will marry you tomorrow if you wish. I want to be your Gwenyth."

Ember, still between them, stretched and licked Nella on the chin.

"Drat that dog!" Bryan exclaimed. He stood up and reached down to her. "Come here. I want to kiss my bride-to-be properly without the help of our furry friend." He pulled her to her feet and into his arms. "You are all I want," he murmured. "My Nella."

EPILOGUE

The deaths of Albert and Gerda joined the other mysteries surrounding Whitestone. The newspaper reported that a terrible accident
had taken the lives of the two, though few knew the "mother and son"
who had lived like hermits in old Dabney Cottage on the Westmoreland Estate.

Of necessity, Lord and Lady Westmoreland learned that Bryan had
been serving in a military undercover operation. He swore them to
secrecy about this as well as his new secret service assignment.

Nella said good-night to Bryan one evening, and the next day he
was gone, having left quietly during the night. It was a painful way to
have him leave, and he wouldn't often be able to write. But she set her
heart and mind to the waiting and prayed fervently for his safety.

In the meantime Nella wrote to Rufe's mother and also to Corporal Peterson's mother after obtaining Mrs. Peterson's address
through the efforts of Captain Evers. To each woman she affirmed the
courage of her son and then gave them each other's address, in case
they wished to correspond.

Lord and Lady Westmoreland, upon learning Nella would become
their daughter-in-law, tried to persuade her to leave the Land Army,
bring Livie, and live with them in Whitestone Manor. Nella gently
refused and settled into a routine that allowed her to stay at the
manse every night with Livie and work only three days a week at
Whitestone. On the days when she helped old Will with the sheep, she
took Livie with her. Ember watched over Livie as if she were one of
the lambs.

Due to a letter of recommendation from Lady Eunice Hilliard and, surprisingly, a note of approval from Lady Westmoreland, Peggy found a teaching position in a private girls' school in Abergavenny. She continued to tutor Annie on many Saturdays. Laurie came out from London as often as he could, and at the manse, Mother and Father Mac welcomed him as warmly as a son. Peggy privately told them he soon might be their "adopted" son-in-law.

Giselle's husband, Claude, wrote to her, agreeing that she could safely return to Lyon in the spring if she went out to the country and lived with her cousins, the Leveques, who had cared for Jacquie and Angie before Giselle's escape. Although Claude couldn't tell her, Giselle knew from the BBC reports that the French Seventh Army was pushing toward the German Rhine Valley. And she knew he belonged to that force.

Jean Kagawa heard regularly from Tom, now back with the Nisei Combat Team. Tom couldn't say where he was, and news reports never mentioned the Nisei Combat Team—the 442nd Division. Tom said he'd seen Em Emerson, with her portable typewriter in one hand, making her way to a tent she called her office. They'd had a long visit. One of his letters included a note from her. She'd seen her sister Marge several times, and all was well with Marge—at least as well as could be while working in a hospital tent near the Front.

While the winter winds blasted over the British Isles in November, the home-front women battened down their hopes and dreams as well as their homes. Surely spring would bring peace, and their men could come home.